WAITING FOR THE SUN

An evocative and heartwarming historical saga

DOMINIC LUKE

Joffe Books, London
www.joffebooks.com

First published in Great Britain in 2023

This book is a work of fiction. Names, characters, businesses, organizations, places and events are either the product of the author's imagination or are used fictitiously. Any resemblance to actual persons, living or dead, events or locales is entirely coincidental. The spelling used is British English except where fidelity to the author's rendering of accent or dialect supersedes this.

Cover art by Jarmila Takač

ISBN: 978-1-80405-915-9

CHAPTER ONE

She had braced herself — not quite sure what to expect, not quite sure how she'd feel, or if indeed she'd feel anything, seeing the old house again. But as the motor car breasted the rise and the once-familiar valley opened up on her right, tears sprang into her eyes, a lump rose in her throat, and Emily Winmer realized that she had not been prepared for this at all.

Chad's open-topped car — his pride and joy — slowed and stopped, easing onto the verge. As he applied the brakes and switched off the engine, Emily raised a gloved hand, surreptitiously wiping her tears. Chad hadn't noticed, had he? But, oh, Alleyn Dene! How could one *not* shed a tear, seeing it again? One's heart strings were tugged in a hundred different directions at once.

From up here, where the road looped over Hoosun Hill, the house looked entirely insignificant. Anyone flashing past in a motor would barely notice it, nestling in its little hollow, all but hidden by the trees clustered round it, tall elms and spreading oaks. Brown sandstone walls peeped between branches green with the first leaves of spring. Windows glinted in the fitful sunshine. Smoke curled from the chimneys. Alleyn Dene. Dear old Alleyn Dene. It meant so much. It meant . . .

But she was not sure *what* it meant. There was too much to take in, too many memories flooding back. It had been so long — thirteen years — and those years included the years of the war. To look back to a world before the war was like looking down the wrong end of Papa's telescope — something she had delighted in doing as a child. Everything looked small and distant, like another world. Which was not so far from the truth. An unbridgeable gap had opened during the war, separating *before* and *after*, *then* and *now*.

Chad held the car door for her. She stepped from the motor and walked across the verge, her low heels sinking into the soft turf. Not far from the road, the land suddenly dipped down, sloping steeply away into the valley, long grass rippling in the breeze. But her gaze was fixed not on the slanting field but on the half-hidden house, the place where she'd spent the first seventeen years of her life. Thrown out of kilter by an avalanche of memories, she found her eyes misting up again — the view blurred before her.

'Mother? Are . . . are you all right? Is anything wrong?'

'I'm . . . I'm . . .'

'You're crying. Are you crying?'

She took a hold of herself. 'No, darling, of course I'm not crying. It's just the wind — the wind in my eyes. It always was such a windy spot, up here on Hoosun Hill. We were lucky, being so sheltered at Alleyn Dene.' She smiled at her son, a smile perfected over the years: a pale copy, perhaps, of Nanny's smile, so comforting and reassuring in the nursery long ago.

The smile seemed to set Chad's mind at rest, as it always had done, and he stood back, watching her — satisfied, perhaps, that his plan had been a success, though it was never easy to guess what Chad was thinking or feeling. He had always been a rather serious little boy. He was certainly not the sort of boy to shed an easy tear, unlike his mother.

They had been getting on so well today that she didn't want to spoil it. She'd been proud sitting to lunch with him in the crowded dining room of a country hotel. For once she hadn't minded people looking, she hadn't been shy at all. If only, though, she'd had some inkling beforehand of what he'd planned, she might have been able to steer him onto another path, something less fraught than a return to Alleyn Dene. But he'd wanted it to be a surprise, her Easter treat, and he'd caught her unawares by his announcement as lunch came to an end. She'd not been able to think, on the spur of the moment, of any satisfactory pretext why she shouldn't want to see her old house again. Indeed, a part of her had leapt at the idea. But there had been misgivings too and Chad — always sensitive to other people's states of mind — had seen it in her face.

'You . . . you do *want* to see Alleyn Dene, Mother?' Doubt had showed in his large brown eyes as he looked at her across the table. He had a rather round, rather boyish face: the face of innocence, Mama had often called it. 'You do want to go, don't you?'

'Well, yes, I . . .'

'You used to talk about Alleyn Dene all the time. I remember the stories you used to tell — about your old nanny, and the stream in the garden with the fish in, and lots of other things.'

Sat in the country hotel, she had gripped the napkin on her lap and said brightly, 'Oh, darling, of course I want to see the old place, it's a lovely surprise!'

As the waiter brought their puddings (Chad had insisted she have a pudding), Emily had tried to recall the stories he had referred to. She must have given him the impression, she realized, that life at Alleyn Dene had been spotless sunshine from beginning to end. As she'd eaten her charlotte russe in the busy dining room, Emily had done her best to silence her doubts about what came next. Everything would be all right, she had told herself. It was only a house, after all. And she was a grown woman, sober and middle-aged (as old as thirty-eight), not given to excesses of emotion.

But standing now on the grass verge looking down at the house in the hollow, she knew that was not entirely true.

'We could go down if you like,' said Chad.

'Perhaps not,' she said quickly. 'It . . . it always looked best from up here, seen in its setting. Besides, we wouldn't want to intrude. Alleyn Dene belongs to someone else now.'

'You're right, of course, Mother. It wouldn't be fair on the new owners.' After a pause, he added, 'I remember once visiting Alleyn Dene — years ago, I mean, when I was a kid.'

'Do you, darling? You would have been five or six, I suppose.'

'Grandpa showed me the stars through his telescope. I wouldn't believe him when he told me that the stars are other suns, millions upon millions of miles away. "Then what are they, young Chadwick?" Grandpa said, "What are they?" And I said, "They are the souls of all the people who have gone up to heaven." That was something you had told me, Mother.' Chad laughed at his five-year-old self.

'I said that, did I? How silly of me!'

'Not silly, Mother. I thought it was rather . . . nice.' He laughed again, as if to underline that, although it *was* a nice idea, he was now old and wise enough to know that it was silly too. 'It's odd,' he added. 'I don't remember any other visits to Alleyn Dene, and yet I suppose we must have come here all the time.'

'Yes, I suppose we must.' Emily thrust aside the question of why she might have wanted to avoid her old home. She considered her son instead, wondered if there might be more in him of her father than she had realized. Certainly Chad's obsession with his motor car reminded her of Papa, who had always thrown himself wholeheartedly into his latest hobby, whether it was astronomy or meteorology or politics. But, for Chad's sake, it might be best if he took more after his other grandfather, Sir Hubert, rather than Papa. No one ever called Sir Hubert solemn or sensitive, it was true, but no one would suggest either that Sir Hubert was ever daunted by life. Emily didn't want Chad to be daunted by life. Then again, neither did she want him to be too carefree and slapdash — to ride roughshod as Sir Hubert often did. What she would have liked most of all, was that he should remain her little boy just a short while longer. Was it too much to ask?

Chad had gone back to his car as she stood lost in thought, respecting her silence with his usual tact. He had the bonnet up, was stooped over the engine, his brow puckered in concentration. He was always fiddling with the engine — he became so absorbed in it that one could watch him with impunity. She herself hadn't the faintest idea of anything to do with motors. She had been born into a world where motors were unknown and she still found them faintly disturbing, if not actually sinister. When Chad was out in his car, she could never rest easy until he was back safe and sound. And the way he drove! She reached up to adjust her hat, a reflex action, for she always felt that it had come loose, despite all the pins, after she'd been out for a spin with her son. The hat was not very practical, of course. The wide brim did tend to catch the wind. One of those cloche hats that were now all the fashion might have been more convenient. But she did not feel at her age — nearly forty — that she would be able to carry a cloche hat off with any degree of success.

As she adjusted her hat, she adjusted her feelings too, damping them down, keeping them in check. She had always been careful not to mollycoddle Chad, not to smother him. She mustn't let herself down this late in the day. He was not her little boy any longer, no matter how much she wished it. He was almost twenty, a young man. She had to accept that, she had to be sensible about these things. She should be sensible, too, about Alleyn Dene.

She turned back to the view, the house peeping between the trees down in the valley. There was no reason to get upset, not when she had so many happy memories to dwell on — the whole of her childhood. She smiled fondly at the thought of the child she had been: an only child, doted on, cosseted — a little spoilt, if the truth be known. The nursery in those far-off days had been a cosy place, a safe place, and Nanny a bastion — she'd had rather an ample figure, dear old Nanny — a bastion keeping the wicked world at bay. Alleyn Dene had been the perfect place for a child. Not as grand, of course, as Nethercote Hall two miles away, nor perhaps as cosy as Cedar Rise in the village where the Barford girls had lived. (Whatever had become of the Barford girls?) To Emily, her home had always seemed — like Baby Bear's bed — *just right.*

She loosened her motoring scarf. The sun had come out again. The breeze had slackened. It was almost warm. But it wasn't too warm for a fire indoors: smoke was still curling up from the chimneys. How snug and homely the drawing room must be this afternoon, with coals glowing in the grate and sunshine on the lawn beyond the French doors. But of course, the drawing room would look quite different now. It was somebody else's drawing room. The heavy velvet curtains that Mama had never quite got round to changing were long gone, as were the Louis XIV armchair and the upright piano and the Empire-style sofa — the armoire, too: how the removal men had sweated and sworn, struggling under the weight of the armoire! And when they came back for the cheval mirror, the auctioneer's assistant with his clipboard had fussed around, insisting they handle it with kid gloves.

Where had all that furniture ended up? In what far-flung rooms was it now installed? And what about the other things, the smaller things: the barefoot Meissen girl whom Emily in her childish innocence had imagined was the likeness of a younger Mama, or Papa's beloved brass telescope? How curious that Chad should remember that telescope! Mama had so often sighed over it, telling Papa he would catch his death standing out in the chill night air. But Papa had refused to be denied. If there was a clear sky and no moon, then conditions were perfect, and he couldn't possibly miss such a golden opportunity. If he was lucky he might even see — Emily forgot what it was he'd hoped to see, some constellation or nebula (she'd never been sure of the terms). Papa had written his observations in his leather-bound journal, along with readings from the barometer and a report of the day's weather. What had become of Papa's journal? No one would have bid for that, the way they bid for the armoire, the sofa and the cheval mirror.

'Oh, Emmy, I can't bear it, all our lovely things!' Mama had wrung her hands, tears had rolled down her cheeks, and Emily had realized that they should never have come, that they should have stayed away on the day of the auction.

But that was much later. Emily had been married by then, she'd no longer lived at Alleyn Dene. It wasn't the auction she should be thinking about, it was the seventeen happy years.

Stood there on the grass verge gazing down at the house amidst the trees, she suddenly had the strangest feeling that she was looking back in time. If she'd had Papa's telescope to hand, she felt sure she would have seen the lawn, the patio and the French doors in finest detail, just as they'd always been. And if she'd focused the telescope still further, she might have glimpsed a little girl in the drawing room, a little girl with her face pressed against the glass of the French doors, a little girl watching the tiny, hazy figures on Hoosun Hill with no idea that she was looking into her own future. For a split second, Emily felt as if she was in two places at once. Both here on the hill, and down in the drawing room. Both a grown woman, and a little girl. How she ached for those lost days before the war — before the advent of motor cars, before the Liberal landslide — before that terrible evening at Nethercote Hall which had changed things forever—

'Mother?'

She gave a start. She had not heard Chad approach. She felt a sense of panic, sure that her thoughts must be written all over her face. But it was all right, he'd noticed nothing. Indeed, he seemed entirely withdrawn from her, his eyes staring into the distance.

As the past faded away, she became aware of Chad's agitation. He was twisting an oily rag in his hands.

'Mother, I . . . I have something to tell you.'

She experienced a flash of comprehension. Of course! Of course he'd got something to tell her! Everything fell into place. This was what today had been all about. He had been building up to this moment all along — whatever this moment was.

An amorphous yet powerful feeling of disappointment swept over her, and it smothered for a moment any sense of curiosity as to what he was about to say. When he did speak, therefore, she was caught completely off guard.

'I've . . . I've met someone, Mother. A girl.'

I've met someone . . . a girl . . . The words echoed in her head. They made her feel dizzy. She was suddenly afraid of falling, standing so close to the edge as she was, and with her head in a spin. She took a step back, a step to safety — but also a step away from Chad.

He noticed. He misunderstood. She could see it in his eyes. He turned abruptly away, flinging the oily rag aside — a gesture reminiscent, not of her placid papa, but of her father-in-law, Sir Hubert, impatient and quick-tempered.

I've met someone . . . a girl . . . Well, what did she expect? That he'd be different from every other boy, that he'd never look at a girl? It had to happen one day.

But, oh, why today? Why tell her today, here, now?

'It's not important, Mother,' Chad muttered. 'It doesn't matter.'

'But darling—'

'I've only known her a few months. I don't suppose anything will come of it. But I wanted to tell you. We've never had secrets from each other.'

Her heart lurched. If only he knew! She felt weighed down with secrets! And the darkest secret of all opened like a bottomless pit that could never be quite covered over.

Avoiding her eyes, Chad stammered, 'I'd . . . I'd rather you didn't tell Grandfather.'

'What do you mean? Why not? Oh, Chad, darling, you've got me worried now.'

'There's no need to be worried, Mother. There's really no need. Honestly, there's nothing to worry about. It's just that she's . . . she's . . . I don't think Grandfather would understand,' he ended rather lamely and turned away, kicking at the turf with his black brogues. After a moment he spoke again, hesitant, unsure, not looking at her. 'Sometimes . . . sometimes I think that Grandfather can be a . . . a bit of a bully. He's . . . he's not always nice to you, Mother. It makes me wonder if—' He took a deep breath, ended in a rush. 'It makes me wonder if you are entirely happy!'

He was staring at the horizon, eyes narrowed, frowning, and she wanted to take him into her arms as she had when he was a little boy, she wanted to hug him to her breast and tell him everything would be all right. But he was too old for that now, and she knew what she had to do. It wasn't so hard. She'd had years of practice. She'd had years of practice, pretending her own feelings didn't exist and hiding the truth.

'Of course I'm happy, darling. Why wouldn't I be? I've got you, I've got a lovely home, there's nothing I want or need. As for your grandfather, you mustn't take too much notice, it's just his way. And he's been good to us, when all is said and done. We'd never have got by without him.'

'All the same . . .' Chad's eyes narrowed even more and he set his jaw. 'I don't see that I need to follow his advice *all* the time. I'm old enough to make my own decisions — nearly twenty.'

'Not for three months.' She bit her lip as soon as the words were out. She'd spoken without thinking. She didn't want it to sound as if she was trying to hold back time, to keep him a boy. She had to face facts. If he'd met a girl . . . well, it was what boys his age did, it was what happened when boys got older. She wouldn't, in her heart of hearts, want it any other way.

She wondered very much about the girl he'd met but was too shy now to turn the conversation back to her. Chad looked so very fierce — so very grown up too — and handsome and earnest. What was he thinking about, as he stared so raptly at the horizon? The girl? Sir Hubert? Or something else entirely? In some ways, Chad had always been a mystery. She remembered watching him at times when he was a very little boy, his tiny fists bunched, his tiny mouth puckered, his big deep eyes lost in thought — thinking, thinking, thinking — thinking for minutes on end, remote from her. It was silly, but she'd always felt incredibly lonely at such moments.

He broke into her chain of thought. 'We ought to make a move, Mother. We should be getting back. I told Aunt Violet we'd be home for dinner, and you know what she's like.'

'Of course, darling. Let's go.'

She took a last look back as the motor car roared down the hill, but Alleyn Dene had already disappeared, lost in a fold of the land. The car ate up the road. The wind snatched at her hat. She wished she'd asked Chad to put the canopy up.

Watching him drive — looking at his hands on the wheel — such big hands, such strong chunky fingers — she found herself comparing them to the tiny, delicate hands that had gripped her fingers as they walked back and forth together, mother and son, along the lane that ran past their little cottage. But that was long ago, before the war, the other side of the great divide: a different world, a lost world.

Engrossed in her thoughts, Emily was not aware of seeing the gates of Nethercote Hall: they came and went in an instant. All she was conscious of was a brief stirring of fear in her mind. Almost at once, the fear was whisked away, and was left behind amongst the fields and the trees and the hedgerows of the green April countryside as the car sped towards home.

CHAPTER TWO

The gates of Nethercote Hall, barely noticed earlier, began to loom large as Emily drifted towards sleep that night in her bedroom at Heartlands. The gates were cast iron, rusty from long disuse, permanently open. Grass and weeds grew thickly all round them. Emily, half-dreaming, found herself hypnotized by the intricate lattice ironwork. The twists and twirls and curves and loops seemed to her like secret occult symbols, spelling out some terrible augury of doom. If only she could read them, if only she could understand — it seemed, in her dream, of vital importance.

She tossed and turned in bed, muttering and mumbling. She could see past the gates, she could see the long, unkempt drive that led like a tunnel beneath the overhanging trees to the gloomy portals of the Hall, hidden from view.

But even in her dreams she had never been back to Nethercote Hall. She had not been back since that night, twenty-one years ago, when she'd left the ball so precipitously and fled into the dark . . .

* * *

Hitching up her skirts, Emily Sutton, aged seventeen, ran sobbing through the black and squally night. She wanted to get home to Alleyn Dene. She wanted Nanny, who always made her feel better. She wanted Mama, who took everything in her stride. But Mama, Nanny, Alleyn Dene: they all seemed impossibly distant as the darkness closed around her. The faster she ran, the further away home seemed to get. The thought of home was leading her on like a will-o'-the-wisp, only to vanish into thin air when she reached out to touch it.

A sense of panic gripped her. Where was she? Dimly she remembered passing the gates of Nethercote Hall. She must now be out in the lane. But was she running in the right direction? She could not be sure. And she dared not stop to get her bearings. Once she stopped, the night would swallow her up and there would be no way back.

The wind was gusting fiercely. There were spots of rain in the air. There were also *things* flying around her. She could hear them, feel them. They were brushing against her face, they were getting tangled in her hair. Bats. They must be bats. She could hear their wings flapping. She could sense their sharp claws reaching to grab her. Their mouths had sharp little teeth that nibbled at her as they swooped. Bats. How she hated bats. How she *loathed* them. But she was at their mercy. Bats, bats, bats—

She screamed in terror. She waved her hands about, fending them off. She ran faster and faster until, tripping over her skirts, she went flying through the air to land with a thud in the mud and watery ruts of the lane. They would get her now. The bats would get her. She lay cowering on the ground with her hands over her head, screaming and screaming until she had nothing left — then she simply lay there, completely drained.

If, at that moment, someone had happened along and come to her rescue — if someone had helped her to her feet and asked what was wrong — she would have said that she'd left her gloves behind: her long, white gloves with the ivory buttons. She'd left her gloves at Nethercote Hall, and it was a calamity. They were new gloves, brand new. They were perfect. They were so white and lovely, the buttons so smooth and round, and now she would never — oh, she would never — oh, oh, oh—

The real reason for her flight she could not have told anyone. She could not even admit it to herself. She had blotted it out completely, because even the bats did not hold such terror as—

But the bats seemed to have missed her. They had gone wheeling and flocking into the night, driven by the wind. Or perhaps there had never been any bats in the first place. Perhaps she'd imagined it. That squeaking sound: it wasn't so much like the squeaking of bats as of trees rubbing together as they seethed and tossed in the rising gale. And the horrible, velvety wings: it was nothing more than the wind gusting in her face.

Slowly, she got to her feet. She looked all round, wide-eyed. The immense, stormy night was utterly impervious to her. This was some comfort. She did not want to be noticed. If she'd only gone unnoticed just now, when—

But she must look a fright, with mud on her face and mud all down her frock, and her hair blown every which way, and her hands — her poor, grazed, bare hands! Oh, those lovely gloves! A present from Granny Drage, and now lost. She'd never get them back. Someone would take them — the Barford girls, perhaps, who were well known for making off with other people's property 'by mistake'. What would Granny say about the gloves? Emily quailed in the dark, for Granny Drage was stern and sharp, and forged through life with a relentless energy that didn't diminish with age.

Oddly, out here in the wild night, lost and bedraggled, the thought of Granny Drage gave Emily a modicum of courage. Granny would not be afraid of the dark. She would not be afraid of the bats. She would swot the bats impatiently aside and march on, indomitable.

Now that she came to look, Emily found that the night was not quite as black as she'd thought. There was no moon, of course, and no stars either. Papa would not be out with his telescope tonight. But there was a sort of shimmer in the sky and she could clearly see the clouds racing. The lane too seemed to glisten faintly. Wasn't that a junction just ahead? Yes, it most certainly was: a familiar fork in the road! One way led to the village and the other wound down into the little hollow in which Alleyn Dene nestled.

Emily took heart. She had come so far, she had done so well, home was much nearer than she had dared hope. She hurried to the fork in the road, took the left-hand lane, then searched along the line of the hedge for the little footpath that was a short cut to Alleyn Dene. Once she found the footpath, it seemed no time at all before she saw lights shining ahead, the friendly lights of home. At last! Oh, at last!

She stumbled through the copse and climbed over the fence, but here she paused. She couldn't just walk in through the front door. She couldn't turn up in this state, dishevelled and muddy, her face streaked with tears. What explanation could she give? What could she possibly *say*?

The truth. She'd been brought up always to tell the truth. Nanny said that—

Emily shuddered. For the first time, cracks began to show. For the first time she began to remember what she'd been trying so hard to blot out. But who would believe her? Who would believe it of *him*? Where in any case would she begin? Were there even any words to describe it?

She began to cry helplessly, bitterly, standing out on the dark lawn, thinking of Mama and Papa snug in the drawing room, Mama no doubt reading yet another Marie Corelli, Papa writing up the day's weather in his log book. The friendly lights of home — the bright, new electric lights, Papa's showpiece — seemed to taunt her. She was an outcast. A ghost. Like Cathy in *Wuthering Heights*.

'Let me in!' she sobbed. 'Oh, please let me in!'

But after a moment she shuddered again and wiped her eyes. It was no good crying. There was no one to help her but herself. She had to harden her heart and make the best of it. She must carry on as if nothing had happened. She could easily tell a few lies. What were lies compared to the way he'd . . . the way he'd *touched* her . . . the way he'd put his hand on her—

She shook her head. She mustn't think about it. She *mustn't.* Once inside, she'd be safe. Once inside, she could forget all about it and pick up the threads of her life. All she had to do was find a way to get inside.

She made her way stealthily round the side of the house. She tried the tradesmen's door. It was not yet locked. Her court shoes were silent on the flagstones as she tiptoed along the dark passage. Light leaked under the door to the servants' hall. Muffled voices sounded inside. Holding her breath, she inched her way past and came at last to the back stairs. She began to climb, as quiet and wary as a thief.

She had only got as far as the first floor landing when disaster struck. A dark figure suddenly loomed up in front of her. For one heart-stopping moment she thought it was *him*, that he'd followed her, that he was here, waiting, that she'd fallen into his clutches again. Then—

'Miss Sutton? Is that you? Stone me! You made me jump out my skin!'

The landing light flared on and there was Perks — only the housemaid Perks. Emily slumped against the wall, weak with relief. For the moment she was quite unable to talk.

'What are you up to, miss, sneaking up the back stairs in the dark? Does Mrs Sutton know you're back? She was just saying, isn't it about time to send Jenkins with the carriage.'

'Th-th-there's no need.' Emily gathered herself, trying to put her thoughts in order. She would need her wits about her. 'I came back with . . . with the Heygates. The Heygates brought me home.'

'I never heard a carriage, miss.' Perks looked at her suspiciously, eyes widening as she took in the full extent of Emily's dishevelment. 'Lawks! Whatever's happened to you? You're soaking wet!'

'You know how the Heygates' carriage roof leaks—'

'But you're covered in mud, too, and your hair — look at the state of your hair, and after I spent so long doing it up!'

'There's nothing wrong with my hair,' said Emily obstinately, trying to swim against the tide. 'There's no mud, it's only rain. The Heygates' carriage—'

'The Heygates my foot! I've got eyes, miss!'

'Yes, and a nose — which you should keep out of other people's business!'

Emily was rather breathless with her own daring, taking that tone with Perks. But Granny Drage would have been even more brusque. Granny Drage didn't believe in mollycoddling servants.

'I want hot water, Perks, and towels. Bring them to my room at once.'

'Very good, miss,' said Perks stiffly, offended.

'Oh, and Perks, you needn't tell Mother anything about this.'

'Whatever you say, miss.' Perks turned to go but then looked back for a moment. There was an expression on her face which made Emily think of the words *sly* and *furtive*. All at once, Emily felt as if she was somehow putting herself into Perks's hands, as if they were complicit in some way, as if Perks now had some sort of hold over her.

'As quick as you can, please, Perks.' Emily tried now to emulate not Granny Drage but Mama, who was firm with the staff but always polite. Emily needed Perks on her side.

In her room, by the light of the fire, Emily with fumbling fingers pulled off her shoes and stockings and clawed at her torn, muddy frock. She couldn't reach round to the fastenings, had to wriggle out of it like a snake shedding its skin. She gathered it up, a sordid little bundle, and threw it with all her might into the far corner of the room. As she did so, she caught sight of herself in the mirror, the merest glimpse. She shied away, putting her hands across her face. At the same moment, a creeping fear and paralysis came over her. She sank down onto the rug in front of the fire. She had rid herself of her grubby clothes but she still felt stained and dirty, as if the mud had seeped into her skin, as if it was working its way into her cuts and grazes. She felt that she would never be clean again. And her room — her dear little room — seemed dirty too, as if a thin green slime was creeping up the walls, spreading across the floor, slowly covering everything, like some hideous moss or mould. She wished Nanny was there. Nanny would never let anyone or anything hurt her. But Nanny had gone, had left two weeks ago to enjoy her retirement by the sea. Emily felt utterly alone. And — like the mud working in, like the slime spreading — the full horror of what had happened was slowly taking hold. Trembling and shaking, sobbing, she clutched at the rug, as if trying to anchor herself, as if trying to stop herself from being swept away.

Suddenly the door burst open and the light came on. It was Perks with the hot water and the towels, but these she put aside at once when she saw Emily's distress.

'Lumme, miss, whatever's wrong, whatever's the matter?'

'Oh Perks . . . Perks . . . I can't stop it . . . I can't . . . I can't . . .'

Emily found herself weeping convulsively in Perks's arms. She clung on.

'Who has done this to you, miss? Who?'

But she couldn't say the name — she couldn't say what had happened — she just buried her face in Perks's shoulder and sobbed and sobbed and sobbed.

* * *

More than twenty years later, Emily Winmer woke with a start in her bed at Heartlands. She lay rigid in the dark, gripped by terror. She could smell his whisky breath, she could actually *feel* his pawing hands—

With an immense effort, as if her arm was made of stone, she inched her fingers towards the bedside table. With a last gasp, she was able to turn on the bedside lamp.

Her arm dropped. She was spent. But now she lay in a pool of protective light and the terror of the dark was retreating. There was no whisky breath, there were no pawing hands. *He* was not here. *He* had never come anywhere near Heartlands.

But as the terror faded, a feeling of hopelessness took its place. *He* was not here, but she would never be free of him. And all because of what had happened in the cloakroom at Nethercote Hall two decades ago.

It had been so unexpected. She'd been dazed, disorientated, meshed in utter confusion, unable to account for the way he'd suddenly changed, dapper and debonair in the ballroom, grasping and groping in the dark of the cloakroom. He'd become a ravening animal: a beast, not a man. And the worst of it was, she'd had no inkling — not the slightest idea — of what he'd been about to do.

Was I really so innocent? Was I really so feeble and helpless? She'd asked herself these questions over and over down the years. She'd asked why she'd done nothing to defend herself. Why hadn't she kicked him in the shins and fled? Why hadn't she opened her mouth and screamed blue murder? Instead, befuddled in the fusty dark, she'd just stood there unmoving and let him do what he wanted.

Lying in bed, she drew the covers up to her chin, holding them tight in her fists. Sweat trickled down her face. Her heart was racing. She felt tired, so tired. She felt ground down and eroded. She was trapped like a hamster on a wheel. There was no escape. It was always with her, always would be.

It. Twenty-odd years ago, Emily had not even been sure what *it* was, what exactly had happened to her. Such ignorance would be impossible now. Girls in this post-war era were worldly-wise, with their bare arms and their ankles showing, dancing with strangers and smoking in public. But even twenty years ago some girls had known more than others. Perks had not been ignorant. Perks had been all too knowing.

'Was it a gentleman, miss? Did he . . . did he force himself on you? Did he have his way with you? Is that it?'

'No, no, no,' Emily had sobbed in her room, hanging on to Perks for dear life.

No, no, no. The words echoed in Emily's head as she lay in the pool of light thinking of her seventeen-year-old self. She had only said no, no, no because she didn't know what Perks was talking about. *Force himself, have his way*: it had meant nothing to her.

'You won't say anything, will you, Perks? Oh, you mustn't say anything, you *mustn't*! Promise me! Promise me you won't tell anyone!'

'Now, miss, don't take on so. I won't say a word, I swear on my life, if that's how you want it. It'll be our little secret, just you and me.'

Emily in bed shuddered, remembering the way Perks had given a sly wink as she said the words *our little secret*.

Or was that, Emily wondered, her mind playing tricks? She couldn't be sure.

Looking back, Emily thought about the days following the ball at Nethercote Hall. She'd wanted to know what had happened to her. She'd wanted to know what it *meant*. She'd been too ashamed, too afraid to ask Perks. She'd thought of Papa's encyclopaedias and reference books. Papa had always hated anything vague or imprecise. He'd liked proper names for things, he'd liked proper, scientific explanations. So Emily had crept into Papa's study when there was no one around and had searched through the shelves of books until she found what she wanted.

Carnal knowledge. Copulation. Coitus.

Rape.

She had stared at the word on the page, *rape*. It had blurred in her vision. It had seemed too fantastic to believe. *Rape* was an archaic word, a medieval word. *Rape* was something that happened in myths and legends and old paintings: *The Rape of Lucretia, The Rape of the Sabine Women*. It was not something that happened in modern times, here and now, in 1905.

All the same, *something* had happened, there could be no doubt about that. And it had been something which hurt, which frightened her, which wasn't nice.

Emily remembered how she'd tried to puzzle it out, sitting not at Papa's desk but under it with a pile of books, sitting there as if she'd been a little girl again, giggling and hiding from Nanny, or merely passing the time, lying on her front and humming to herself as she traced with her finger the pattern in the carpet. Yet even when she was a little girl, nasty things had sometimes happened. A bee had once stung her: that had hurt. Then there'd been that day when the cows in Hobber Meadow had rushed her, thinking it was milking time: that had been terrifying. But Nanny had always been there. Nanny had soothed, cured, reassured. Nanny had made everything better.

In the autumn of 1905, there'd been no Nanny. Nanny had gone, had retired. When one was seventeen one didn't need a nanny. At seventeen, one should be able to soothe and cure oneself. *There, there, it's only a little sting, it's only the silly cows. You'll be all right now, you're safe now, it's all over, my little poppet.*

Lying sleepless in her bed, Emily remembered how she really had believed the wound would heal, the scab fade, that she could *make* herself forget, that everything would go back to normal. Little had she realized that her experience in the cloakroom at Nethercote Hall would gnaw away at her, gnaw her from the inside. Little had she realized that the details would never fade but would remain fresh and vivid in her mind so that even twenty-one years later there were times when she felt it had happened only yesterday.

She had never forgotten. But she had, over the years, learned to push the memories aside, to keep them out of focus. She had learned, on the whole, to live with them. But today, seeing Alleyn Dene again after so long, her head had been turned upside down and now her mind was whirling like a merry-go-round.

She would make it stop. She would get it under control again. She always did. But it took so much out of her. It had taken half her life, all her youth, holding the lid down. Lying now in the pool of light with the bed covers up to her chin, she felt old and worn out, as if she had nothing left. She couldn't even shed a tear for the girl she'd once been, the girl called Emily Sutton who'd been lost to the world a long time ago.

CHAPTER THREE

Chad couldn't sleep. He was walking in the garden, humming to himself, 'Tea for Two', a silly song. He knew very well it was a silly song. But—

Picture you upon my knee . . .

To picture Lily upon his knee made him almost giddy with pleasure. It hadn't happened for real yet, but it could, it might.

Just me for you, and you for me . . .

Love, he said to himself. This must be love, this feeling of . . . of . . .

Of what? Well, it was a clean and pure feeling, like being able to breathe properly. It was like stepping from the stuffy confines of the house to walk in the midnight garden, with the night opening around him, wide and unexplored. A liberating feeling. An all-encompassing feeling. He'd never have guessed love was like this, until it happened.

'*Tea for two*! *And two for tea*!'

He laughed, shushing himself. His tuneless singing would wake the whole house if he wasn't careful. Grandfather would growl and bluster, call him a hedonist, a libertine, a flagrant epicure (but was it so wrong to want a bit of fun, a bit of *life*?). The aunts would purse their lips and shake their heads — Aunt Violet most of all: she probably thought it was immoral to walk in the garden at midnight in one's shirt sleeves. Not that Aunt Violet was in need of an excuse these days to make her little remarks. Grandfather passed comment because he felt it his duty, but Aunt Violet seemed to take pleasure in doing it.

'*Picture Lily upon my knee*,' Chad sang under his breath, turning round to look at the house which loomed as a wall of shadow against the paler sky. Anyone who was looking out could hardly fail to miss him, ambling across the lawn. But all the windows were dark — all except one. Mother's room, was it? There was the faintest glimmer through the curtains. It was unlike Mother to be up so late.

Dear old Mother! She was such a gentle soul, so quiet and timid. He was awfully fond of her. But to ask point-blank if she was happy, as he'd done that very afternoon — to come right out and say it! He blushed to remember. But this was obviously something else love did for you. It opened your eyes — it made you see people clearly. And it made you fearless, absolutely fearless.

Today had not entirely gone to plan. He'd wanted to tell Mother about Lily but hadn't banked on being quite so tongue-tied, nor on Mother backing away as if she didn't want to know. Taking Mother to see Alleyn Dene now seemed rather a mistake. He'd wanted to give her a treat, but he hadn't stopped to think how she would feel, seeing her old house again, her childhood home, knowing it was now in the hands of strangers.

How did Mother actually feel about Alleyn Dene? Was it possible to love a house in the same way one loved a person? Think how he would feel if he saw Lily in the arms of a stranger! But perhaps Mother had got upset for quite different reasons. She might have been thinking about Grandpa, for instance — poor old Grandpa. Or maybe even Father. But Father had never had any real connection to Alleyn Dene, so it couldn't be that.

Chad shivered. It was rather cold. His breath was steaming. Walking briskly, he made his way round to the side of the house and let himself into the large double garage, purpose-built, as the whole house had been, to Grandfather's specifications. Turning on the light, he feasted his eyes on his motor car, his beloved Sunbeam, so stylish, so graceful. The curves of the wheel arches filled him with exquisite joy. The headlamps like staring eyes made him feel that the vehicle was all but alive. How different it was to its companion, Grandfather's stately, lumbering Rolls! He caressed the bonnet of his car, experienced an all but overwhelming urge to leap into the driver's seat, roar off into the night, drive to London, to Lily: to Lily's street, to Lily's house — except he didn't know where she lived, not yet. That, too, like taking her on his knee, would come in time. Until then . . . well, he admired her caution, he heartily approved of the way she looked before she leaped. She was not a girl to rush into things, which made it all the more wonderful that she'd rushed into this romance with him! For that was how it had been so far, a veritable whirlwind, less than four months since they met, six weeks since they began holding hands, only two weeks since first he'd kissed her . . .

He sat down on the running board of his car, elbows propped on his knees, resting his chin in his hands, thinking back to the beginning. Serendipity. That was how they'd met. If he'd not been walking down that exact street at that exact moment, just before Christmas . . . He shivered to think how different things might have been. But Fate had taken a hand. Fate had it all planned. It was Fate that had sent him to stay with Great Aunt Margery in Belgravia, Fate that had prompted a Cambridge chum to ask him to luncheon that day of all days, Fate which had made him run late — well, perhaps that hadn't been Fate so much, he was always late for everything. And so, he'd been in a hurry, buttoning his waistcoat, arranging his watch chain, not looking where he was going, which had resulted in him colliding with a girl coming the other way along Ebury Street. To be fair, she couldn't have been looking where she was going either, or else she'd have stepped out of his way, but he'd done the gentlemanly thing and taken all the blame, apologizing profusely as he picked up her hat, desperate to be off.

Where had she been going that day? The purlieus of Belgravia were surely far from her usual haunts. Funny that he'd never thought of this before. He'd have to ask her. No doubt that, too, had been arranged by Fate. At the time, all he'd been thinking was that he'd be late for lunch. He'd been on the point of rushing off, when something clicked in his head and he'd looked at the girl again — really looked at her this time. And that was when it happened. It had taken only a split second for him to be bowled over — to be captivated by her smile, her eyes, her voice. Smile first. Eyes second. Then her voice. Her voice!

'Please, sir, don't take on so, it's my fault I'm sure, I walk round half the time with my — oh, my hat, tah very much — with my eyes shut, I hope you've not done yourself a mischief or nothing.'

He'd stood there staring: staring at her shy smile that faded in and out like sunshine between the clouds. Staring at her cautious eyes, extraordinarily blue, like sapphires. Listening to her voice, sweet and unaffected, with the faintest of accents (cockney, was it?) and perhaps the merest hint of a lisp, which made his heart turn over.

But what was the use of words? Words didn't do her justice.

It was most odd. He'd had the strangest feeling that he knew her already, that he'd met her before — impossible, of course. Perhaps what he'd really been feeling was that he *ought* to know her, that their meeting had been ordained.

Sitting on the running board, chewing his lip, Chad tried to put the events of their meeting in the proper order — it seemed terribly important he should do so. He'd handed her the hat, which had been knocked off in their collision, she'd put it back on, she'd said — or was it he who'd said? — No. He simply couldn't remember which of them had spoken first. All he knew was that, if he'd been in full possession of his faculties, he'd never have been so forward as to suggest — unless it was Lily who'd suggested — someone, anyway, had suggested that they meet again later.

He'd torn himself away from her. He'd been late for lunch. Strange to say, his chum's people hadn't minded in the least. They'd been quite taken with him. They'd thought him (his chum had told him later) witty, clever, modest, polite. This was all the more extraordinary because he wasn't the sort of person who usually made much of an impression — not all at once, anyway. Too shy, too solemn, too reserved: those were the words that had been used of him over the years. But that day, that lunch . . . He had a vague recollection of explaining at length why it was a good thing for Britain to be back on the gold standard, and he'd followed this with a lucid and cogent analysis of the Locarno Pact. He'd been incisive, informative and hugely entertaining. He'd made them all laugh with his humorous asides. And it had all happened without him even trying, without him giving it so much as a thought. He hadn't been able to think, because his mind had been full of Lily (he hadn't known her name then). Would she turn up as promised? What would they find to talk about? Where would they go? Were her eyes *really* that blue?

And so here he was, three and a half months later. He'd met her a dozen times. He'd held her hand. He'd kissed her. He wanted to tell the whole world about her. But he hadn't even been able to tell Mother, not properly. And Grandfather — was Lily the sort of girl Grandfather would approve of? Chad had not considered this until today. Or maybe he hadn't *allowed* himself to consider it. What he'd found most disconcerting today was that, in telling Mother about Lily — in starting to tell her — he had begun to see Lily in a different light. Or, rather, it had made him see her as other people would see her — her clothes slightly shabby, her accent slightly cockney (definitely cockney, there was no denying it), her station in life rather lower than one might have wished. None of this had seemed to matter until today, and even then it hadn't put him off wanting to tell Mother.

But Mother was one thing, Grandfather quite another. Grandfather had a habit of dismissing people — whole classes of people. Then there was Aunt Violet. Aunt Violet liked nothing better than to look down her nose. And where Aunt Violet led, the other aunts would follow. Also, what about his chums at Cambridge? They would raise their eyebrows a bit, no doubt about it. They would be sure to rib him. Not that they themselves never flirted with girls like Lily. Some of them had done more than flirt, if you could believe them. But *love* — love was another matter entirely.

Chad set his jaw. Let them all raise their eyebrows and look down their noses! Let them think what they liked! He could take it. He was old enough to know his own mind.

He frowned, remembering what Mother had said that afternoon about them needing Grandfather. It was true. Grandfather provided a home, paid for Cambridge — even the beloved Sunbeam was a present from Grandfather. Did that make one beholden? Grandfather probably thought so. What about Father — would he have thought so too? Or would Father have seen things differently? If only Father hadn't died!

The furrows in Chad's brow deepened. Fancy thinking about Father. What had brought that on? He didn't think of Father from one month to the next.

Father, his dead Father, the war hero.

The war. Chad did not like to think about the war. Thinking about the war gave him an odd, cold, tight feeling inside, which he couldn't explain. Father was mixed up in this feeling somehow, but there was more to it than that. Why was it one should feel so oddly about the war? He wasn't the only boy who'd had to grow up without a father, he wasn't the only boy who'd been too young to fight. Did all the other boys in the same boat get this odd, cold feeling too? Sometimes, when this feeling came over him, he wanted very much to get drunk, to dance the night away instead of going to bed, to smash crockery and roister in the streets, like the bloods at college.

He jumped to his feet and paced restlessly around the garage, but there was hardly any room to move and he felt trapped. Switching off the light, he let himself out, pulling the door to behind him.

The air was icy now outside, and his feverish mood soon cooled. High in the sky, the clouds had parted in places. Stars glimmered in deep pools of blackness. Chad craned his neck, looking up, remembering what Grandpa used to say about the stars being other suns and how he, Chad, had refused to believe it. He'd stuck stubbornly to his contention that the stars were souls, the souls of the dead. Later on, aged ten and eleven, unhappy at prep school, homesick — grieving too, suddenly fatherless — he'd often lain awake for hours in the dorm, whilst the others were fast asleep. Sometimes, he'd crept to the window and leaned out, looking up at the night sky. He'd told himself that he could see Father's star, that Father's star would burn all the brighter because it was so new. It had comforted him to think of Father up there in the heavens looking down, watching over him.

As your bright and tiny spark
Lights the traveller in the dark . . .

Chad sang a different song, a song from his childhood. His breath steamed in the cold air.

Twinkle, twinkle, little star . . .

Mother had sung this to him in the days of the cottage when he was a very little boy.

Which of all these myriad stars was Father's star? Chad's feet crunched on the gravel path as he turned and twisted, trying to remember, to pick out Father's star — Father's soul.

What had Father been like, exactly? It was strange that one knew so little about him, just old photographs and a sense or reverence. Father the war hero. Would Father have approved of Lily? Had Father ever experienced this overwhelming sense of being alive, of wanting to walk in the garden at midnight and sing silly songs? Had Father ever felt like this about Mother?

It was impossible to know. Father really was like a star, fixed and immutable and ever more distant. Father was a fading star in the firmament of one's memory.

Rubbing the crick in his neck as he gazed up at the unfolding sky, Chad sang softly under his breath, '*Father, Father, twinkling star, how I wonder who you were*!'

CHAPTER FOUR

'Must you bring those flowers in here, Emily?'

'Violet! Oh, hello, I didn't see you there.'

'Perhaps if you opened your eyes . . .' Violet, seated on the Chesterfield sofa, looked at Emily sourly. 'Those flowers. The smell. It makes me feel quite nauseous.'

'I'm sorry, Violet, I forgot.'

'Well, really, I don't see how you could. You know what a martyr I am to my sinuses. Do you never think of anybody but yourself?'

Emily summoned a smile, trying to foster charitable thoughts about her sister-in-law — never an easy task. Violet — frosty, pinch-faced, with greying hair, dressed in the fashions of twenty years ago — was sorting through some papers: the week's menus, by the look of it.

Emily brought her nose close to the cluster blooms in her hand, gave a surreptitious sniff. Such a heavenly smell. Was it really possible that anyone could object to it? Or was Violet just being awkward?

As Emily retreated to the far end of the morning room, taking her bunch of tulips, hyacinths and daffodils with her, along with a vase to put them in, the thought popped unbidden into her head that someone, once upon a time, might have, or actually had, called her sisters-in-law *the three witches.*

It wasn't me, Emily hastened to add, *I would never be so cruel.* Although she was forced to admit that she'd been rather interested in witches as a child, and had purloined Papa's telescope on occasion to try to spot them flying on their broomsticks across the face of the moon.

Searching for a suitable place to put the vase, Emily dismissed from her mind the image of a feisty, witch-obsessed little girl who could not possibly be her younger self, and must be pure invention. Perhaps it had been Alan, then, who had called his sisters *witches.* Certainly he had not been blind to their faults. They were spoilt, he'd said. They were Father's little angels, and they could do no wrong. It made them impossible to get along with, which was why he'd argued with them all the time when he was younger. But he'd loved them in his own way, just as they in their way had loved him.

Emily bit her lip. As if on cue, there was Alan himself. The photograph on the sideboard had become so familiar by now that one usually never noticed it. Today, though, she saw it afresh. It must have been taken around 1915. Alan was in uniform. He looked much younger than his thirty years, round-faced, dimple-chinned, an uncertain smile on his lips, his eyes rather apprehensive behind his little round spectacles. A gentle-looking man. Not the type of man to call *anyone* a witch, let alone his own sisters.

Alan had been very different to his father, and it was his father who dominated this room. The painting of Sir Hubert, unlike Alan's photo, was impossible to miss, a vast, imposing portrait over the mantelpiece. Sir Hubert in all his glory, grave and majestic, swathed in flowing robes, one hand resting on — of all things — the hilt of a sword. This portrait had been painted soon after his investiture. It showed a man at the height of his powers. He gazed out, meeting the future head-on.

Sir Hubert was an intimidating man, so much so that it was all but impossible for Emily to believe that once, long ago, she had found him not intimidating but *boring.*

Emily placed the vase of flowers on the sideboard. 'Perhaps here, Violet?' Next to Alan. Alan had liked flowers. The garden of their little cottage had overflowed with them. It had been a rather wild sort of garden, very secluded, almost secret, like Mary Lennox's. Emily smiled to remember it. 'Perhaps here?'

'Oh, very well, if you must.' Violet's voice was querulous. 'Though I don't see why we *need* flowers.'

'They brighten the place up. Don't you think so?'

Violet snorted, went back to the papers in her hand. 'Will that boy of yours be in for luncheon? I really must get these menus to Cook.'

That boy, Emily wanted to say as she arranged the flowers, trying to make them look as unarranged as possible, *is your nephew*. 'I'm not sure if he will, Violet. Chad has gone into town this morning and—'

'What, *again*? I suppose he'll be late back. He won't want lunch *or* dinner. You ought to put your foot down, Emily. You ought to put a stop to this gallivanting. He will get corrupted. London is a dangerous place these days, all those cocktails and that Negro music and heaven knows what else: it's always in the papers.'

Emily recognized in Violet's pronouncement a favourite theme of Sir Hubert's: London's debauchery, the city of sin. *They parrot their father,* she thought, *they never stop to think for themselves.* Alan had often said the same thing.

But why am I thinking of Alan? she asked herself, turning away from the sideboard and looking out of the window, her back to Violet. *Why think of Alan now, after nearly nine years?*

It was because of her day out on Sunday, that glimpse of Alleyn Dene. Ever since then, memories had come tumbling into her mind like a waterfall released from the frost: at first a slow trickle, soon building to a deluge. Oh Alleyn Dene! Dear Alleyn Dene! (Alan. Alleyn Dene. Had not Alan's father once made a tasteless remark about the similarity of the names, something along the lines of Alleyn Dene being Alan's destiny? But when . . . when . . . ?)

Whilst her mind was groping into the murky past, she looked out at the terrace and the steps down to the lawn. The shorn grass, the clipped topiary, the line of trees beyond: it was all neat and orderly, just as Sir Hubert liked. But it wasn't perfect. There was moss growing between the flagstones on the terrace, there were weeds in the grass, the tops of the trees made a decidedly ragged line against the grey of the sky. These were the sort of details Sir Hubert noticed. He railed against the *untidiness* of nature. He railed against the untidi-ness of people, too. People, like nature, were bent on going their own way. Why must everything in life be so *haphazard*? It was wasteful and inefficient. It offended his sensibilities.

Watching grey clouds scudding across the space of sky above the untidy tops of the trees, Emily was jolted out of the past by Violet's just-spoken words, still reverberating in her head: *that boy . . . he will get corrupted . . . London is a dangerous place . . .* Did Violet know something? The girl, for instance: the girl Chad had mentioned on Sunday. Was she somehow connected to London? Chad had been reticent about the girl and it was unlikely he would confide in his aunts. But Violet and her sisters could be cunning — they winkled things out, they were like a dog with a bone. It came, Alan had said, from having nothing to do, from being thwarted. They squandered their talents on idle gossip and petty intrigue.

Poor Violet! One ought to feel sorry for her. One ought to be more understanding. If only she didn't make it so difficult for one to like her!

'Violet! Violet!'

A trumpeting voice resounded along the passage. Moments later Sir Hubert stomped into the room. Gruff and white-haired, stiff-looking, eyes glaring. He was clutching two envelopes in his gnarled hands.

'So this is where you've got to, Violet. Didn't you hear me calling? I've had that infernal woman — Cook — muttering in my ear, something about menus. It is of vital impor-tance, and so on and so forth. See to it, Violet, would you?'

'I have the menus here, Father. I was just checking—'

'Never mind all this prevarication! Get on with it! You can't expect your mother, in her condition . . .'

'There is nothing wrong with Mother,' said Violet coldly, getting to her feet.

'How can you say that, hmm, hmm, with all that your mother's had to suffer — Alan and so on and so forth?'

'And I suppose we haven't suffered? I suppose *I* haven't suffered? He was *my* brother!'

Violet swept from the room in high dudgeon. Sir Hubert was unimpressed. 'Suffer? Suffer? What does she know about suffering — what do any of them know? They've had every advantage, every comfort. They've always had far more than I ever had when I was growing up, eight of us in a terraced two-up two-down. That's suffering. That's hardship. But what has all this luxury done for them? They are albatrosses round my neck. Albatrosses!' He stuck his lip out, white eyebrows bristling.

How and when, Emily wondered, had Alan's sisters changed from angels to albatrosses? The days when they could do no wrong had long passed. But they'd never been allowed to *do* anything. That was part of the problem. Alan had been right.

Sir Hubert made a rumbling noise in his throat but slowly his expression changed, his eyebrows relaxed. A calculating look came into his eyes. He brandished the envelopes, one in each hand.

'Now then. Now then. I've letters here, letters to be posted, important letters. There's wind of a by-election. It could be the chance I've been waiting for. *This* letter is to the constituency party, offering my candidacy. And *this* letter is to Lloyd George, asking for his endorsement. I'm sure he'll be able to pull a few strings, and so on and so forth. He'll only be too glad, I think, to have me back in the House, someone he can rely on, hmm, hmm?' An eager light shone on his face. He lowered his voice, confiding. 'I can't trust these letters to the servants, do you see? Far too important! But I know I can rely on you, Emily. I can always rely on you. You'll take them straight away, won't you? You'll take them to the village and post them? Good, good. Well then, off you go! No time to lose!'

Reluctantly, Emily took the letters. Sir Hubert's words were a weight on her shoulders. She didn't *want* to be relied upon. She had no idea how she'd gained this reputation for reliability — unless, perhaps, in producing Sir Hubert's heir, she had put herself in clover forever. The nuisance of it was, that Sir Hubert's favouritism rankled with her sisters-in-law and made things awkward — especially now that the sisters were *albatrosses*.

As she pulled on her coat and slipped the important letters into a pocket, Emily found herself doubting whether this latest scheme of Sir Hubert's would prove more successful than any of the others. His one wish was to get back to the House of Commons. He spent his days plotting his return.

First elected in the Liberal landslide in 1906, Sir Hubert had held his Northamptonshire seat for sixteen years before being ousted by a Unionist opponent in 1922 — a bitter blow. He had found himself a West Country constituency in time for the snap poll in December the following year, scraping home with a wafer-thin majority, but less than eleven months later, in the election brought about by the fall of the first Labour government, Sir Hubert had been amongst the countless Liberal casualties. He had immediately begun to plan for his inevitable return to Westminster. Now aged seventy-six, he was waiting for the next election, searching for the right constituency, whilst nursing hopes of sneaking in via a by-election. But Emily had begun to doubt whether any of this would ever happen. Sir Hubert, during the war, had nailed his colours firmly to Lloyd George's mast. He was convinced even now that, if only the Coalition could be revived, all the country's ills would be cured. But one heard less and less of the Welsh Wizard these days. Was it possible that Lloyd George's day was done? Not that Emily would dare suggest such a thing to Sir Hubert. Nor did she confess that, if she was honest, she preferred Mr Baldwin as Prime Minister, a most soothing man.

Emily let herself out of the front door and walked down the drive, pausing to look back just before the house disappeared from view. Alleyn Dene having been so much on her mind these last few days, it seemed natural to compare the two. Brick-built Heartlands came off worse, square and modern and rather ugly. It had been constructed during the heyday of 1919 when Sir Hubert's stock had been riding high and the economic boom had pointed to an early return to pre-war prosperity. That hope, of course, had proved a chimera. But no one had foreseen it at the time, so soon after the Armistice. No one had realized that the pre-war world had gone for good.

Sir Hubert had got rich in the war, dabbling in this and that —profiteering, some said unkindly. When the fighting was over, he'd been able to pay upfront for his new house. He'd also, it was suggested in some quarters, paid for his knighthood too. 'But that's not true!' Violet insisted. 'It's just jealousy and lies! Father would never do anything that was *immoral*! He wouldn't, he just wouldn't!'

There was something cloying about Heartlands, thought Emily as her eyes traced the neat rows of brickwork. It was somehow angular and unyielding, very different to Alleyn Dene with its warm sandstone walls. Alleyn Dene was a homely sort of house, welcoming and alive. But it was a long time since Emily had lived there. She'd moved out after her marriage, and later her beloved childhood home had been sold. She had made a new home for herself — and for Alan and Chad — in a little country cottage miles from anywhere. Afterwards — after Alan was killed in the war — she had lost the cottage too. She'd had to throw herself on Sir Hubert's mercy. That had meant, eventually, coming to live here in new-built Heartlands. She'd had no choice.

She sighed and turned away. Remembering the letters — her urgent and important mission — she hurried down the drive, heading for the village.

* * *

Violet Winmer watched through the glass panels of the front door as Emily dwindled down the drive. Lingering in the hallway, Violet was putting off the moment when she had to face Cook. Cook would make problems about the menus. Cook always made problems. She was obstinate. What made things so much worse, was that one did not quite know how to talk to her. All one wanted was that Cook should see reason but Cook, being naturally contrary, often refused to do so. One ended up by raising one's voice. One couldn't help it. Cook, of course, could not answer back. And yet, somehow — in some subtle and devious way — one always felt that Cook ended with the upper hand.

Why did one have such trouble? It was not as if one *wanted* to behave like that, shouting and hectoring, laying down the law. No doubt, thought Violet bitterly, it was all down to breeding. One did not come from a family that was *used* to servants. Indeed, one's forebears (Violet used the word *forebears* instead of *grandparents*, distancing herself) had been servants themselves. One was not like Emily, with her genteel ways. One did not have an aunt who'd married into the aristocracy, or a grandmother like old Mrs Drage with her airs and graces, able to make servants jump to her every whim.

Oh, but Emily, Violet said, unable to stop herself sneering even though she knew it pulled the muscles of one's face in all the wrong places. ('If the wind changes, you'll stay like that!' Father had used to joke, in the days before he'd become too pre-eminent for jokes.) *Emily*, who seemed so inoffensive, as if butter wouldn't melt, as if she wouldn't say boo to a goose — so very, very *prim*! But what about that book — that shameless, unspeakable book — hidden in her room? Not that one had been *snooping* when one found it. Of course not! One was entitled to go into any room one chose, when one ran the household — which one did, with Mother pretending to be ill so much of the time.

What if everyone pretended to be ill? *What if I*, said Violet, who got headaches, dreadful headaches: *what if I . . . ?*

She flexed her hands and scotched her rising hysteria, refusing to acknowledge it. She turned her attention instead back to Emily, who was not as innocent as she made out, who never had been. Some people were taken in, but not Violet Winmer. Violet had known from the start. She had seen the way that Emily set her cap at Alan, the way she'd trapped him. Poor Alan, her baby brother, starry-eyed and green as grass!

'You don't *have* to marry her, Alan! You don't owe her anything!'

'But I'm to blame, Vi. It's my fault. I'm the one who . . . who . . . who got her into trouble.'

'And *she* had no part in it, I suppose? She could have said no!'

'I don't think she quite realized . . . she is very innocent—'

'Humph!'

'Oh, but she is, Vi! I don't blame her in the least for any of this. I was the one who should have known better. But I was drunk, Vi. I was drunk. I can't think how I got in such a state. I feel so ashamed.'

'Shame is no reason to marry.'

'But love is. And I do love her, Vi. I love her very much.'

Alan had insisted that his love for Emily was real. But Emily had not loved Alan, Violet was convinced of it. Emily on her wedding day had not looked like a blissful bride. She had looked more like Andromeda chained to a rock and awaiting the dreadful sea monster. Alan had married from a sense of duty (Violet, all these years later, dismissed his professions of love as an irrelevance). But what was it that had driven Emily down the aisle? This question had nagged and niggled at Violet over the years, until finally she had fitted the pieces together in a way that suited her. Ignoring the fact that Emily had been with child — which was all the reason one needed for the hasty marriage — Violet told herself, quite illogically, that Emily must have known what a success Sir Hubert would make of his life, and had been determined to have her share of it. Emily had backed a winner and was now reaping her reward. Emily, who had no responsibilities, who never had to speak to Cook. Emily the tragic war widow, who everyone felt sorry for. Emily, who was spoilt and cosseted—

'Violet! Violet! Where are you?'

Violet sighed. Father again. Always Father. How she hated him! Yes, hate. Hate, hate, hate. Why at her age pretend otherwise? Why dissemble, extemporize? She didn't have the energy for all that anymore. She didn't have the will.

She could see all too clearly what was going to happen next. Father would put her in a rage and then she would take it out on Cook. For the rest of the day she would feel wretched and tarnished and helpless. Was this any sort of life? Well, was it?

Taking one last look through the glass panels (Emily had long gone), Violet experienced a pang of regret for the years before the war when Mother had been her old self and had shouldered all responsibilities (they had lived in a smaller house back then, less bother). Often in those days left to her own devices, Violet had been wont to drift and daydream. She'd been fond of lying on her bed and picturing the man she was going to marry, a tall and steadfast figure silhouetted against a golden sunrise. But somehow — somehow — she had never quite been able to make out his face. And now, after so long, if she searched through her mind, she found there was nothing left. The golden sunrise had faded away. The tall and steadfast figure was gone. All she had was a blank space where once her dreams had been.

'Violet! Violet!'

Father had hunted her down, he was stomping along the passage towards her. She had no choice but to turn and face him.

'What is it, Father? What is it *now*?'

* * *

Emily emerged from the village post office, having despatched Sir Hubert's letters (not that they would do any good: they never did). She paused now to put her gloves back on, looking round at the church, the pub, the terrace of little cottages, the village green, all so familiar after six, nearly seven, years. Her eyes shied away from the stark, fresh-cut stone of the war memorial and came to rest on something else, something she had never seen in the village before, a rather stubby-looking, single-decked, green-painted omnibus parked opposite the church. *The Sparrowhawk* was written in gold letters on its side. Its destination board read *Tottenham*.

Tottenham? Tottenham in London? Well, it was quite possible. She always thought of London as being a world away, but Chad had laughed when she'd happened to say so. 'I can be in Piccadilly in less than an hour, Mother, if I go in my car. London, in any case, gets nearer all the time. It's growing, getting bigger, coming to meet us.'

And here was the evidence, this omnibus out of the blue. She felt there was something almost sinister about it. The tentacles of London were snaking out into open country, and even this quiet, sleepy village wasn't safe: less than an hour from Piccadilly, inextricably linked now to Tottenham. She thought of Violet's words earlier about London being a dangerous place. She felt that Violet was right.

What did this mean for Chad?

Emily always liked to think of Chad having a life of his own, able to escape the stultifying atmosphere at Heartlands by going to school or to Cambridge, by visiting friends, sometimes going on holiday with them. And now he had his motor. But just how often did his motor take him to London? What did he *do* there? If she'd been an interfering, smothering sort of mother, she would have asked. But she wasn't and she didn't. She could only guess. And Violet's words had made those guesses much more disturbing.

With a start of surprise, Emily realized that she had — quite unwittingly — walked within touching distance of the sinister, alien omnibus, almost as if she was being drawn to it against her will. She reached out a tentative hand to touch the dusty green paintwork — and at that very moment, a man came strolling round from the front of the bus, hands in his pockets, whistling.

She snatched her hand away as if she'd been caught touching the exhibits in a museum. Clutching her bag, hugging it against herself, she looked at the man warily. He had stopped stock-still. The whistle died on his lips. He seemed, if anything, as much taken aback as she was.

He was a young man, in his mid-twenties perhaps. He was wearing some sort of uniform: a peaked cap, a jacket with polished buttons. A conductor's uniform, thought Emily. Of course. He must belong to the bus. He was a bus conductor. And, indeed, he had a ticket machine slung over one shoulder, a money bag over the other. The two straps met slantways across his chest.

The young man quickly recovered his composure and touched his cap in a sort of salute. He broke into a grin. 'How do, missus? Er, good morning, ma'am, I should say. Can we tempt you to take a trip on our bus? There's every comfort on board *The Sparrowhawk*. Satisfaction is guaranteed. And only a tanner return. Cheap at half the price.'

He was putting on airs, talking posh in his role as conductor, but traces of an accent kept breaking through, *owny* for *only*, *haff* for *half*. North country, was it? Or Midlands, perhaps? His accent only added to Emily's sense of alarm. She shied away from his wide grin, his bright eyes, all his rough edges. If she'd stumbled across a wolf in the woods, she could not have been more alarmed.

Backing away, overcome with confusion, she stuttered, 'Oh . . . um . . . no . . . I . . . er . . . no . . . thank you . . . no.'

It was all she could do not to break into a run. She took one last glance behind her and got a confused impression of him standing there, leaning against the bus, a rather puzzled expression on his face, then she turned into the lane that led past the churchyard and the omnibus was lost to sight.

She stumbled in her haste and nearly fell, and this brought her to her senses. She forced herself to slow down, to take more care. Her breathing began to get back to normal.

It was silly, to get so flustered. Why did she always get so flustered? She wished she could be more like Violet, able to look down her nose, able to make 'good morning' sound like an indictment. It was not as if the bus conductor had been all that alarming. Just a man. An ordinary man. A rather cloth-cap sort of man, at that.

She had left the village behind. The lane rambled on through a beech wood bright with the green of new leaves. Overhanging branches swayed in the slackening breeze. The sky was a patchwork of white and grey clouds. It was brighter now than earlier, a fine spring morning, getting on for lunchtime.

Emily, however, could not shake her sense of unease. What if the bus conductor followed her? Even ordinary men could be dangerous, unpredictable. She couldn't stop thinking about the way his provincial accent kept breaking through, as if underneath the thin veneer of respectability — the smart uniform, the 'Good morning, ma'am' — there was a different sort of man, a rough, coarse, libidinous man. She had glimpsed it in his glinting eyes, in his wolfish smile, in his rasping voice. It had shown in his hands — those great, chunky, masculine hands, like grasping paws—

Terrified, she spun round in the middle of the lane, quite sure he'd be there: her mouth was open, ready to scream. But there was nothing, nobody. The lane stretched empty back towards the village, the church spire just visible between the trees. She listened. No furtive footsteps. Just the wind in the trees, and the faint sound of birdsong echoing from deep in the wood.

She took a deep, shuddering breath. Tucking her bag under her arm, smoothing her long, pleated skirt, she turned to continue her journey. She felt a little shaky on her feet after so much panic, and the lane wound on and on ahead of her through the endless wood. Heartlands was three-quarters of a mile away at least. She baulked at the distance but she had no choice, she simply had to grit her teeth and get on with it.

As she toiled along the lane, her mind seemed determined to torment her, turning from thoughts of the disquieting bus conductor to all the memories that had been raked up the other night when she'd been lying sleepless in bed after seeing Alleyn Dene again. In the days and weeks following the ball at Nethercote Hall twenty-one years ago, she had convinced herself that it would be possible to forget what had happened, to put it behind her. She had told herself over and over, day after day, that tomorrow she'd feel better, tomorrow she'd be back to her old self, tomorrow life would return to normal.

'Emmy, dearest, what's wrong? Are you quite well?' Nothing much had ever got past Mama, though people had often made the mistake of thinking her scatter-brained. 'You haven't been right since that ball at Nethercote Hall. Late nights and too much excitement are obviously not good for you. Go up to bed, dear, and have a little sleep if you can. I'll come and see how you are by and by.'

Lying in bed had been neither restful nor soothing. It had given Emily too much time to think. She had found herself crying for what she had thought, at the time, was no reason at all. Looking back now as she walked along the lane, Emily recognized those tears as a perfectly natural reaction to the shock and stress of her ordeal.

Thus, she had naturally been in floods of tears when, without warning, the door had flown open and Perks had come marching in with a tray.

'I do wish you'd knock, Perks!' Emily had mopped her face on the bed covers.

'How can I knock, miss, when I've my hands full with this tray?'

'A tray? Is it teatime already? What cakes are there today?'

'No cakes.'

'No cakes?'

'Just chicken broth and rice pudding, as you're not feeling yourself.'

'I don't *want* chicken broth! Take it away!' A sense of disappointment out of all proportion had swept over her.

'Now, then, miss, what's all this?' Putting the tray aside, Perks had sat on the edge of the bed in a way that Mama would have termed *over-familiar*. 'Why are you so upset, miss?' A look had come into Perks's eyes that Emily in hindsight called *calculating*. 'You're all right, I suppose? You aren't—' Perks had lowered her voice, leaning ever closer. 'You aren't *in trouble*, are you, miss?'

'I don't know what you mean, Perks. I wish you'd leave me alone.'

'I'm only thinking of you, miss, after what happened and all.'

'Nothing happened. I don't want to talk about it.'

'That's all very well, but you'll have to face up to it, if you're—'

'If I'm what? Stop looking at me like that! I don't understand you!'

'You don't understand? Stone me! Anyone'd think you were born yesterday! Do I have to spell it out?'

'Spell *what* out?'

'Have you had your courses, miss? Have you had them at the proper time?'

'Have I had my *what*? What are you talking about, Perks?'

Passing beneath the overhanging branches, Emily wondered if, by being disagreeable and offhand, she had hoped in the autumn of 1905 to keep Perks at arm's length. But it had been too late for that. Perks had explained exactly what she meant by *courses*. Emily's cheeks, as she walked along, burned in sympathy with her seventeen-year-old self, who had been shocked to the core by Perks's words. To talk of such things openly — in broad daylight — it was indecent, it was *shameful*! Even Nanny had beaten around the bush when it came to what she called *women's affairs*. *All very nasty*, she'd said with a shudder: *nasty and unhygienic*.

Perks had faced Emily head-on. 'There's no need to think the worst quite yet, miss. I'm not regular myself all of the time. But it's best to be prepared.'

Perks had told her bluntly what it was for which she should be prepared. Emily had gaped at her in horror. A baby? Growing *inside* her? No! No! It was monstrous, abominable, impossible! How could Perks say such things — as if people were no better than cats and dogs and cattle! It wasn't true. It *couldn't* be. She wouldn't *allow* it to be true.

'Lawks, miss! Where do you think babies come from, then?'

'From God. From Jesus. Under the gooseberry bush.'

Emily, twenty-one years later, could not bring herself to believe that she had been quite so ignorant. Wishful thinking must have played a part, she told herself as she turned off the lane, taking the driveway that led to Heartlands. She had refused to believe what was happening, but she must — she insisted now — have known in her heart of hearts: she must have known she was pregnant.

'The gentleman concerned, miss — I don't suppose there's any chance he'll . . . ?'

Emily had shaken her head violently.

'Not to worry. There's more than one way to skin a cat. We'll just have to think of something else.'

That was how it had begun. That was how they had become complicit. They had been bound together by Emily's dreadful secret.

Her footsteps slowing, Emily left the driveway to cut across the grass, wading through it out here, where the lawnmower never came. She remembered that she had not been at all grateful for Perks's help and advice. Just the opposite. She had resented Perks inordinately. She had felt as if she was being hoodwinked in some way, made a fool of. She had felt that Perks was drawing her down, gleefully, inexorably, into an unspeakable underworld of lies, deceit, depravity.

Trailing to a halt, Emily stood by the linden tree where the long grass ended and the neat lawn began. Gazing at the brick-built harshness of Heartlands, she wondered what would have happened, all those years ago, if she'd come clean and confessed. (Was that what one did, *confess* to being raped?) It had not seemed an option. She had barely been able to explain it to herself, to explain to someone else would have been impossible. And even if she had managed to confess, what then? Would anyone have believed that it wasn't her fault? Would anyone have believed that *he* was capable of such iniquity?

'It's always the girl's fault,' Perks had said. 'It's always the girl who's to blame. That's what folk say. That's what they think.'

Emily rested her cheek against the smooth, grey bark of the linden tree. In the random way of memory, it was the disappointment of chicken broth and rice pudding which had lingered longest and gained over the years a distorted importance. Cook had made such wonderful cakes. Teatime had been a treat, one of the highlights of the day. But thinking back now, by a trick of the mind it seemed to Emily that after that day, the day of the chicken broth, she had never tasted Cook's cakes again. Events telescoped in her memory so that she now had the impression it was the very next day when Granny Drage and the Winmers had come to luncheon and she had been forced to fall back on the terrible plan which Perks had devised for her.

And so the jaws of the trap had snapped shut.

CHAPTER FIVE

'Well really, Beatrice, what *were* you thinking!'

Granny Drage, arriving at Alleyn Dene just after midday in the autumn of 1905, was most put out when she learned who else was coming to lunch.

'You *know* how much I detest that man,' she continued, removing her stole and her gloves in the hall. 'What made you think I'd want to sit to luncheon with a Uriah Heap of *his* sort?'

Halfway down the stairs, Emily stood irresolute, wondering if she dared creep back up again. She ought to have known that Granny Drage would be early. Granny Drage was always early. But it was one thing greeting the old woman in the genteel comfort of the drawing room, quite another to meet her face to face and unprepared in the functional surroundings of the front hall. Would Granny ask about the gloves? She was bound to ask about the gloves!

'What is wrong with Jago, I should like to know?' Granny was now pulling out handfuls of hatpins and handing them to the maid. 'Jago has *always* been our MP. I see no reason to change.'

'It's time for someone new,' said Mama equably. Mama had a quiet way of dealing with Granny. She never allowed herself to get flustered. 'Gerald says that we must give the Liberals a chance.'

'His latest craze, I suppose. I've never known such a man for crazes. I don't know *why* you put up with it, Beatrice. This is what happens when you marry a *shoemaker*.'

'Gerald is not a shoemaker, Mama, he is a businessman. Sutton's Shoes are renowned, and rightly so. Gerald moves with the times. He is a very *modern* sort of man.'

'Humph! There's far too much emphasis these days on being modern. It will all end badly, mark my words.' Granny Drage's roving eyes finally came to rest on Emily, who flinched. 'Ah, Emily, there you are. Come down and let me look at you.'

Emily descended, trembling. When would Granny ask about the gloves? And what about Uncle Walter — where was Uncle Walter? Emily peered round Granny's substantial form, looking for her uncle, who tended to loiter.

'Hello, Emily.' Granny kissed the air near Emily's cheeks, took hold of her, inspected her closely. Granny's sharp eyes seemed able to penetrate to one's very soul. 'You are looking pale. Too much reading of books, I shouldn't wonder. You shouldn't be reading books at your age. How old *are* you, by the way? I forget.'

'Seventeen, Granny.'

'Ah. An awkward age. Your mother was *very* awkward at that age.'

'Emily has not been feeling well.' Mama took Emily's hand and gently drew her out of Granny's orbit.

'Not been well? Humph! I don't know! What are young people coming to? One would think they were hothouse flowers. Walter is just the same. Said he was too poorly to come today. What nonsense! But he wouldn't be moved. I had to leave him. He was being most *extraordinarily* vexing.' Granny sighed. It was like the exhalation of a volcano. 'What can be done? My children were sent to try me. *You* in particular, Beatrice, inviting this Winmer person. He's nothing but a freeloader and a social climber. You should refuse to have him in the house, whatever Gerald says. I would *never* have let your father get away with anything like this.'

Granny Drage's voice faded as she led the way to the drawing room, Mama trailing behind. Emily hesitated in the hallway. The gloves had not been mentioned — not yet — which was a blessing, and Uncle Walter had not come, which was even more so. But, knowing what faced her later, Emily could not feel any sense of relief. Luncheon would be torture.

Still trembling, Emily made her way to join the others.

* * *

Granny Drage from the outset had ruled her children with a rod of iron. She was implacable, set in her ways, and she always knew best. Granny planned her children's lives and expected them to bend to her will. She had not reckoned on them having ideas of their own. Thus it came about, despite her best efforts, that each of her children had, in one way or another, proved a disappointment.

Emily's Uncle Frank — the third child, but the eldest son — had rebelled in the most spectacular fashion of all. Emily had no memory of Uncle Frank, for he had run away to sea when she was a very tiny child. Later, the merchant ship on which he was serving had foundered somewhere off the west coast of South America and that had been the end of Uncle Frank.

'I blame myself,' Granny often said (it was not in her nature to let matters lie). 'I should have put my foot down.'

Frank's defection had served as a warning. Granny had doubled her efforts. By then it was already too late to put her foot down where her eldest daughter was concerned. Beatrice, like Frank, had gone her own way: less ostentatiously, perhaps, but with just as much determination. She had committed what were, in Granny's eyes, two cardinal sins: she had married beneath her, and she had married for love.

'Love!' snorted Granny Drage, who could speak volumes in a single word. Love, it was to be understood, was deserving of infinite contempt. 'But I'm afraid, Emily, that nothing I said would change your mother's mind. She can be decidedly *obstinate*. It is perhaps the worst of her *many* faults.'

There were two other children, Margery and Walter. Emily's Aunt Margery behaved herself. She was the golden girl, so to speak. She always did as she was told, which included marrying who she was told to, as well. The husband Granny had chosen for her was eminently suitable, a scion of the aristocracy. Aunt Margery had duly become Lady Ainsleigh and Granny had congratulated herself on a job well done. But even here her satisfaction was short-lived. Time was ticking on and still there were no children from the marriage. (Emily, indeed, was Granny's only grandchild.) The fault, of course, had to lie with Margery. The golden girl, by 1905, had begun to lose her shine.

Which left Uncle Walter, the youngest. As a boy he'd been what Granny described as 'a handful'.

'It was glaringly obvious from the moment he was born that I'd need to keep a close eye on Walter,' Granny was in the habit of saying. And so she had — two *very* close eyes. She had battled long and hard to bring him to heel, to curb his wayward ways. From his earliest days, Walter had been kept on a short leash — which was why it had come as something of a surprise when he'd gone against Granny and refused point-blank to attend the Winmer luncheon that particular day in 1905.

'Perhaps he's learning to stand on his own two feet at last,' Mama had said. 'About time, at twenty-eight.' But she'd not said it in Granny's hearing, and Emily had kept her own counsel.

* * *

Twenty-one years later, sitting up late reading an old Marie Corelli of Mama's and most definitely *not* listening out for Chad's motor (where could he be at this hour?), Emily found that she could remember every detail of that long-ago luncheon at Alleyn Dene. Tomato soup, roast partridges with bread sauce, apple tart and cream: Cook had pulled out all the stops.

Looking back, it seemed to Emily that food had been different before the war, partridges more succulent, bread sauce more piquant. Cook's pastry had melted in the mouth — the cream had been wonderfully rich and thick and yellow. Emily's mouth watered at the memory. She was filled with a very belated regret that she'd not been able that day to manage more than an eyeful.

Nobody had noticed. Nobody ever noticed much when Granny Drage was amongst the guests. Granny simply *demanded* attention by her very presence. She dominated any room she was in. She monopolized every conversation. As she set about her tomato soup that day in 1905, she had turned her attention to a rumour she'd heard: the Balfour government, it was suggested, was on the way out. Could this possibly be true? It hardly bore thinking about! A general election in the current climate could prove disastrous. The Liberals (here she'd cocked an eye at Papa) might even win a *majority*! Heaven help the country if *that* happened! What, she'd cried as the soup plates were removed and the partridges brought in, was the world coming to? The natural order of things was being turned wholly upside down. Take the Russian war, another example. One had thought it a foregone conclusion. The Japanese hadn't a prayer. The Russians, after all, were European (just). The Russians, after all, were *white*. But — *well*! The Russian army routed! The Russian navy sunk! One's blood ran cold! Where would it end? Was there no defence *whatsoever* against the Yellow Peril?

'If I might be permitted to say—' Sir Hubert had been plain Mr Winmer in those days, had looked plain too, had been dull, unprepossessing, rather self-effacing.

'No, you may not be permitted to say!' Granny had glared at him across the table. 'I will not be lectured on foreign affairs by a man who supports *free trade*! If the Russian war proves anything, it is that we can no longer afford to be complaisant. British trade, like the British Empire, must be *protected*!'

'But the Japanese, Mrs Drage, are our allies.'

'Allied with Japan? Don't be absurd! I've never heard such nonsense!'

Granny had always adjusted facts as she saw fit. Her infallibility had been established long before the Pope's. It had never occurred to Emily, twenty years ago, that Granny could ever be wrong, just as it had never occurred to her that Granny's manner might be considered somewhat rude, if not downright offensive. No one sat round the table that day would have dared to suggest it. Probably no one had even dared *think* it, such was the force of Granny's personality.

Mr Winmer in those days had still been working in a very junior position in the legal profession, but he'd begun to take an interest in politics. He'd had high hopes in that direction, particularly after he'd been taken up by Papa and mooted as a Liberal hope for the Northamptonshire division in which they lived. Papa had been all for the Liberals. He'd had what Granny Drage termed 'an outmoded and misguided belief' in free trade. All this talk of protection, he'd said, was damaging to international commerce. The bombastic attitude taken by Austen Chamberlain was having a detrimental effect on the order books. Sutton's Shoes could only flourish in a tariff-free environment. If the Liberals got in, the matter would be favourably settled and business would finally boom. That, anyway, was the theory, or as much of it as Emily had understood. She had not paid much attention. It had all been so boring. Mr Winmer had been particularly boring. Emily had tended to agree with Granny Drage where Mr Winmer was concerned.

On the day in question, Mr Winmer had been accompanied to Alleyn Dene by his mousey wife and four children: his three dutiful daughters, and his boy Alan. When Papa had first taken up with Hubert Winmer, Alan had been conspicuous by his absence, away at college studying, but Emily had made up her mind about him even before she met him. It was the way they went on about him — his doting parents, his adoring sisters — that was what rankled. Alan was clever and handsome, Alan was modest and well-mannered, Alan was the nicest boy you could meet. Emily wrinkled her nose. Alan sounded horribly spoilt. He must be insufferable. He was nothing more than a twenty-year-old booby.

But when in the summer of 1905 she finally met him — as Papa set about persuading the local Liberals to look on Mr Winmer as their prospective candidate — she had found to her chagrin that Alan was almost impossible to dislike. He really was modest and well-mannered — if he was clever, he didn't rub one's nose in it, and if he was spoilt, there was no sign. Whilst it might have been something of an exaggeration to call him *handsome*, he certainly wasn't *unpleasant* to look at, with his earnest, youthful face, his straight brown hair, his little round spectacles. He was quiet, unassuming and scrupulously polite.

Unable to dislike him, Emily had done her best to ignore him. Who needed boys anyway?

And then she'd happened to overhear Granny Drage talking to Mama.

It was perhaps a month or so before the fateful luncheon. Granny had coincided with the Winmers at tea. After the Winmers had gone, Granny had sat on with Mama in the drawing room. Emily in the garden had happened to be loitering by the French windows, which were wide open in the August heat.

'That Winmer boy will need to be watched, Beatrice. I don't want him getting ideas above his station.'

'I'm sure he doesn't . . . you don't *really* think that he . . . ?'

'I know what I'm talking about, Beatrice. The signs are there. Keep him away from Emily, or there'll be trouble.'

Emily's interest had been instantly aroused. Had Granny got it right, did Alan Winmer *like* her? What did it mean to be liked by a boy? She'd had no one to ask. Nanny had gone. One couldn't talk to Mama. The Barford girls, it was true, knew a thing or two, but one hesitated to ask their advice, they were so smug and self-satisfied. There'd been Perks, of course. Perks was wise in the ways of the world, or so she made out — she often boasted how the village boys made eyes at her and followed her round, as if she was the Pied Piper. But one couldn't really demean oneself by making friends with Perks.

Sitting by the fire in the drawing room at Heartlands in April 1926, Emily was mystified to have discovered a contrary streak in her seventeen-year-old self, a contrary streak that later vanished without trace. What had possessed her to start being nice to Alan Winmer when Granny had warned of trouble? Was it the same impulse that had made her swing on an old rope over the stream at the bottom of the garden, despite the very real risk of falling in? Was it the same impulse that had got her to inveigle Watkins, the gardener, into teaching her how to catch fish in that same stream, by tickling their bellies? Why on earth had she wanted to do such things? Pure contrariness. That was the only explanation. No one would ever guess, to look at her now.

Putting her book face down on her lap and staring into the dwindling flames, Emily remembered that she'd been quite at a loss as to how one could be *nice* to a boy. Her only guide had been to think of Juniper, her dog. Juniper as a puppy had been a dear little thing. She had pampered Juniper, and Juniper had grown up to adore her, as devoted as a slave. What fun it would be to have Alan Winmer as a sort of pet, a lesser version of Juniper, running after her and wagging his tail! It would be one in the eye for Perks, who only had clodhopping village boys chasing her, not the son of a prospective parliamentary candidate.

What a silly child I was, said Emily to herself, watching the glowing embers. *So contrary and thoughtless, wrapped up in my own little world. Poor Alan! I never stopped to think how he would feel, playing second fiddle to a dog!*

But, in currying favour with Alan, she had unwittingly paved the way for what came later.

Staring unseeingly at the dying fire, Emily could not help wondering what would have happened if that silly, contrary, sometimes daring girl from the summer of 1905 had survived to grow into a woman. But of course she hadn't. *That* Emily Sutton had vanished forever on the evening of the ball at Nethercote Hall.

Her eyelids fluttered. Her head nodded. As she teetered on the edge of sleep, suddenly Perks was in the room with her. A subtle change had come over Perks that long-ago autumn. She had stopped calling Emily *miss* quite so often. There had been sly and knowing smiles. And here she was now, leering and crowing, leaning over the sofa in the drawing room at Heartlands, just as Emily remembered her from 1905.

'Well, well, Miss Emily! How the mighty have fallen. Turns out you're no better'n the rest of us, for all your airy-fairy ways. You won't be able to hide it much longer, you know. Everyone will be able to see. You've one chance, and one chance only, and that's to do exactly as I say. You must put yourself in my hands. Only I can save you. Ha ha ha! Ha ha ha!'

'No . . . please . . . Perks . . . don't make me!'

'It's the only way! Ha ha ha! The only way!'

* * *

'Are you cold, Miss Sutton?' asked Alan Winmer anxiously in the garden at Alleyn Dene, in the autumn of 1905. 'We can go indoors if you're cold.'

'No, I'm quite . . . quite—'

'But you're . . .'

'I'm . . . ?'

'Shivering. You're shivering.'

'It's the . . . the fresh air. So invigorating, don't you think so? Let's not go indoors. Let's not.'

There was a blustery wind. Grey clouds were scudding across the sky. Rooks clamoured in the denuded poplars, but the lawn had been swept clear of autumn leaves. Swathed in her hat, coat and muffler, Emily was caught off guard by sudden hysterical laughter bubbling up inside her as she walked beside Alan. This conversation was inept. They were stumbling over their words, interrupting one another. Alan looked flushed, his cheeks bright red. Embarrassed? Or drunk? Possibly both.

Emily had watched out of the corner of her eye as Perks, at luncheon, surreptitiously filled Alan's glass again and again, whilst Alan — transfixed by Granny Drage, the way everyone always was — drank it all back, unaware. Hovering in the background with the decanter, Perks had winked and nodded, darting meaningful looks. Emily had wanted to laugh. She had wanted to scream. She had wanted to roll on the floor and shriek. She couldn't stand it! She couldn't stand it! But she had to stand it. She had no choice.

'Are you cold, Miss Sutton?'

'I—'

'Did I ask that already? I asked that already.' He whipped off his spectacles, which had steamed up, he dropped them, he stooped to pick them up off the muddy lawn.

More hysterical laughter bubbled up. Emily gulped it back, hiccupped. As quickly as it had come, the laughter drained out of her, leaving her feeling hollow and wretched. She wondered if it might not be better — easier — to simply throw herself into the stream. She pictured herself floating in the rushes like Ophelia, a pale dead face turned up to the overcast sky.

She felt sick.

You must stir him up, Perks had said. *You must make him mad for you*. Perks had looked at her sidelong, as if doubting Emily's ability to do this.

Emily flogged herself into action. She forced herself to speak. She would show Perks — she would *show* her. 'Do you—?'

'Do I—?'

'Do you . . . like . . . walking? Do you like walking, Mr Winmer?'

'Oh, yes. Oh, rather. I like walking *very* much. I-I-I like walking with you, Miss Sutton.'

'I'm . . . I'm glad.'

'Are you? Are you really? Oh, Miss Sutton, I do so . . . I do . . .'

'Do you?'

'Oh, *yes*! Rather!'

'Perhaps you'd like to—'

'Yes?'

'Hold my . . . hold my hand?' Her cheeks, she was sure, must be a match for his, claret red. She was acting so shamelessly, so brazenly. What would Nanny have said!

But it was not Nanny's voice she could hear in her head, it was Perks's. *This is no good, Miss Emily. Hold his hand? How in heaven's name will that help? You can't afford to be a namby-pamby. His hands have to reach other places, if you're to make this work.*

She felt his finger tips brush against hers, timid. Then, abruptly, and with great daring, he took hold of her hand in his own. His fingers were thin and bony, his skin warm, his touch gentle, as if he was handling the most delicate Chinese porcelain — as if he was holding the hand of the barefoot Meissen girl on the sideboard in the drawing room.

Emily's heart was racing. She felt like a hussy. She was sure they were being watched.

She looked over her shoulder. They were out of sight of the house. No one could see. No one would come running in horror. ('Holding hands, Emily! How could you!') If only he would ask her to marry him, if only he would get down on one knee right here by the privet hedge, then all her troubles would be over.

Except Perks had scorned the idea. *Don't be daft, miss! The arrangements would take months! And what do you think he would say when you start to show, when you get big with the baby inside you? Don't you think he'd break it off at once?*

But Perks, Perks, I can't do it, I can't!

You must. It's the only way. No one's going to come to your rescue. You must rescue yourself.

Shaking, Emily tried to remember what came next. Perks had schooled her punctiliously. She only had to do as she'd been taught.

‘I’m so—’ Her mouth was dry, her voice a croak. She swallowed, forced herself to go on. ‘I’m so happy, being here with you. I’m—’

Her words sounded empty and false, as withered as dead leaves. Why didn’t he notice? How could he not see? Even Juniper had noticed the change in her over the last few weeks, whining pitifully and licking her hand.

She hardened her heart. The fact that he *didn’t* notice only went to show that men must be stupider than dogs. They didn’t *deserve* any consideration. All their polished manners and fancy clothes were simply a thin veneer. She’d found out what men were *really* like in the cloakroom at Nethercote Hall. She drew a breath, gritted her teeth. She needed to be indomitable, like Granny Drage. She needed to forge ahead, taking no one’s feelings into account — least of all her own.

There were spots of rain in the air, which made it perfectly natural to suggest taking shelter in the summerhouse. She shut the door behind them. Every fibre was telling her to run, run, run. It took a great effort for her to stand her ground.

‘I should like you to kiss me.’ The words were Perks’s, not hers: wanton, shameless words. But Perks had drummed it into her. Even when men knew what they wanted, Perks said, they had little idea how to go about getting it. They had to be shown. They had to be led by the nose.

Alan seemed amenable to kissing, but it was all very clumsy and awkward, like a puzzle where the pieces don’t fit. They bumped foreheads, their noses seemed to get in the way, his spectacles were knocked skew-whiff. He took them off, put them in his breast pocket, then they tried again.

It was horrible, his lips, his mouth, all wet and slimy. It must be terribly insanitary. She felt she would much rather have kissed Juniper.

What next? She cudgelled her brain, trying to remember.

Once you get him hooked, Miss Emily, you mustn’t let him go. You must—

Must what? What, what, what?

The image of her dog was stuck in her head, the idea of wanting to kiss Juniper instead of Alan. She thought of how Juniper jumped up at you with his front paws outstretched when he was seeking affection. She thought of the little snickering noises he made in his throat. He licked your hands and your face with his soft wet tongue. He wagged his tail furiously.

She patted and stroked Alan, as she would have Juniper. (*I mustn't call him Juniper by mistake.*)

'Oh, Miss Sutton . . . Miss Sutton . . . if only you knew how much I . . . how much . . .'

He looked so strange without his spectacles, blinking like an owl in the daylight, and he was stammering, his voice hoarse. She clung to him like grim death, remembering to bite her lip and flutter her eyelids, the way Perks had shown her. She averted her face and guided his hands onto her body. Time was running out. Someone might come at any moment.

'Oh, Mr Winmer . . . you'll think I'm so . . . but I *do* feel safe with you . . . there's no one I'd rather . . . I'd do anything.' In her desperation, she was getting Perks's words all mixed up, had to ad lib. 'Oh, please, Mr Winmer, *please*!'

'Oh, Miss Sutton!'

'Oh, Mr Winmer!'

'Alan. Call me Alan.'

'Alan, oh Alan.' (*Hurry up, please hurry up.*)

'Oh, Miss Sutton, I never guessed — I never dared hope — that you — that you—'

'But I do — I do!'

'D-d-darling!' He spoke the word with stuttering reverence, as if he'd been holding it in a secret place inside, worshipping it and waiting for the right moment to use it. 'Miss Sutton! My darling!'

'Yes, yes, that's right! Oh, do please—' (*Please hurry. Hurry, hurry, hurry.*)

Their clothes had endless buttons and fastenings. They seemed to get into an awful muddle, fingers fumbling. His shirt came loose from his trousers. He was wearing, underneath his outer clothes, white woollen combinations with rubber buttons. The sight of them made her feel giddy with shock. The summerhouse was spinning round her.

'Miss Sutton, we can't, we *mustn't* . . .' He snatched his hand away, as if the hooks-and-eyes of her frock had burned him.

He was slipping away. It would all be for nothing.

'Mr Winmer . . . Alan . . . I thought . . . I thought you liked me . . . you're . . . you're not a mouse, are you?' (*Prick his pride*, said Perks. *Men will do anything to make themselves look big.*)

'Oh, Miss Sutton, I do like you, I really do!'

'But if you did, if you really did . . . if you liked me — if you *loved* me—'

'I do love you, you don't know how much!'

'Then it's all right. It's quite all right. It won't be wrong, if we love each other. Oh please! *Please*!'

She shut her eyes tight. Her frock was slipping off her shoulders. He must be able to see her camisole. The degradation was almost beyond endurance. She could hear his staccato breathing. He was swallowing repeatedly. She felt him tentatively touch her. She pressed herself against him, frantic, trying to drive him on, on, on. His vile male body was hot and stifling.

Now her petticoat was riding up her legs. There was cold air on her ankles, on her knees, on her thighs. There was cold air on the naughty places, the nasty places, those parts of the body one must only ever touch with one's flannel.

All at once, she felt herself go rigid. She had no control now. She couldn't move a muscle. She was locked away inside herself. And then—

Pain, pain, pain, like knives ripping into her. She wanted to scream. She couldn't. She was paralyzed. It was worse, far worse, than in the cloakroom at Nethercote Hall. She had not known then what was happening. It had all passed in a blur. This time she knew. This time she lived every second.

She was going to die. The pain was too much. And she couldn't breathe. She was suffocating. How much longer . . . how much longer . . . how much—

She felt him give a convulsive shudder. His head came to rest on her shoulder. There was a moment of silence and stillness. Was it all over? She had to be certain it was over. What had Perks said? She couldn't remember. Her mind was a blank.

'M-M-M-Miss Sutton—'

The paralysis was lifting. She could move again. The pain, too, had lessened. It was throbbing now, not slicing.

She opened her eyes warily. He was flushed and sweaty. His hair, that was usually so neat, was all tousled and sticking up. He looked in disarray. He looked stricken. He looked like a little boy.

'Miss Sutton I — we — did we just get carried away? We . . . I . . . I shouldn't have — shouldn't . . .'

He began buttoning himself up. She hurried to do the same. She couldn't bear to look at him. It made her gorge rise. She had to get away.

She pulled at the door, she tugged at it and tugged at it, making it rattle. Suddenly it flew open.

'Miss Sutton. Miss Sutton!'

Miss Sutton, Miss Sutton: he was like a parrot in a cage. She glanced back at him. He was putting his spectacles on, hooking the arms over his ears — all the better to see her with. She held up her hand to block him out, then she turned and ran.

She ran, ran, ran through the cold autumn air with the spots of rain in it. Squeezing through a gap in the hedge, she fell to her knees on a patch of dug-over mud. At once, she was violently sick. Everything went black.

After a time, she became aware of the smell of smoke. Watkins must be burning the leaves that he'd raked off the lawn. There was a smell of mud, too, and of vomit. She blinked and screwed up her eyes. Her vision slowly cleared. She shied away from the sight of her sick. Her eyes fixed instead on a worm wriggling amongst the clods of mud. She watched it wriggling, a senseless, helpless thing. She watched it wriggling and wriggling, her mind a blank.

* * *

Emily jerked awake, found herself in the drawing room at Heartlands with the dying fire and her book in her lap. There was no Perks, there was no Alan, there was no worm wriggling. She was alone.

She sat back, her heart rate slowing. What a dream. What a horrible dream. All the more horrible because it was real, it had happened — and it was all Perks's doing.

Rubbing her tired eyes, relaxing just a little into the sofa, Emily remembered how, in the autumn of 1905, she'd tried to dismiss her seduction of Alan Winmer, she'd tried to forget about it, she'd tried to pretend that she wasn't pregnant at all. *Wishful thinking*, Nanny would have called it. But Nanny had not been there. Nanny had been far away, enjoying her retirement by the sea. She had sent a picture postcard which Emily had cried over and then, in a rage, had torn into little pieces, blaming Nanny for her predicament, blaming everyone, blaming Perks most of all. She'd known nothing about being pregnant until Perks had told her. It was Perks who'd made her pregnant. Flying in the face of the evidence, Emily had all but convinced herself that she had not been with child until Perks had tricked her into going into the summerhouse with Alan Winmer.

But rewriting history hadn't helped. However it happened, the problem had remained. 'Now you must tell the missus,' Perks had insisted. But Emily hadn't been able to. It was too much.

In the end, Perks had taken matters into her own hands, dropping hints, making leading remarks. 'Miss Emily's looking peaky. Miss Emily must be sickening for summat. There's summat up with Miss Emily.'

'Stop it, Perks, stop it!'

'It's for your own good, miss. You can't bury your head forever.'

'I'll never forgive you, never! You're simply hateful!'

'And that's all the thanks I get, is it?' Perks had tossed her head and gone off in a sulk.

Her hints had eventually struck home.

'Oh, Emily, how *could* you!'

The hurt in Mama's eyes had been too much to bear. Emily had thrown herself onto the sofa in floods of tears, covering her head with her arms.

'I'm sorry, I'm sorry, I'm sorry! Oh, I'm sorry!'

Papa had wrung his hands. He'd always been at a loss when things came out of the blue. He liked fair warning, he liked plain facts. This was not something he could write up in his almanac.

So it was Mama who had taken charge, doing everything in Papa's name (she had known her place). She had taken Emily to London. It had been far too delicate a matter for old Dr Woodhouse in the village. Emily's condition had been confirmed. There had no longer been any room for doubt.

'Very well,' Mama had said crisply. 'Alan Winmer has brought all this about. He must now face the consequences.'

In truth, neither Alan nor Emily had much say in the matter. It was all arranged by what Emily in those days had still thought of as 'the grown-ups'. Hubert Winmer had fallen over himself to smooth things over. Thinking about this in later years, Emily was never able to decide on his motives. Had he been worried that this shameful episode might wreck his nascent political career? His hopes of being selected as prospective Liberal candidate had largely rested on Papa's patronage, and events at that time had been moving swiftly to a moment of decision. Or had he seized on the marriage simply as a serendipitous match for his son? In those days, it must have seemed advantageous indeed. Emily, as an only child, had been set to inherit everything: Alleyn Dene, the shoe factory — not to mention the Drage family fortune (such as it was).

Politics and nuptials had been oddly juxtaposed in the last weeks of 1905. On Monday 5 December, Mr Balfour had resigned as Prime Minister, triggering a general election. Next day, at a small anonymous ceremony in London, Miss Emily Sutton had been married to Mr Alan Winmer. It was a subdued occasion, hushed up beforehand, only announced afterwards. Alan had been pale and death-like. Emily had barely been able to face him. She had felt sick to her stomach. She had been wracked with guilt. She had believed that—

Well, her thoughts and feelings about Alan Winmer had been in such a tangle by then, that it was easier to thrust them all aside, rather than try to unpick them.

Hubert Winmer had been the only one smiling that dull, squally December day. Emily could still see him rubbing his hands with a glee that, in all probability, had been grossly accentuated in her memory by the passage of time.

'*Alan* Winmer. *Alleyn* Dene.' He had chuckled. 'It's too much of a coincidence to be blind chance. It must be destiny, my dear. Destiny!' He was thinking, she had realized, of the day when his son would take possession of her childhood home. In those days, Alleyn Dene had represented, to Hubert Winmer, almost unimaginable opulence. The brash splendour of Heartlands had come later, much later.

In the event, of course, Alan had never lived at Alleyn Dene. Emily's old home had been lost for good long ago, before the war. But no one that drab December day could have predicted that.

Papa and Hubert Winmer had gone off in a rush, dashing back to Northamptonshire for the selection meeting. Emily and Alan had travelled to Margate to begin their married life with a few days' holiday. The weather had turned milder. It had been wet and breezy. Emily remembered an empty beach, a grey sea, a misty horizon.

She had never been back to Margate since.

* * *

Her eyes flickered and opened. She must have nodded off again. She yawned and sat up. The fire was all but out now and her book had fallen to the floor. She had been dreaming about the sea. The sound of the sea had been loud in her ears. But now another, muffled noise replaced it: the growling of a car engine. So Chad was back at last. He was home and safe.

It was late. Everyone else was in bed. But Chad must have seen the light and he came to investigate. He brought in with him a waft of cold air which made the dying embers glow. Tall and smart in his evening wear, he was pink-cheeked and bright-eyed, looked young and vibrant and immortal.

'Mother! What are you doing up? Not waiting for me, I hope.'

'No, darling, of course not. I was reading and I fell asleep.' She never fussed, it was her cardinal rule. But Violet's words from the other day had been fermenting inside her and, still muzzy from sleep, she suddenly found herself wailing, 'Jazz! Oh, Chad, *jazz*!' She invested the word with all her doubts and misgivings.

Chad laughed. 'There's nothing wrong with jazz, Mother. It's all the rage. You should try it. You might like it.'

'But all this — this gallivanting!' *Gallivanting* was another of Violet's words.

'All I want is a bit of fun, Mother. There's nothing wrong with that, is there? I'll be going back to Cambridge before you know it, then I'll knuckle down, I promise.'

'What about . . . this girl?' The words were out before she could stop them. She felt a sense of despair. She was doing everything she had always promised herself she wouldn't — interfering, *prying*.

She was turning into Granny Drage.

'Lily isn't just any girl, Mother.' Chad's vibrant smile only served to fuel Emily's fears. 'That's her name, by the way: Lily. She's — she's . . .' His smile for a second grew even wider, then abruptly it was gone. He seemed to reach a snap decision. Taking a breath, he said, 'Her name is Lily and she's a waitress in the ABC tea shop on Cheapside.'

Thrown off balance, Emily could not begin to imagine what was showing on her face. Whatever it was, it seemed to sting Chad into action. He came swiftly across the room and sat next to her on the sofa, staring into her eyes. 'It's not like it sounds, Mother. She's beautiful, she's clever — well, not *clever*, but you know what I mean, she has her wits about her.

She's not forward or anything, you mustn't think that. She's the most modest, unassuming girl you could ever wish to meet, and she's awfully decent and respectable. She's eighteen. And — oh, Mother, she's simply wonderful!'

He turned away, hung his head, as if he could sense her doubts. But she could see in profile that his jaw was firm and set, determined.

'I know that Grandfather won't approve, but I thought that you . . . I hoped that you . . .'

The reproach in his voice pierced her. But then he turned to her again and unexpectedly he smiled, changing the subject as if there was nothing more to be said, as if he'd made up his mind about this girl and wouldn't be moved.

'The stars were so bright tonight, Mother, as I was driving home. You should have seen them! Do you remember that song you used to sing to me, *Twinkle, Twinkle, Little Star*? I found myself singing it the other night and, I don't know why, but I-I found myself thinking about Father.'

A strange, tingling sensation swept over her. How odd — how uncanny — that Chad should mention Alan, when she'd been thinking of Alan — dreaming of Alan — all evening.

She cocked an ear. Was that the sound of the sea she could hear? But no, of course not. Heartlands was miles from the sea, miles and miles. It was just the last echo of her dream. She had been dreaming about Margate in December 1905, so bleak and desolate. And yet — and yet . . . She had never thought of this before, but Chad had been there in Margate too. Chad had been growing inside her. Somehow this made all the difference. Suddenly she almost felt nostalgia for Margate.

'What was he like, Mother? What was Father actually like?'

'He was — he was . . .' Emily floundered. The claustrophobia of the summerhouse came back to her vividly. She could see in her mind's eye the worm oozing in the mud. Her flesh crawled.

'Grandfather is confusing,' said Chad after a pause. 'Sometimes he talks about Father as a war hero, other times he says Father frittered his life away.'

'Your father went his own way, made his own plans. They didn't always tally with the plans Sir Hubert had for him.'

Emily reached a full stop. There was nothing more she could say about Alan without opening a hornet's nest. It was best to say nothing. To underline this fact, she reached down to pick her book up off the floor. But as she did so, a picture took shape in her mind: the tiny front room of the cottage, the curtains closed, a fire glowing, the oil lamps lit, her and Alan in opposite chairs. How many evenings had they sat like that, Chad tucked in bed upstairs, the deep silence of the country night lapping round their walls? Alan might have been reading a book, or turning the pages of the newspaper. She might have been sewing or embroidering. Or maybe they'd had the gramophone on, Gilbert and Sullivan, such beautiful music. They'd sat there spellbound, listening, not speaking, each in accord with the other.

Emily straightened up, her book in her hand. The vision faded. Yet it had been so real — so unexpected — so . . . so . . .

'Mother?' Chad was watching her closely. What had he seen in her face? His voice was gentle. 'Mother? What is it?'

'It's — it's nothing. It's nothing.' She shook her head. 'It doesn't matter.'

He smiled at her, his deep smile, the smile from deep inside. 'Everything will be all right, Mother. You'll see.' The smile broke off, turned into a yawn. He stood up, stretching. 'Bed for me, I think. Good night, Mother.'

The room seemed big and empty with Chad gone — it seemed more than usually soulless. The fire had gone out. The electric lights blazed remorselessly, so unlike the flickering oil lamps in the cottage. Emily made to get up, then suddenly paused, with her hand on the arm rest of the sofa. She tried to summon again the picture she'd seen just now, and the feeling that had come with it: all those evenings sitting with Alan in the cottage, absorbed in their books and their handiwork and listening to music. She found her eyes misting over at the memory. How odd that she should feel so — so what? What was it exactly, this great sweet swelling sadness inside her? It was almost as if—

Could it be true? Yet it really did seem to her, just then, that in the days of the cottage, without ever realizing, she had actually grown to be happy.

CHAPTER SIX

Her name is Lily . . . she works in an ABC tea shop . . .

Emily, in the days after her late-night conversation with Chad, could not stop thinking about the girl called Lily — could not stop worrying. It might be nothing, a passing fancy on Chad's part: a *craze*, like Papa with the weather and the stars and the Liberals, or like Chad himself with his beloved motor car. But Emily sensed that this was different. A girl was different. Dangerous.

Emily shied away from it, but that was no good. It was no good burying one's head — as Perks had said all those years ago in a different context. Emily knew she had to face it. Her boy, her little boy, had grown up. Chad was now a man. He was prey now to his appetites, just like any man. Prey to them, driven by them — trapped by them? Surely Chad was too sensible to fall into a trap, to let himself be used? And yet such things happened, Emily knew only too well. Perks had shown her. Perks had schooled her. How to use a man's weaknesses against him, to inflame his wanton passions for your own ends. She herself, Emily Sutton, naïve and ignorant, had snared Alan in just that way. Alan had been Chad's age, more or less. She had been just seventeen, younger even than this Lily who worked in a tea shop. What was she like, this

Lily? Chad had begun to talk about her the other night but then, as before on the hilltop above Alleyn Dene, the subject had changed, and Emily's many questions had gone unasked.

Alone in the morning room at Heartlands, Emily debated with herself. Chad was back at Cambridge now. But was he safe? For all she knew, he could be dashing down to London at every opportunity. How soon could one reach Piccadilly from Cambridge?

There's nothing you can do about it, said a voice inside Emily's head, fatalistic.

Maybe — maybe not, said another, more insistent voice, *but that doesn't mean you just sit back and let him make a terrible mistake, fall headlong, get hurt.*

I don't interfere, I never interfere. That's my rule.

So be it. But there's nothing to stop you going to see this girl. You could see for yourself what she is really like, just to set your mind at rest.

I don't know who she is or where to find her.

Yes, you do. Chad told you. Her name is Lily and she works in an ABC tea room on Cheapside.

Cheapside! The very name sent a shudder through her.

I couldn't, oh, I couldn't!

But the other voice, the insistent voice, said, *You could — you must!*

It was impossible, though. She would have to ask permission to use Sir Hubert's motor. What excuse could she give for wanting to go to town? She couldn't tell the truth. She couldn't betray Chad's confidence. Unlike her, Sir Hubert had no qualms about interfering in other people's lives. Public office had made him bombastic, a characteristic which the passage of time had only served to accentuate. There would be a terrible row over this girl. Chad would dig in his heels, the way he did sometimes. Sir Hubert would throw his weight around. Who could say where it might lead?

So it was best to do nothing. It was best to let events run their course.

Emily picked up the newspaper from where Sir Hubert had left it, inside out. Signor Mussolini in Tripoli. The coal crisis. She turned the pages, trying to damp down the agitation inside her. Births, marriages and deaths. The personals. Wimbledon tickets wanted. Miracle cures. And all those cryptic little messages, the meaning of which one would never discover:

> *HR. Yes, to the utmost — there can be no half measures. W*
> *Muleteer. You missed a splendid opportunity. 84.*
> *S. Thank you: it will give so much happiness. ES*

What exciting lives people led, other people! How much one missed out on, here at Heartlands!

She put the newspaper aside absent-mindedly, thoughts piling up in her head. She could say that she was going to visit Mama. Sir Hubert always let her use the motor when she went to Mama. Once in London — well, it would be easy to take a detour via Cheapside. But could one trust the chauffeur? Violet said that the servants spied on them and reported back to Sir Hubert. Violet was prone to exaggeration. But it only needed one careless remark, a passing hint, and Sir Hubert would pounce. He would not be satisfied until he knew everything.

Emily experienced a sudden, terrible feeling of claustrophobia, as if the house was shrinking around her, as if the walls were closing in. She was trapped here, the village the limit of her travels — unless Sir Hubert said otherwise. Time was ticking by. She was growing old, desiccated. Her life had dwindled to a routine of arranging flowers and waiting for Chad. When Chad was away in term time, the weeks stretched ahead like a desert.

Just as she felt that despair was about to swallow her up, there came a spark, a sudden idea, a recollection. Last week, in the village. She had gone to post Sir Hubert's letters. There'd been a green omnibus parked opposite the church, *The Sparrowhawk* in gold lettering, *Tottenham* on the destination board. She had been afraid of it — the tentacles of London. But now it seemed like a chink of light, a door opening, her escape route.

She caught her breath, her heart thumping. Dare she?

Oh, stop dithering! The insistent voice lashed her. *Stop dithering and fetch your coat!*

She ran into Violet in the hall, but it was too late to back out.

'Oh, Violet, I shan't be in for luncheon today.'

'Where are you—' Violet began, but Emily slammed the front door and was running down the drive before Violet could finish her sentence.

* * *

Emily could not decide, as she hurried along the lane through the beech wood, which she wished more: that the omnibus would be there, or that it wouldn't.

She reached the village. The omnibus was there, parked opposite the church as before.

She hesitated, lurking round the corner, hugging the churchyard wall, fingering the wide revers of her coat, her heart gambolling. The insistent voice had abandoned her at the very moment when she needed to be braced and bolstered.

She thought of Granny Drage. Granny Drage would not hesitate. Granny Drage had never hesitated in her entire life.

Emily drew herself up. She took a deep breath. She marched towards the omnibus, purposeful, insouciant — that, at least, was what she was aiming for.

The young man in the conductor's uniform must have been watching from inside the bus. He came to the door in a flurry and jumped down onto the road. He touched his cap as before but he did not smile this time. He seemed instead rather wary, looking at her with cautious eyes.

And no wonder, thought Emily, the way she had treated him last week. In running away, she had been rather brusque. It must have seemed to him as if he was being brushed aside. Emily felt a horrible tightening and twisting inside her. Why, why, why must people so often mistake her shyness for rudeness?

She faltered, wanting to turn and run: it would be so much easier. Heartlands, contradictorily, now seemed like a retreat and a refuge, a place where she was safe.

She *wanted* to run. But instead she fumbled in her bag and then took a step forward, holding out a shilling.

'A return ticket, please.'

* * *

She was the only passenger as the omnibus got going. She had taken a seat near the front. The conductor was sitting at the back near the door, sideways in his seat, his feet in the aisle. She was sure he was watching her. She could almost *feel* his eyes on her back. But when, as the bus picked up speed, she finally dared to glance over her shoulder, she saw him hunched over, his chin propped in his hands, staring out at the passing countryside.

Her heart stopped thudding quite so hard. She found she could breathe more easily. It was even possible to relax a little. She put her bag down on the seat beside her. A sense of achievement slowly welled up. How brave, how daring she was! This must be the sort of life that other people led, the people who put cryptic messages in *The Times*. She felt free, she felt exhilaration, as the village receded, and Heartlands dwindled to a mere shadow in her mind. The sun was shining, the countryside was decked in April green. Fields, trees, hedgerows passed in wonderful profusion.

As the omnibus made its juddering way along narrow, winding lanes, Emily found herself wondering why she spent so much of her life trying *not* to be noticed, wanting to fade into the background. Maybe it was high time she stopped. She was tired of being timid. It took so much out of her.

But she was getting ahead of herself. All she'd done was get on a bus. People got onto buses all the time. One did oneself in London without even thinking. There was nothing heroic about getting on a bus.

Picking up her bag again, she gripped it, resting it on her lap, swaying and bouncing on her seat as the omnibus jolted over potholes, paused at a junction, turned onto a wider, smoother road. The buzz and hum of the engine rose a notch as the bus accelerated. Under cover of the noise, Emily began to plan her day.

First she would go to Mama, who was due a visit. Going to see Mama would somehow justify this jaunt into town, make it legitimate. No one needed to know that, after leaving Mama, she would head for the city and — and . . .

She baulked at the thought of the girl, Chad's girl. Perhaps it was best not to make plans. She might lose her nerve when it came to the point, and then she would feel that she'd failed. She would play it by ear, she told herself, using a phrase that she recognized as one of Alan's, surprising herself: how odd that she should bring this phrase out now, after all this time. Odd, too, that Chad should have asked about his father the other night. Why had he?

They were in some ways very much alike, her son and her late husband. She had worried about Chad digging in his heels over this girl, and Alan too had sometimes been stubborn: he had needed to be, battling against his father, wanting to do things for himself, decrying paternalism and nepotism, sticking to his principles. Sir Hubert — still plain Mr Winmer in those days — had been furious when Alan got himself articled to a country law firm. Alan was wasting his talents, he would never get anywhere, why not come to London, instead of hiding in the sticks? There were opportunities in London, Mr Winmer had insisted. He had contacts, now he was in Parliament. He could open doors. But Alan had stood his ground.

It had been due to Alan's stubbornness, thought Emily, that they'd ended up in the little cottage in the middle of nowhere, a mile from the small market town where Alan was working.

Emily shifted uncomfortably in her seat. The warm glow that had risen up inside her at the thought of the cottage now died away again, swamped by feelings of guilt. Alan, who for a moment had been taking shape in her mind, faded into the background once more, fuzzy and indistinct — kept at a safe distance, where he'd always been.

She glanced out of the omnibus window. Instead of fields and hedgerows, there were now building plots and half-finished houses. They were passing into the suburbs of London, the ever-growing suburbs.

Without thinking, she looked over her shoulder. A little shock ran through her as she realized that this time the conductor *had* been looking at her. For a split second their eyes met along the length of the bus. Hurriedly, she looked away, feeling her cheeks burning. At the same moment the omnibus began to slow. There was a welcome distraction as it came to a stop and more passengers got on. Emily clutched her bag against her chest, wrapped in anonymity. She waited anxiously for the bus to start off again.

* * *

She got off the omnibus at the new tube terminus. It would be quicker, the conductor advised her, using his studied enunciation and disguising his East Midlands vowels, for her to catch the tube rather than stay with the bus as it meandered its way to Tottenham. Tottenham was out of her route.

She took a train to Charing Cross, where she got the District Railway to Richmond. Here she made her way across the river and came at length to a secluded house set back from the street, once a rather grand family villa and now converted into what was termed a 'rest home'. A nurse took her through to a big room with a bay window which looked out on a wide lawn fringed with pollarded trees and surrounded by a tall brick wall. Mama was sitting in a wing-chair, watching the sparrows chirping and hopping on the grass outside.

'Mrs Sutton?' The nurse touched Mama's shoulder. 'A visitor for you, my love.'

Mama did not look up. Emily hesitated a moment as the soft-shoed nurse retreated. How frail Mama looked, how old, yet she was only sixty.

Emily leaned down to kiss Mama's cheek, before drawing up a chair and sitting next to her. 'Hello, Mama, dearest.'

Still Mama did not look round, her eyes fixed on the sparrows. Suddenly they took fright and flew away. The lawn was empty. Mama slowly turned her head. A bewildered expression came over her face as she stared at Emily. Then, without warning, she smiled, a smile as warm as the sunshine.

'Hello, dear, how nice to see you. Who are you again?'

'It's me, Mama. It's Emily.'

'Emily? Emily? I had a daughter, once, called Emily.' Mama's face clouded over, she peered with narrowed eyes. '*Who* did you say you are? Are you my mother?'

* * *

Emily stepped off a red London omnibus and made a dash for the pavement, dodging horse dung squashed on the road. Behind her, the omnibus crawled forward a little, then came to a halt once more as the policeman up ahead on point duty raised an imperious hand. The road was clogged with traffic, the pavement clogged with people. Emily picked her way, overtaking the now stationary omnibus, stepping off the kerb to go round two bowler-hatted gentlemen deep in conversation. She eyed nervously a blinkered horse prancing restlessly between the shafts of a cart. The driver of the cart flicked the reins impatiently. A horn tooted. Engines throbbed and buzzed.

Stepping back onto the pavement, Emily saw the sign for the ABC tea room up ahead. As she reached the door, the traffic began to move. The horse clip-clopped smartly past, pulling the cart — the omnibus trundled behind.

The door banged shut behind her, cutting her off from the street. The tea room was busy — there was a crush of people, a babble of voices. Emily weaved between the chairs and tables, found somewhere to sit, took off her coat and hung it on her chair. She picked up the menu then looked at it unseeingly, her heart in her mouth.

Almost at once a girl came.

'Oh, tea please.'

'Cup or pot, Empire Blend or China?'

'A . . . a pot, I think, please. Empire Blend. And some currant bread.'

'Two slices or three? Two is it? Very good, madam.'

The waitress was already moving away when Emily reached out and touched her arm. 'Excuse me . . .'

The girl looked back, expressionless. 'Yes, madam?'

'Is . . . is Lily here today?'

'Lily? Lily Perks, you mean? I believe she is, madam, but I'll enquire for you.'

'Please don't go to any trouble—'

'No trouble at all, madam.' Turning to the next table, the waitress continued in the same breath, 'Good afternoon, sir, madam, what can I get for you?'

Emily leaned down to put her bag on the floor but then had second thoughts, wondering if it would be safe (London was full of pickpockets and thieves). She moved her foot surreptitiously, placing it over the strap. She kept her head down.

She had never been in an ABC shop before. She had never been able to shake the feeling that there was something faintly disreputable about them. It had been common knowledge at one time that tea rooms were frequented by suffragettes and women of that sort. But that was long ago, before the war. Young people these days seemed to go anywhere, everywhere, without giving it a thought, without worrying what might or might not be respectable. *Loose living*, Granny Drage called it. But, oh, if only one could be free of all the doubts and niggles, of worrying what people might think!

I am an anachronism, thought Emily. *I am old.*

She checked that her hat was straight, keeping her eyes lowered, feeling horribly conspicuous, a woman on her own.

In the street one could blend in, pass unnoticed, dash along in a blur — but in here one was stuck to one's chair, pinned and labelled like an exhibit.

Her tea came, and the currant bread. She poured. Her hand was shaking. The hot tea, however, soothed and revived her. After a few sips she felt bold enough to look around. No one was staring at her. No one was looking at her at all. They were all too busy with their companions, and with their teas and coffees, their cutlets and chops, their liver-and-bacon, their fried plaice, their Bakewell flans and apple turnovers and cabinet puddings. The food looked appetizing, the different aromas enticing, but she couldn't even manage her currant bread. Her empty stomach was closed-up, clenched tight.

As she took a tiny sip of tea, she heard a voice from the past: 'Oh, darling, it's a waste of time, taking you out to dine! You never eat more than an eyeful!'

Alan. She remembered the laughter in his voice. But he had not been mocking or poking fun. Alan had never poked fun at anyone.

'Maybe it's just as well that you haven't got a taste for the high life, darling. We can't really afford restaurants.'

A jocular remark with a hint of contrition. Had she recognized this at the time, or had she been too busy worrying about the uneaten food on her plate, and what a waste it was, and was anyone watching, and what could she say next to keep the conversation going? She wondered where exactly they had been eating and when. It must have been on one of their rare trips into town. The details were lost in the past — lost, like so much of the world before the war. And yet she suddenly had the strangest feeling that Alan was very close, almost as if he was sitting there with her in the ABC tea room on Cheapside. It ought to have been disconcerting, like meeting a ghost, but oddly enough it wasn't. Rather the opposite, in fact.

She picked up a slice of currant bread, bit into it, her eyes following the waitresses as they hurried back and forth, balancing trays and plates and dishes, neat in their uniforms and efficient, yet giving the impression of being somewhat frayed round the edges, harassed. One's feet ached in sympathy.

'Poor fellow.' Alan again. That same restaurant (where?). She had been sitting opposite him, she remembered. He had been looking over her shoulder, watching something that was happening behind her. His brow had been furrowed. Candlelight had glinted on his spectacles (there had been candles, cut crystal glasses, red wine). 'Poor, poor fellow.' The *poor fellow* had been a waiter, a young man — a boy almost — in a white shirt and black waistcoat. He, too, had given the impression of being frayed round the edges. An irate customer had been haranguing him: the fish was cold or hadn't been properly filleted, she couldn't remember which.

'We shall leave him a tip,' Alan had said in the same tone of voice he used when railing against his father's attempts to steamroll him, a tone of voice that was resolute yet somehow brittle too. 'We shall leave him a tip, and prove to him that not all his customers are ill-mannered boors!'

Dear Alan! Sometimes she had felt that he would have given away his every last penny had there not been her and Chad to provide for. He'd seen deserving causes at every turn. He'd always done what he could — it had galled him that he couldn't do more. But he'd also gone through agonies, feeling that his family deserved better. If only he wasn't so stubborn, sticking to his principles, refusing his father's help! But how could he go against everything he believed in? How could he live with himself, if he abandoned all his principles? Not that he'd said any of this in so many words. But Emily had become adept at reading between the lines where Alan was concerned. There'd been his eyes, too. His eyes had often given him away. Such expressive eyes, brown and gentle.

Why had she never told him — reassured him — that the cottage was enough — the cottage and Chad and the life they had? Why had she never told him it was all she wanted or needed? She ought to have put him out of his misery. She should have told him she was happy. Except that she hadn't known she was happy — or she'd refused to acknowledge it. She had hankered instead after Alleyn Dene. She had told herself that Alleyn Dene was the only place where she could truly be happy. She'd fostered resentment towards Alan for taking her away from her cherished home, as if *he* had been the one who'd seduced *her*. She wanted Alleyn Dene: this was what she'd told herself, plastering over her feelings of guilt, and ignoring the fact that she had come to love the little cottage, defects and all.

The tea room around her grew blurred as tears sprang into her eyes. Why was Alan haunting her now, after all this time? Why had he come back? He'd been dead nearly nine years, dead and buried — or perhaps not buried, for no one knew what had become of his body, lost in battle.

As she blinked away the tears, Emily saw through the mist a waitress come out of a door marked *PRIVATE*, tying her apron strings. The waitress was obscured for a moment as another waitress flashed past — the very waitress, Emily realized, who'd taken her order.

'Oh, Lily, there's some lady asking after you.'

Emily's vision slowly cleared. She found herself staring wide-eyed at the girl still fumbling with her apron strings. Lily Perks. The name that the waitress had used registered at last. It exploded in her head like a delayed-action bomb. *Lily Perks!*

Emily's eyes grew ever wider. It was unnerving. It was quite uncanny. It was like stepping back in time. Because this girl was the spit-and-image — the very spit-and-image — of Mabel Perks, the maid from Alleyn Dene.

Emily was gripped by a sudden all-consuming fear. She must avoid this girl at all costs. Nothing else mattered.

She got unsteadily to her feet, scooped up her bag, grabbed her coat, keeping her eyes on the girl — on Perks, Lily Perks. At the very last moment she remembered that she hadn't paid, scrabbled for her purse, put a coin on the table. She turned away, stumbling towards the door. She dropped her bag, picked it up, bumped into chairs, tables, earned curious or irritated or blank-faced looks. As she neared the door, reaching blindly for it, she heard above the hubbub of conversations and clattering crockery the voice of her waitress. 'Well, she *was* here. I call that *most* peculiar . . .'

Out in the hurly-burly of the street, Emily's one thought was to get away, as far away as possible. She blundered along, heedless of which direction she was going, her coat in her hand and dragging along the pavement. Mabel Perks seemed to loom up everywhere. In her head she could hear an echo of that long-ago voice.

What are you doing, miss, sneaking up the back stairs . . . I have got eyes . . . it's for your own good, you can't bury your head forever . . .

CHAPTER SEVEN

The tube train rattled and rolled, streaming out from the tunnel into the open night, ascending quickly to an embankment. It was so late, thought Emily, looking out. How had it got so late?

Leaving the ABC shop, she had wandered in a daze. She remembered seeing a street sign, *PUDDING LANE*, and thinking automatically, *the Great Fire*. She remembered seeing the tall, pale Monument with its gilded pinnacle. And then what?

Sitting in the tube train, she tried to piece it together in her mind. She had found herself standing on a bridge whilst traffic streamed behind her. London Bridge, she realized now: it must have been London Bridge. The wide river had looked deceptively sluggish, as if it wasn't flowing anywhere much. The surface of the grey-brown water had rippled in the breeze. The river had been clogged with boats, masted ships with flags and pennants, other ships with funnels belching smoke, barges and lighters moored in rows. She remembered seeing Billingsgate Market on the left-hand bank and the pillared portico of the Customs House. Further off rose the frowning walls of the Tower, with the majestic span of Tower Bridge beyond. Warehouses lined the opposite bank, where there was a forest of cranes. Everywhere, people were on the move. She had felt swamped by it, weighed down by it. She had felt utterly insignificant, like dust on the wind. And all the time something had been niggling away at her. Slowly it had come to the surface of her mind, floating there like flotsam on the river. She had left half a crown on the table in the tea room. She had left half a crown and not waited for her change. Oh, how silly! How silly, silly, silly! To leave half a crown and not wait for her change! Her tea and currant bread could not have come to more than fourpence-ha'penny. Yet she'd left half a crown.

She would go back, she'd decided. She would go back and explain. She would try to get her change. Half a crown was half a crown, after all. She couldn't afford to just throw it away.

But even as she'd resolved to return to the tea room, a sense of urgency had overtaken her. What was the time in all this? How long had she been standing there, staring at nothing? She would be late for dinner if she didn't get a move on. She would not get back at all if she missed the omnibus. What time had the conductor told her, the last trip?

She had broken into a run.

She was still racking her brains even now, trying to remember the time of the last trip, as the tube train rattled through the suburbs of north-west London. But what was the use in fretting? There was nothing she could do to make the train go any faster.

Perks. Lily Perks.

No! She wouldn't think about that. She mustn't. Couldn't.

She closed her mind, leaned back, watched the passing scenery through the opposite window, the rows and rows of houses at right angles to the embankment, all the slate roofs and brick chimney stacks, streets stretching away into the distance. Street lamps. Lighted windows. So many windows. So many different rooms. She thought of all the different lives going on inside those rooms, all the different people. There they all were, and here she was, on this train. It was chance, blind chance, that she was here, and not there. She might easily have been in one of those rooms living a different life. Instead she was trapped in this life, her own life, a life that went on day after day, following its set path: a mindless, mechanical sort of life, like this train mindlessly and mechanically following the rails on which it ran.

She closed her eyes, blocking out the rows of houses and all the other lives. She had been set on the same track now for so long that she couldn't imagine things any other way. Once, perhaps, there had been junctions, branch lines, chances to veer onto another course, but all that seemed long ago, endlessly remote, and the war, as ever, was an insurmountable barrier. The four years of war seemed more like forty — or four hundred — as one fumbled in the dark trying to remember the world as it had been before 1914.

The train rattled and rolled. The journey went on and on. But the sense of urgency had gone. She was in no hurry now. She was in no hurry to reach the end of the line. The thought of returning to Heartlands left her cold. Heartlands, where she spent her days simply keeping idleness at bay, where she hardly dared do anything for fear of treading on someone's toes, where even putting out a few flowers was enough to earn Violet's ire. What a wretched and diminishing life! It was as if she had been miniaturized and placed in Queen Mary's dolls' house, stood in the same room, holding the same pose, forever.

The train began to slow. She got to her feet and made her way to the door, passing from one dangling strap to the next. The train jerked to a halt. The doors hissed open. She crossed the platform with the few remaining passengers, hurried up the stairs. The station clock told her that the omnibus would be long gone. Her heart sank as she crossed the black-and-white tiled foyer, thinking of all the trouble she would have in getting home.

But as she passed through the doors and looked round outside, she saw, parked in the forecourt, the snub green shape of *The Sparrowhawk*, as welcome as an old friend. The young conductor came leaping down as she approached, his money bag and ticket machine bouncing against his hips.

'Evening, madam.'

She looked at him wonderingly. 'You waited.'

'Aye, well, we had to honour your ticket.'

He seemed abashed by the excess of gratitude in her voice. She was so happy, out of all proportion. She felt he'd rescued her from some terrible nameless fate.

'Thank you. Thank you so much, Mr — er — Mr . . . ?'

'Midgely. George Midgely at your service.' He touched his cap, gave her a curious glance, quickly looked away, fiddling all the time with the handle of his ticket machine.

She was the only passenger. It would have seemed churlish, when he'd been so gracious, to sit at the opposite end of the bus as she'd done that morning. Instead, she took a place two rows along. George Midgely remained standing, his legs braced against one of the seats, his body swaying with the movement of the bus as it lumbered through the suburban streets, then past the building plots, finally heading out into the dark countryside.

At length he said, rather hesitantly, 'Did y'have a good day, madam?'

No, she wanted to say — to shout, to scream — no, no, no! First Mama — it always wrenched at one's heart, seeing Mama like that — and then — well, she didn't even want to think about the rest of the day.

'Yes, thank you, Mr Midgely. I had a very good day.' Even as she spoke, a savage anger surged inside her. Always so polite. Never wanting to make a fuss. Treading softly. Abrogating herself.

She shivered. Cold air was flowing in through the open doorway. The unseen countryside was blanketed in darkness.

'The poor driver,' she ventured, feeling it beholden on her to pass some remark, tit for tat after George Midgely's asking about her day. 'Doesn't he get cold, sitting out in the open?'

'Old Ginger? He's all right. He don't feel the cold. He's known worse. We both have.'

She groped for something else to say. 'How . . . how many of you are there, working for the Sparrowhawk Omnibus

Company?' This was the name on the printed ticket. 'Such a splendid name, the Sparrowhawk Omnibus Company.'

'It's the thing to do, to give your bus a grand name. But there's only one bus, and there's only Ginge and me: we're the Sparrowhawk Omnibus Company.'

'Oh. I see.' She looked round at the empty seats. How did they ever make a living?

He seemed to sense her unspoken question and said rather defensively, 'Weren't always this way, the bus half-empty. We used to do all right for oursen. There were money to be made.' Without thinking, or so it seemed, he took a seat opposite her, sitting sideways as he had that morning, his feet planted in the aisle between them. 'We used to do all right. Then rules changed. We had to gi' up profitable routes. The General forced us out.'

'The General? Who is the General?'

'Not who, what. It's the combine. The London General Omnibus Company.'

'Of course, yes.' She remembered now the word *GENERAL* emblazoned on the sides of the red omnibuses in London. She had ridden in one herself earlier that day, on her way to Cheapside. Inexplicably, she felt a sense of guilt about this now. She did not want George Midgely to know.

'We're pirates, missus. One of them pirate buses there was so much fuss on a few year back.'

He didn't look much like a pirate, thought Emily, as she listened to him talk. His accent grew broader as he warmed to his theme, explaining how you had to take every chance you could get, when unemployment was so prevalent, and opportunities for work few and far between. In 1922, when independent buses had started to appear on the streets of the capital — buses that soon became known as *pirates* — he and his friend, Ginger, had decided to pool what little money they had, take out a loan, and buy a second-hand omnibus. For a while, business had been good. You could have your pick of the routes. But then, he said, aggrieved, the government had stepped in, introduced new restrictions. The independents had been forced off most of the more lucrative routes. This was done deliberately to favour the combine, the London General. The combine had all the muscle — plenty of money, and friends in high places. The little man got trampled on.

Not much like a pirate, Emily repeated, watching George Midgely as he spoke, his eyes roaming round the bus or straying out into the dark, his hands constantly fidgeting: fingering the ticket machine, tapping the back of the seat, adjusting his cap. Finally, he took his cap off altogether and laid it on the seat beside him. Not like a pirate. Too neat and self-contained. Very smart in his conductor's uniform, scrubbed and trim. Tow-headed, grey-eyed, clean-cut, bursting with restive energy.

But if he wasn't a pirate, what sort of man was he? The more she watched him, the harder it got to pin him down. He was a mass of contradictions. He was young — about twenty-eight or so — but often gave the impression of being much older. He was plain-looking, yet somehow handsome too — rough-edged, yet scrupulously polite. It seemed absurd to Emily now, that she'd ever thought him the sort of man who would follow her for nefarious ends, as she'd imagined when they first met. And yet, despite that — and for reasons she couldn't put her finger on — she felt there were other and different ways in which he might prove dangerous.

She looked away. She didn't want to be caught staring. He, meanwhile, carried on talking. He was telling her now about Ginger, his old mate Ginger, who he'd met in the war. Of course, she thought, the war. That would explain a lot: his young/old demeanour, the sense of there being more to him than met the eye. And yet he glossed over the war as if it wasn't important. He spoke of it — many now did — in a strangely impersonal way, as if it was something that had happened to other people, as if it had become symbolical only.

For me, thought Emily, *the war was never quite real at all.*

It took place off-stage. It was presented as a fait accompli. One's only part in it was to pick up the pieces once it was all over.

But that wasn't quite true. Looking out from the omnibus window as it sped through the dark, she found herself remembering a day when the war had seemed suddenly very real — when it seemed almost to reach out and touch her. She'd been at the south coast, walking by the sea. There'd been a strange, ethereal throbbing in the air. One had *felt* it as much as heard it.

'The guns in France.'

Overhearing this remark in passing, Emily had experienced a little shock, as if she'd touched an electric current. The guns, the distant guns. Some massive bombardment at the front, endless miles away across the wide, blue English Channel.

She shivered inside the omnibus, shook herself free of this disquieting memory. George Midgely, she realized, had changed the subject, was asking again about her day, but in a casual, conversational way, so that Emily did not feel she was being put on the spot. Her vague replies — what else could she be but vague? — seemed to satisfy him, and before she knew it they were talking about London, talking easily, naturally, without any awkwardness at all: about how she always found London faintly menacing, about how George Midgely had come to make it his home. He'd liked to explore on Sundays, he said, walking miles, getting lost, finding his way, getting acquainted. His steps had often led him to Parliament Hill, which was still his favourite place, a place where you could sit and think, or not think, where you could see London spread out in front of you, where you could marvel at the size of it, or simply sit and stare at the distant horizon, and the wide, over-arching sky. Not that he had time for sitting and staring these days, he added. There was too much work to do now, Sundays the same as any other day. He missed his walks, but needs must.

Engrossed, when Emily finally glanced out of the window again, she was surprised to find how close to home she was. The journey back seemed to have taken no time at all.

George Midgely insisted on their driving the extra mile, dropping her by the entrance to Heartlands. He jumped out to hand her down. She could feel the warmth of his strong fingers through the thin material of her gloves (why did she always wear gloves, so old-fashioned?).

'You've been very kind, Mr Midgely.' (Oh so stiff and formal.)

'Our pleasure, madam. All part of the service.' (The careful diction, like a mask.)

She hesitated, then ventured, 'Mrs Winmer. Please, do call me Mrs Winmer.'

'Mrs Winmer,' he echoed. Yet it was not quite an echo, there was a subtle difference in his pronunciation — a trace of his East Midlands accent, perhaps. She found herself forming the sound with her lips, trying to repeat her name the way he'd just said it. Quickly she smiled to cover her mimicry.

He let go of the hand she hadn't realized he was still holding and touched his cap, that characteristic half-salute. They both wavered, still face to face, as if they were trying to remember the common courtesies, as if they'd forgotten how to say *goodnight.* The headlamps of the bus made long pools of light on the rutted lane. An owl hooted in the darkness of the wood.

'Come on, Midge, get a bloomin' move on!' The cockney voice of the driver came floating through the cold air.

George Midgely grinned, his teeth showing white in the deep shadow cast by the peak of his cap. 'Old Ginger's anxious for home. His missus'll be waiting.'

'What about you, Mr Midgely? You will want to get back to your family too, I expect.'

'Not me. I've nobody waiting. Just mesen.' He laughed, as if he had made some sort of joke, and then he stepped up onto the platform. 'G'night, Mrs Winmer.'

He was moving away even as he spoke. The omnibus dwindled along the lane. The light of its headlamps faded. The sound of its raucous engine slowly dissipated and dissolved into the dark. In the silence that followed, she heard the owl again, tu-whooing deep in the wood, a faint and eerie sound. But it was not just the owl making her shiver. There was something else — something more. She felt — she felt . . .

She was not sure how she felt. As if there was a spark inside her. As if she was coming to life. London, she supposed. Sometimes, London had that effect. She had almost forgotten what London was like, it was so long since she'd been there (visits to Mama in Richmond did not really count). It must be years, for instance, since last she'd stayed with Aunt Margery. What had she been doing all this time? How had she spent her days?

As she made her way up the drive, the night closed in round her. Suddenly, she was conscious of Lily Perks. The thought of Lily Perks loomed up out of the dark like a phantom of the woods. Lily Perks, with her mother's eyes, her mother's nose, and the voice . . . the very same voice . . .

With an effort, Emily thrust Lily Perks aside. She couldn't cope with Lily Perks just now. Anything, rather than Lily Perks. But the very name *Perks* was enough to extinguish the faint spark that had kindled inside her as she listened to the omnibus fading into the night. All she wanted now was to get to the house. She was tired, footsore, could feel a headache coming on.

She hurried on. Her footsteps sounded loud in the silence of the wood. The throbbing of her incipient headache made her think once again of the throbbing of the guns long ago — 1916, had it been, or 1917? She had been on a visit to Mama who, after Papa died, had retired to the coast, living in a modest bungalow grudgingly provided by Granny Drage. They had been walking along the sea front under a blue, autumnal sky, waves breaking endlessly on the pebbly beach, gulls on the wing flashing white in the sun. And then — the throbbing and rippling of the air, fading in and out, pressing infinitesimally on one's ear drums.

'Listen, Mama. Listen. Can you hear it? Can you hear the guns?'

'No, dearest. That isn't gunfire. That's just thunder.'

Thunder, she'd called it. Yet there'd not been a cloud in the sky.

Was that the day, Emily wondered as she saw the bright lights of Heartlands glimmering through the trees ahead, when she first noticed that Mama was getting vague? Like a great, inexorable, obliterating wave, Mama's amnesia had slowly spread, sweeping over her past.

'Have you come to take me home to Alleyn Dene, Emily? When are we going home? Papa will be wondering where we are.'

Hysterics, Granny Drage had called it. 'Pull yourself together, Beatrice! Stop this *disgraceful* behaviour! There's no excuse for it, absolutely no excuse! I shan't come again, if this is all I can expect from you.'

Granny Drage had refused to countenance that Mama needed help, had washed her hands of her unworthy daughter. And so it was Sir Hubert who'd paid for the doctors (there had been little the doctors could do), who'd found the rest home in Richmond, who'd covered the fees: Sir Hubert, who would have been nothing, but for the Suttons. And now the Suttons — Emily, Mama — were totally reliant on him. Fate's wheel had turned. Fortunes had been neatly reversed.

Poor Mama! As Emily hurried towards the lighted windows, shivering with cold, she experienced a fierce pinch of regret. What made it worse was that one had never truly appreciated all that Mama had done. One hadn't realized, until it was too late — too late to tell her how much one admired her, too late to really get to know her. Mama had kept always in the background, demure and modest, the model wife, an unobtrusive mother. But it was Mama who'd created Alleyn Dene, a whole separate world, a safe place, unchanging — home.

Emily climbed the steps to Heartlands' front door, but then paused on the threshold, turning to stare into the dark, thinking of Alleyn Dene, of Mama's part in it. The illusion had been complete. One had assumed that the house ran itself. One had imagined that life was always like that, calm and ordered and inherently civilized. Mankind had tamed the world. It was God's will. How else to account for the peace and plenty of Alleyn Dene? But whatever the explanation, it could hardly have anything to do with that mild-mannered woman in a tea gown, cutting slices of cake and handing round the sugar basin. One would have laughed, in the old days, if anyone had described Mama as *brave* — one would have scoffed at any suggestion she could be *intrepid.* And yet, how else could one describe it but brave and intrepid, the time when Mama had contrived to arrive at the cottage in a carrier's cart on a hot summer's day long before the war?

CHAPTER EIGHT

'Dearest Emmy! You don't know how glad I am to see you! I thought I would never get here. This heat, I can't tell you. I am half-dead.'

Mama collapsed into a cast-iron garden chair in the shade of the apple tree, fanning herself with her ostrich feather hat, her eyes rolling, her bosom heaving.

Putting her sewing hurriedly aside, Emily said in some surprise, 'Mama! How lovely! But I wasn't expecting you!'

'Not expecting me? How can that be? I wrote and told you I would be coming.'

'That was before the rail strike. I really didn't think—'

'I'm a woman of my word, you should know that, Emmy. I couldn't let you down when I'd promised. But you can't *imagine* the trouble we've had getting here. It's been awful, quite awful — hasn't it, Gibbs?'

'Yes, ma'am. Awful.' Mama's maid, swaying where she stood, looked dazed. Sweat was pouring down her face.

'We came by carrier's cart, the last few miles.' Mama was getting her breath back. 'You are so out of the way here, Emmy, miles from anywhere. I was beginning to think I would end up in one of those lists in *The Times*, people killed by the heat.'

But Mama, thought Emily as she got to her feet, was not someone who could be finished off so easily. She looked with affection at her parent, dusty and dishevelled, and still fanning herself. Dear old Mama. So scatter-brained. So *silly*. Fancy setting off on such a journey in this heat and with a rail strike on and the whole country — from all that one gathered — in uproar. Not that one gave the world much thought, here at the cottage. The world seemed too far-removed and chimerical, too unimportant — never more so than on this baking August afternoon. The back garden of the cottage was particularly secluded, tucked away from the lane, edged round by crumbling walls and overgrown hedges, just like the Secret Garden in the book.

The Secret Garden, thought Emily sheepishly. At her age — twenty-three — she really ought to have outgrown children's books. But here, one could be a child again if one wanted. One could be anything, do anything. The normal rules didn't seem to apply. Only rarely was it necessary to be stuffy and sensible and adult.

Mama summed it up precisely, succinct as ever. 'What a little Eden you have here, Emmy!' She was slowly recovering her poise, sitting in the shade of the old apple tree and looking round at the wisteria and the straggling roses and the clematis cascading over the walls. A blackbird trilled, perched on the mossy statue of a Greek or Roman lady. Blue cornflowers grew in the untidy lawn, invaders from the fields beyond. The air was thick and somnolent. Sunshine gilded everything, dazzling the eye.

But — poor Mama, melting in her chair — and her maid fit to drop. Emily stirred herself and set about organizing things, taking the maid to lie down in the cool interior (every door and window was open wide), asking her own girl to bring lemonade, sandwiches, cake. In the main room, with the lattice windows overlooking the lane, little Chad was having his afternoon nap on the sofa. Emily gently brushed the curls off his forehead. Let him sleep. There was plenty of time to see Grandma later.

The heat hit her as she stepped out into the garden once more. It was almost unbearably bright after the dim and shadowy indoors. The sun blazed high in a cloudless sky. Not a breeze stirred. All sound was stifled. Even the blackbird had fallen silent. Its wings were unfurled over the head of the statue, its orange beak was open, as if panting.

Emily settled herself back in her chair, sipped cold lemonade, so refreshing.

'How is poor Gibbs?' asked Mama. 'I had almost to carry her up the path to your door. She was quite overcome.'

'She's resting now. Is she new, Mama?'

'Well, no, not really; she's been with us for some time. Have you never — but I suppose not: I can't remember the last time you came to Alleyn Dene.'

'Oh, Mama, it's not been that long!'

Or had it? One forgot. The days passed in a blur here. And then travelling was such a nuisance, said Emily to herself as she watched the bees in the lavender, and Northamptonshire so far away. That must be the reason why she'd neglected to go back to Alleyn Dene for so long. What else could it be?

'Gibbs has been a godsend,' Mama continued. 'Such an *obliging* sort of girl. There was an awful lot of interest in her when she became available. Mrs Barford, in particular, was very persistent. But I managed to manoeuvre Mrs Barford aside, and bring Gibbs to Alleyn Dene.'

Swirling her lemonade, Emily said casually, 'Whatever happened to Perks, Mama?' She tightened her hold on her glass. Why mention Perks?

'Perks? Perks? I can't quite . . .' Mama knit her brows. 'It's not like me to forget a face. Oh, yes, Perks, now I remember.' Light dawned but her frown lingered. 'Do you know, I really had almost forgotten Perks. How very strange. It must be — oh, let me see — four, five years, since we let her go. We had to let her go, of course. It was all rather awkward. But you must know all this, Emily, surely you must know?'

'Oh, yes, I . . .' Emily grew confused. *Did* she know? Or had she, too, forgotten? What had prompted her to bring up the subject of Perks in the first place? She slowly sipped her lemonade, trying to put her thoughts in order. But she'd never been able to put her thoughts in order when it came to Perks.

Out of the corner of her eye, Emily saw Mama glance at her curiously, and for a split second the sunshine seemed to falter, as if the shadow of some vast, predatory bird had fallen across the garden. But Mama did not pursue the subject. The shadow passed. Perks dropped out of sight once more. The sun beat down. The bees buzzed. The blackbird watched with a beady eye, sunbathing on the statue. Its spread-out wings looked like scraps of ragged-edged black cloth.

'This weather, Emmy! Will it never end?' Mama was fanning herself again. She had drunk her lemonade in one go. 'It's hotter even than the summer of ninety-nine. Or was it ninety-eight? I can never remember. It doesn't seem quite natural, such heat in England. But then again, this has been an odd sort of year all round, what with one thing and another — the Coronation in June, and the bank making such a to-do over Papa's loan, and now this rail strike. There was all that fuss, as well, over the German gunboat in Morocco. I can't begin to imagine what all that was about. Papa said that it might mean war. But really, it would be too, too silly, to have a war over *Morocco*. And as if all that wasn't enough, now there's . . . well . . . is it true, dearest, that Parliament has voted to abolish the House of Lords?'

'They have voted to abolish the veto, Mama: it's quite different.' (Alan had explained it all to her. Alan found that he was drawn to politics despite himself.)

'It's beyond me, Emmy, but I suppose Mr Asquith knows what he is doing. Your papa is convinced of it. You, of course, must hear all the latest news, with Alan's father in the House. I've heard it whispered, dearest, that Mr Winmer might soon become a *right honourable*.'

'I really couldn't say, Mama. We don't see much of Mr Winmer.'

Alan had rather blotted his copybook, as far as his father was concerned, by taking up with a country law firm, instead of making full use of the doors that could be opened for him in the capital. Alan said it was important to be one's own man. His father, self-made, ought to understand better than anyone. His father ought to be aware of the corrosive nature of privilege.

Emily, in the beginning, had found this rather alarming, Alan in his adamant mood. Gradually, she had got used to it. She'd come to realize that he wasn't just being pig-headed and bombastic, the way his father often was these days. Alan only ever dug his heels in when his cherished principles were at stake. Nothing could move him, when he thought something was right, or when he'd given his word. He was always true to himself, which Emily found rather comforting. One knew where one stood with Alan. He was a man who could be relied on.

It was impossible to explain all this to Mama. Emily wouldn't have known where to begin. She changed the subject instead.

'How is everyone, Mama? How is Papa?' Emily liked to hear news from what she still thought of as home, even though she seldom went back there. (It made it easier, not going back. Easier to remember Alleyn Dene as it used to be, before — as she put it to herself — 'Perks spoiled everything'.) 'How is Granny? Have you heard from Aunt Margery?'

'Granny is just the same, as you might expect,' said Mama. 'Your Aunt Margery was quite well, the last time I heard — your Uncle Walter, too (you forgot Walter, dearest). As for your papa . . . there's his indigestion, of course . . . and he does worry so about the business. I'm hoping, once this big order comes in . . . I told you about the big order, didn't I? No? How silly of me! I don't know the details — it's all beyond me — but Mr Winmer (so kind) has promised your papa a government contract for . . . now let me see . . . is it boots for the army? Yes, I rather think it is. Boots for — oh, but here's little David!' Emily turned to see her son stumbling out from the cot-tage, rubbing his eyes with his fists and squinting in the glare.

He went straight to his mother and stood very close, clutching at the sleeve of her dress, looking at the visitor dubiously.

'He — he's rather shy, Emily,' ventured Mama, equally dubious.

Grandmother and grandson eyed each other with mutual misgiving.

'He's always a little shy of strangers at first,' said Emily, stroking the boy's little fist, trying to get him to loosen his grip on the fabric of her dress.

'But I'm not a stranger!' cried Mama. She put on a smile. 'Hello, little man. Hello, David. You remember me, don't you?'

'We call him Chad, Mama. Chadwick. His middle name.'

'Do you, dearest? Such an *odd* sort of name.'

'It was Alan's mama's name, before she was married. I rather like "Chad".'

'Ah. Hmm. I see.' Mama's tone suggested that this business about the name might lead some people to suspect Alan of being a mummy's boy — which, of course, he wasn't. At least, he wasn't in any of the ways people might mean. He was not like Uncle Walter, for instance, dominated by Granny Drage, tied to her apron strings. Nor was he bluff and patronizing, the way some men were with their mothers. Alan's affection for his mother was manly and mature, as befitted him. Watching Alan with his mother had been one of the things which, in the weeks and months after the rushed wedding, had made Emily wonder if being married to him might not be as awful and hopeless as she'd imagined.

'Hello, Chad! Hello, little man.' Mama held her hand out, wiggled her fingers. Chad looked on in alarm, as if he'd come across a nest of snakes. 'How old is he now, Emmy? Five? As old as that? We really rather thought, dearest — your papa and I — that there might have been another happy event by now.'

For a split second, as these words broke over her, Emily almost succumbed to the horrific illusion that it was not

Mama sitting in the chair opposite, but Perks — Perks, nodding and winking, a sly and salacious smile on her face.

Now, miss, you know what you've got to do, I've told you all about it, it's easy as riding a bike . . .

Emily blinked, and the illusion vanished like a puff of smoke. Perks was banished once more from the garden.

But as Emily deftly turned the conversation to other matters, Mama's remark — *we really rather thought there'd have been another happy event* — seemed to hang in the air, pointing like an accusing finger.

* * *

Nearly fifteen years later, walking in the gardens at Heartlands, Emily mulled over Mama's visit that long-ago summer before the war. It had been a perfect interlude in so many ways, perhaps the best week of all, in her time at the cottage. She had breakfasted with Mama at leisure each morning, after Alan had left for the office. They had ventured out into the lane. They had strolled in the surrounding fields, where haymaking was over but the harvest not yet begun. They had walked at a snail's pace so that Chad could keep up on his little legs. They had held Chad's hands and swung him between them. He had laughed and kicked his feet. Every day had been bright and hot, the heatwave never-ending.

It seemed to Emily, looking back, that there had been something different about Mama on that visit. She'd not looked any different. She'd taken her bag and her parasol with her, as usual, wherever they went. Yet she had seemed somehow unencumbered, as if a weight had been lifted, as if, for a short while, she could truly relax. She had sat on the ground without demur in the shade of the trees on Spinney Hill, never a word about the damp and the dirt. She had laughed when ants crawled up inside her petticoat, she had flicked at wasps fearlessly with her bare hands. Far from worrying what time it was and whether they'd be late for tea, she had been content to while away lazy hours in the wilds of the countryside, enjoying the view, talking in a desultory way about this and that, and teaching Chad to say *yellow* instead of *yerro*.

In the evenings, with Chad in bed and Alan home, the three of them had sat to dinner with the windows open and the lamps lit. Alan had been his gentle, charming, serious self, and Mama at long last, after five years, had begun to thaw towards him, had begun the slow process of forgiving him for the shameful seduction of her daughter. That was the effect that the cottage had. That was the magic it worked. *What a little Eden you have here*, Mama had said. She'd been right.

Walking along the gravel paths at Heartlands, with a trug on her arm and the wind in her hair (it looked like rain), Emily reflected how different the gardens were here compared to the cottage. Here everything was neat and ordered, somehow sterile, the paths raked, the grass cut inch perfect, not a blot or blemish in sight. Everything at Heartlands had its proper place, flowers in one section, vegetables in another. The cottage garden, by contrast, had been all higgledy-piggledy, runner beans tangled with the clematis, raspberries amongst the roses. Obviously, it had been terribly neglected over many years. Yet somehow it worked. And in that long, hot summer — the summer of 1911 — it had been at its most bewitching.

Passing through a perfectly neat gap in a perfect privet hedge, Emily came to the allotted place for the spring flowers. She paused for a moment, letting a bittersweet nostalgia sweep over her. How wonderful it now seemed, that time before the war, when motor cars were a rarity, and no one had heard of wireless receiving sets. At the cottage, there'd been oil lamps and an outside well. The market town, a mile away, might have been at the ends of the earth. She thought of the riotous profusion of the cottage garden on that August afternoon when Mama arrived, of the zesty tang of the cold, cloudy lemonade and of Mama, so stalwart, and little Chad, so shy. All in the past now. All just memories. Lost, like the real Eden. Mama, too, had gone. The woman in the rest home was nothing but an empty shell, like one of Madame Tussaud's waxworks.

The heady feeling of nostalgia seeped slowly away and Emily sighed, taking her secateurs from the trug. But even as she considered which flowers to cut, she suddenly shivered. It seemed so perfect, looking back, that long-ago summer of 1911. But there'd been a snake in Eden. And Mama had put an unwitting finger on it, when she asked about the next 'happy event'.

Abruptly, Emily put the secateurs back in the trug. What was the use in cutting flowers? Violet would only complain of the smell, the other sisters would also find fault, and Sir Hubert wouldn't notice if there were flowers or not. Abandoning the trug on a varnished bench, Emily walked aimlessly, heedless of where she was going. She didn't know what was the matter with her today, she couldn't settle to anything. What was it, this deep-rooted yearning inside her, almost like a physical pain? A yearning for what? For days gone by — for the cottage and Mama — for Alleyn Dene, too, and her lost childhood? But it wasn't that. It wasn't anything to do with the past. Almost she felt she wanted to look forward. But what was the point in that? She had nothing to look forward to.

Moping about, Nanny would have called it. Granny Drage would be harsher. 'Hysteria. That's all it is. Hysteria, plain and simple.' It was always hysteria to Granny Drage. Hysteria was the cause of all a woman's problems. 'There's no excuse for it, wallowing in that sort of nonsense.'

What would Granny Drage have thought, if she could have looked into a certain hotel room in Margate in December 1905 and seen her granddaughter shedding silent tears in the watches of the night, overcome by hopelessness and despair? The worst moment of all, thought Emily. The night after her wedding. And in Margate, of all places.

Why Margate?

'It's just the sort of place to which the Winmers would go,' Granny had said dismissively. 'A vulgar place for vulgar people.'

Emily had found it all strange and beyond her ken, the spotless, impersonal hotel room, the mortifying embarrassment of seeing Alan in his pyjamas, the shame and humiliation of having to share a bed with him. Worse was the feeling that she'd lost everything she'd ever cared about — Mama, Papa, even Juniper, and dear Alleyn Dene: her whole life. And on top of this, she'd been weighed down by the looming fear of what might happen when she was called on to fulfil her wifely duty.

Alan did not importune her in Margate, barely laid a finger on her at all. He'd been worried, he admitted much later, that marital relations might in some way harm the baby. Which made Emily realize, in hindsight, that he'd been almost as ignorant as she was — almost, but not quite.

They had moved to the cottage. Alan had been articled to a law firm in the nearby market town. He'd had exams to study for. He'd been kept busy. He'd 'buried himself in the country', as his father disparagingly put it. Meanwhile, Emily grew bigger and bigger, and the baby occupied more and more of her thoughts. She'd forgotten all about her wifely duty.

The months wore away. Chad finally arrived. Weeks later, in the miniscule front bedroom of the cottage, with the curtains closed and a candle burning, the moment she'd feared, and then forgotten, had suddenly arrived. It had been an evening in early autumn, the days drawing in, a chill in the air. Alan had hovered near the end of the bed in his pyjamas and his dressing gown.

'Darling, do you think we could . . . I would so like to . . . I want you very much, you see.'

She'd still been living in the bubble of happiness that had enveloped her when Chad was born. She'd got used to Alan, too, by then. She'd felt safe, tucked up in bed in their little cottage.

Anything, she had said to herself: *I can cope with anything, now*.

Even her wifely duty.

And so she had nodded shyly, averting her eyes.

Alan had taken off his dressing gown, folding it neatly. He had taken off his spectacles, placing them carefully on the bedside table. Her eyes had been drawn to his hands as he did so, and she'd seen that they were shaking. That was when she'd felt the first presage of fear.

He had blown out the candle. He had got into bed in the dark. The bed had creaked and sagged. Her heart had been racing, her stomach in knots. Fear had taken full hold of her.

Rigid as stone, she had felt the weight of him on her. His touch, his breath, had made her skin crawl. What was that smell? Whisky, was it? Whisky, and fur and leather and mothballs. As if she was back in the cloakroom at Nethercote Hall. And then—

Pain. Excruciating pain.

'Oh, please, no, no—'

'What is it, darling, what's wrong?'

'I can't . . . I can't . . . it's too horrible.'

'But it's all perfectly natural. It's what a man and wife do.'

His deep, gentle voice had seemed to her tinged with exasperation and she'd been sure he was about to force himself on her. She'd wanted to fight him off, but she couldn't, lying paralyzed in the dark, barely able to breathe.

'Darling, oh, darling . . .'

'I can't. Oh, please don't make me. It hurts, it hurts, it hurts so much!'

'Darling, I say, you're shaking. You're shaking all over — oh, darling, I'm so clumsy, what have I done to you? I'm sorry, I'm sorry, please forgive me, please say you'll forgive me. See? I'm not touching you now. I shan't lay a finger on you. I shan't touch you ever again, if that's what you want. I promise. I *promise*. Oh, darling, I love you so much! I wouldn't hurt you for the world!'

'Alan, oh, Alan!'

'Hush. Don't cry. Come here. Let me hold you. You don't mind if I hold you? That's it. You're safe now. You're quite safe. I won't ever hurt you. You know that I won't. I've promised, and I always keep my promises.'

He'd been true to his word. He was Alan Winmer, his word was his bond. Thus it was, when Mama came to visit in August 1911, there'd been no happy event, nor would there ever be.

This terrible secret was the snake in Eden.

Emily shuddered, surfacing from her memories. She looked round. Where was she? She hardly ever came to this part of the gardens, a neglected corner at the back of the house, separated off, shaded by trees, a place where there were sheds and compost heaps and piles of old trellises and disused plant pots. A rusty, upturned wheelbarrow lay on a patch of threadbare grass, a ladder had been tossed aside, broken panes of glass from the greenhouse, green and mossy, were stacked against a leaning fence. It was an untidy place, somehow sordid, hidden away like a guilty secret. No visitor was ever allowed here. Visitors only ever saw the immaculate places, the perfect gardens.

Emily picked her way across the patchy grass, stepped over a heap of roof tiles, squeezed between two ramshackle sheds. At the back of the sheds was a rusty chain fence with bindweed growing up it and barbed wire along the top: the perimeter of Heartlands. Beyond was a secluded meadow, yellow with buttercups, and bordered on the far side by trees. The treetops made a ragged line against the grey horizon but, above the meadow, the sun was gleaming through tattered clouds.

As she watched the buttercups shimmering in the breeze, Emily asked herself if she ought to have been more accommodating with Alan. She could at least have tried. But she'd not given much thought to the sacrifice Alan was making in order to keep his promise. At first, she'd remained wary, unsure if his promise would really hold. As she grew more sure of him, bedtime had ceased to be an ordeal. She had even grown to like having him near, lying next to her — so much so, that she'd missed him dreadfully when he went away to war.

She wondered what might have happened if they'd tried again. Once she'd grown more comfortable around him, would she have learned to submit to his attentions? Or was the damage wrought in the cloakroom at Nethercote Hall too deep, too permanent? She'd always been far too afraid to try and find out. She'd lacked the courage to absolve Alan of his promise.

Why had she ever married him? She had spoiled his life as well as her own. She should never have listened to Perks.

This reminder of Perks filled her with anguish. There was still the problem of Chad's girl, the ABC waitress — the girl who must be, who could only be, Mabel Perks's daughter. Lily Perks had to be confronted. She had to be confronted for Chad's sake. Because it couldn't be a coincidence, Chad's meeting her, even though Emily, since her trip to London, had tried so very hard to pretend that it was. She had, as usual, buried her head. But this time she couldn't afford to. Despite her cardinal rule, she *had* to interfere, there was no other way round it.

Which would require another trip to London.

She hugged herself and got ready to face down all the doubts and trepidations that London engendered. But instead of the doubts, she found herself flooded by an up-rush of joy. She couldn't explain it. She couldn't explain it at all — unless it was a residue of her sense of achievement after last time, going all the way there, and coming all the way back, and all on her own, without any help, without anyone at Heartlands knowing half of what she'd been up to. Rather a paltry achievement, it was true, and not deserving of such euphoria. But the thought of escaping Heartlands again, if only for a little while — the thought of having a whole day to herself, the thought of *The Sparrowhawk* and George Midgely — oh! it all seemed such an adventure, so much so that she could hardly wait. In this mood, Lily Perks seemed no obstacle at all.

She hugged herself ever tighter, looking at the buttercups spread like gold dust in the long, green grass. The grey clouds on the horizon were receding, leaving only white clouds, pure and fleecy, and a space of sky, infinitely blue.

Walking back, Emily forgot all about the trug on the bench until she glanced up at the house and saw Lady Winmer looking out of an upstairs lattice window, a pale, forlorn face, gazing into the distance. Alan's mother, whom he'd been so devoted to. Alan's mother, who had always been so kind. 'Now, dear Emily, you must call me mother, for I am your mother now — your other mother. I am so glad that Alan chose you, for I can see in your eyes that you will love him as much as I do.'

Standing on the gravel path, Emily waved impulsively, smiling. But Lady Winmer was lost in a world of her own and didn't see her. They had once seemed so very different, her two mothers, her own mother and Alan's: like chalk and cheese. Now they were oddly alike, Lady Winmer perhaps not as confused in her mind as Mama, but both of them lost, adrift, harbourless.

Emily turned back for her trug and the secateurs, making her mind up to cut some flowers after all. Never mind Violet and the others. There was little enough she could do to repay the kindness Lady Winmer had shown her over so many years, but perhaps a few flowers might help to brighten her day — if anything now could.

CHAPTER NINE

It was the height of folly, thought Emily, to be walking up and down the pavement, just across the street from the ABC shop on Cheapside. Anyone watching would think she was mad. But no one was watching. No one in London noticed anything. They were all too busy with their own affairs, swarming along the streets in such numbers that it made one's head ache. And the noise of the traffic, on and on, grating on one's nerves, leaving one feeling raw and shredded.

She didn't even know if Lily Perks was working today, or what time she would finish if she was. Pacing up and down the pavement, Emily could not bring herself to go into the tea room. She had a horror of the place now — of all ABC shops. A vague, pre-war feeling that they weren't entirely respectable had coalesced with the shock of seeing Lily Perks, giving rise to a morbid dread of such places. She'd seemed to see them everywhere today — at Piccadilly Circus and Parliament Square, at Charing Cross and outside Mansion House tube — as she made her circuitous way to Cheapside, carefully timing her arrival to lunchtime as before, only to find she was too afraid to go in.

Afraid of what? She wasn't sure. All she knew was that it was ridiculous, pointless — the height of folly — to go on walking up and down the pavement like this. Her feet were aching, she was hungry, she didn't even know what she would say to Lily Perks if she met her. How Violet would sneer and snigger if she could see her sister-in-law now! 'What *are* you doing, Emily? Who do you think you *are*?' And Sir Hubert — well, Sir Hubert must *never* know about his beloved grandson — his heir — and the ABC girl.

No. This was not the way to go about things. She would have to come up with a different plan.

She turned to go, glancing over her shoulder one last time across the street at the tea room — and there, coming out of the door, unmistakeable, wearing a drab coat and a mean little hat, was the girl Lily Perks. As Emily watched, Lily Perks set off purposefully in the direction of St Paul's. She was almost immediately lost to view. An omnibus (London General) came sweeping from the other direction, only to get snarled in traffic. It slowed and stopped, blocking all sight of the other pavement.

Emily, on impulse, darted across the road, edging round the stationary omnibus. A horn tooted. There was a motor bearing down on her. She dashed towards the far pavement, reached it in a fluster of stumbling feet, her heart beating fast. She looked around. She expected Lily Perks to be nowhere in sight, but no, there she was, dawdling now, pausing to look at a shop window, but in a desultory manner, as if she wasn't much interested. Emily weaved her way along the pavement, keeping her eyes on Lily Perks, making a detour round an old woman sat on the kerb selling apples from a huge basket. Emily kept her distance, trying to make up her mind whether to approach the girl or not. A pretty girl, thought Emily, observing from a distance: dark hair, a small nose — so very like her mother. Yet Mabel Perks hadn't been pretty. She'd been hard and sly, her features worn down. Was it some sort of trick — like a sleight of hand — that made Lily look so appealing? Trailing after her, Emily watched closely, as if waiting for the girl to betray herself, to show herself as her mother's child. But there was nothing hard or sly about her, she seemed only tired and a little despondent. (Emily remembered the waitresses in the tea room, flustered and frayed. She remembered her feet aching in sympathy.)

The dome of St Paul's loomed ahead against an indifferent sky, the grandeur of it arresting, eye-catching. Emily could not help but stare. Even so, she would have sworn that she'd only taken her eyes off Lily for a matter of seconds. But when she turned her attention back to the pavement in front of her, Lily was right there, face to face with her, barring her way: indeed, Emily almost ran into her, stopped just in time.

'I do beg your . . .' Emily's voice trailed away. The girl was watching her, suspicious. Something of Mabel Perks's hardness showed in her eyes now.

'You were following me.'

'No—' But what was the point of lying? It sounded feeble and obvious — blatant. Emily summoned her courage, her Drage indomitability. 'Miss Perks? Miss Lily Perks? I am Mrs Winmer, Chad's — Chad's mother.'

'His — his mother?' Lily went pale. Her face suddenly looked more worn than ever, pinched, malnourished. 'Oh, Mrs Winmer — you have to believe me — I didn't mean no harm — I didn't want to do it, I really didn't, but Mum said I must, Mum said—'

'Mum? Do you mean Perks, Mabel Perks?'

'Yes, that's her name, that's Mum. It was her idea to—'

'To deceive him, to trick him, to use him?'

'No — well — you don't understand! She said — she said—' Lily was bright red. For some reason, the colour in her cheeks reminded Emily of the deceptive bloom of the consumptive.

'What exactly did you hope to gain? Revenge?'

'Revenge?' Lily seemed puzzled. 'Revenge for what?'

But this conversation was monstrous — in broad daylight, in the shadow of St Paul's. Emily had half expected Lily to scream and struggle, and to scratch like an alley cat, but instead she looked stricken — almost as if she might have a conscience after all.

Emily hardened her heart, finding strength in the thought of her son. She felt buttressed with steel.

'I shall have to tell him. You do see that, don't you?'

Lily hung her head, said quietly, 'Yes, I see. But—' She looked up again, anguish showing.

Caught out, thought Emily: her deception uncovered.

There was nothing more needed saying. 'Well, goodbye, Miss Perks.'

Emily stepped off the kerb. She could hear behind her Lily's voice: 'Wait — Mrs Winmer — please — let me explain—' But the voice was quickly lost in the sound of the traffic, the trundling wheels and brisk hooves, the roar of an omnibus, the shrill neighing of a rearing horse. Emily broke into a run, pressing through what suddenly seemed like chaos all around her, the traffic and the people and the endless noise. The sky seemed to be swaying, the dome of St Pauls' tottering. The ground suddenly disappeared from under her feet.

It was a tube station, the entrance to a tube station. She staggered down the steps, nearly falling head over heels, clutching the handrail. Then she ran along the echoing passages of a subway. All at once, the ticket barrier appeared — then she was on the platform — a train came, the doors hissed shut and the train pulled away. Soon, it was rocking and rolling in the dark wormhole of a tunnel, taking her away from Lily Perks, who looked so much like her mother. Taking her to safety — to safety.

Emily sat back and breathed a sigh of relief.

* * *

There were several other passengers on *The Sparrowhawk* this afternoon and Mr Midgely was busy with his ticket machine, but Emily barely noticed, looking out of the window as the omnibus eased its way through clogged streets and then onwards along emptier suburban roads. The sun was dipping down. The half-built houses of the building plots cast long shadows.

She was still in a daze. She felt sordid, unclean. London had left its stain on her, a stain that felt like a thin layer of grease covering her from head to foot. Last time — on her last trip to London, not much more than a week ago — she had skimmed across the surface of the city and not let it touch her. This time, she'd been immersed — she'd begun to sink into London's squalor. Her clothes were smudged with London's dirt. She had London's sooty air in her lungs. She'd escaped in the nick of time, before she was dragged under completely. But she wasn't out of the woods. Now she had to decide what to tell Chad. She had to tell him something. She had to warn him.

Warn him about what? She was not exactly sure. But whatever it was, Perks was behind it, Mabel Perks. Perks had coached her daughter, set her up in a deception — sly, manipulative Perks was pulling the strings once again. What could she possibly hope to gain? Not revenge, no. Money. That was it. She wanted money, like last time.

Emily felt sick at the thought of last time, remembering how Perks had reappeared like a ghost from the past one bright summer morning in 1921. Emily had been staying with Aunt Margery in Belgravia. The butler, tall and proper, had presented himself in the drawing room, where Emily had been reading the paper.

'There's a woman wishes to see you, madam.' A *woman*, not a *lady*. 'I haven't asked her in,' he'd added significantly.

And then — an awful scene on the doorstep. Chad, aged fifteen and on holiday from school, had come along just at the wrong moment. He'd been at the Science Museum with a friend all morning, they'd returned for lunch.

'This your boy, is it?' Perks had shown interest. If that had seemed menacing at the time, it was much more so in retrospect.

Perks, that day, had not mentioned children of her own, there'd been no talk of a daughter — or had there? Reaching back five years, Emily found she could not be sure. So much of that encounter was now a blur in her memory.

Perks had asked for money, Emily remembered that much. 'Your family owes me, I reckon.'

How on earth had Perks managed to find her at Aunt Margery's? But she'd always been devious, had Perks, she'd always been—

'Are you all right, Mrs Winmer?'

She looked up, startled, and was alarmed to find a man looming over her. She flinched, her heart thumping. She'd all but forgotten where she was. It came as a shock to see the bus, the empty seats. The other passengers had got off and she'd never noticed. Outside, the passing countryside was green and peaceful, the colours of sunset splashed across the sky. And the man standing next to her was George Midgely, down-to-earth George Midgely with his East Midlands vowels and his plain-handsome face. He seemed to her just then, after all her thoughts of Perks, the very antitheses of menacing.

'Are you all right?' he repeated, looking at her anxiously.

'I-I was miles away.' She couldn't manage a smile.

'You was in a world of yer own, I didn't like to disturb you, but you went so pale all of a sudden—'

'Did I? I wonder why. But I'm quite all right, Mr Midgely, thank you.'

He hesitated a moment, then sat down opposite, sideways in the seat, planting his big feet in the aisle, the money bag at his hip squashed against the upholstery. He took off his cap, ran a hand through his tousled hair. Abruptly, as if he'd been weighing his words in his mind and suddenly thought, *What the hell?*, he said, 'I wish you'd call me Midge, Mrs Winmer, everyone does.'

She was taken aback. This was unexpected. She didn't know what to say. Then, all at once, she felt pleased, as if he'd singled her out for an act of special kindness. A little less tense now, she was able to breathe again. London was behind them. They were out in the open countryside. She was alone and safe with George Midgely. What was it about him that seemed, well, almost *soothing*? It wasn't gentleness, he was too rough and ready for that, but it was something very much akin.

But — *Midge*? It sounded so offhand. A street name. A pub name. What 'everyone' called him.

'Everyone?' A smile came stealing onto her face, she didn't have to force it. 'Not your mother, I'm sure.'

'No. Yer right. Not Mam. I were always Georgey to Mam.'

A strange expression crossed his face and he looked away. She wondered if his mother was dead. He'd made it sound as if she was. Emily didn't have the nerve to ask.

She felt, suddenly, that she'd made a mess of things. He'd asked her to call him 'Midge', offering the hand of friendship, but she'd hesitated, not knowing what to say, so that he must think that she'd wanted to rebuff him. Perhaps he even fancied he'd offended her, by being so forward. Then she'd made things worse by mentioning his mother.

'Mrs Winmer . . .'

She looked up, found him watching her.

'If there's summat troubling yer . . .'

Once more, she found herself at a loss for words. Once more, he hurriedly looked away.

'I'm sorry, it's note to do wi' me.'

'No, please, it's — it's good of you to ask. But it's nothing.' Without knowing the full story, he'd only think her silly. Yet she suddenly felt an almost overwhelming urge to confide in someone, and who else was there? It seemed easier, too, telling a virtual stranger. 'It's my son and — and a rather unsuitable girl, I'm afraid.'

'Boys'll be boys, they say.'

'You think I'm being over protective.'

'Note wrong in that. Me mam were same. "Keep yoursen away from all them bad girls, Georgey," she used to say to me. And I used to think, "Chance'd be a fine thing!"'

He laughed. It was a strange laugh, brief, even a little bitter. But all Emily could take from it just then, was that he seemed to find it funny, a mother's concern for her son. Men were such brutes, with their raucous, hard-nosed laughter, making a joke of everything — trampling over everything — trampling even over their own finer feelings.

'You don't understand—' He didn't know what she was dealing with. He didn't know about Perks.

He stiffened a little, as if he sensed her hostility. 'How's she unsuitable, then?' he asked bluntly. He added, almost as if he was challenging her, 'Poor, you mean?'

'No,' said Emily firmly (but she sounded to herself rather prim than firm). 'It's not that. Of course it isn't.'

Then the ground shifted, and she thought: *Or is that just it? Am I nothing but a snob?*

But, no. She shook her head. No, no, no, it was nothing to do with whether Lily was poor or not. Money came into it, of course, but only because that was what Lily hoped to gain. But it wasn't money that made her actions unforgiveable, it was that she'd deceived Chad, played him false — used him. Or maybe that wasn't Lily so much. Lily was still a child, after all, younger even that Chad. Perks was behind it. Perks was to blame.

Emily felt as if a heavy weight was pressing down on her, making her head ache intolerably. Perks. Always Perks. The bane of her life. Why, oh why, had she ever listened to Perks? Why had she agreed to Perks's monstrous plan all those years ago? She had placed herself entirely in Perks's hands, she had given Perks a hold over her. And it hadn't really made anything right, Perks's plan. Poor Alan! He could have married any other girl in the world, and he'd have had a better wife. He could have taken his pick. He could have had a proper, dutiful wife and lots of lovely children of his own. He could have been happy.

Midge had fallen silent, slumped in his seat, sunk in gloom. Emily felt remorse. She'd not disguised her sense of irritation, even though it wasn't Midge she was angry with. She was wrong, as well, to think him a brute. He'd only been trying to help. Men had their own ways of going about things, that was all.

‘Listen to me, going on!’ Emily spoke brightly, trying to make amends, but her words seemed to chime the wrong note, they sounded false and gaudy. Why, why, why could she never get it right with people? ‘I’m sure it’s not part of the service, listening to your passengers’ problems. You’ve problems enough of your own, I expect.’

‘What do you mean by that?’

He looked at her suspiciously and she realized that she’d hit on something quite by chance, possibly the very thing he’d been brooding about.

‘Oh, don’t mind me, Mr — er — Midge. I didn’t mean to pry.’

‘You needn’t worry about me. I’m all right.’

‘Well, you know what they say about a problem shared.’ (Oh, false, false, false! How could he be taken in by it? And her smile, fixed on, so sickly.)

Midge grimaced and shifted his position. For a second she thought he’d seen through her, but then she realized it was his money bag — it had obviously been digging into his hip. He took it off now. A few coins rattled. He hesitated, then rattled it again, deliberately this time.

‘Don’t sound much, do it? Don’t sound much for a day’s work. Happen you wonder how we manage, Ginger and mesen. Happen you’re right to wonder.’

‘I’m sorry.’ But what was the use in being sorry? What use, for that matter, had she ever been to anyone? At least that girl, Lily — at least she had a job, paid her way — at least she *did* something.

The omnibus slowed and Emily, looking out, realized that they had reached the turning to Heartlands. They had passed right through the village without her even noticing. The sky above was pale. Dusk was thickening under the beech trees.

Midge jumped up and put his cap back on. He handed her down, as before.

She found herself fumbling in her bag.

'Here.' She held out a coin, a half-crown. 'Call it a tip,' she added brightly, after a moment's silence, pasting over sudden misgivings.

Midge stared at the coin in her hand as if he'd never seen the like before. Abruptly, he turned away. His face darkened.

'I don't want yer money,' he said curtly, swinging back onto the bus. 'We've no need of charity just yet, missus.'

His words were stiff and bristling. They stung her like the lashes of a whip.

'You ain't a clue, woman like you, wi' yer silver spoons and yer afternoon tea. You ain't a clue how it is for blokes like me and Ginge.'

He stood on the platform, looking down at her, scowling, as the noise of the growling, chugging engine grew louder, discordant, matching his mood.

'Summat else, and all—' He raised his voice, rasping and angry as the bus eased away from the verge and headed off down the lane. 'You oughtta gi' yer lad's girl a break. Her can't help being poor!'

For a split second, Emily had the strangest illusion that the bus wasn't moving at all, that it was getting further away from her because a crack had opened at her feet, a crack in the world getting wider and wider. She was on one side, Midge on the other, and they being torn apart. There was an unbridgeable chasm between them.

The omnibus roared, receded, rounded a bend in the lane, was gone. The sound of it faded into the dusk. Emily looked down at the coin she still held in her hand — the offending coin. She put it away in her purse. It was Sir Hubert's money, in any case. He wouldn't approve of her simply giving it away. He believed people should help themselves, not rely on charity.

She had to blink away sudden tears as she began to walk up the drive. Nothing had gone right today, and this was the last straw. How had they got it so wrong this evening, her and Midge? It had been so easy last time. They'd talked about London. She'd admitted she found the capital daunting. He'd told her about Parliament Hill, his favourite place. Conversation had flowed naturally, effortlessly. She'd not even had to try. But this evening they'd seemed to talk at cross purposes, they'd both been prickly and defensive. A casual, innocent friendship: it shouldn't be too difficult to pull off. But she couldn't even manage something as simple as that. To top things off, she'd offered him money, setting the seal on her failure. She'd spoiled things forever. She wouldn't have the heart to face him again.

Maybe it would be better all round if she didn't leave the seclusion of Heartlands in future. At least she knew what to expect at Heartlands.

But then she remembered that she had yet to face Chad. She had to tell Chad about Lily. She baulked at the thought, but there was no getting away from it.

She would just have to grasp the nettle.

* * *

Midge tore off his cap and hurled it as hard as he could along the aisle, as the bus roared and jolted through the gathering dusk, Ginger taking the corners of the winding lane at speed in his hurry to get this last run of the day over with. Midge was blazing mad. He was in a towering rage. With her. With himself. With everyone.

He was not exactly sure what had brought it on. The insult, he supposed. Offering him a half-dollar like that. A handout. Charity. But he was at fault too, mithering about the takings. She must have thought he was giving her a hint. She must have thought he *wanted* her to offer money. Another time, he'd know better. Another time, he'd keep quiet about his and Ginger's private affairs. No one else needed to know.

But it wasn't just that. It wasn't just the money. She'd been in a funny mood all journey. He couldn't make her out. He'd wanted to — to—

Oh, bugger it! Best forget the whole business. He should forget the whole thing. She was a passenger, just another passenger, nothing more. Passengers. You sold them a ticket, you gave them some chat, you dropped them off and they went on their merry way. What you *didn't* do was get in rage with them. You didn't get in a rage over nothing.

The bus continued on its way back to London. By the time they reached the last stop, Midge had regained his composure. Several passengers had got on en route, more than he'd expected. He'd sold tickets, he'd smiled, he'd given some chat, he'd kept his cool as well as his distance. He was helping the last one off now on Tottenham High Road, not far from the corner with White Hart Lane. Some old dear, it was, who was 'ever so grateful, thank you ever so much, what a nice, well-mannered young man you are, not like all those others!'

Ginger came round from the cab, smoking a cigarette, as the old dear finally went tottering off. 'Reckon you're sweet on her, Midge.'

'Give over! She's about ninety!'

'Not *her*, you peanut. The posh bird. Special delivery to her doorstep.'

'Get on with yer. Don't be so daft. It's end of her drive, any road, not her doorstep.'

'It's not on the blooming route, more like it. And *she's* not on *your* route, me old son. You want to think about that.' Ginger tossed the end of his cigarette aside, slapped Midge on the back. 'Come on then, cocker. Let's park the bus and get back for some grub.'

'You go ahead, Ginge. I'll take bus back to garage.' He wanted some time on his own.

'If you're sure, mate.' Ginger was not about to look a gift horse in the mouth. 'I'll get Nell to keep your grub handy.'

'See yer at home, Ginge.'

Midge began to whistle as he swung into the driver's seat, trying to perk himself up. But as he set off for the garage, he remembered that the rent on it was due: another millstone round their necks. He grimaced, thinking of that half-dollar of Mrs Winmer's. Perhaps he'd been a fool, after all, to turn it down. Ginger would probably think so. They needed all the help they could get just now.

Driving through the back streets as dusk came on, manhandling the big steering wheel, wrestling with the gears (Ginger made driving this thing look easy), the air was cool on his face, a savour of spring in it, and Midge found himself thinking — quite out of the blue — of Evie, his girl Evie. Well, she *had* been his girl, once upon a time, in the old days. They'd walked out together on evenings like this, and on Sunday afternoons. He remembered how they would linger in the shadows under the railway bridge, the only private spot they could find. He remembered the sound of water dripping, echoing. He remembered the glint of her eyes in the gloom. What a precocious little tyke he'd been, giving her all the chat, putting his arms round her, bold as brass. He'd been no more than fifteen, but he'd thought himself the bee's knees. It made him laugh now to think of it.

The laughter died on his lips and suddenly, on this still April evening, he could almost imagine he was under that old bridge again, with his back pressed against the slimy brick wall and Evie in his arms. He remembered what it was like to hold her, to kiss her: that feeling which ran up your spine, which clenched in the pit of your stomach, which set your knees trembling. Her soft, moist, susceptible lips — her arms looped round his neck, the feel of her body pressed against his — his arms tight round her waist. Evie, his Evie. She'd said she'd wait for him when he went off to war. She'd said she'd be there when he got back.

He grinned wryly as he pulled on the brakes and jumped down to throw open the doors of the back-street garage. Soppy wazzock. Why think of her, of Evie, of kissing her under the railway bridge? Why think of her now, after all this time? Those days were long gone. What girl would look at him now? What girl wouldn't run a mile, when she knew all about him?

He jumped back into the driver's seat and eased the bus into the garage, forcing himself to face hard facts instead of getting carried away. Even so, he couldn't quite shake the feeling, that feeling in the pit of his stomach — as if he'd been kissing Evie under the railway bridge that very afternoon.

CHAPTER TEN

Chad stopped his motor car in a field gateway, turned off the engine, leaned over the steering wheel, tired and sick at heart. He snapped off the headlamps. Darkness closed in. The countryside all around was shrouded deep in shadow.

He was not quite sure where he was — the topography of this midnight landscape was like another world, distances had grown vast, landmarks had disappeared — but he had an idea he was somewhere in the vicinity of Heartlands. The temptation to seek it out was almost overwhelming. He wanted to go home. But that would entail all sorts of questions and explanations, and Grandfather wouldn't be happy: he hated surprises, didn't like his routine disturbed. Aunt Violet, too, would sniff at the inconvenience and point out to him his thoughtlessness in turning up out of the blue. The other aunts were sure to join in and peck at him, too. As for Mother—

Well, he was not sure he could face Mother again so soon.

He'd never known her come to Cambridge, not without being invited, so it had been obvious straight away that something was wrong.

'Darling, it's rather awful, I'm so sorry.' But it had been none of the things he'd imagined, death or illness or family disaster.

He'd refused to believe it. He'd refused to believe it of Lily.

'I'm so sorry, darling.'

'No, you're not! You don't want me seeing her, so you make up these lies! You're as bad as Grandfather, interfering!'

His heart burned now, remembering how he'd spoken to her — his own mother — as they walked along the Backs. But all he'd been able to think of at the time was Lily.

He'd left Mother standing when he reached the point where he simply couldn't bear to hear any more: he'd simply walked away. A moment later, he'd broken into a run, going straight to where his motor was garaged. He'd driven non-stop to London, made his way to the city, parked in a side street, waited outside the tea rooms on Cheapside. As he hung around on the pavement, a feeling had taken hold of him like a heavy, icy hand gripping his heart. He knew nothing about Lily, not even where she lived. She was little more than a stranger.

He'd waited a long time. When finally she emerged from the ABC shop, she'd been very surprised to see him. They'd not arranged to meet, it wasn't one of their days. He'd watched her closely, alert for any clues. Was that a guilty look in her eyes? Oh, but her smile!

He'd taken her arm. 'Let's go somewhere. A picture palace.'

'Mum'll be expecting me, she'll be waiting. Besides, you know I don't like those places, the words come and go too quickly on the screen, I can't keep up.'

'Only an idiot would say that! Only someone who's *illiterate*!'

He'd known then, by the way he'd spoken to her, that he believed everything Mother had told him. He hadn't wanted to believe, he'd told himself he didn't believe, but deep down he knew Mother would never lie. He'd been angry because he didn't want it to be true but he knew it was, and there was nothing he could do to change that.

She'd shaken free of him. 'I'm not illiterate! That's such an unkind thing to say! Why are you being like this?'

Grabbing her wrist, he'd said, 'Tell me the truth, Lily—'

'You're hurting me!'

She'd twisted and struggled, trying to get away as he shouted accusations at her.

Finally, she'd burst out, 'All right, all right, it's all true, everything your Mother told you! Are you satisfied now?'

She'd begun to cry but it had seemed false to him, entirely false. His heart, by then, had turned to stone.

'I didn't know it would be like this, I wish I'd never started,' she'd sobbed. 'Mum told me it'd be easy. I just had to play you for a fool, she said. All toffs are fools, she said. I didn't want to play anyone for a fool, I really didn't, but Mum kept on at me, and she's so poorly now I don't like to upset her. I couldn't say no to her, I couldn't.'

'How can I believe a single word you say after this!' he'd yelled at her, dragging her along the pavement by her wrist. But passers-by had begun to stare, people had cast dark looks at him, so he'd let go of her wrist, straightened his jacket, tried to get a grip on himself.

She'd backed away, rubbing her arm: rubbing it and rubbing it. 'I never asked you for nothing and you can't say I did. I couldn't do that to you, once I got to know you. Mum told me not to be so daft, she wanted me to fleece you. But it was too late, it was too late. I-I'd fallen in love with you!'

With his head resting on the steering wheel, Chad wracked his brains, trying to remember if she really had said the word *love*, or if that was just his wounded heart speaking. It was all so hazy in his mind; everything had happened so quickly. She'd run away, disappeared. He'd blundered along the street. Had he been crying too? But no, he wouldn't cry, he hadn't cried in years, he was nearly twenty. Besides, what was there to cry about? His relationship with Lily was fake, totally fake, every second of it an illusion. The serendipity of their first meeting, that was all a lie. There'd been nothing magical in it, it hadn't been destiny. He should have realized. He should have *known*. He'd been so *naïve*. Well, he wouldn't get taken in again, never, never, never.

London had seemed busier than ever today, the last Saturday in April. There'd been swarms of people everywhere, he'd had to fight his way through crowds, he couldn't find a moment's peace. Whether the Cup Final had anything to do with it — Bolton Wanderers against Manchester City — he wasn't sure, but he'd got the distinct impression that the lower classes were far more in evidence than usual: the great unwashed, getting above themselves (Lily was one of them).

There were certain chaps at Cambridge who said it was high time all the riff-raff were put back in their place. They talked of a big strike in the offing. All the workers were going to down tools. 'It'll be us against them,' the chaps said. 'We can't allow them to win.' To make sure of that, some of the chaps intended to volunteer as special constables. The police would need specials, they said, when the time came.

Chad jumped out of his motor and slammed the door. He was so restless all of a sudden that he couldn't sit still. He walked round in circles by the field gate and, when that wasn't enough, he broke into a run, debating with himself the whole time. He ran up and down the narrow lane. He ran at full pelt, with the darkness all round him. He began to feel better. He could breathe. He could stretch his limbs. He didn't feel squashed and trapped anymore.

He ran himself to a standstill. He came to a halt, exhausted. He leaned back against his car, looking up at the sky. The clouds had broken, a few stars glimmered. Stars were—

What? Not souls. He knew that much. Stars were not the souls of the dead.

'I'm a gullible idiot!' he shouted fiercely at the top of his voice, addressing the night sky, addressing the empty dark. 'A gullible idiot!'

He'd been waiting so long for something bigger and better than the little life he led. He'd thought Lily was it. He'd been wrong. But now he knew what he had to do. He'd volunteer to be a special. He'd stand against the riff-raff. This was his chance. This would be his war.

He'd found his role at last.

* * *

Emily looked around in puzzlement. Why was she sitting on the floor? Where was she?

But of course, she was in the drawing room at Alleyn Dene, the drawing room as it had been twenty, thirty years ago. She was sitting cross-legged on the Persian carpet. A dazzling light was coming in through the French windows, white and golden, like sunshine through mist. Outside was blank, nothing could be seen.

She became aware of other people in the room, moving around, silent and purposeful, faceless men in cloth caps and long brown coats. They were carrying everything away. The room was being dismantled piece by piece around her. Even the Persian carpet was whisked away from under her. Two men carried it out, a long, sagging tube. Soon there was nothing left. She was sitting alone on the dusty floorboards, the walls bare except for the wires dangling from the light fittings. The white, glowing fog outside had faded. Now there was just a grey, dim nothingness, pressing against the windows. Someone or something was tapping on the glass, tap, tap, tap — trying to get her attention perhaps — or trying to get in. Fear took hold of her. She sat frozen in place, waiting. All was silent except for the sinister tapping. Tap, tap, tap — tap, tap, tap—

She awoke with a jerk, feeling as if she'd tumbled from some high place down into bed: her own bed, in her own room, at Heartlands. But still she could hear someone tapping: tap, tap, tap — tap, tap, tap. The paralyzing fear from her dream lingered a moment as she tried to work out where the sound was coming from.

The tapping stopped. The door slowly opened, cautious. A young and timid-looking maid appeared with a tray. It was she who'd been tapping.

'Tea, ma'am?'

Emily sat up, shaking off the last shreds of her dream, and she forced herself to smile. One had to smile: she was such a mouse, this girl, she needed every encouragement. 'Good morning, Quinn. Tea is just what I need, thank you.'

Emily leaned back against the pillows, sipping hot tea with a spoonful of sugar, watching Quinn open the curtains, shaking each one conscientiously to make the folds hang correctly. It was so strange, thought Emily, to have had that dream again, after so long. It had been quite familiar to her at one time, that dream. She'd almost got used to it. Not the tapping. That was new, brought about by Quinn's timid attempts to wake her. But the rest of the dream had been exactly as she remembered. What made it so real were the details, the feel of the dusty, gritty floorboards, the sight of the dangling wires (Papa had been so proud of the electric lights, so proprietorial). That Alleyn Dene — the Alleyn Dene of Papa's electric lights, of the Louis XIV armchair, of the armoire and the Persian carpet — had vanished irretrievably. It had been broken up and scattered to the four corners of the earth. This had happened in real life much as it happened in her dream: the removal men, the slow but steady disintegration. But in real life she'd not been sitting on the floor in the drawing room whilst it was going on. In real life, she'd stood watching at a distance with Mama. Both she and Mama had been there.

Emily sipped her tea, asking herself, as she had many times over the last thirteen years, why she'd ever agreed to take Mama back to Alleyn Dene on the day of the auction. She couldn't help wondering if it was this which had finally tipped Mama over the edge, seeing the home she'd created being broken up. Watching her whole life — what was left of it after Papa's death — disintegrating before her eyes.

Quinn came to stand diffidently at the end of the bed. 'Shall I get your clothes ready now, ma'am?'

'Yes, please, Quinn. My blue blouse, I think. And my pleated skirt, the grey one.'

* * *

It was an overcast morning, a dismal Monday. Breakfast was long and drawn-out. Viola, Ivy and Ada were gathered like mummies in a museum, Lady Winmer fragile like old porcelain with the cracks showing. Sir Hubert had the newspaper open: it always set Emily's teeth on edge, that he should read at the meal table.

'Budget Day . . . hmm . . . hmmm . . .' He perused the headlines. '"Mr Churchill's task". That turncoat, that traitor! "The Prime Minister to resume mediation between the colliery owners and the miners . . ." Humph! Man's a fool! Far too soft!'

The footman came into the room, discreet. 'The post, sir.'

'Ah, good, good, excellent!' Sir Hubert's eyes lit up, gleaming and avaricious. His gnarled hands reached eagerly for the letters, grasped them.

But soon his face fell. His candidacy in the forthcoming by-election had been rejected. The news was greeted around the table by a strained air of suspense. All eyes were on Sir Hubert.

He threw the letter down, outraged. 'A disgrace! A travesty! I've been swindled! It's the Asquith faction, conspiring against me, because I always supported Lloyd George, and so on and so forth. Well, I'm not finished yet. We'll see about this. Emily, I shall need you. We have work to do.'

Whilst Emily was experiencing a sinking feeling inside at this summary demand, Violet had the temerity to speak, her voice thin and uncertain. 'Perhaps I could help, Father?'

'What? Hmm? No, no, no, no. Not you! You're useless! Useless! You're all useless, all three of you. Albatrosses! Why don't you ever *do* something, hmm, hmm?'

The three sisters sat as if frozen, staring into the distance.

Lady Winmer chose that moment to smile, but it was not a smile that had anything to do with what was happening in the room. She was lost in a world of her own — she so often was.

After a long pause, Violet got to her feet with ponderous dignity, putting her napkin aside. 'Will you be in for luncheon today, Emily?' she asked pointedly, spitefully. 'You are so often out these days. I can't imagine what you find to do. You were seen the other day getting into an *omnibus*!'

Violet swept from the room. Ivy and Ada dodged after her.

* * *

Once she'd finished helping Sir Hubert draft his letters of protest, of appeal, of lordly condescension — letters which would all, no doubt, be ignored — Emily escaped to walk in the beech wood before lunch. The sky was still grey and it was really rather cold for the time of year — only a few primroses and cowslips spoke of spring. Emily shivered as she waded through the beechmast and last year's dead leaves. Her mind turned this way and that, trying to find soothing thoughts to calm her nerves, but everything she came up with only served to increase her agitation. Violet's remark about the omnibus. Sir Hubert's letters. Her dream. She also found herself dwelling on her interview with Chad two days ago. It had not been much warmer that day, walking along the Backs, the river grey and flat, and Chad—

But no, it was too painful to remember. ('You're wrong, Mother! You're as bad as Grandfather, interfering!') She shivered again inside her coat, the wind seething in the upper branches of the trees, the silent woodland stretching in every direction.

On another spring day — a brighter, sunnier day, thirteen years ago — a telegram had arrived at the cottage. Emily's mind had been a blank as she opened it. What on earth could it be?

She'd had to read the words three times before they sank in.

Papa was dead. Dead.

* * *

An accident, they called it. He'd been crossing the railway line, hadn't heard the London express.

'You know how deaf he'd got, dear, these last few years.' Mama, swathed in black, was pouring tea in the drawing room at Alleyn Dene: pouring tea and pouring tea, sitting in her favourite Louis XIV armchair.

'But Mama, what was he *doing* on the railway?'

'I can't imagine. I can't think. But you know Papa.'

It was inexplicable. A bolt from the blue. A terrible shock. But that was not all. The business had gone bankrupt. Sutton's Shoes was no more.

'I don't understand it, Emmy. Mr Carson says we have lost everything — *everything*. How can that be?'

Mr Carson, the family solicitor, had been quite clear. He had left no room for woolly thinking.

'Of course,' Mama continued, 'it isn't Mr Winmer's fault. We mustn't blame Mr Winmer. A slice of cake, Emmy?'

Mr Winmer, it transpired, had promised a government contract — army boots — the solution to all Papa's business problems, the problems no one had known he had. But the contract had never come about. Hubert Winmer, not even the most junior of junior ministers, had no say in the awarding of government contracts. As always, he had made himself out to be far more important than he actually was. Had Papa been taken in? Or had he clung to this desperate straw, even whilst knowing it wouldn't save him? Either way the business had foundered. The boots had piled up, more in hope than judgement, and lay unwanted in a Northampton warehouse. They would be sold cheap to pay Papa's debtors — everything would be sold.

'I had no idea, Emmy, that the house had been mortgaged to pay for the boots. But there it is. Your papa didn't like to trouble me. More tea, dear?'

Emily, sitting on the empire sofa watching Mama pour tea, tried to recall every detail of the last time she'd seen Papa, on her most recent visit to Alleyn Dene before this tragedy. He'd looked older, white-haired, spectacles perched on the end of his nose. 'Speak up!' he'd said, cupping his hand to his ear. 'Speak up!' His hand had been shaking.

Had he known, even then, that the business was doomed, that Sutton's Shoes, which he'd built up through his own hard work, was teetering on the edge? But it wasn't just the business that was lost. Mama was going to lose the house, too. She had always trusted Papa implicitly in all financial matters. She'd run the household, kept within her budget, and felt she was doing her bit. And all the while — it now emerged — Papa had been getting deeper and deeper in debt.

It would have been this that Papa found hardest to bear, thought Emily, the feeling that he was letting Mama down. Perhaps, in the end, he'd decided he couldn't live with the guilt.

* * *

Walking in the wood, dead leaves rustling underfoot, the *cawk* of a distant pheasant echoing though the trees, Emily thought about Papa's funeral all those years ago. The misery of it. The sordidness. So many different emotions. All these years later, those long-ago emotions had solidified into a hard kernel, deep buried but enduring.

Mama had looked terribly pale that day, dressed in black from head to toe, hesitating in the hallway at Alleyn Dene.

'What will I do, Emmy? What will I do without him?' But she had faced the funeral with her usual fortitude.

Me, Mama, Alan, thought Emily. And who else? Who else had been there? Granny Drage, of course. Aunt Margery had come alone. Uncle Walter had been present, and Mr and Mrs Winmer. There'd been others, curious villagers, distant relatives, long-lost acquaintances.

'Such a terrible loss. Such a tragic accident. Our deepest condolences.'

Oh, but they'd known. They'd all known. They'd known how Papa had died. And Emily had been only too aware of what they were thinking, and that was what had made the whole affair so sordid.

Wading through dead leaves, musing on death whilst seeing everywhere signs of new life — emerald green and white tipped leaves on the branches of the beeches, flowers beginning to come out on some of the older trees — it occurred to Emily that only after Papa was gone had she realized how much love there had been between her parents. It had never showed much on the surface. They'd never been a demonstrative couple. But what was it Papa had often said? *Still waters run deep*. That was it. Mama had been enough in love to go against Granny Drage, which few ever dared to do. Granny had never approved of Papa, calling him a parvenu and a dilettante, a social climber — which, of course, he had never been. Emily had never known anyone *less* conscious of class than Papa. Her parents' love for each other had pervaded Alleyn Dene. That had been the secret. The reason why people had been so keen to visit. The reason why one looked back now with so much nostalgia.

Emily came to a stop, listening to the wind in the branches and the deep, underlying silence of the wood. Her heart ached. She felt a piercing longing, a wish that she could have known love the way Mama and Papa had known it. But any such chance had been destroyed that night at Nethercote Hall. She had been ruined and broken, at seventeen. She'd had to get on with life afterwards as best she could. But always, like her shadow following her, she never quite escaped thoughts of what-might-have-been.

Looking round at the endless ranks of trees, Emily remembered standing at the graveside after the funeral service thirteen years ago. The Barford girls — the Barford girls had been amongst the village contingent — had leered and gaped, unashamed, indiscreet. Had one of them, Emily wondered, been wearing her gloves, the white gloves with the ivory buttons which they'd purloined from Nethercote Hall? But no. The Barford girls that day had been all in black. Everyone had been in black, Granny Drage too, swathed and veiled, as indomitable as a battleship, cowing even the Barford girls who, looking shifty and sheepish, had shuffled hurriedly away from the grave. Mama had leaned on Granny's arm, and Granny had walked stiff and straight, facing the world with a fierce defiance that no one could stand against.

Granny Drage was ruthless. She had always been ruthless. She was most ruthless of all with her own children.

'You made your bed, Beatrice, and now you can lie in it,' she had said, back at the house. Alleyn Dene had been hushed and strange, like a fading photograph, as if it had been mothballed, as if it was doomed. Which it had been, for Mama had nothing, not a penny to her name, and Papa's debtors were clamouring at the door, queuing to pick over the bones — as Granny Drage had been quick to point out, for this was what she'd meant by *making one's bed.*

'Society is falling apart,' Granny had continued, holding court. 'Young people these days marry whomsoever they please, without so much as a by-your-leave. Children disobey, go their own way. Everyone insists on being *modern*. This rush to be modern will end badly, mark my words. There are consequences to one's actions. There are always consequences — as you, Beatrice, are now finding out. Let this be a warning to you, Walter. This is where it leads, the ceaseless pursuit of frivolity, the chasing of unsuitable girls. It leads to perdition. If your husband, Beatrice, had spent less time contemplating the stars and more time on his business—'

So cruel, thought Emily, walking in the beech wood, and yet so true. Granny's truth had always had the sharpness of a knife.

When war eventually came, Granny had felt vindicated. She had warned people what would happen. They had ignored her. Now they were paying the price. War, death, destruction: these were the fruits of being *modern*, of making one's own bed, of going one's own way — of not listening to her, when she knew best.

But what about Aunt Margery? Aunt Margery had listened. Aunt Margery had done as she was told. Where had it got her? She'd come to the funeral in all her finery, glamorous in black, but she'd been pinched and cold and childless — and that made her a failure in Granny's eyes.

After one too many whiskies-and-soda, Aunt Margery in a hushed, dead voice had elaborated at length on Lord Ainsleigh's neglect and cruelty, his other women, his refusal to do anything for her, even to come to the funeral. Emily remembered thinking that this — this empty life in which Aunt Margery seemed to have lost the ability to be happy — this was where Granny's propriety led one.

Leaving the woodland behind, Emily began to make her way round the edge of the buttercup meadow at the rear of Heartlands, picking up her pace so as not to be late for luncheon (Violet would be only too ready to make the most of it, if Emily had the temerity to be late). Sir Hubert, of course, had been plain Mr Winmer at the funeral in 1913, but Mr Winmer MP, a man on the up, making his presence felt. He'd talked at the top of his voice about the Home Rule Bill and the war in the Balkans. He'd fulminated against Mrs Pankhurst, who'd had the insolence, the audacity, to plant a bomb in Lloyd George's country house, and who'd spent nine days in prison for it instead of three years, simply because she'd gone on hunger strike! The Cat and Mouse Act would put a stop to all that, Mr Winmer had declared. They'd see how far they would get, those suffragettes, trying to outface a Liberal government — trying to get the better of *Lloyd George*!

'My dearest Emily,' he'd added in an aside, wringing his hands, 'it's so sad, all this, such a tragedy, the business gone, the house too. I wish I could have done more, but it was out of my hands. I promised your father I would try, but government contracts are not like sweets to be handed out willy-nilly. I was in no position . . . I can't be held responsible . . .'

Had Mr Winmer already by then, Emily wondered as she opened the gate that led into the grounds of Heartlands, developed that reputation for slipperiness which had grown ever more marked during the war?

'I'll do all I can for your poor mother,' he'd continued. And to be fair he'd been true to his word: not then, but later, when Granny had washed her hands of Mama ('this pretending to forget things . . . this hysteria . . . I won't have it, Beatrice . . .'). It was Sir Hubert who'd arranged for the rest home where the empty shell that had once been Mama still lingered.

Rounding a high topiary hedge, Emily saw Heartlands ahead of her, the rather plain rear facade. As she walked up the gravel path towards the back door, she remembered returning to Alleyn Dene one last time a few weeks after the funeral. The auction had been a harrowing experience, like watching someone you loved being operated on. The house, which Mama had created and brought to life, had been taken apart piece by piece. The world, so long kept at bay, had broken into the charmed circle of Alleyn Dene at last. People had swarmed all over the house and out into the garden, dealers and bargain hunters and the idly curious. Everything had been carried off and lost forever.

Emily had not wanted to go to the auction. It had been Mama who'd insisted. *I should have put my foot down*, said Emily, walking on the raked gravel as drizzle began to fall listlessly out of the grey sky. *I should have refused to take her. It would have been cruel-to-be-kind. It might even have saved her. It was surely the auction which finally broke her mind.*

Emily stopped, turned on her heels, looked back. Her footsteps made an untidy line in the gravel. The tall topiary hedge was green and clipped. The beech trees in the surrounding wood raised green rounded heads against the grey April sky. The wind had momentarily dropped and the drizzle fell in straight lines, pattering on the grass. But Emily saw none of this. Instead she saw, in her mind's eye, a slowly forming picture: Alan as he'd been on the day of the funeral, standing by the graveside in his black suit, a black tie, his black hat in his hands, his chestnut hair oiled, his gentle eyes blinking behind his small round spectacles. How kind he had been that day — and yet it had been a kindness so unobtrusive, so instinctive, that she'd barely noticed. He had put his arm round her in church as if shielding her, he had taken her hand by the graveside and squeezed it, he had stood guard at the house, warding off the worst of Granny Drage's strictures, nipping in the bud the barbed remarks of the Barford girls. It had been Alan who'd found her in the garden where she'd gone to escape it all (it had proved a futile hope).

'Emily. You're shaking — crying.' He'd put his arm round her once more. 'What is it, darling?'

'Everything. Aunt Margery. Poor Margery.' (It hadn't been Aunt Margery's misery that had thrown her off balance in the garden, it had been something else entirely, but that was neither here nor there.)

'Hush, darling. Don't think about it. It wasn't right of her to burden you at a time like this.'

'But Alan, she's so unhappy. Marriage has made her unhappy.'

'Ainsleigh is a cad, an absolute swine.' Alan had tightened his grip. 'Our marriage is different, darling. We'll never be like those two. I'd never treat you that way. You do believe me, don't you?'

Standing in the drizzle thirteen years later, Emily wondered how she could ever have forgotten just how safe she had felt with her head resting on Alan's shoulder and his arm round her: safe and cradled and comforted. But always the guilt had been there, always she had tried to sidestep Alan, tried not to think of him. Alan had seemed content, had said he loved her. But had he merely been making the best of it, trapped in a marriage where there was no real intimacy? He'd been so kind to her that day, so very dear and gentle. What had she ever given him in return?

A sudden gust of wind blew the drizzle in her face, which washed away the tears that were streaming down her cheeks.

CHAPTER ELEVEN

Emily rearranged her room to pass the time, to keep busy, but as she emptied her wardrobe and spread her clothes across the bed, as she piled books on the floor from the shelves of her bedside table, she found it impossible to stop her mind from wandering. Here, for instance, were some of Mama's old Marie Corellis. Mama in the days of Alleyn Dene had often had her head buried in a Marie Corelli. Later, she'd taken them all with her to the south coast. They'd been amongst the few things saved from the auction. Later still, in a rare lucid moment towards the end of the war, Mama had suddenly decided to throw them away. Marie Corelli was a food hoarder, it said so in the paper. She was unpatriotic, her books were tainted, they had to go. But Emily, when it came to the point, had been reluctant to lose these landmarks of her childhood and she'd rescued them. And so here they were, on the bedside table, yet another reminder of the past.

Emily abandoned her rearranging with a sigh and drifted across to the window, looking out at the nondescript day. Alleyn Dene, Nethercote Hall, Papa's funeral, Alan — and now Mama's books. It seemed to her she'd been besieged by the past these last few weeks. One tended to think of the past as fixed, woven immutably into the fabric of one's memories.

And yet, when one came to look — when one tried to summon up those memories for close examination — so many details were lost, that it was like peering back through a haze. She wondered if the war played a part in this. Had the war thrown up so much dirt and detritus that the very pattern of the past was obscured?

Emily, standing by the window, sighed again. She was unable to settle to anything. Why did she feel so restless? What was it she wanted?

To see Mama. She wanted to see Mama.

She latched on to this idea. It was only two weeks since her last visit to the rest home, but so much had happened since then — mostly in her head, of course — that it seemed like months ago. To see Mama was just what she needed. There was something comforting about being in Mama's presence, even now.

She would go. Why shouldn't she? She was not a prisoner. Let Violet make as many remarks as she liked. Let Sir Hubert fulminate. Emily didn't care. Strangely enough, none of that seemed to matter much anymore.

A surge of excitement swept through her. It was silly — silly to get so excited. But — oh! — to escape, to get away for a few hours, to be *doing* something! And Richmond wasn't London, not really. She wouldn't need to brave London's perilous streets. She'd be quite safe in Richmond.

Her mind made up, she lost no time, grabbing a clean skirt off the bed, kicking off her slippers, kicking over, as she did so, one of the piles of books on the floor. She hesitated. But the books could wait. She must be as quick as lightning. She needed to go before it was too late, before she changed her mind.

She was halfway to the village, dashing along the lane, when it occurred to her that she had taken it for granted she would go into town by omnibus. Why not Sir Hubert's Rolls? She had nothing to hide today. She was going to see Mama, and that was all.

Or was it? Was it Mama she wanted to see — or Midge?

She laughed out loud. What a stupid question! What a meaningless question! Where had it come from? Midge was nothing to her, she was nothing to him. And after last time, her crass attempt to offer him money, he'd probably want nothing to do with her.

She paused. Oh goodness! She'd quite forgotten how awful it had been. How could she face him after what had happened?

Debating with herself, she looked back along the lane, unsure. But it was Mama who was important, she told herself. It was Mama she was going to see. Nothing else mattered. And she'd miss the bus if she didn't run.

Midge was very cool with her, avoiding her eyes as she boarded the omnibus. It was all most awkward. She sat clutching her bag as the bus juddered along the country lanes. She tried to think of something to say, an opening, but everything she came up with seemed fraught with social constraints and possible misunderstandings. This was worse than trying to get through to Mama.

All too soon, other people got on and the chance had passed. She couldn't possibly speak to him in front of so many people (she had never known *The Sparrowhawk* this popular), and in any case, he was busy now. He issued tickets and answered questions about the schedule, he was cheerful and unassuming, he went up and down the aisle lithe and balanced, his body swaying with the movement of the bus.

Emily focused on the view from the window, tried to put Midge out of her mind, looked forward to seeing Mama.

But when she finally reached the rest home, it was to find Mama vague and disinterested, as she sometimes was: almost a stranger. Even her voice sounded different, not like Mama's at all. Emily struggled on for half an hour, but it all seemed pointless. With a sense of failure, she got up to go.

She was on her way out — walking along the main corridor towards the entrance, pulling on her gloves, buttoning her coat, her bag tucked under her arm — when, for no reason she could think of, she suddenly remembered Jarvis.

She stopped dead, puzzled, looked all around as if she half expected to see Jarvis somewhere in sight. Why else would she have thought of him after all this time? But the corridor was empty. There was just a faint echo of distant voices, the rattle of a trolley, all the usual sounds of the rest home.

Absently doing up the last button of her coat and then undoing it again, Emily stood in the corridor trying to account for Jarvis popping up like this. It was because she had been thinking so much about Alan, she decided. It was thinking of Alan, and then coming here: for this was where Jarvis now resided.

He was lodged in a wing of the rest home that had been separated off for soldiers wounded in the war. He could never have afforded this place by his own means, of course, but Sir Hubert had stepped in and insisted, Lady Winmer too. Jarvis had been a private in Alan's platoon, and Alan's servant. ('Officers are gentlemen, and gentlemen must have servants, even at the Front,' Alan had said, half-mocking, half-bitter.)

Jarvis was also living proof of Alan's heroism.

Emily found herself being drawn almost against her will towards the soldiers' wing. She passed through some double doors. There was a subtly different atmosphere here, less soporific, a touch volatile, wholly masculine. She could only remember coming here once before, when Jarvis had first been admitted and Sir Hubert had insisted on making a fuss of him. She wondered if Sir Hubert had done a deal, negotiated a discount, Mama and Jarvis as a package. But that was unkind. Sir Hubert had made all the arrangements and paid for it all. All the same, Emily was taken aback to think that she'd not been back to this part of the rest home since then. And yet, why should she? What was Jarvis to her?

Reaching another set of doors, Emily hesitated and nearly turned back. But she'd come this far, she might as well see it through. She refused to be so feeble as to turn tail now. Giving herself no time for further thought, she walked straight through the doors.

She found herself in a large chamber that might once have been a ball room, when this house was still a family home. There was a wooden floor with the polish rubbed off, and tables and chairs spaced out. A series of arched windows overlooked a rock garden with clipped hedges around it. She felt very self-conscious, having so many pairs of eyes on her — men's eyes. It took an effort not to turn and run.

She made enquiry of an orderly. He pointed. Jarvis had his back to her. He was sitting a little apart, as if he was the odd one out — which, in a sense, he was. Most, if not all, of the other men in the room had been officers. This was an establishment really meant only for officers, but Sir Hubert's money and position (the Right Honourable Hubert Winmer) had opened doors. And nothing was too good for Jarvis, the symbol of Alan's heroism, the man Alan had rescued from death.

From the back Jarvis looked ordinary, mundane, a slight figure hunched in a wheelchair. But as Emily moved round, a little shock ran through her, even though she knew what to expect: the trousers folded and tucked up, an empty space where his legs would have been, and one jacket sleeve wrapped over the stump of his right arm. His face was pallid, and perhaps a little chubbier than she remembered, but there was still something very youthful about him, as if he'd been frozen in time. He was neat and tidy, like a half-finished drawing. He was making a basket, weaving with his one hand, using his chin to hold it in place.

He looked up suddenly and was startled to see her. She felt herself colouring up, embarrassed, watching as his basket slipped from his hand and rolled away across the floor. She stooped quickly to retrieve it and handed it to him. He took it, his cheeks flaming — just as red as hers must be. He avoided her eyes.

'Thank you, miss — Mrs Winmer.'

He knew her. After all this time, he knew her.

She felt a sudden fierceness grip hold of her. She thought of Alan who, in letters and on leave, had always been so concerned, so solicitous, about his men — his platoon — and about Jarvis in particular: little Jarvis, no more than a boy, so afraid all the time — petrified — and yet so dogged, gritting his teeth and bearing it.

Her fierceness turned to anger, taking her by surprise, burning her. What had Jarvis got to blush about? It was everyone else who should be blushing — who should be ashamed — who should be made to come and see him as he was, in his wheelchair, working at his basket.

The orderly brought her a chair and she sat down. She found it quite easy to talk. She forgot, in her fierceness and her anger, that she had been worried about what to say, worried about finding the right words. The conversation, once begun, flowed quite naturally. He called her *miss*, persisted with it even when, now and again, he corrected it to *Mrs Winmer*. It made her feel odd, being called *miss*. It made her feel young. It made her, strangely, feel more on a level with him. He told her about his basket making, about the food, about his room, about the gardens. She listened with interest, asked all the right questions: it was no effort at all. She wondered why she couldn't be like this always, why she couldn't be at ease with people.

And then, as they continued to talk, she slowly became aware of herself, sitting there preening. What had she got to be so proud of? All she'd done was conduct a conversation. Most people wouldn't think twice about that. There was nothing clever in conducting a conversation. Here was Jarvis — a man half-drawn, a man tucked away in a forgotten corner — whereas she was a woman richly delineated and housed in a palace like Heartlands. She ought to be counting her blessings, as Nanny had taught her long ago, and never mind what had happened to her in the past.

There was a lull. She fingered the strap of her bag.

'I wonder . . .' She hesitated. Suddenly she was shy and unsure of herself. She felt there was something important she wanted to ask. What was it?

She remembered, suddenly, standing on the gravel path at Heartlands the day before yesterday. She remembered standing in the rain, and thinking about Alan. That was what she wanted to know. She wanted to know about Alan. Jarvis was the one person outside of the family that she could talk to about Alan.

'I wonder, would you mind very much if we . . . if we talked a little about my husband — and — and the war?'

'The war, miss?' Jarvis licked his lips. A strange expression came over his face that might have been termed crafty if his innocent, boyish looks had admitted of such a description. 'The war, miss, the war was — was a long time ago. Sometimes it seems like a dream now.' He glanced at her, then lowered his eyes and dredged up from some deep place a few hesitant words: simple words, like a child's story. 'I got seasick, going over. I'd never been on the sea. All the villages had funny names — French names, I suppose. We marched along French roads. Very straight, they were. We marched till our feet was raw. Our feet used to get red raw.' (He had no feet now.) 'But—' He licked his lips again. 'If you want to know about Lieutenant Winmer, miss, he was — he was — Lieutenant Winmer was . . .'

* * *

A line of poplars shone silver in the moonlight. A patchwork of French fields — fields without hedges — stretched colourless and cross-hatched with shadow into the infinite dark, the white ribbon of a road glimmered faintly, dipping then rising, following the contours of the land before disappearing over a low ridge. The moon, high above, blazed with a cold white fire, not quite full.

Alan Winmer gazed wide-eyed at the scene in muddle-headed awe. (*I'm drunk. Drunk.*) It looked unreal. It looked like a ghost land. There was a deep, ageless silence. (*Ageless silence. I like that.*) Far off, on the very edge of sight, lights flickered: flares, perhaps, or the flash of big guns — the terrible splendour of the guns. (Had he read that somewhere, some poem or other, 'the terrible splendour of the guns'? Or had he made it up here and now, on the spot, drunk as he was?)

'Winmer! Come on, man!'

They were waiting for him, Beaulieu, Walton and . . . and that other one. (What was his name, the other one? He was new.) They were waiting for him, in the middle of the street, in this little French town on a hill, a little French town called thingy, wotsit (another name he'd forgotten).

'Do buck up, Winmer! We haven't got all night! What are you *doing*?'

'I was looking at the ageless silence.'

'Can one look at a silence?'

'The terrible splendour of the guns.'

'You're tight as a tick, old man.'

'Drunk. I'm drunk. I really oughtn't . . . oughtn't to get so drunk.'

'There's no harm in it, no harm in a chap getting drunk on his birthday. It's quite in order on a chap's birthday. A chap's allowed to enjoy himself then — even you, Winmer.'

'No, no, no, you don't understand. Bad things happen when I'm drunk. I was drunk when — when — oh, Emily!'

'Who's Emily?'

'My wife, my darling, I hurt her . . .'

'Surely not, old man? Surely not you, most worthy Winmer, pure as the driven snow?'

'You're laughing at me.'

'My dear fellow, you should see yourself — you should *hear* yourself — you'd be laughing too. Now do buck up and come this way: we're going this way tonight.'

'But this isn't the usual way, this isn't the way to that place, the drinking place.'

'You'll like this other place even more, you'll see.'

Alan stumbled. It was a dark and narrow street. Where were they taking him? He wanted to ask, but he couldn't remember which of them he had just been talking to. It might have been Walton. It might have been the new one. But it was easiest to simply address his remarks to Beaulieu.

'Where are we going, Beaulieu?'

'You'll see. Nearly there.'

'Beaulieu?'

'What's up, old man?'

'Can I ask you something?'

'Ask away.'

'What's it like, do you think, when you stop one? What does it *feel* like?'

'Haven't the foggiest. But the brass hats seem determined that we should find out. This new show's as much of a muddle as all the others, from what I've heard. Fritz knew all about it beforehand, of course. Fritz was waiting as usual.'

'Shut up, Beaulieu, give it a rest!' The other two shouted him down. 'Enough shop talk! Today is Winmer's birthday. We're celebrating. We're having fun. And this is just the place.'

'What sort of place is it?' Alan peered. 'Why is there a red light in the window?'

'It's a different sort of *estaminet*, Winmer, a special sort. You'll like it here.' This was spoken in a suggestive tone, with a lecherous glint in the eye: Beaulieu was a man of the world.

I may be drunk, but I'm not stupid, thought Alan as he lurched through the doorway. *I know what this place is. A bawdy house. A bordello. A brothel.*

It was very discreet, very tasteful. There was wine — more wine. There was—

He wasn't sure what there was, but it was all very nice, very soothing, very interesting, a new experience. Everything was so very, very interesting this evening (*. . . the terrible splendour of the guns . . .*). He wished he could remember the half of it. (*I'm drunk.*)

He found himself being led upstairs. (*Oops, mind your head! Where's Beaulieu got to?*) A girl was holding his hand. A girl. A woman. (*Is she a—?*) There was a room with a sloping ceiling, the curtains closed, a lamp giving out a subdued glow, a bed. He felt large and clumsy in this confined space.

He took off his coat. (*Why have I taken my coat off?*) He sat down on the edge of the bed. (*The ageless silence of a whore's boudoir.*) The girl/woman standing before him let her dress fall, let it cascade down her body. She had on a — he was not sure what it was called, that flimsy, silky thing: *a shift*, was it? *A shift*. It sounded faintly disreputable. The soft lamplight caressed her skin. Her mousey hair was tumbled round her shoulders. So much in the world was ugly just now but she was beautiful — so beautiful it tore his heart in two. (*I'm drunk.*)

He stared up at her. What to say? 'I-I can't remember any French, mademoiselle. *Pas de français*. I've never been in a place like this before. I'm drunk, you see. I'm blind drunk. It's my birthday.'

She parted her red lips and spoke. '*Je m'appelle* Claudette, monsieur.'

'Claudette,' he repeated, fascinated by her lips. He wanted to touch them with his fingers, but he felt that might be indecent. 'My name is Alan. I'm Alan. *Moi*, Alain.'

She sat next to him. He reached out a tentative hand. The silky feel of her shift. The warmth of her skin. How beautiful she was. A cornucopia of beauty. He was filled up by it.

She smiled at him.

Such a smile!

A sad smile.

Feeling suddenly brave, he touched her lips. 'It's my birthday, mademoiselle. I'm thirty-two. Thirty-two today. *Aujourd'hui, trente-deux*.'

It was a rotten way to spend one's birthday, out here, in France. He wanted to be home. He wanted his cottage and Emily and little Chad. But Emily — oh, God, Emily! He wanted to give her everything, to give her the world, but his pride, his stupid pride, got in the way. What did pride matter, the way things were? He ought to have accepted his father's offer of help. He ought to have made money whilst he could. Then he'd have been able to give Emily whatever she wanted (what did she want?).

He shook his muzzy head. He needed to think clearly. He'd promised. He'd promised Emily that he would never,

ever treat her the way that cad Ainsleigh had treated her aunt. He'd promised not to betray her. He always kept his promises. Well, of course he did! He was Alan Winmer!

'I promised, mademoiselle: I promised.'

'Monsieur?'

'You don't understand, how could you? I'm a beast, a lustful beast. I hurt her — I hurt my darling wife — my darling Emily. I was clumsy, I botched it, and now—'

But did the promise still hold? Out here, did it hold? Everything was different here. And what if—?

The terrible splendour of the guns. The new show.

This, here, now, tonight: this might be his chance — his only chance — his last chance—

Did the promise still hold?

He groaned and held his head. The room was spinning. He'd drunk too much wine. 'Oh, God, mademoiselle — Claudette. It's madness. The world's gone mad. What am I doing here? I should be at home with Emily and Chad.'

'Monsieur—'

'No, no, listen—'

'Monsieur—'

'Listen, will you, listen!' But what did he want to tell her? What was so urgent? He'd forgotten. His mind groped. 'In the last show, Claudette — do you understand *show*? An attack. An offensive. Over the top. *Boom, boom*! You understand? Yes? Good. Good. In the last show, mademoiselle, I watched our guns shelling no-man's land. I watched them shelling our wounded, all the men that hadn't been brought in. Our own guns. Our own wounded.'

But she wasn't listening. She was pulling off his boots, undoing his tunic. She was practised, proficient, handling him as if he was a boy, undressing him like a boy, as if he was four years old and she was his mother. They'd not had servants or a nursery in the old days, Alan reminded himself. They'd not had servants when he was four. But Mother had never undressed him quite like this. Practised and proficient, yes. But also sensual and intimate, caressing him.

He took her hands. He had to stop her (the promise). He wanted to explain, but how, how? He looked into her eyes, such beautiful brown eyes, so deep and mysterious — so alive — so sad too: yes, he was right about the sadness. Perhaps she had understood after all, about the guns, the wounded, the pity of it.

'When they are dying, Claudette, they scream for their mothers, they always scream for their mothers.'

'Monsieur—'

He knew that much, *monsieur*, but the rest was lost on him. He couldn't remember the little French he knew. He was drunk. Drunk. And yet the words seemed to shine like lights inside his head. He could see them even though he couldn't understand them.

'Vous devez vous dépêcher, monsieur. Il y a d'autres qui attendent. Êtes-vous venu à parler ou à baiser?'

She was so beautiful, her hands so soft and warm. He wanted to touch her lips again. He wanted to take off her stockings. A desperate need was dammed up inside him.

'Mademoiselle — Claudette —' He choked on the words. He took hold of her hands. He wanted her to tell him, he had to make her tell him: in a world gone mad — the terrible splendour of the guns — did his promise still hold?

Did it still hold?

* * *

Yes, thought Claudette, whose real name was Veronique Colbert, a widow at twenty after her husband had been devoured by the mincing machine of Verdun, a mother whose baby had no father now. Yes, she thought with a vague, bored bitterness, infinitely weary: it was always their wives, their sweethearts — whatever the word was in English for sweetheart. Not that you needed to know the word: you could read it in their eyes. It was better not to know the word. Better, safer, more convenient. That way you could keep your distance. That way you could keep them at bay. The words they spoke meant nothing to you, were like the empty cries of beasts, like cattle lowing, impatient for milking time.

All the same, she could tell, she could always tell. She knew what they were saying. She didn't need to understand the words, she could read it in their eyes. *Our wives, our sweethearts — they are pure and virtuous and unsullied — whereas you — you—*

But they didn't know what it was like, to be a widow at twenty. They didn't know what it was like to have nothing. Nothing.

Never mind. It didn't matter what they thought of her. It was of no importance. She had a job to do. She got back to it. She unbuttoned his shirt, unfastened his trousers. She hoped he would take the hint. He was drunk, and drunks were always the worst. They prevaricated. They were unpredictable. To an unseasoned girl, they often presented a problem. But not to 'Claudette', skilled in the arts of her profession. Her fingers worked quickly, nimbly, as expert as a factory girl's. She unfastened, she unbuttoned, she stroked, she coaxed.

At the very last moment, he shied away. It came as no surprise. It often happened. They didn't want the responsibility. They liked to pretend it was none of their doing, that they'd been backed into a corner. This was no obstacle, not usually. There were ways and means of getting the job done. But this one — *mon Dieu*! — he was hard work! He was crying now, the way drunks sometimes did. And yet he wasn't crying quite like a drunk. These weren't just drunken tears. He was sobbing, actually sobbing, crying his heart out. *Mon Dieu*! *Mon Dieu*! She would certainly earn her money with this one!

She cradled him on the bed. He was half-undressed, the job half done. Time was ticking by, and time was money. She craned round to look at his face. Had the tears stopped yet? Not quite. Not quite. Her eyes lingered, appraising. He wasn't young, this one. He must be thirty at least. And yet . . . what was it about him . . . something almost naive. It wasn't that he was inept. They were often inept, like untrained dogs. But this one . . .

She took off his spectacles. She dried his eyes on her chemise. He looked up at her, his head on her lap. He looked up at her in a way that made her shiver. No. No. Inept wasn't the word at all. He wasn't inept. It was more like he was . . . unspoilt.

He looked much nicer without his spectacles. He looked almost handsome. It was not often she noticed what they looked like. She gently stroked his face, thinking of her dead husband, thinking of her baby, which she never usually did at work.

He was trying to tell her something. She leaned down to listen, her long hair brushing against his cheek. *Two*, he was saying, or was it *twice*. What did he mean? That this would be his second time tonight? But he wasn't a braggart. No, no, he most definitely wasn't a braggart. His second time, then, with a professional lady. Was that it? She wondered who the other had been. She felt an unwonted twinge of jealousy. But tonight she'd show him what a *true* professional was all about.

She knew her job. She did it well. No one had ever had cause for complaint where 'Claudette' was concerned. But there were times — a few, rare times — when she took a real pride in her work.

* * *

'It was an eye-opener, miss, and no mistake,' said Jarvis. 'I never realized how big the world is, or what it's really like.'

Little Jarvis, poor kid. Emily remembered snatches of Alan's talk, but she had never really taken much notice. The war had been a horror she couldn't take in, didn't want to. Jarvis and all the others — Private This and Corporal That — had been faceless people she didn't care about. All Alan's new jargon — *up the line, a strafe, the show* — had meant nothing to her, it had been beyond her imagination. Now, as if a fog was clearing, she was beginning to get glimpses. Or maybe it wasn't so much a fog, as a steamed-up mirror, reflecting darkly. Jarvis's face was the mirror. His eyes were sunken, haunted, faraway.

She became aware that his mouth was twitching. As she watched, the twitch spread from his mouth, across his cheek, and up to his eye. Briefly, half his face was twitching. She looked on, appalled. Had she done this to him? Had she done this, stirring up memories he'd much rather forget?

After a moment or so, he appeared to gain some measure of control. She felt very near to him now, as if they were wrapped in a cocoon here in the corner of the room, cut off, alone together.

'I'm so sorry, Jarvis. All these questions.'

'I-I don't like to talk about the war, miss. I don't know the right words.'

'It's perfectly all right. You don't need to say any more.'

'But Lieutenant Winmer, miss. You wanted to know about Lieutenant Winmer. I must tell you about him. If it hadn't been for Lieutenant Winmer . . .'

* * *

Another cock-up, thought Alan savagely. Another bloody balls-up. The brass hats couldn't organize a piss-up in a brewery. That was what the men said, and the men were right. Their words were the right words, the only words, brutal and unlovely.

The explosion had bowled him over, flattened him into the mud. He'd been deaf and blind for quite some time. His ears were still ringing even now. On top of which, he'd completely lost his bearings, he'd lost touch with the attack. He was crouched like a rat in a sewer, hiding in a shallow dip in the churned-up desolation of no-man's land. There was a grey sky and grey earth, a lunar landscape pitted with endless intersecting shell craters. Mud was everywhere: stodgy, clay-like mud. He was covered in it.

He slapped his cheeks, trying to liven himself up. The bombardment was continuing, but the whistling of the shells through the air sounded muffled, as if he had cotton wool in his ears. Slowly, as he crouched there in the mud, it came back to him. These were British shells, fired by British guns. Their own guns. Shelling their own men. Again.

What was the point? What was the fucking point?

He remembered now that he'd sent a man back to try to get an urgent message to HQ, wherever HQ might be in this featureless desert, because they'd been pinned down by their own guns, the few of them left of the first wave. They'd been pinned down by their own guns, because the bombardment hadn't lifted — though it was possible they were in the wrong place, not where they should have been. They should have been halfway to Berlin by now, if everything had gone according to the briefing. What had it been, again? A, B, C: position A, objective B — and C for fucking cock-up.

Christ, his language! He'd not be fit for civilized drawing rooms ever again. Not that he cared. He wished all civilized drawing rooms to the devil. He wished this bombardment would strafe them all to bloody hell. But he ought to make one last effort, try to gather his men — if there were any men left to gather.

He curled his lip. One last effort. Always one last effort. You never gave up. You always went on, however hopeless it was. Human beings had an infinite capacity for self-deception. He'd never have believed it before the war.

Slowly, cautiously, he raised his head. There was a ruined pill-box just ahead and a little to the right. There'd been a machine gun in it earlier. It was now silenced. One of the shells must have hit it, the shells coming from behind, from their own lines. So they had done *some* good.

He looked back — back towards the British trenches, or as near as he could make out. There was a rim of sky, broken clouds stained red, gold, purple: sunset, was it? In this grey desolation, the scene held his eye. It was like seeing colour for the first time. It smote his heart. It brought tears to his eyes. Oh, God, it was so lovely!

He thought how much he'd taken things for granted: sunsets, the cottage, Emily — darling Emily — little Chad, too — and his parents, his long-suffering parents. What would Mother think if she could see him now, covered head to toe in mud? And Father — Christ, he'd happily sit and listen to Father now, he'd only be too glad for Father to tell him what a stubborn fool he was, how he'd wasted his chances in life. He'd happily sit and listen to Father forever and a day. And what about Violet, Ivy, Ada? He'd thought them spoilt. They'd irritated him. He'd lost patience with them. But, now, all he wanted was to kiss them, he'd never kissed them nearly enough.

The colours in the sky, blurred by the tears in his eyes, were fading already. But the shells kept coming. Who was it he'd been talking to not long ago about the British guns killing the British wounded? Oh, God, yes, that tart. He'd been so drunk he barely remembered. But he remembered enough. Too much. Claudette. Beautiful Claudette. Would she still be there when — if —?

Christ, what was he thinking? What was he turning into? His sense of decency must be all shot to pieces, if he could cherish the memory of a night of depravity like that! Guilt had been eating away at him ever since. Only — if that was what it could be like — if that was what he'd been missing out on — he'd never imagined it could be like that. If Emily — he and Emily . . . When he got back he'd—

He shook his head. Thinking of home was a luxury he couldn't afford. He had to stick to the here and now — the show — objective B—

No, actually, bollocks to that, fuck it, as the men would say. And it was the men who mattered. He needed to find out what had happened to his men. He was the lieutenant, they were his boys. His fellow subalterns might laugh at him — worthy Winmer, pure as the driven snow — but no one could say he'd ever shirked his responsibilities. Men mattered more than bloody objective B. If war had taught him anything, it had taught him that.

He steeled himself, got up, began to crawl, to run, every sense on full alert, his service revolver in his hand. He went slipping and sliding, sinking into the mire, the mud sucking at him, trying to wrench off his boots. *Boom, boom, boom.* There was still no sign of Jerry, but now Jerry's guns were joining the party.

He stopped, dropped down. Had he heard something? No, it must be the whistling and humming of his ears, louder even than the guns. But wait — yes — a voice. Over there.

He crawled. He peered over the edge of a shell hole.

'Sir! Sir! Here, sir! It's me, sir, me.'

It was Jarvis. Or what had once been Jarvis. Now—

Alan swallowed. He had to force himself not to flinch, not to get on his feet and run away screaming. Sliding down the slope, he came to rest next to the mangled carcass that was all there was left of Jarvis. Why wasn't he dead?

'Sir, am I finished, sir?' The whites of Jarvis's eyes showed up lucent. His face was covered in thick mud and yet, beneath, it was perfect, not a scratch. 'I d-d-don't want you to think I'm a c-coward, sir, but I'm not sure . . . not sure how . . . how much more . . .'

This had always been Jarvis's mantra: *I don't want you to think I'm a coward, sir . . .*

Alan reached for Jarvis's hand, but there was no hand: Jarvis's right arm had vanished. Alan drew his own hand back, suddenly afraid of touching the boy in case his body disintegrated altogether.

'You'll be all right, lad. You'll be OK. Where are the others? What happened? I was knocked over. It was a bomb, I think. I've rather lost track.'

'J-J-Jerry came at us, sir. Jerry c-c-came out of nowhere.'

'A counter-attack.'

'Hobbs, Nixon, Gately were hit. B-B-Billings got blown to pieces. B-B-Billings got blown to pieces right in front of me.'

'A bit of a balls-up all round, then.'

'Y-y-yes, sir. A balls-up, sir.'

'All right, Jarvis. Hang in there, lad.'

'But, sir, I can't feel my legs, sir.'

His legs? His *legs*! Christ, there was nothing left of him except his face, his white eyes.

Alan felt a fierce anger. He wasn't going to let Jarvis die. He wouldn't let it happen again, their own wounded blown to smithereens by their own guns. He *refused* to let it happen.

'I'll get a stretcher party, Jarvis—'

'Don't leave me, sir! P-P-Please, sir, please don't!'

'Don't worry, Jarvis, everything will be all right. I won't be long. I'll pop back to the lines, find out what the hell is happening, fetch a stretcher party. I'll be back before you know it. You're not going to die, Jarvis, do you hear me? You're not going to die. I promise. I *promise*.'

* * *

'He went back to the line,' said Jarvis, his face a pale grey, his eyes staring, the fingers of his one hand clenching and unclenching. 'Lieutenant Winmer went back to our front line. He went to fetch a stretcher party. He said he'd come back. The stretcher party came, but not Lieutenant Winmer. I never saw Lieutenant Winmer again.'

* * *

Running, dodging, his revolver still clutched in his hand, Alan made his way across the torn-up ground that was devoid of all landmarks. He ran through the dusk, crouched over, driving himself on. To the whine and whizz of bullets was now added the shriek and crunch of shells. Jerry had fully woken up now. Jerry was active all along this sector, just to make life more interesting.

HQ, of course, had been in turmoil when he finally found it. Wires had been cut, contact lost. Runners simply vanished, blown up or swallowed by the mud. Alan had made his report, sent for stretchers, asked in the foulest language possible for the bombardment to be lifted (but no one at HQ had any idea how to contact the artillery). He'd stirred them all up, he'd thrown his weight about, now he was on his way back to Jarvis. Jarvis would not die. He'd made this solemn promise.

But what were his promises worth, Alan Winmer, the great betrayer!

Well, if he could do this one thing — if he could save Jarvis — then it might go some way towards his rehabilitation. He'd betrayed Emily, but he would make amends. Things would be different when he got home. He'd make sure of it.

But he mustn't tempt fate. He mustn't, mustn't, mustn't.

He paused, ran a few yards, paused again. Every time he stopped, he could feel himself slowly sinking into the mud.

Suddenly he felt a blow like a punch to the abdomen. It winded him. It knocked him off balance, so that he sat down heavily, like an unsteady toddler. He was angry at the delay. Yet another delay. All he wanted was to get to Jarvis, to save Jarvis.

He staggered to his feet, rubbing the spot where the punch had landed, the heavy fist of an invisible man. His fingers came away sticky. Mud, liquid mud, always mud. But when he looked down he saw, mingled with the grey of the mud, a streak of vivid colour that reminded him of the sunset earlier: a brilliant, vibrant red, red like blood.

Like blood? It is blood, he thought with a sense of surprise. *Blood. My blood.*

He stared at it, his mind clunking. Blood? Blood!

Then I must have been hit. I've stopped one.

And what had it felt like? Like nothing. A punch in the belly.

Christ, it's getting very dark all of a sudden. It's going pitch black. Why is it so dark? Am I d————

CHAPTER TWELVE

Sat in the omnibus going home, Emily felt a strange sense of detachment, as if she was both here on the bus, and also still in the officers' room at the rest home, listening to Jarvis, watching his face, his expression at times almost childlike in its clarity.

'There's lots I can do now one-handed, miss: lots and lots. I'm getting better at it all the time. I'm getting more used to it.'

After nine years, that was just as well.

'That's good, Jarvis. I'm glad. Your family must be pleased, too. They must be very proud of you. Do you see them often?'

'Oh, yes, miss. As often as they can manage, any road. My ma comes when she can, but it's a long way for her to travel, see, and she can't always afford the coach fare. My old dad, he came the Christmas before last — or was it the Christmas before that? I can't remember. There's our Vera, too, and her nippers. Vera's my sister, miss. To tell the truth, I've not seen Vera in a while, nor the nippers. They must have growed up quite a bit by now. I daresay I'd hardly recognize them. Never mind. It can't be helped.' And he'd smiled his stoic smile.

Emily on the omnibus felt powerless, felt sad. What was it Alan had called Jarvis? *Dogged*, that was it. And still Jarvis carried on in his dogged way, as if there was nothing else but to stick it out — to smile, smile, smile, in the words of that old song, the one the soldiers sang in the war.

What's the use in worrying?
It never was worthwhile.
So pack up your troubles in your old kit bag,
And smile, smile, smile.

That was Jarvis in a nutshell.

Emily had never had much to do with Jarvis. She'd not been interested in the circumstances of Alan's death. It was enough to know he was dead, the minutiae didn't matter. Lady Winmer felt differently. She wanted to know everything, down to the last detail. She'd swiftly become disillusioned with Jarvis. He was one of the last men to see Alan alive, it was true, but he could not tell her exactly how Alan had died, nor where Alan's body lay. Lady Winmer had written endless letters to everyone she could think of, asking for information. She'd written to the men in Alan's platoon, to his fellow subalterns, to his commanding officer. She had appealed to the War Office, she had put notices in the papers, she had got her husband to pull all the strings he could — all in her ceaseless pursuit of 'the truth'.

Sir Hubert had no patience with his wife's obsession. Like Emily, it was enough for him to know that Alan was dead. But at least he had the consolation of Alan's not having died ignominiously or in vain. Jarvis was living proof that Alan had died a hero's death, saving a man's life. Jarvis was the very symbol of Alan's heroism. Jarvis must be feted and rewarded.

We rewarded him, thought Emily, *and then we abandoned him.*

Poor Jarvis! He had been installed in that rest home, no expense spared. But no one had given any thought as to how far his mother would have to come to see him. No one had considered that his nephews and nieces, of whom he was so fond, would grow up without him. He was alone in that place — cut off, not just from his family, but also, as Emily had seen today, from the other inmates of the officers' wing. Jarvis was a ranker from the lower classes: not quite our sort, what!

This was not what Alan would have wanted for him.

Sat silent in the omnibus, guarding her thoughts from the other passengers as she watched the spreading suburbs swing by, Emily was taken aback by how certain she was: how certain of what Alan would have wanted for his dogged little servant. She had spent so many years trying *not* to think about Alan, trying not to bring him into focus, that it came as a shock to find she knew so much about him.

Ironically, having rejected his father's plans for him, having eschewed politics, Alan had nonetheless come to politics by a different route. The war had accelerated a process begun whilst they lived in the cottage. Working for the local law firm, Alan had fallen into the habit of accepting for his services a payment people could afford, rather than what was due — he had been known to refuse payment altogether. This got him into trouble with his firm. He'd dug in his heels. 'The law should be there to help everyone,' he'd said, 'not just those who have the money to make use of it.'

At the outbreak of war, there'd been no doubt that Alan would do what he saw as his duty and volunteer. Life in the army had opened his eyes. Mixing with the men of his company, he'd been appalled how some of them had lived in peace time, the poverty in which they'd grown up.

'How can such poverty still exist in this day and age — in Britain, in the twentieth century? How is it possible?'

Something should be done, he'd said. Something *must* be done. And if no one else would do it, he'd have to do it himself. That was when he'd begun to toy with the idea of one day becoming an MP — but not for his father's party.

'Labour? The Labour Party? Don't be absurd. My son was not a fool! He would never have wasted himself on Labour!' Sir Hubert insisted on rewriting history after Alan's death and he'd brushed aside Emily's testimony about Alan's change of heart. 'Alan believed in the Coalition. He always believed in the Coalition. He'd have joined me before long on the government benches — I can just see it now!'

But who could say what Alan would have done, if he'd lived? He'd been just as dogged as Jarvis, going his own way, sticking to his principles. Of one thing Emily was certain, however. He would never have left Jarvis to moulder away in that rest home.

Placing Jarvis in the rest home was Sir Hubert all over: Jarvis should count himself lucky, he was much better off than those poor devils on the streets, limbless, disabled, on crutches, begging. The professional staff in the rest home would be able to look after Jarvis much better than his own family could. Sir Hubert was often kind, Sir Hubert could be generous, Sir Hubert was always ready to help — but only on his own terms. He always knew what to do. He always knew what was needed. He could run the whole world on exactly the right lines, if only the whole world would let him.

He'd been in his element during the war and he'd risen high on the strength of it. Life in the war had been properly organized: that was Sir Hubert's firm opinion. There'd been rules, regulations and — latterly — rationing. People had been *forced* into a better way of living. The country had improved out of all recognition. For the first time Britain had been on the right track. It galled him that all the progress made during the war had been dismantled in the Peace. If only he could get back into the House, if only the Coalition could be revived, there might still be some hope for the future.

On a more personal level, Emily knew she would not have survived without Sir Hubert. She remembered only too clearly her sense of panic in the late summer of 1917 after Alan's death. What would become of her, how would she ever get by? She was a widow with a young son, and all but penniless.

Mr Winmer (as he'd still been) had stepped in. 'You will come and live with us, my dear — you and the boy, my heir. It's the least I can do.'

The cottage, which had once been a little Eden, had become by the autumn of 1917 a millstone. It was ridiculously remote and impossible to keep up under wartime restrictions. With Chad away at school much of the time, she'd been horribly lonely. In the end, it had come as a relief to leave it behind.

There had been no Heartlands in those days, of course, just a rather modest (by comparison) town house in Holland Park. Here, in the autumn and winter of 1917, and on into 1918, Emily had witnessed the full impact of Alan's death on his family. His sisters, pale as ghosts and decked in black, had seized on their grief and made mourning their raison d'être. Sir Hubert, on the other hand, had been angry. He had often worked himself into a towering rage. He'd held Field Marshal Haig personally responsible for Alan's death: Haig, that bungler, that butcher, that *murderer*, architect of the senseless slaughter of Passchendaele in which Alan had perished. Haig ought to be stopped, but Haig could not be stopped. Haig was a runaway train, he was a rabid dog. Lloyd George had tried his best to muzzle him, but Haig had friends in high places — privileged friends, powerful friends. He was untouchable. That bungler, that butcher would carry them all to perdition.

Mrs Winmer had reacted differently again. She had not wept or wailed like her daughters, she had not laid blame like Sir Hubert. She had become ever more obsessed with her quest for the truth. She was certain she wasn't being told the truth. Alan's body had never been found, nor his effects (his watch, his spectacles), so how could anyone say with any assurance that Alan had been killed? If only she could get at the truth. He might be lying in some hospital, for all they knew, his memory gone. He might be a prisoner of war. Surely she would have known if he was dead, her own son. Surely she would have *felt* it.

After several few weeks of this — the grief and the anger and the obsession — Emily had reached breaking point. She had been desperate to get away. And so she'd escaped on a visit to Mama on the south coast.

But why, she'd asked herself in the late autumn of 1917, should it just be a visit? Why not stay with Mama permanently? Chad could come to them during the holidays. It would be perfect.

'Well, I'm not sure, Emmy . . . I have my own routine . . . and my little bungalow, so tiny . . . I don't really have the room . . .'

Mama by then had begun to live in a world of her own and the war had become unreal to her.

'It's true, Emmy, that the news was bad before, but now Lord Roberts has gone out to take command . . . and ever since the relief of Mafeking . . .'

Emily had realized, as they walked along the sea front, that Mama was talking not of the war raging in France and Flanders, but of the South African War fifteen years before. Emily had wished she could obliterate the war from her own consciousness as completely as Mama. Almost it had seemed possible that golden afternoon, with gentle waves lapping on the stony beach, and gulls on the wing flashing white in the sun, and the sky vast and blue and permanent. But then, as they walked along the esplanade, there'd come that rippling of the air, that faint pressure on her ear drums, which was the sound of the guns far away across the Channel.

'No, dearest, that isn't gunfire, it's thunder.'

Sat in the omnibus nine years later, Emily had a vivid recollection of her sense of betrayal as she realized the extent of Mama's withdrawal from the world. Back at the bungalow after their walk, Emily had packed her bags and left. She'd turned her back on Mama, the way Mama — this was how it had seemed — had turned her back on her. Emily had not understood then, as she did now, that Mama's apparent callousness was a symptom of that illness which had led her in the end to the rest home.

Emily looked up. To her surprise, she found that the omnibus had emptied whilst she'd been lost in her thoughts. She was now alone with Midge. He was standing nearby, wedged against the seats, his body swaying with the movement of the bus in the now familiar way. He was close, and yet not close, as if he hadn't quite made up his mind to approach her — or as if he was waiting for her to make a sign. Outside, the countryside at dusk flashed past. The fading sky was pockmarked with cloud, stained pink and purple at the edges.

She turned from the view and began, without further thought, without preamble, to tell Midge about her day. It seemed the most natural thing in the world, as if the awkwardness that had existed between them that morning had never happened. And, indeed, why should there be awkwardness? What was a little misunderstanding over money? It was nothing, absolutely nothing, when the world outside on this calm April evening was so peaceful and so beautiful.

She told Midge about visiting Mama, and about seeing Jarvis again after so long. Midge responded to her overture, came quickly to sit opposite, listened intently, nodding, asking the right questions, as if he really was interested. He was always so pleasant and polite. He was always so easy to talk to. She was flooded with a feeling of warmth towards him.

She found herself, unpremeditated, trying to put her thoughts about the war into some sort of order, searching for the right words — thoughts to which she'd never given expression before.

'It seemed so very exciting at first, like an unexpected holiday. One felt that . . . that life had got a bit dull, and that now, at last, one could start living in earnest. Everyone was of one mind. That was how it felt — that the whole country was united. It was all rather thrilling, those first few weeks.'

Then weeks turned into months, months into years. The war became ubiquitous. Slowly, imperceptibly, it smothered everything, insidious, stifling. A creeping horror had overtaken the world.

Her thoughts had outrun her words, and she suddenly realized that she'd fallen silent. Gathering herself, she glanced at Midge shyly.

'Were you in the war, Mr Midgely — Midge?'

She already knew the answer. He'd once told her that he'd met Ginger during the war. Plus, there was that air about him, what she called his young/old demeanour: it was something she often saw in men who'd been soldiers.

'Happen you're right about it being an adventure,' he said, by way of an answer. 'Seemed one big adventure at outset—'

He stopped, his face expressionless, his eyes blank, as if a shutter had come down. It was understandable that he might be reluctant to talk about his experiences in any detail, but this sudden and complete shutdown was unexpected, especially in a man usually so open and affable. It was even a little disturbing.

He seemed to sense her speculations and drew back, like a snail into its shell. Taking a quick breath, he said briefly, harshly, 'What were it all *for*? It did note for nobody.'

He turned away from her, staring out of the window.

She thought she understood what he meant but she didn't believe it was entirely true. Some people had done very well out of the war, Sir Hubert for one. But she was thinking, rather, of Aunt Margery. In the months after Alan's death, living with the Winmers in London, Emily had begun to see more of Aunt Margery. A transformation had taken place. The forlorn and desolate woman from the day of Papa's funeral had gone and a new and ebullient Aunt Margery had taken her place.

'It's too awful of me, Emmy, and I know I shouldn't say it, but I really don't want the war to end! I'm having too much fun!'

This was in the early spring of 1918, around the time of the great German offensive. Emily had called on Aunt Margery at her Belgravia home and stayed for lunch, as she often did in those days. The atmosphere at Aunt Margery's acted as an antidote to the Winmers' house in mourning. On that particular day, luncheon had gone on well into the afternoon. Aunt Margery had opened one of her husband's expensive bottles of wine and had drunk more than her share.

Under the wine's influence, the tenor of her talk had become ever more intimate. She had been in confessional mood.

Lord Ainsleigh, of course, had been absent. He'd been in France, doing his bit. He'd secured a comfortable staff posting, well behind the lines.

'Living the high life in those French chateaux,' as Aunt Margery put it. 'Up to his old tricks, no doubt. Enjoying the company of the French *mesdames*. He prefers *mesdames* to *mademoiselles*. Married women make less of a fuss.' Aunt Margery had laughed, gulping her wine and smoking a cigarette in a long, elegant holder. With a glint in her eyes, she'd added, 'Well, Emmy my dear, what's sauce for the goose . . .' She had winked knowingly.

If Emily had been shocked at this change in her aunt, she'd been even more shocked to discover that Aunt Margery was far from being alone in this. There'd been a whole section of society who, when they thought of the war at all, thought only of its advantages. Life for them was an endless round of pleasure, one lavish party after another, at which they conducted their amorous intrigues. *Dancing whilst men are dying*: that was how Emily had put it to herself eight years ago, on that cold April day more like winter than spring. Having finally taken her leave of Aunt Margery, she'd walked across Hyde Park on her way back to the Winmers', with her aunt's words still ringing in her ears, more chilling even than the weather: 'I really don't want the war to end. I'm having too much fun.'

It had been all too easy, in the spring of 1918, to believe that Aunt Margery's wish would be granted. Certainly, Emily had seen no end in sight as she walked across Hyde Park, huddled in her coat. The war, she'd felt, would go on and on and on, until there were simply no more recruits left to send, and England was emptied of young men. Already that April day, the Park had seemed strangely deserted.

Looking back after eight long years, Aunt Margery's talk of parties and pleasure — dancing whilst men were dying — had got mixed up in Emily's mind with Mr Pemberton-Billing and his revelations over the 'German black book'. The newspapers had been full of it around that time. Pemberton-Billing had hinted at vice and corruption in the highest places, of which the Germans were well aware and using to their advantage. Blackmail and treachery, Pemberton-Billing had declared, were undermining the prosecution of the war. Emily remembered that she'd felt as if there was a canker at the very heart of England — that men were fighting and dying in unimaginable squalor for something rotten and degenerate, a glittering, gluttonous *haut monde* utterly indifferent to their suffering and sacrifice. Decadence and death had seemed partnered in a callous and macabre dance. The thrilling early days, when the war had seemed an adventure and the whole country united, had by then been lost in a mythical past, replaced by an endless nightmare from which there was no awakening.

But the nightmare had come to an end eventually and it now seemed almost unreal.

'One can hardly believe one lived through it. It makes one feel so . . . so *old*.'

'You aren't old, Mrs Winmer.'

Emily looked up, startled, suddenly aware that she'd spoken aloud, and that Midge had replied. Midge had been sitting so still and so quiet that she'd almost forgotten he was there.

She met his eyes, and he said in a rush, 'You . . . you don't look old, any road. You look like . . . like Gladys Cooper!'

He got up abruptly and moved away, as if trying to distance himself from what he'd just said. She caught a brief glimpse of colour flaring in his cheeks before he disappeared out of her eyeline, blundering towards the far end of the bus.

Emily found that she was blushing too. What on earth had possessed him to say such a thing? She wasn't beautiful and glamorous like Gladys Cooper. She was nothing like a film star. Impertinent, Violet would call it. Even Mama — the old, irrepressible Mama of Alleyn Dene days — might have raised an eyebrow at a compliment paid by a bus conductor. Was it pity? Was that what had prompted his clumsy piece of flattery? Did he feel sorry for her, so crabbed and worn and tired as she was? Yet it hadn't sounded like pity.

How had it sounded, exactly? She mouthed the words the way he'd pronounced them: *Yo int owd.* Violet would sneer. Granny Drage would be scathing: those common people, they were even incapable of speaking their own language correctly. But that was just the point. He'd made no attempt just now to put on airs and talk posh, as he'd done when they first met, as he did so often. These were real words that meant something. This was the real Midge. It was like getting a glimpse of the man behind the mask.

She felt the bus slowing and glanced out of the window. They were pulling up by the turning to Heartlands. The journey was over already.

She got to her feet. Midge was waiting by the door. He avoided her eye, didn't offer to hand her down. Was he embarrassed by what he'd said? Did he now regret saying it? She couldn't tell. Just as, a moment before, she had felt she'd caught a glimpse of the real Midge, now she felt sure that she didn't know him at all, he was a complete stranger — which wasn't so far from the truth. She knew nothing of his family or where exactly he was from. She knew nothing of his life before the war, and very little of his life since. She wanted to know. She wanted desperately — fiercely — to know. But she was too afraid to ask. She'd always be too afraid, too much of a mouse, too much of a shadow of a woman.

With a feeling of helplessness, she said tonelessly, 'Thank you, Midge.'

He didn't respond and, as she stepped down from the platform, she was seized by a sense of anguish that seemed wildly out of proportion. She heard the bus's engine revving behind her; she heard the engine begin to rattle and roar.

And then, over the noise: 'G'night, Mrs Winmer!'

The sudden, shouted words startled her and she swung round instinctively. The omnibus was already moving away down the lane. Midge was perched on the very edge of the platform, holding on with one hand, leaning out, reckless.

He looked very young, like a daredevil boy revelling in danger. But his dark eyes were not a boy's — the eyes that were watching her, fixed on her, as the bus gathered speed. It rounded the bend in the road and disappeared. The sound of its engine echoed a moment amongst the beech trees then faded away. An empty silence fell.

Emily remained where she was for a moment, gazing along the empty lane. Finally, with an effort, she turned from the road and began to make her way up the drive.

It seemed to her almost as if she'd lived through the whole war again on her way home — she'd lived through it all in her mind. She now found herself thinking of something that had happened afterwards — after the Armistice — the trip she'd made with Lady Winmer. Lady Winmer was the one who'd wanted to go, who'd seen the advertisement in the newspaper for battlefield tours.

'I want to see those places, Emily, I want to see them all: the places where Alan was.' Lady Winmer had looked on the trip by way of a pilgrimage.

Sir Hubert had flatly refused to have anything to do with it. He said it was a waste of money. It was *wallowing*, he said. Violet and her sisters had followed their father's lead. And so it had been left to Emily to accompany Lady Winmer across the Channel in the summer of 1919.

It had all been very well organized, hotels booked, cars at the ready, an ex-officer to guide them. A day's outing to the 'devastated areas' had formed the centrepiece to the tour.

'Oh, Emily! Emily!' Lady Winmer had clutched Emily's arm as they walked across the wasteland, treading warily, gingerly — for there were unexploded bombs, there were daily casualties, some tourists had even been killed.

Lady Winmer had seemed to welcome the danger, to *wallow* in it, as Sir Hubert might have said. She had looked all round with wide and ravenous eyes, drinking in every detail. The churned-up ground, pockmarked with shell holes, looked like the surface of some ghastly frozen sea. The stumps of trees stuck out of the ground like old and rotting fence posts. Barbed wire, trailing across the mud and tangled in great clumps, resembled the fossilized remains of torturous, writhing snakes. Scattered across this dreadful landscape were endless shell cases, rusting rifles, abandoned machine guns, piles of rubble. A fire-blackened and overturned tank had every appearance of the decaying corpse of some monstrous, antediluvian animal. It was not unknown, their guide had told them cheerfully, to come across a corpse or two.

Emily had wanted to shut her eyes, to blot it out. She could barely believe it was real. Had human beings created all this?

Countless ammunition boxes had littered the ground. Their guide and his assistant had upended some of them and placed them in a circle. One they had covered with a cloth and laid it with sandwiches. They had sat there, the four of them, picnicking in perdition.

Emily had eaten mechanically, her mind numb. The sandwiches had tasted of nothing. The sky had been blue, and the sun very bright, but it had seemed to have no power to warm. A deadly chill had settled on her. Dumbly, she had watched distant Chinese workers in large flat hats filling in the trenches and making vast heaps of rusting metal.

At long last it had been time to go. They had made their slow and steady way back towards the car. Lady Winmer had lagged further and further behind. She had seemed reluctant to leave. Emily had stopped to look back and had seen her mother-in-law some way off on her knees. Mindful of the danger of sharp edges and barbed wire — not to mention the unexploded bombs — Emily had retraced her steps, to lend Lady Winmer a hand.

She had found Alan's mother rooting through the dirt, digging the soil with her bare hands, letting it trickle through her fingers, her nails clogged with earth as she dug ever more frenziedly. Eyes wide and staring, she had repeated over and over, over and over, 'Where is he? Where is he? Where is he?'

Granny Drage would have called it hysteria, Granny Drage would have spoken sharply and told the bereaved woman to pull herself together. But Emily, silent, sympathetic, had helped the old lady to her feet — Lady Winmer seemed very old indeed just then, though she'd only been sixty-four — had led her back to the car. Lady Winmer had walked with heavy, clumsy steps. She had held her soiled hands out in front of her, her arms stretched rigid.

They had driven away from the scene of desolation. Emily did not look back.

The battlefield tour did not put an end to Lady Winmer's desperate search for her son. She had gone on waiting, hoping, exploring every avenue. Soon after they moved to Heartlands, she had taken up with spiritualism.

'Madame Bobatska is calling today,' she'd announced one morning at breakfast. 'Madame Bobatska comes highly recommended. She has helped countless families. You'll join us, won't you, Emily dear? You'll help us try to contact Alan on the Other Side? And if he's not there — if even Madame Bobatska can't find him — think what it will mean!'

Sir Hubert had leapt to his feet without any warning, nearly overturning the table.

'Stop it, stop it, stop it! Stop this nonsense, Elizabeth! Stop it *at once*!'

He had turned bright red, erupting with rage, leaning down to yell into his wife's face, whilst Emily and the sisters sat frozen with shock.

'Alan is dead, you stupid woman. He is *dead*. Why can't you get that into your vacuous head? Our son was killed, he has gone, he is never coming back. He was murdered by that butcher Haig and left to rot in France. We have lost him, lost him forever.'

Lady Winmer had been utterly unruffled. She had stirred sugar into her tea and, as if she was conducting any ordinary breakfast conversation about the weather or their plans for the day, she'd said, 'There must be some mistake. There is no body, there is no grave, we can't be sure that he was ever killed at all. If he was dead, I would know — I would *know*.'

That morning, given the circumstances, the old litany, repeated endlessly, had seemed more than chilling.

Sir Hubert, after a moment, had sat down. He had continued with his breakfast in silence, as if nothing had happened. But from that day on, he had started referring to what he termed Lady Winmer's 'condition'.

'You must do more around the house, Violet. You can't expect your mother, in her condition . . . Will you sort out my letters, Emily, Lady Winmer can't be expected to manage, in her condition . . .'

Lady Winmer took no notice. She carried on believing. She still believed now, seven and a half years after the end of the war. She no longer said as much. She said very little at all, these days. But one could read it in her eyes, that same litany: *there's no body, there's no grave, he can't be dead, I'd know.*

Walking up the drive in the dusk, Emily paused to look up at the brick-built facade of Heartlands. It was a modern house, but steeped in the past. There was Lady Winmer, clinging to her forlorn hope. There was Sir Hubert, still dreaming of a triumphant return to the Commons. There were the sisters, all in their forties now, but somehow suspended in time: the mummified remains of 'Father's little angels'.

And me, thought Emily. *What about me?*

She brushed aside this uncomfortable thought and went indoors.

In her room, as she changed for dinner and then replaced the clothes she'd taken from her wardrobe that morning, she noticed the pile of books she had kicked over in her haste to be gone. She knelt to put them back on the shelves of the bedside table. One book had slid right under the bed. Stretching for it, her fingertips brushed against something else, a wooden storage box that she'd not thought about in months. Almost reluctantly, she dragged it slowly out and opened the lid. Here were her bits and pieces, the flotsam of her life, which she slept over, like a dragon on its hoard. What had she got in her hoard? Nothing much. An old photograph, curling at the edges, of Mama and Papa. Some pictures of Chad, and some of his childish drawings — his first baby shoes too. Gramophone records from the cottage. A book Aunt Margery had once given her (she put the book hastily aside, embarrassed). There were letters, too. Mostly they were letters from Mama, but there were also a few Alan had sent from the Front, still in their envelopes.

She backed away on her knees from the wooden box. She got to her feet, walked blindly across the room, opened the curtains. Dusk was giving way to dark night, but as she peered through the window it seemed to her that she could see shadows out there, shadows moving in the blackness, floating eerily in mid-air like mist over the meadows. As she watched the ever-moving mist, she heard Jarvis's voice in her head, words he'd spoken earlier.

'Worst bit of all, miss, was one morning, early, before we went over the top. Got myself in a right state, no two ways about it. Shi — shaking like a leaf, I was. Didn't think I could face it.

'Next minute, Lieutenant Winmer's there, Lieutenant Winmer comes along the trench. He sees straight off I'm in a funk. He stops and talks to me. Gets out his wallet. Shows me a picture inside — a picture of his little boy, and of you, miss: a picture of you.

'"See here, Jarvis," says he, "you've all this to look forward to, a wife and a family of your own."

'"What's it like, sir," I asks him — to keep him talking, like — "being married?"

'"Best thing that can ever happen to a fellow," says he. "Do you know, Jarvis," says he, "I never realized just how lucky I am until I came out here. My Emily—" these are his words, miss, not mine "—my Emily means the world to me. She's made me the happiest man alive."

'"I don't have no luck with girls, sir," I says to him — which was the God's honest truth.

'But he says, "Just you wait, Jarvis, my lad. You'll have the girls queuing up when you get home, a war hero like you."

'Funny thing, but I did feel a bit of a hero, after Lieutenant Winmer'd had a word. He put some heart in me, and I found I could face it, going over the top.

'"Chin up, Jarvis," he says to me. "You'll pull through, you see if you don't."

'And he was right about that, miss. I'm still here. I count my blessings, too, when there's plenty others who never did come back — don't think as I don't count my blessings. But I should have liked to have got married, miss. I should have liked to have got married one day.

'Ah, well.'

Staring out at the strange grey mist, Emily felt she could see dimly through it into the past, she could see Alan in the days of the cottage getting ready to go to work, buttoning his shirt, brushing his hair, hooking the arms of his spectacles over his ears — those little, round spectacles that made him look like an owl. With nimble fingers, he knotted his tie. He pulled on his waistcoat, arranged his watch and chain. The same routine, every morning. She'd watched him as she lay in bed in the tiny front bedroom with the sloping ceiling and the uneven, creaky floor. She'd watched him idly, lazily, not taking much notice, for it all seemed so commonplace, so unchanging. And yet—

I never realized how lucky I am . . . the happiest man alive . . .

He'd been happy. Alan had been happy. He'd said so, he'd told Jarvis. And she'd been happy too. She'd been happy and she'd never noticed. And now it was too late. Alan was dead and gone, she'd missed her chance, she was alone.

She found tears rolling down her cheeks, because everything was so hopeless. At least, that was how it seemed. That could be the only explanation, for why else would she be crying? But where — deep inside — there should have been nothing but gloom and misery, she felt something else: a spark, a tremor, a sense of excitement — almost like hope.

CHAPTER THIRTEEN

Sir Hubert paced up and down the drawing room. 'Four days!' he bellowed. 'The strike is four days old. Now is the time for Lloyd George to act. Why doesn't Lloyd George do something?'

Sir Hubert's tone expressed no doubt, merely puzzlement. His faith in the Welsh Wizard had never wavered. Lloyd George had only to work his magic, and the crisis would be over.

There had been no mention of Lloyd George on the news that morning. They'd huddled round the crystal set, sharing the headphones. The detached and ethereal voice of the BBC had offered nothing, no real news at all. It had reminded Emily of the days of Madame Bobatska, sitting in a hushed circle, vainly trying the contact 'the Other Side'.

To Emily, this crisis had come completely out of the blue but Sir Hubert insisted it had been brewing for months — since last July at the very least when, on 'Red Friday' (as it had become known), the government had given in to the miners' demands and agreed to a coal subsidy. What this meant exactly, Emily wasn't sure, nor had she any memory of Red Friday. She'd seen, in recent weeks, newspaper headlines about the coal dispute but had not taken much notice. Strikes were ten a penny. There were strikes all the time, or so it seemed to Emily. Not a year had gone by when there wasn't a strike since the long, hot, fractious summer of 1911, the summer when Mama had arrived at the cottage in a carrier's cart. Even during the war there had been strikes, for all the talk of a nation united.

But this strike, Sir Hubert insisted, was different. This strike was unlike any that had gone before. This was a *general strike*.

'Baldwin, that slippery eel!' boomed Sir Hubert. 'I see his game. Red Friday my eye! That was just a ploy, to buy time, and so on and so forth. It was a delaying tactic. It gave the government time to prepare for a day of reckoning.'

Sir Hubert gave Mr Baldwin short shrift, but he had no time for the miners either. They had to learn to face reality and accept a pay cut. Most of them would probably agree to it, had they not been hoodwinked by their union, and by Mr Cook in particular, a troublemaker and a Bolshevist, who took his orders from Moscow, and who led the TUC by the nose.

Having thus dismissed the government and the miners, Sir Hubert turned his attention to the mine owners, for whom he had even less sympathy. The mine owners were nothing but a bunch of bull-headed, superannuated—

On and on he went, until Emily's head was spinning. And still she had little idea what it was all about.

The first she'd heard of the strike was on Monday (it was Friday now), when Chad had suddenly appeared at Heartlands.

'The general strike is on! It begins at midnight! I'm off to London, to see what's what. They'll need help at the docks, they'll need people to drive the trains. Or I might volunteer as a special constable. I can stay with Aunt Margery if necessary.'

'Foolishness!' Sir Hubert's bushy eyebrows had bristled. 'Don't be so hasty, young man! We must wait to hear what Lloyd George says. Lloyd George will know what to do.'

'Lloyd George? No one listens to Lloyd George anymore. Lloyd George is obsolete.'

Chad, in the past, would never have dared be so scathing. Emily wondered if his bitter experience with Lily Perks had changed him.

'Chad, darling, you will be careful, won't you?'

'Of course, Mother! Don't worry! I'm old enough now to look after myself!'

And so he'd gone, and there'd been no word from him since. Emily could not help but worry. She sensed that events had taken a very grave turn. She didn't need Sir Hubert to tell her, she could see for herself that the situation was fraught with danger. But what exactly was happening? Here at Heartlands they were cut off from the world. The newspaper had stopped coming. The ponderous voice of the BBC gave little away.

Emily paced round her bedroom, just as earlier Sir Hubert had paced in the drawing room. She had to find out what was going on, she simply had to. She bit her lip. Could she — dare she — go to London? If she caught *The Sparrowhawk* and—

Something bubbled up inside her at the thought of *The Sparrowhawk*: a wild feeling, almost joyous. A sense of adventure, perhaps? But that was impossible! She was the least adventurous person on Earth!

She bit her lip again in an agony of indecision, walking back and forth between her bed and the window. As she turned on one of her circuits, her foot connected with something and she stubbed her toe. She looked down and saw the wooden storage box which she had still not replaced under the bed. Her eyes lingered on it. A sense of unease took hold of her. There was something that she'd not noticed until she came to put her bits and pieces away last week. Only as she was replacing them in the box had it occurred to her that they'd not been in the right order when she took them out. They'd not been as she left them, the last time she'd looked in the box.

But that had been months ago, perhaps even years, so she couldn't be sure. She had dismissed her suspicions and abandoned the box where it still lay. Seeing it now, her suspicions returned, and this time they quickly hardened to a certainty. Someone *had* been through her things. And there was only one person it could be: Violet.

The thought of Violet looking at the photographs, reading the letters, was deeply disturbing. More than disturbing.

Almost intolerable. And what would Violet have made of that book, the book Aunt Margery had given to Emily in the summer of 1921? Emily blushed to think. Why had she not got rid of the book ages ago? She didn't want or need it.

She sank down to sit on the edge of her bed. Everything suddenly threatened to get on top of her — the uncertain atmosphere of the strike, worry over Chad, Violet's snooping. But almost at once Emily jumped to her feet again and, as she did so, she reached a snap decision. She *would* go to London. She *would.*

She got ready in a mad dash. She grabbed her handbag and stuffed into it the photographs, the letters, the mementoes of Chad, Aunt Margery's book. That would put pay to Violet. (But it wasn't Violet's fault that she was the way she was. It was society, Alan had said, it was their father. Women were pushed aside and ignored, their talents squandered. And Alan was right. Alan had always been so sympathetic, so understanding, so full of compassion. If only Alan had lived! The world needed Alans. The war had left the world with Sir Huberts instead.)

Emily could not bear to face Sir Hubert or Violet and all the explanations that would be necessary. She told the maid, Quinn, instead. She was going to London to visit her aunt, she would not be back for dinner, and she might be away for several days. Could Quinn remember all that? Could she tell the master and Miss Violet?

Quinn nodded solemnly, a conscientious girl. Emily left her mouthing the important message — committing it to memory — and went running down the drive.

* * *

There was no omnibus parked opposite the church.

The sense of disappointment was crushing. All her plans lay in ruins. So much for her vaunted sense of adventure.

But she should have known that of course *The Sparrowhawk* wouldn't come, with the strike and all the disruption it was causing. It was silly of her not to have thought of this. Silly, too, to have got dressed up, and for what? She felt quite ridiculous in all her finery, which might not have been out of place in London, but which made her stick out like a sore thumb in this sleepy village where nothing much had happened for half a thousand years.

Her sense of urgency evaporated. She wandered disconsolate across the village green. Spots of rain began to fall. It was cold for May, and rather dismal.

She glanced in passing at the war memorial. She had already walked by when something made her stop and go back and look again. She looked at it properly this time, facing the war full-on. All those names, carved in stone, those unknown men whose lives had been cut cruelly short. For a boy like Jarvis, however, there was no memorial. There was no memorial to his lost arm, his missing legs, the sweetheart he'd never had, the life he might have lived. So many of the war's victims went unrecognized, unremembered. Even Chad was a victim, in a way, forced to grow up without the man he'd called father. Emily felt humbled. She felt ashamed. In the face of such suffering and such sorrow, why was she worrying that her best coat and polished shoes might look out of place? It was so trivial. But that was all there was to her. Her life was entirely composed of trivia.

Sobered by her thoughts, she turned away and went meekly to the shop in the hope of finding a newspaper. There were none. But the price of milk was up, vegetables too. She picked over some sorry-looking cabbages, thinking of the cabbages that had grown in the cottage garden, sprouting from nowhere of their own accord, green and delicious.

As she inspected the slug-ravaged cabbages, she slowly became aware of a sound outside: a faint sound getting rapidly louder. She left the cabbages and hurried out of the shop. She was just in time. Rattling, humming, growling, shattering the age-long peace of the village, *The Sparrowhawk* appeared around a bend, swept past the row of cottages, circled the green, and came to rest in its customary place opposite the church.

Emily's heart danced. It was like meeting an old friend. And the fact that she was still here, the fact that she'd lingered in the village almost as if waiting, made it seem like destiny.

Ginger did not turn the engine off today. Emily hurried towards the omnibus, fearing that it might zoom away at any moment.

Midge jumped down to hand her up. They both began to speak.

'Hello! I wasn't sure you'd—'

'How do, Mrs Winmer—'

They both stopped, they both laughed. She felt rather shy of him, and sillier than ever for getting dressed up. But how smart he looked today, scrubbed and polished, his buttons gleaming, his boots shining, clean-shaven and bright-eyed.

Emily took a seat. Ginger wasted no time in getting going. The omnibus accelerated out of the village. Emily and Midge had to talk over the roar of the engine.

'First time we've seen you this week,' Midge ventured, pronouncing *week* as *wick*.

'I know. I wasn't sure, with the strike and everything—'

'We've tried to keep to timetable for sake of regulars, but with some changes.'

Most of the men who worked for the General, Midge told her, were out on strike — their union had called them out. This had proved an opportunity too good to miss. He and Ginger had extended their route into central London, to take advantage of the General's absence. With fewer buses on the streets, and the tube at a standstill, they'd been busy.

They were busy again today. As the omnibus reached the building plots, and then the outer suburbs, people began to pile on in numbers. Midge was soon hard at work, issuing tickets, handing out change, answering queries, signalling to Ginger when to stop and when to go. The babble of voices grew louder. There was an air of excitement. All ordinary, everyday reserve fell away.

'. . . I trekked all the way to the office yesterday, walked every step . . . one hears the most incredible rumours . . . it's all being funded by the Russians. The Russians are behind it all . . . soldiers guarding Hyde Park, soldiers on Oxford Street . . . somebody told me there was a pitched battle at Poplar . . .'

Emily half listened to the conversations going on around her, but most of her attention was centred on Midge. Every so often as he worked, he'd glance across or look over his shoulder, seeking her out with his eyes. She experienced a little shock every time. It made her blush to be caught staring. She mustn't stare, she told herself, it was rude to stare: Nanny had drummed this into her.

She forced herself to look out of the window, where rain was streaming down the glass, but it wasn't long before — inexorably, inevitably — her gaze was drawn back into the bus. He was making his way along the aisle, lithe and balanced and swaying with the movement of the bus. Their eyes met. His eyes seemed very brown, very big and round. He wasn't smiling. He looked rather grim, almost fierce. She saw colour flare in his cheeks as he brushed past her. Her heart was beating fast. It cost an effort not to turn in her seat and follow him with her eyes. But even though she couldn't see him now, she still knew exactly where he was. She didn't need to look.

She heard a voice in her head: Granny Drage's voice, sharp and reproving. *Shameless hussy, making sheep's eyes at men!*

Gradually, however, and for all her heightened awareness of Midge's presence, she found herself looking out more and more often at the passing streets, a feeling of unease growing inside her. Some streets seemed oddly deserted; others were teeming. There were very few motor vehicles, but many bicycles. She saw some people hurrying along, as if they had places to be. She saw others milling on street corners, as if killing time.

They met an omnibus coming the other way. Strangely, it had boards nailed across the windows either side, and barbed wire on the bonnet. And there, on the platform, standing to attention, with a rifle in his hand, was a soldier.

The bus flashed past. She craned her neck to see. Surely she had been mistaken. Surely what she had taken to be an armed soldier had in fact only been a uniformed conductor. But the other bus was already out of sight.

She hadn't been mistaken. It was no good pretending. She *had* seen the soldier, a soldier standing guard. Guarding against what? She gripped her bag, unease budding into fear.

It had stopped raining. There were gleeds of sunshine. The streets went on and on. The milling crowds grew bigger. There were some people standing now right in the road and they moved aside reluctantly, grudgingly. Others watched from the pavements, their hands in their pockets and badges on their lapels, hostility clear on their faces. Emily shrank into her seat, afraid of the truculent eyes. She was beginning to regret her journey.

Suddenly — and without any warning — the omnibus jerked sharply and began to skid across the road. Emily was nearly thrown from her seat. Desperately, she clung on. The bus was out of control. The buildings outside whirled past in a blur. Passengers were shrieking all round her.

There was a sickening crunch and the bus came to an abrupt halt. Emily's arm was almost wrenched from its socket as she clung to her seat. The pain, for a moment, made her giddy. When at last she was able to take stock, she found that the bus had come to rest at an angle, the floor tilted backwards and also sideways. She could see, out of the upturned windows, roof tops and chimney stacks, and the grey sky above. Inside the bus, bodies were rolling in the aisle and people scrambling to their feet. There were shouts of alarm, moans of pain. It was a scene of chaos.

It had all happened in the blink of an eye. Emily tried to steady herself. Her mind groped for some sort of explanation. But, at that moment, a window near her suddenly exploded. There was a deafening sound of shattering glass. Shards rained down on her. A brick bounced off the empty seat immediately in front of her and landed with a thump in the aisle.

'You dirty blacklegging bastards!'

The voice came from outside. Other voices joined in: harsh voices, angry voices. There was a pattering sound, as if it had started raining again, but Emily realized it was stones, a hail of stones. She put her arm up automatically, to shield herself, even though the stones were outside. She cowered in her seat as chaos became pandemonium — there was a mad scramble for the door.

The bus began to rock from side to side. Taken unawares, Emily lost her balance and tumbled off her seat. She landed awkwardly in the aisle, arms and legs flailing. People stepped over her, pushed past her. She tried to curl up into a protective ball but one of her legs was jammed and she couldn't get it free. She couldn't stand up, she couldn't protect herself, she was trapped, she'd be trampled. Struggling frantically, her rising sense of panic threatened to smother her.

All at once, she felt someone lifting her, freeing her leg, setting her on her feet. Strong arms were holding her.

It was Midge.

'All right, Mrs Winmer. All right. I've got you.'

She clung to him. He was like a rock in the shifting confusion. But though his words were reassuring enough, his voice was unsteady, and the tension in him was transmitted to her by the way he was holding her.

He ushered her towards the door. They floundered together along the aisle, staggering from side to side as the bus rocked ever more violently. Their feet crunched on broken glass.

She hesitated on the platform. Because of the tilt of the bus, the pavement seemed a long way down. Midge jumped then turned back for her. She flung herself forward. She seemed to fly through the air for an age, her heart in her mouth. Then Midge caught her and she was safe.

But she wasn't safe. She found herself in the midst of a vast crowd — a rabble — people pressing round her on every side. 'Scab! Blackleg! Traitor!' Someone spat in Midge's face. She saw the spittle slide stickily down his cheek, before he wiped it off on his sleeve. Nearby, a group of burly men were manhandling the bus, reaching long arms underneath it, rocking it back and forth. As she watched, they finally succeeded in tilting it right over. The crowd surged away from it as, slowly, almost majestically, it toppled onto its side. It came to rest with a crash, windows shattering, metal buckling.

It was then that she heard the sound of whistles. The crowd suddenly thinned. Gaps appeared. She could now see along the street. Several policemen were running towards the seething crowd, accompanied by some other young men wielding batons. Parts of the crowd turned to face this onslaught — others turned tail and began to run in the opposite direction.

Midge shouted in her ear. 'Mrs Winmer, we oughtta—'

But already the police were upon them. Whistles blew wildly. People were yelling, howling. Emily felt Midge tugging at her, trying to get her to move, but she couldn't, she was rooted to the spot.

A young man came wading directly towards her through the sea of faces, a young man in a Fair Isle jersey and plus fours. He had a police cap on his head, and was lashing out with a wooden baton, carving his way through the crowd, and yelling so hard that the tendons stood out in his neck like ropes.

'Come on then, you Bolshevist scum! Come on!'

She knew he was going to hit her: she was right in his path. There was nothing she could do but try to duck out of the way.

She ducked just in time. Instead of hitting her full-on, the baton landed a glancing blow across the side of her head. Pain erupted like a blinding light. Her knees buckled. She stumbled, clutching her head. There was a terrifying, heart-stopping moment, when she seemed to have gone blind. Then the world around her began to come muzzily back into focus. She saw Midge and the young man in the Fair Isle jersey, eyeball to eyeball. The young man raised his baton but Midge was quicker. He aimed his fist. It slammed into the young man's face. The young man reeled. His baton fell from his hand. Blood fountained from his nose. There was an expression of utter surprise on his face. Then he fell backwards and disappeared, swallowed by the seething crowd.

A shrill whistle pierced Emily's eardrums as a policeman bore down on Midge. The policeman's face was stern and inflexible. A long arm reached out to apprehend.

Suddenly, the policeman was shoved aside. In his place Ginger appeared — the bus driver, Ginger. He was waving, beckoning, calling.

'This way, Midge! Follow me!'

Ginger's hatless, carroty head showed up like a beacon in the melee. Emily did her best to follow him as he thrust his way through the streaming crowd. She had lost sight of Midge, Ginger was her last hope. But her head was throbbing, blood roaring in her ears. The world began to blur again. A feeling of terror seized her. She would be left behind. She would be lost. There was no knowing what might happen to her.

And then someone grabbed hold of her hand. She was tugged and pulled along. She stumbled, running blind, had no choice but to trust in her unseen helper.

Gradually the noise grew less, the chaos began to fade away behind her. She was brought to a halt. She blinked repeatedly. The fog before her eyes began to clear once more. She found she was standing in a narrow side street. Ginger was there, blood running down his face. Midge was there too. Like Ginger, he was hatless and dishevelled. He was still holding her hand. They were all three gasping for breath and shaking. It had begun to rain again.

'Our bus, Midge!' groaned Ginger. 'Our bloody bus!'

'Never mind the bloody bus. Look at state of you!'

'Some bastard—' Ginger didn't listen to Midge, carried on talking '—had poured oil all over the road. Didn't see it, did I, till it was too late.'

'Bugger that. Ginge mate, yer bleeding like a stuck pig.'

As if he'd only just noticed, Ginger reached up to wipe the blood out of his eyes, smearing it with his fingers across his face.

'It's nuffin. Just a scratch. Listen, cocker, we don't want to hang round here. They'll be rounding people up soon, if I know Old Bill. Let's go home. We can get cleaned up, decide what to do. Bring yer lady friend, if you like.'

But Midge had other ideas. 'You go 'head, Ginge. Get yoursen home, get yoursen sorted. I'll see Mrs Winmer right, then I'll follow on.'

Ginger hesitated. 'You sure, mate? Don't like leaving yer.'

'Give it a rest, Ginge!' said Midge roughly. 'I'm a big boy now. I can look after mesen. Stop mithering and gerron home, afore you bleed to death.'

They argued about it some more, but Midge would not be moved. To Emily's ear, their words sounded harsh, almost brutal, but there was also something reassuring — almost comforting — in the way they looked out for each other. Finally, with some reluctance, Ginger went on his way. He looked back a few times before disappearing round a corner, but Midge didn't notice. He had turned his attention to Emily. Her hand was still in his.

'Where can I tek yer, Mrs Winmer? Have you got somewhere to go?'

Emily frowned, trying to think. 'There's . . . there's Aunt Margery. She lives . . . she . . .' But the address wouldn't come. The pain pulsating in her head made it impossible to concentrate. She was shaking, too, and felt terribly weak. What was happening to her?

'You need summat for shock,' said Midge firmly. 'I could do with summat mesen. There's pub round corner, if I remember right. We used to come round these parts with *Sparrowhawk*, afore General kicked us out.'

He led the way, keeping hold of her hand. Emily felt like a little girl, walking with Nanny, holding Nanny's hand. But

Nanny would most definitely not have approved of going into a public house. If an ABC shop could be considered somewhat disreputable, then a pub was beyond the pale. Emily wanted to explain this to Midge, but couldn't summon the words. She was desperate to sit down.

They turned out of the side street onto a wider thoroughfare. The pub was on a corner. It had frosted windows and a sign over the door. Emily dragged her heels, troubled, afraid, but Midge forged on, pulling her with him, their stretched-out arms linking them. She had no choice but to follow.

The bar was busy. There was a babble of voices, smoke drifted and the smell of beer and tobacco was overpowering. Emily kept her head down, didn't dare look round. She felt horribly out of place, horribly conspicuous.

'Sit yoursen down, Mrs Winmer.' There was a little round table in one corner, with a bench against the wall. It was a huge relief to take the weight off her feet.

He let go of her hand to search in his money bag. He still had the money bag slung over his shoulder, but the ticket machine — like his cap — was gone. His mousey hair was tousled, tufts sticking up like the bristles of a broom.

He fished out a handful of change. He gave her a brief smile. 'Won't be a minute.'

As Midge moved off, an elderly man on a stool nearby said crustily, 'I don't hold with women in boozers.'

Midge, pushing his way to the bar, said over his shoulder, 'Hold your sweat, mate. Times is changing. Ant yer heard? There's a revolution going on out there.'

He disappeared into the crush at the bar. Emily sat hunched up, trying to be as unobtrusive as possible, avoiding the disapproving looks of the crusty old man.

In no time at all, Midge was back. He sat astride a stool opposite, the wobbly table between them, and handed her a glass. 'Brandy. For shock.' He'd bought a pint of beer for himself.

She felt a little better, now he was back. His broad shoulders blotted out a large part of the room, as if a defensive wall had been thrown up. She watched him take a long swig of beer. His adam's apple bobbed as he swallowed. The table trembled as he put his glass down. There was a rim of white foam on his top lip. He wiped it away with the back of his hand.

'Well, that were an adventure!' He tried to make light of it, grinning a little shakily, but there was a trace of bitterness in his voice. He took another swift swig of beer, then spoke again.

He spoke of the old days, when the pirate buses first appeared on London's streets, and the General had tried to get rid of them, sending buses out to tail them, to chase and harass them. 'Used to bumped up kerbs, run us off road — but they never tipped us right over, like today,' he added ruefully.

Emily shuddered, remembering. 'I don't understand. Why did they attack us? What had we done?'

Midge shrugged.

'Aren't you angry?' Emily demanded, getting angry herself. 'You ought to be angry, after what they did to us — to *The Sparrowhawk*.'

'They're right, though. I *am* a blackleg, Ginger and all.'

'What is a blackleg?'

'Them as won't support strike.'

Emily was confused. Midge and Ginger weren't blacklegs. They weren't in a trade union, they'd not been called out. But Midge explained that he and Ginger had taken advantage of the situation, extending their route to take the place of London General services stopped by the strike. He'd refused to have a police guard or an armed soldier on *The Sparrowhawk*, hoping to show that he and Ginger weren't taking sides, that they were staying out of it. But you couldn't stay out of it, he said grimly. You *had* to take sides. If you weren't *for* the miners, you were *against* them, and he should have realized that. But all they'd been thinking about, him and Ginger both, were their debts, and Ginger's wife and kids. They'd not stopped to consider the wives and kids of the strikers. They'd not stopped to think of the miners and their families, whose livelihoods the strikers were trying to defend.

Midge raised his glass to his lips but then a shudder went through him and he set the glass down again without having taken a sip. 'What were I thinking? I must be soft in the head. I could've got us all killed. I'd never forgive mesen if summat had happened to you, Mrs Winmer.'

'It wasn't your fault, Midge! You mustn't blame yourself! It was those people, those horrible people, like animals.'

'Oh, aye? And worrabout coppers? Worrabout them specials, throwing their weight about? It's one big game to folk of that sort. They've no idea what's like to live on miner's wages. I do. I know. Me dad worked down pit, me brothers too, and all they got for it were pittance.'

There was no mistaking the bitterness in his voice now. Emily was taken aback by just how bitter he sounded. She couldn't help feeling that some of it was aimed at her. If you weren't for the miners, he'd said, then you were against them. But she didn't know enough about it to be on anyone's side. And why should it matter about the miners anyway, here in London, miles from any colliery?

She racked her brains, trying to recall everything that Sir Hubert had said about the coal crisis. The miners' slogan, she remembered, was *not a penny off the day, not an hour on the day*. Sir Hubert had dismissed this as unrealistic. The miners had to face facts. The coal industry was in a mess. It was in desperate need of change. The miners must be prepared to make sacrifices for the greater good. But that went for the mine owners, too, Sir Hubert had added. If he had his way, he'd—

But she couldn't remember what he would do if he had his way. It was all too confusing. It didn't help that her head was still fuzzy with pain, that she was still shaken up. She couldn't feel any sympathy for the strikers, after what she'd just been through: she simply couldn't.

She watched Midge take another swig of beer, his hand curled around his glass: a big, brutal hand, it seemed to her just then, thinking back to how he'd used it as a fist in the melee by the omnibus. She could see it slamming into the face of the young special — and he had been very young, that boy, no more than Chad's age.

She shuddered at the thought of Chad — at the thought of Chad in London, in the midst of all this chaos. She'd been worried about him, but she'd little realized how much danger he might be in.

She wished she'd never left Heartlands. She wished she was back there now. She didn't want to be in this nasty, smoky public house, amongst strangers. She felt very alone. An unbridgeable gap had opened up between her and Midge. He seemed a long way off. She barely knew him. What sort of man was he? How could he possibly defend those thugs who'd attacked the bus? How could he be worried about the miners, when the miners wouldn't face facts, when they'd plunged the entire country into turmoil?

Cradling her brandy glass, she became horribly aware of the silence between them, a silence all the more pronounced because of the noise all around, a silence which made it seem as if they had nothing more to say to each other.

She glanced across at him. He was looking down, scowling, picking at the edge of the table. What was it he'd said just now about his father and his brothers? She'd not been listening properly, her head throbbing, but she thought he'd said something about them being miners. If that was the case, it would go some way to explaining his support for the strike.

She found herself curious about the brothers. How many brothers? Where were they now? He'd mentioned his father. What about his mother?

She might, under ordinary circumstances, have baulked at expressing any curiosity. Her natural timidity would have taken over. But here in the pub, with the brandy glowing inside her, she found her tongue loosened, she found it suddenly possible to bridge what had seemed unbridgeable.

'Were . . . were you a miner too, Midge?'

He shook his head. 'I never went down pit. Mam weren't keen on it — not after me dad and me brothers kicked they clogs — they was killed, I mean, they was killed down the mine, all of 'em.'

'Oh, Midge, I-I'm so — so sorry.'

'Nature of job, Mrs Winmer. Men have always died down pit.'

He spoke offhand, as if it was nothing, but his scowl deepened, and he picked and picked at the table. Oddly, she was put in mind of Chad, of Chad as a young boy. He'd frowned just as fiercely as Midge was frowning now, on the day he set off for school, his first term away from home. ('I'm all right, Mother. I'm not scared. I'm not scared at all.')

Emily almost laughed. As if there could be any real resemblance between Midge and a boy of eight! But thinking so made her less shy of Midge, gave her the confidence to continue the conversation, instead of letting it lapse, as she would have if she'd let her embarrassment get the better of her.

Midge needed only a little prompting before he offered up more. There'd been an explosion, he said, underground. The roof had caved in. His father and two brothers had been buried. He'd been just a lad when the accident happened and it had made a deep impression on him. When he left school at fourteen, he found work as a delivery boy, instead of signing on at the colliery.

'I dint have the guts, that's long and short on it. I dint have guts to go down pit. That's what they told me later, any road, when I were—' He stopped abruptly. He moved his now-empty glass around, nudging it with his fingers, his eyes focused on it. The little table wobbled slightly with each nudge.

A delivery boy's wages, he continued after a pause, weren't enough for them to live on, him and his mam, even with the extra she earned charring, and he'd begun to realize he had no alternative but to go down the mine: it was his only option. Then, out of the blue, something happened which changed everything. The war began.

'So I became a soldier—' (He pronounced it *sowjer.*) '— instead of a collier. I were only sixteen. Passed mesen off as older. No one asked no awkward questions. They dint, back then.' He nudged his glass again and the table wobbled. He laid both hands on it, palms down, to steady it.

Silence fell again between them, but to Emily this seemed a different sort of silence, not empty but intimate. The pain in her head had reduced to a dull ache. The fog in her eyes had melted away. Everything looked bright and sharp and clear. All the bustle of the pub, however, had receded into the background. Only Midge was in the foreground. He seemed very close now, just the tiny, wobbly table between them.

She finished the last of her brandy. She put her empty glass down next to Midge's. Her hand lingered there, curled up a little, as if still holding the glass. She looked at Midge's hands, pressed flat against the scoured surface of the table. She looked at his pared nails, his thick fingers, the lines and ridges of his skin. She looked at the tiny hairs growing, at the veins showing faintly blue. On his left hand was a pucker of red skin, a thin jagged line from knuckle to wrist, an old scar. A war wound, perhaps? Or the result of some hot-headed brawl?

She saw once again, in her mind's eye, the image of him punching the special.

He did it for you, said a voice in her head. *To protect you. He did it for your sake.*

He had come to her rescue. He had fended off the special, he had steered her clear of danger, he had led her to safety. He'd led her by the hand, keeping hold of her until they left the melee behind. His savage strength — his belligerence — had saved her.

What had it felt like, holding his hand? She'd been too dazed to really take it in. Now she'd never know, for why would he ever need to take hold of her hand again? A sense of regret swept over her, and a fierce longing to know how it felt to hold his hand. Her fingers seemed to move of their own accord, uncurling, extending. She watched them, feeling they belonged to someone else. The very tip of her middle finger brushed, as if by accident (it was a very small table), against the tip of Midge's middle finger. It seemed to Emily that a spark passed between them, as between the fingers of God and Adam in Michelangelo's painting in the Sistine Chapel, but the contact was so faint, so minimal, that Midge, with the calloused skin of his hands, probably hadn't even noticed.

She wanted him to notice — to know how grateful she was.

'I'm so glad—' Her words came out as a whisper, barely audible above the babble, so that, like their touching fingers, she was not sure he'd notice. 'I'm so glad you were with me today. I don't know what I'd have done without you.'

Even as she was speaking, it seemed to her ever more astonishing that they were sitting here, in this public house, somewhere in London, the two of them together. She might easily have been at Heartlands now, never having caught *The Sparrowhawk*, her courage having failed her. Or they might never have met at all. It was pure chance that had taken her to the village that day, the day she'd first seen the strange omnibus parked by the church. Pure chance, too, that he'd survived the war years almost unscathed, when he'd been a soldier from the tender age of sixteen, when so many had not been so lucky, when Alan was dead, and Jarvis crippled. It was miraculous — a miracle — this moment. So very unlikely. And yet they were here.

Her eyes met his. They looked at one another.

'I'm glad,' she whispered, wanting him to know, wanting it very much, 'that you came through — the war, I mean — and that I got the chance to meet you.'

'I came through—' He too spoke softly: it gave his voice a husky note. 'Safe and sound. Just my hand. My leg. Note but scratches. But . . . but after . . . when it were over—' He grimaced, turned his face away. As if through gritted teeth, he said, 'I'd a . . . a sort of breakdown. They put me in this place . . . a madhouse . . . an "asylum", they called it. Only right you should know.'

The sound of his voice set something vibrating inside her. The words barely seemed to matter: she was aware of them, yes, but only as part of a pattern, part of a greater whole. She felt that his outer layers had peeled away — the bus conductor putting on airs, the ruffian with his fists — leaving her sat opposite someone who was both different and yet the same: as if those other Midges were pale copies of this, the real Midge.

She didn't want him to feel ashamed of what he had told her. She didn't want him to think she was shocked or repulsed. After all, she knew only too well how fragile the mind could be. She had only to look at Mama. But in Midge's case, whatever it was he'd been through, he seemed thankfully to have recovered. He was luckier than Mama.

Her hand slid over his. She wanted to set his mind at rest and this was easier than words, a simple gesture, a quick reassuring pat. But somehow their fingers became entangled. He gripped tight. His face, however, was still turned away. She wanted him to look at her, to see it was all right, that she didn't think any the less of him — just the opposite. She squeezed his hand. She willed him. Slowly, slowly, his head began to turn. She braced herself for the nerve-racking moment when their eyes would meet.

And then—

'Time, gentlemen, please!'

A hand bell began to ring. There was a sudden surge of movement. All around people were draining their glasses, getting to their feet. The pub quickly began to empty.

Abruptly Midge stood up, removing his hands from the table, so that Emily, for a split second, felt completely bereft — as if there had been delicate threads beginning to weave between them, joining them, but now those threads had been snapped. They were two separate people once more. They were falling into the background, too, no longer alone and detached from it all, but part of the crowd. They were being swept away into the heedless ebb and flow of the city.

'Time, gentlemen! Can I have your glasses please!'

They made their way to the exit, Midge leading, Emily following. He set his shoulder against the door, pushed. Emily blinked in the daylight. It had stopped raining. The sun was shining. An age seemed to have passed since last she breathed fresh air. Yet it was still early, less than half the afternoon gone.

They were jostled along by the little crowd pouring out of the pub, but as the crowd thinned out along the street, Midge slowed and stopped — Emily too — as if they had no volition of their own, as if only the jostling crowd had kept them moving. She suddenly sensed that she'd been wrong to think all the threads had snapped. She must have been wrong, because she still felt herself drawn to him. Neither of them had spoken, not a word had passed between them since before they left the pub, but that didn't seem to matter.

She found herself in a shop doorway, sheltered from the tides of people on the pavement, cut off from the few cars, and the many bicycles, and a horse clip-clopping, drawing a laden cart which was covered with a tarpaulin. Midge was standing facing her. She looked into his eyes. Everything else faded away. She was aware only of him.

He took her in his arms and kissed her.

At once, she froze. Her body went stiff and rigid. She couldn't move.

It always happened. It had happened with Alan. Suddenly it wasn't Midge gently holding her in a shop doorway, it was *him*. She could feel his groping hands, she could smell his whisky breath.

Midge could not fail to notice. He would have needed a hide thicker than an elephant's, not to have noticed. She had become utterly unresponsive, her body as cold and hard as stone.

He stepped back. His eyes showed doubt, they showed confusion. And still she couldn't move, still she couldn't speak. She was locked away inside herself and had no way of putting things right.

'Mrs Winmer, I-I'm dead sorry — I never meant no harm—' He grew distressed, angry. His hands went up to his head and tore at his tousled hair. 'Christ! Bugger! You bloody fool, George Midgely! You bloody idiot! You've gone and ruined everything! Mrs Winmer, I don't know what come over me, I-I — oh, *bugger* it.'

He was gone. There was a blank space where he'd been standing just seconds before. It was as if he'd vanished into thin air.

Emily drew breath — and at once, as if at the touch of a button, all the noise of the street switched on again: the traffic and the people, a distant barrel organ, the endless hum of the city. A cold wind was gusting. It swirled in the shop doorway. She huddled in one corner, clutching her bag — but then she suddenly realized that her bag wasn't there, she didn't have it with her.

Somehow, somewhere, she had lost her bag.

* * *

Aunt Margery opened her own front door.

'Why, Emily, what a surprise! Is it really you? You're the last person I expected. Isn't it all thrilling! I'm quite buzzing with it! Charles says that— But, oh, Emmy: your head! You've a lump the size of a golf ball! You *do* look a state! What on earth has happened? No, don't tell me here on the doorstep. Come in. Come in. Andrews, help her. I think she's going to faint. What's that, Emmy? What's that, dear? You walked? Walked from where? What omnibus? I don't know what you mean. No, no, I can't see your bag. I can't see it anywhere. Are you sure you had it when you arrived? I don't think you did, you know.'

Emily, in the opulent drawing room, lay back exhausted on the chaise longue, footsore and aching. She was not quite sure how she'd managed to find her way, threading through a maze of London streets, until at long last she'd reached the purlieus of Belgravia.

'I walked and walked. I simply guessed the way. I didn't dare ask. I saw soldiers, I saw an armoured car. It didn't seem like London at all, it seemed like— Oh, no, Aunt, not more brandy, I couldn't!'

‘But you haven’t touched a drop yet. Do try to sip it, Emmy, I’m sure it would do you good. You’re white as a sheet.’

This was a different Aunt Margery — different to the pinched, cold, empty woman who’d come to Papa’s funeral all those years ago, different again from the woman in 1918 who’d snatched at every pleasure, bright but brittle. Now well into her fifties, Aunt Margery, if anything, appeared to have got younger with age. She had a girl’s zest for life, and a seemingly boundless source of energy.

She was full of news and she relayed it all with great relish. Five buses had been wrecked in Hammersmith yesterday. Street battles were raging all over London. Four policemen were dead, a Cabinet Minister seriously wounded. It was true, all true. Absolutely gospel. She swore to it. And now it was rumoured that two divisions of the Red Army were on their way from Russia, and the gas supply was going to be shut off at six o’clock — or was it seven?

‘Where will it all end, Emmy!’ cried Aunt Margery, her eyes gleaming with excitement. ‘We shall all be murdered in our beds! We shall be ruled by soviets! Charles, of course, says I’m talking nonsense. He insists there’s no danger at all. Men are going back to work in droves, he tells me, and the TUC are simply *desperate* to find a way to call it off. But you know Charles. So very down to earth, the darling!’

She laughed at her husband fondly. He was not at home. He was busy with this committee, and that committee, spent all day dashing from one meeting to the next. To hear Aunt Margery talk, one would have been forgiven for thinking Lord Ainsleigh was settling the dispute single-handedly.

‘He’s hardly ever home, Emmy. But guess who we have had! We’ve had Chad! You should see him in his police uniform, he looks simply gorgeous! Yes, yes, darling, he’s safe, quite safe. He’s enjoying himself almost as much as I am. You mustn’t worry about him. Now, Emmy dearest, have some more brandy. Oh, yes, do! It’s putting the colour back into your cheeks. Andrews! The decanter.’

It was not the same butler as on that day five years ago when there'd been a *woman* at the door not a *lady*, the same day on which Aunt Margery had given her that indecent book. Holding her glass up to be refilled, Emily wondered why she should notice this in particular — that there was a different butler — when there was so much else going on. But thinking about the butler, and then about the book, reminded her of her bag. She'd lost her bag. She must have left it behind in the omnibus. She would never get it back now. With her bag gone, she'd lost the whole of her life. Alan's letters. The mementoes of Chad. The picture of Mama and Papa. Lost, all lost. She had nothing left. She was already a woman without a future. Now her past, too, had slipped through her fingers and vanished.

Sipping her brandy on Aunt Margery's chaise longue, she felt infinitely old and tired.

CHAPTER FOURTEEN

Hyde Park was closed, cordoned off, the public not allowed in.

Midge turned away, not sure why he'd wanted to go to Hyde Park in the first place, not sure why he was here, in this part of London, though he'd always liked the look of the Park — all that space, all that green — passing it on the Bayswater Road in *The Sparrowhawk*, on the way to and from Hampton Court. That was in the old days, of course, when the pirate buses had been going strong, before the government stepped in, heavy-handed, giving all the profitable routes to the General, and driving the independents to the outer limits — or out of business.

He glanced behind him one last time, regretting that he'd come all this way and still hadn't properly seen the Park. But as he looked up at the imposing entrance — those big arches, all those white columns — it hardly seemed designed for a bloke like him, it was much too grand.

He trudged along a street. There was a wall on his left, running alongside the pavement. Trees were growing the other side of it, as if there was another sort of park in there. This, too, he was excluded from: the wall made that clear. Eyeing the big houses on the opposite side of the street, he wondered if Mrs Winmer's aunt lived round here somewhere. He had an idea that she did, but he wasn't sure.

He smiled grimly. So that was it, was it? That was the big idea? He'd come all this way on the off-chance of finding Mrs Winmer's aunt — or, more accurately, of finding Mrs Winmer herself. As if either of them would want to see him! Mrs Winmer, earlier, had made it all too clear what she really thought of him. She hadn't needed words. The look of terror on her face had been enough. But he should have expected it, a woman in her position, and him a lowly bus conductor. It must have come as much of a shock to her as if her footman or her gardener had made a lunge for her. (Did she have a footman and a gardener? But she must have, living in that big place out in the country.)

Midge groaned out loud. 'Why'd you do it, George Midgely? Why'd you kiss her, you great wazzock?'

Christ! Talking to himself! He was tuppence short of a bob, no two ways about it. They'd got it spot on at that asylum place. They'd hit the nail right on the head. And the fact he was traipsing all over London, chasing castles in the air, only went to confirm it.

One disaster had followed another today. He'd nearly got her killed when *The Sparrowhawk* came a cropper. (Oil on the road: that was deliberate, that was. It had been an ambush.) Then, in the pub, he'd talked too much, spilling his guts — as if she was interested! To top it all — the piece de resistance, as the Frogs would say — he'd shoved her into a shop doorway and put his great mucky paws all over her. No wonder she'd frozen up. No wonder she'd been horrified. He ought to have known better. He ought to have kept in his place. She was like Hyde Park — she was like the garden on the other side of this wall. She was out of bounds, out of his reach, forbidden. He really ought to have *known*.

He *had* known — to start with. He'd got the measure of her on their first, brief meeting, in that little village with the church and the pub. She'd been off with him that day. She'd given him short shrift. She'd turned her nose up at

The Sparrowhawk. An uppity cow, he'd thought. A right toffee-nosed snob. But then, later, when he'd got to know her a bit, she'd seemed all right, she'd seemed down to earth, she'd talked to him on the level. She was posh, yes, but she didn't rub your nose in it. She was always painstakingly polite. She was quiet and shy. There was no side to her at all. And she wasn't the least bit vain. Just the opposite. It was as if no one had ever told her how beautiful she was. It was as if she'd never looked in a mirror. She was like a closed-up flower, her full splendour hidden. She was like a closed-up flower, waiting for the sun. Why was it the sun had never shone for her? It made his heart hurt to look at her, all closed-up like she was.

Slogging through the streets, taking little notice of his surroundings, Midge's mind was full to bursting, full of Mrs Winmer. He pictured her as she'd looked in that pub earlier, sitting in the corner in her cream coat with the big lapels, a string of beads round her neck, a neck so very white and delicate and slender. He remembered how she'd watched him from under the wide brim of her hat. He remembered their fingers touching on the table top and the way he'd come up in goose pimples. He'd felt it, sitting with her: he'd felt that feeling, the feeling that ran up your spine, that clenched the pit of your stomach, that made your knees tremble. This was what she did to him with just a look, with the merest touch of her finger. He'd been rocked on his heels. He'd been bowled over.

But he'd got the wrong idea. He'd misread all the signs. He, George Midgely, with his one-track mind—

Oh, yes. They'd got that right, too, in the madhouse. They'd shown him up for what he was. What were the words they'd used? His *lewd thoughts about women*. That was it. They hadn't half been clever, those people in the madhouse. They'd seen right through him. And here he was now, exactly as they'd described him, his lewd thoughts and his talking to himself, his walking round in a dream. He was cracked, that's what he was. Cracked, crazy, doolally-tap. No two ways about it.

'No two ways,' he repeated out loud, startling some old dear with a walking stick who was coming the other way.

That's it, madam. Mind the loony. Make way for the loony. Steer clear of the bloody loony.

He laughed bitterly and stopped to look round, taking stock. Where was he now? Some sort of big square. And there — you couldn't mistake it — the Houses of Parliament. He'd never seen them so close before. He gawped at their gothic splendour. Were they inside right now, he wondered, Mr Baldwin and all that lot, passing laws and making plans and plotting the downfall of the strike? It was nothing but a talking-shop, that place, but it was so big and grand that it sort of weighed you down. This city was full of buildings like that, massive buildings that made a bloke feel small, that made a bloke feel as if there were people out to get him.

Or was that just his doolally brain playing tricks?

There were spits and spots of rain in the air. He hunched his shoulders, not looking at the Houses of Parliament, looking at the pavement instead as he shuffled along, aimless. People passing seemed not to notice him, as if he wasn't there. He was a nobody, the ghost of a man.

There were times when he liked it, when it suited him, being on his tod. Those Sundays when he'd hiked round London, when it was all new to him and there'd been so much to discover: he'd enjoyed himself back then. But every so often he was ambushed by a feeling of loneliness. He tried to fight against it, the way they'd told him in the asylum, but you couldn't alter the facts. He had no one. No family. Nothing. Even his memories of Mam and Dad and Sid and Ernie seemed somehow to have no connection to him, as if he'd stolen someone else's childhood and passed it off as his own. If he tried to picture them now — Dad and Sid and Ern — he saw them all black from the pit, with black hands and black faces and the whites of their eyes showing. He saw them in their caps and jackets and moleskin trousers, with straps tied round the knees to keep the coal dust out. He remembered their wooden clogs and their water bottles and their stooped and sloping gait, coming in from work.

'Here he is!' Sid and Ernie had grinned at him, showing their teeth. 'Here he is, Mam's little darling!'

They'd roughed him up, getting him all mucky, as they waited for Dad to finish with the bath. They'd been bigger and stronger, and there'd been two of them. He'd fought like a tiger, but he never stood a chance. How he'd hated them, as they knocked him about, laughing. How he'd sworn at them, and wished them dead.

And then they *had* died, Dad too.

'How do you feel about that, George? Do you feel it's your fault? Do you imagine that it was you who brought about their deaths?'

This was what they'd asked him in the madhouse. But he wasn't as cracked as all that. He'd not caused the explosion. It had nothing to do with him.

'You feel guilt. You feel ashamed. You blame yourself, because you survived and they didn't.'

The know-alls in the madhouse had been only too keen to tell him what he was thinking, what he was feeling.

It was raining properly now and he meandered to a stop on the pavement. He wondered if he should seek shelter, but there didn't seem much point when he was already wet. He leaned over a parapet. He looked out at the river. There was a bridge to his left, there was a bridge to his right, he wasn't sure of their names, he always got the names wrong, as Ginger was never slow to point out. ('That's not London Bridge, you doughnut, it's Tower Bridge. Tower Bridge has towers. Clue's in the name.') The Houses of Parliament were now away to his right, looming over the river, massive, fastidious, self-important. Across the water was yet another of those immense buildings which weighed you down, which made you feel empty and listless and helpless.

He conjured up Sid and Ernie, who'd never been listless, who'd always had the energy to rough him up, even after a shift down the pit. It was funny to think that he was older now than they had been when they died — funny to think that he was older now than his big, bullying brothers. He'd like to have seen them get the better of him now. He'd have liked to see them try.

The rain streamed down his face as he thought of the explosion which had brought down the roof of the mine and buried Dad and Sid and Ern, killing them. Had they been crushed instantly to death by the vast weight of the groaning earth falling on top of them? Or had they been trapped underground in the dark, had they slowly suffocated as the air ran out? In the weeks and months after the accident, he'd experienced both kinds of death for himself, waking up night after night fighting the blanket, thinking he was being crushed and asphyxiated.

'Dunna send me down pit, Mam! I dunna wanna go!'

Mam had shushed him and stroked his brow and told him he didn't have to go down the pit, she wouldn't let him go.

Staring at the grey river, pockmarked by rain, Midge thought of how, at age eleven, you believe your mam, you think there's nothing she can't do, but at sixteen you start to see things differently. He'd seen how she went without so that he would have enough. He'd seen how thin she'd become and hollow-eyed. He'd seen that it was time he started earning more than a delivery boy's small change. Mam would never send him down the pit: she'd promised. Which meant he would have to send himself.

Then the war had started: deliverance.

The rain was falling heavily now. Rain was flattening the hair on his head, running down inside the back of his collar and seeping in through a hole in his boot.

Don't get your feet wet, Georgey.

That was what Mam had said to him when he set out on his big adventure, going off to war.

Look after yourself, Georgey, she'd said (he tried to recall her voice, couldn't). *Look after yourself. Don't get in with the wrong crowd. Keep away from bad girls. And be sure not to get your feet wet.*

'Aw, Mam, gerroff, yer smothering me! I'll be dead afore I reach the war, this rate!'

She'd stood on the front step with her hands in her pinny, where he'd seen her standing so often down the years. Had he looked back and waved? He liked to think that he had. He couldn't after a dozen years be sure.

He turned away from the parapet. He walked in the pouring rain. Water squelched in his boot. His wet woollen sock rubbed against his foot. As he walked he clenched his fists. He would have liked nothing better than to give his sixteen-year-old self a clout round the head, the boy who'd been embarrassed by the fuss Mam made, the boy who'd hadn't kissed her goodbye, the boy who'd not looked back or waved (face facts). Now — now he'd let her fuss him all she wanted. He'd let her fuss him non-stop day and night until the end of time, if only he could hear her voice again, and see her, and smell her and feel her cool hand on his brow, the way he'd felt it in the dark of his tiny bedroom as she soothed away the terror of the nightmares.

He'd come home on leave for the first time in 1917, fresh from fighting in the Flanders mud, and with his hand bandaged. They'd gone over the top less than two weeks before. It was the third time in three years that his battalion had been cut to pieces. Somehow he'd come through it yet again and he'd been sent on leave. Dog-tired and footsore, with blood seeping through the bandages where his wound had reopened, he had walked the weary miles from the station, taking a footpath that was a short cut and which led him up to a low ridge of land where he could look across at the village on the far side of the little valley, rows of grubby cottages with grey slate roofs. *Home*, he'd thought. Not a word, but a feeling — an ache inside, which had sliced into his heart that afternoon, the way two weeks earlier shrapnel had sliced into his hand. The tall colliery chimneys had been belching white steam and black smoke. Golden sunshine lay on the stark, grey slopes of the slag heap. Stencilled against the cloud-dotted sky, he'd seen the big, round gin-wheel which, ever since the day of the explosion, had taken on a sinister significance for him. Ragged, coal-stained colliers had been streaming in long lines across the threadbare fields below him. He'd followed in their wake. He'd lingered for a moment under the railway bridge, staring at the slimy wall where he used to stand with Evie, kissing and cuddling whilst coal trains rattled overhead. He'd listened to the sound of water dripping, echoing. He'd been caught unawares by a stirring in his loins, the first for many, many months.

Leaving behind the twilight under the bridge, he'd climbed the slope and walked along the cobbled street where children were playing, their voices shrill in the evening air. Women on their doorsteps had watched him pass. He'd felt their eyes on him. Everything had been just as he remembered, but he'd felt like a stranger. He wasn't Georgey anymore, he was Midge: that was what they called him in his platoon. He was a well-worn old soldier, hard-bitten at nineteen.

He'd reached his home. The door had been locked. There'd been no answer when he knocked. He'd looked in at the front parlour window. The curtains had gone, the furniture too. Had Mam fallen on hard times? So hard she needed to sell the furniture?

Mrs Crossley had come out from the next cottage. She had stood on the threshold with her arms folded.

'How do, Mrs Crossley. Where's me mam?'

'How do, George. You're back, then. Yer mam's not here, duck. Her's gone.'

'Gone? Gone where?'

'Ant you heard, then, George? I'd a-thought you'd a-heard.'

'Heard what, Mrs Crossley?'

'Were letter what done it, the letter as come. "Missing believed killed," letter said.'

'Who's killed, Mrs Crossley?'

'You, George. You. "Missing believed killed." Her thought you were dead.'

'But I int. I int killed. I int missing. I'm here. I'm back.'

'Ah. Well. Her dint know that, did her.'

'Where is she, Mrs Crossley? Where is she?'

'They . . . they found her in cut.'

An accident, Mrs Crossley said. Mam had often been seen wandering round at all hours, after the letter came. She'd missed her footing in the dark. She'd fallen in the canal and drowned. An accident, Mrs Crossley had insisted. But there'd been a hint of doubt in her voice.

He'd missed the funeral by a week. The cottage had been cleared beforehand, the contents sold, to pay for the burial.

Mrs Crossley had told him all this, then she'd fallen silent, watching with patient eyes as he stood there not knowing what to say.

Walking back along the now-deserted cobbled street as dusk fell, all he'd been able to think was: *Where do I go now, then?* He was on leave, with nowhere to go.

And then he'd seen Evie.

He'd have known her anywhere. He'd run to catch her up. His army boots striking the cobbles had sounded loud in the evening silence.

'Evie! Evie! Wait!'

She'd lingered in the street. Breathless from running, he'd reached her.

'Evie.'

'How are yer, George? We heard you were dead.'

She'd looked at him — or *not* looked at him, would be nearer the mark: as if he wasn't really there. There'd been a shawl round her shoulders. She'd held it close to her.

Words had seemed great, ungainly things that he struggled to get his mouth round. 'Do you remember, Evie, what you said to me afore I went away?'

'I said lots of things. I canna remember them all.' She'd glanced behind her, along the empty street. 'I'll have to go, George. I only popped out for a bit o' marge.' She'd hesitated, then added, 'I'm wed now, George. Tom Shawcross axed us, and I said yes. Tom Shawcross earns good money down pit.'

'But Evie . . . Evie . . .'

She'd looked him full in the face at last. She'd been defiant. He'd changed, she said. He was not the boy she remembered. He looked different, he even spoke different, she'd never have known him.

She'd hurried away. She'd dwindled into the dusk. He had never seen her again.

Never mind the trenches, thought Midge mordantly as he walked along the Embankment in the rain nine years later. Never mind the bleeding trenches. He'd been more shell-shocked by his leave than by anything he'd gone through in the trenches.

It had come as a relief to leave Blighty behind and get back to the front.

The rain was easing now. A grey light, like a film of dust, marked the first onset of evening. Midge, bedraggled, limping a little where his foot had rubbed, made his way once more to the parapet. He gazed up at Cleopatra's Needle, pointing cryptically at the overcast sky. He watched as a lone locomotive came steaming across the railway bridge that was now to his right, trailing a long string of carriages from the direction of Charing Cross. He wondered where the train was going, to what far-flung corner of England, places he had never seen, probably never would.

He rubbed the smooth stone of the parapet. He looked at the scar on his hand, the wound of 1917. Later he'd been wounded in the leg, more serious. That had left a scar too. But his mutilated mind, that had no scar, there was no outward sign.

When was it the symptoms had first started to become evident? Not during the war. There'd been no time during the war to notice anything. Nothing, in any case, had been normal during the war. Afterwards — after he'd been demobbed — he'd found it hard to settle, somehow. He hadn't been able to sleep. He would get angry for no particular reason. He'd often found himself weighed down with worry — sweating and shaking with it — but when people asked him what exactly he was worrying about, he hadn't been able to say. He'd resented them asking. He'd felt they were trying to trick him in some way.

There'd been lots of questions of this sort — trick questions, he called them — in the madhouse. Much of that time was now hazy in his memory. The demeaning moments, the degrading moments, the despairing moments: they were the only clear memories that remained.

They'd fired questions at him, one after another.

'Do you have lewd thoughts about women? What are your experiences with prostitutes? How often do you masturbate?'

He'd tried not to listen to the questions, hanging his head. He'd been ashamed — ashamed of them, as well as himself. He'd watched what he said. But he'd made mistakes, all the same. And they'd read things into his silences. He'd begun to think they could read his mind.

'Self-abuse is a serious affliction. It undermines the entire nervous system. It causes weakness and lethargy. Unchecked, it leads to madness.'

Their pointed remarks had seemed to serve a purpose of which he was only dimly aware. They had watched him. They had written things down. They had spoken to each other as if he wasn't there.

'He admits to a pathological fear of coal mines.'

'Ah. I see. So symptoms of cowardice were manifest long before the war.'

'It's become fashionable to blame the war for everything, for all manner of underlying conditions. Nine times out of ten, we find the war has nothing to do with it.'

To his dismay and distress, they had somehow found out about Mam.

'Your mother, I've been informed, took her own life. Is that true? Well? It's a straightforward question. Was she fished out of a canal, or wasn't she? Yes, yes, I hear what you're saying, but you have to realize that people often claim an accident in such cases. The facts, I'm afraid, usually speak for themselves. Suicide is classic evidence of congenital mental weakness, a weakness which will have been passed down to you. What you are suffering from is an inherited degeneracy. Do you see?'

Midge remembered sitting slumped in a chair in the middle of an office. He remembered it vividly, the distempered walls, daylight seeping in through a grubby window, a grubby floor beneath his feet. His chair had seemed adrift from the large desk that dominated the room, a big space separating him from the white-coated doctor perched on the edge of the desk, swinging his foot. The doctor had been speaking to him in an offhand, conversational tone.

'Lunatics. Idiots. Imbeciles. Epileptics. Deaf-mutes. Deviants.' The list went on and on, the doctor ticking off each item on his fingers. 'Criminals. Tramps and vagrants. Suicides and prostitutes and perverts. The feeble-minded, the backward, the congenitally blind. These are all inherited characteristics — and they are characteristics which are on the rise. It's evidence of an increasingly tainted blood stock. The population at large is being slowly but inexorably swamped by degenerates. This degenerate strain proliferates because of unregulated procreation. It's a problem that threatens the very survival of our race. We need urgent solutions. If I had my way, you'd all be sterilized.'

By this casual use of 'you', the doctor had lumped Midge in with the rising tide of degenerates.

'Sterilization, in my opinion, is the only humane answer.'

Midge, in the asylum, had often been overwhelmed by a dark mood beyond even the realm of despair. He'd described it to himself as like being encased in a giant egg. Numb, immobilized, he had sat on his bed and hugged his knees, alone inside his egg, inside the impervious shell.

Standing on the Embankment, he remembered what it was like, being cut off from the world, encased. Almost he felt himself back there, enveloped by the numb feeling, the nothing feeling. But slowly he became aware of something breaking in on him. A sound. A bell. Attacking the shell around him. Attacking it like the beak of a bird, pecking, pecking, pecking — each chime another peck. The chimes of a clock, shivering through the grey dusk. But not just any clock.

Aloof, magisterial, immeasurably dignified, Big Ben was ringing the hour.

Midge looked round, as if waking from a deep sleep. The Embankment was all but deserted. But sweeping now towards him along the road, the noise of their engines growing rapidly louder, a long convoy of vehicles came swiftly from the direction of the Houses of Parliament. He shrank against the parapet as they passed, trucks and armoured cars, guns pointing, soldiers standing on alert. The pavement trembled under the weight of their heavy wheels. He watched them speed on their way, disappearing into the dusk. The sound of their engines faded.

He wondered where they were heading. To force open the docks? To keep supplies moving? To crush the strike with the government's iron fist? The strikers stood no chance in the face of such ruthless, such regimented, such naked force.

He turned back to the river, shivering in his wet clothes as a thin breeze blew along the Embankment. Where could he go now? Ginger would be waiting for him, and Nell, but somehow he couldn't face them. *The Sparrowhawk* was wrecked. His and Ginger's bus service was at an end. What was left? Just debts to pay. That was all he had: debts, and Mrs Winmer's pity. It stung, her pity. But he was a fool if he thought it could ever be different. He was a fool if he thought a man like him could make the sun shine for a woman like her.

He leaned over the parapet, staring at the river, its wide surface whipped into waves by the breeze, the grey-brown water lapping at the walled banks, a strong current flowing, swirling round the piers of the bridge. He'd be better off feeling nothing, than feeling like this, so full of anguish. He'd be better off locked inside the impervious egg. But as he watched the river — as he stared at it and stared at it — the ceaseless moving current seemed to draw him out of himself. He felt as if he was floating on the tide. He felt as if he was being tugged from his moorings. He was in danger of being swept away. He clung on. But a voice inside him whispered, *Let go, let go!*

The voice inside him said, *Let go*. And all he wanted was to obey.

CHAPTER FIFTEEN

Emily awoke for a second morning amidst all the luxury of Aunt Margery's guest room, stretched out in a vast bed, in a borrowed nightdress, silk (she had forgotten to bring one of her own, having left Heartlands in such a hurry). She lay there, listening to the quiet of a London Sunday. Solitary footsteps sounded outside in the street. They slowly faded to silence.

It was the sixth day of the strike. The BBC was reporting a mass return to work, but there still seemed no end in sight. Emily wondered how they were getting on back at Heartlands. Was Sir Hubert even yet waiting for Lloyd George to speak? Yesterday evening, it had not been Lloyd George but the Prime Minister who'd delivered an address on the wireless. He was a man of peace, he'd said. He desired to maintain the living standard of every worker. Have faith in him and he would see that justice was done.

'Dear old Stanley.' Aunt Margery had switched off the wireless and reclined on the chaise longue. 'He is always so *reassuring.*'

They had been alone together in the drawing room. Lord Ainsleigh had gone rushing off to one of his committees.

'And then to his club, if I know Charles,' Aunt Margery had added. 'There's nothing men like more than a good gossip. And they have the cheek to mock women over it!'

Emily, lying in bed, looked round the guest room. Her eyes lingered on the simple, elegant lines of the Heppelwhite wardrobe, on the rich pile of the Persian carpet, on the intricate patterns of the painted ceiling, on the velvet curtains draped languorously across the wide window. Her mind gaped to think that one day all this would be hers. And yet that was what Aunt Margery had told her last night.

Emily had been sipping coffee in the drawing room and inspecting a Gainsborough landscape on the wall — wondering if such an Arcadia had ever really existed outside of the imagination of the artist — whilst Aunt Margery watched her from the chaise longue. At length, Aunt Margery had said, 'You do realize, Emmy, that one day it will be yours?'

Emily had looked round, nonplussed. 'This painting?'

'Not just the painting, dearest Emmy: everything.' Seeing Emily's blank expression, Aunt Margery had gently chided, 'Well, really, Emmy, I thought you'd have worked it out. Charles and I do not have children. Charles is an only child. And I have only the one niece: you. There really is no one else we would rather leave everything to. We're awfully fond of you, Emmy dear, always have been. There are, of course, some distant relatives on Charles's side who will need to be taken into consideration, but the bulk will go to you.'

Emily had stood with her mouth open, trying to make sense of Aunt Margery's words. She had never thought of Lord Ainsleigh's fortune as having anything to do with her. 'I-I don't know what to say, Aunt.'

'There's no need to say anything. I just wanted to be certain that you knew. We were thinking, however, Charles and I—'

'Must we talk about it, Aunt Margery? I'd really rather not. It won't happen for years and years. You will go on forever.'

'Yes, well, I *do* feel rather sprightly for my age, I must admit. But that's all the more reason, as I was about to say, for us to— Well, it can't be much fun for you, cloistered away at Heartlands.'

'I've never said—'

'No, of course not, Emmy, you never complain about anything. You are such a dear, so wonderfully forbearing. But that doesn't mean you have to go on living as you are. Charles and I were talking. We really ought to have thought of it before. We'd like to give you a little something now: a lump sum or an allowance, whichever you prefer.'

'Oh, Aunt Margery, don't, please don't! I couldn't. I couldn't possibly!'

But Aunt Margery had been adamant: she and Charles were quite decided. Lying now in bed, Emily found her mind racing, thinking of all that this might mean. She could escape from Heartlands. She could set herself free. She could find a little place to rent, or maybe to buy, somewhere Chad could come in his holidays. Her time would be her own. She could shape her days to her own devising.

But what exactly would she do? What would she do all day? She pictured, automatically, a home like the little cottage where she had lived with Alan. But, really, the cottage had been terribly inconvenient: no electricity, water from a well, the nearest town miles away. It had been made bearable, it had been transformed, because she had Chad — and, she was ready now to admit, because of Alan. But Alan was dead, and Chad would soon fly the nest for good. What would become of her then?

She baulked at the idea of living alone. Yet other women had to face it. Thousands, perhaps millions. So many men had been killed in the war, husbands and sweethearts and potential bridegrooms: bridegrooms who would now remain forever unknown to the brides they might have married. Other women had to face life alone. Why should she be any different? She would manage. She would have to.

But the world since Friday seemed a much more dangerous place. She had seen just how thin was the veneer of polite society and cultured civilization. Underneath, and ready to rise up at any moment, was a different world, a world of cruelty and brutality and violence. She had seen this for herself. She would not forget.

Somehow, though, it was impossible to feel anything but safe and secure, coddled in all the luxury of Aunt Margery's guest room.

Sighing with contentment, Emily allowed herself a little longer to relax in bed before she peeled back the covers and prepared to get up.

* * *

When they got back from church, Lord Ainsleigh went straight out again: he had an important meeting before lunch.

'Oh, Charles, on a Sunday!' Aunt Margery reproved him. Then, brightening, she had added that she might just pop out herself on a little fact-finding mission.

'You want a good gossip with the neighbours, is what you mean,' her husband had teased her.

Aunt Margery had given Emily a look. 'What did I say, Emmy, about men and their clubs?'

Husband and wife had set out together, laughing and joking, at ease.

Sat now with the depleted Sunday papers, and the latest edition of the government's emergency news sheet, the *British Gazette*, Emily looked up as she heard the doorbell, wondering who could be calling at this hour on a Sunday.

A moment later, Andrews appeared. 'There's a gentleman to see you, ma'am.'

'To see *me*?' She couldn't think who. Not Chad. Chad would have walked straight in. (Where *was* Chad?)

Emily waited on the sofa, the newspapers forgotten. After a moment, Andrews showed in a man wearing a cheap Sunday suit. The man doffed his cap, revealing a mop of carroty hair. It was the hair which gave her a first clue, and then of course she recognized at once the bus driver, Ginger.

He looked different out of his driver's uniform, somehow diminished, slim and slight with a boyish face and freckles across his nose. Cuts and bruises showed as evidence of the fracas on Friday.

'Beg pardon, Mrs Winmer. I hope you don't mind me calling on you like this.'

'That's quite all right. Do please sit down.' (What was his name? She only knew him as Ginger.)

'I brung you this.' He took a pace forward, holding something out.

'My bag!' She had been so sure she would never see it again. She took it from him, almost reverently. 'It's so very kind of you to bring it. I thought I'd lost it forever.'

Ginger sat gingerly on the edge of a chair, fiddling with his cap. 'Your bag was still on the bus, missus, where you dropped it, seemingly. I went to have a butchers at our bus. It's badly mashed up.'

'I'm so sorry, Ginger — but I can't keep calling you "Ginger".'

'Ginger'll do, missus. Even me old gal calls me Ginger.' He twisted his cap, glanced at her, reticent. 'To tell the truth, I didn't just come about the bag. I was wondering, Mrs Winmer, if you'd seen Midge?'

'Well, no, I haven't, not since Friday.' She blushed to remember Friday, yet she'd done little else these last two days except remember. Midge had been so much on her mind, that it came as a relief to be able to talk about him — and to someone who knew him, too. 'But isn't he with you, Ginger? I thought he lived with you?'

'Yeah. He does. But he's not been home since Friday. We're getting worried, me and Nell.'

'Oh, Ginger, you don't think anything's happened, do you?'

'Midge can look after himself, missus.'

'Yes. Yes, of course.'

But she sensed that Ginger was not quite as sure of this as he sounded — he was just sticking up for his mate, the way she would defend Chad if anyone spoke against him. She was reminded of how solicitous Ginger had been of Midge after the fight by the bus, and how irritated Midge had been by it — by all the 'mithering'. It seemed to put a new slant on the relationship between these two former comrades-in-arms, but she could not quite work out what it meant. She hesitated to mention the asylum.

Ginger looked at her guardedly and she wondered how much he could guess of what she was thinking.

He said slowly, as if feeling his way, 'I know him, missus. He'll not get hisself in any scrapes. He'll not do nuffin stupid. Least — what I mean to say is — he'll not do nuffin all at once. But he winds hisself up. He gets down on hisself. He starts thinking the worst. Who can blame him, after all what he's been through, the old mucker.'

'Everything he's been though?' echoed Emily. 'The — the war?'

Ginger glanced at her charily. 'That's right. The war, and all that carry-on. Enough to make anyone think the worst, that was — know what I mean?' Ginger grew suddenly anxious. 'Don't go getting the wrong idea, missus—'

'Of course not.'

'I'm not saying he's a nutter or nuffin.'

'But he did have some sort of — of breakdown.'

'He told you that, did he?'

'Yes.'

They looked at each other, both rather breathless — or so it seemed to Emily. They'd come into the open, giving voice to what they'd both really been thinking.

Ginger regarded her with some surprise. 'He don't usually like to talk about all that.'

'He — he didn't go into much detail.'

'He weren't raving, nuffin like that — he weren't *violent*. Think I'd have had him in the house if he'd been violent, with the kiddies and all? He had a bit of a funny turn, that's all. He weren't near as bad as they made out. But this old bag next door — interfering busybody, she was — she reported him, and they come and took him away. We told 'em he was right as rain, but would they listen? Would they hell as like.'

'And was he — right as rain?'

'He weren't A-1, to tell the truth. But he'd have got back on his feet if they'd let him alone. Way I see it, weren't no different to any other wound — weren't no different to the Blighty he got in his leg.'

'He told me about that, too.'

'Did he? Did he, now?' Ginger shot her another glance. 'He told you a lot, seemingly.'

She sensed that Ginger was weighing her up, reassessing her. She almost felt that he might respect her: not the 'yes ma'am/no ma'am' respect of a lackey, but the respect one gives to an equal.

After a pause, Ginger continued. 'His leg: it needed time to heal. Shrapnel wound, it was. Just below the knee. He's still got the scar. Reckon it gives him gyp now and then — not that he'd let on. But this trouble of his, up here—' Ginger tapped his own head. 'That was a wound, too. Not the sort what you put bandages on, but a wound all the same. All it needed was time to heal. Then they go and cart him off to the nut-house, and—' Ginger frowned, which, with his red colouring, gave his sharp-eyed but honest face a startlingly fiery look. 'All I know is, they never fixed him up in that place, they only made him worse.' Ginger's knuckles grew white, as he twisted his cap into a tight spiral on his lap. He burst out, 'I know their game. They tried to make out as he's not right in the head, that he's never been right, that the war had nuffin to do with it. That way, see, they won't have to pay him any sort of pension — a what-d'you-call-it — an invalidity pension. Not their fault, so they needn't cough up. I reckon they went on at him in that place so much that they had him half believing it, they got him thinking he was coward born and bred, just because he never fancied going down the pit. You heard as his old man copped it down the pit, his brothers and all? Well, mean to say, if that'd been me — my brothers, my old man, and me just a kid — you'd not have got me down no pit for all the tea in China. Daresay that makes me a coward in their book.' Ginger leaned forward. He let go of his cap as he did so. It fell to the floor between his feet. He didn't seem to notice. Looking Emily in the eye, he said earnestly, 'Mrs Winmer, me and him, we were together nearly three year all told — same battalion, same company — so I should know. And I'll tell you this for nuffin: Midge ain't no coward, I swear on my old gal's life.'

He held her gaze. She couldn't have looked away even if she'd wanted to, mesmerized by those pale blue-green eyes that seemed to be looking deep into her, as if he was searching to make sure she'd taken him at his word. Not that she needed convincing. Ginger's vehemence would have been enough in itself, even if she'd not already been predisposed to believe him.

Abruptly, he looked away: whether because he was satisfied with her, or because he was overcome with embarrassment, she couldn't say. He flushed, seeming suddenly ill at ease. His knee was jigging up and down, and his fists curling and uncurling as they rested on his thighs.

Wanting to reach out to him in some way, she said impulsively, 'You — you've been very good to him, Ginger.'

'Least I could do.'

'It's true, though. Taking him in, when you'd a wife and children to think of.'

'He'd nowhere to go, when we left the army. I wasn't about to see him on the streets. My Nell, she didn't make no fuss, she knows what she owes him.'

Emily wondered what he meant by this. She sensed an immeasurable, unspoken history behind Ginger's words, a friendship so deep it would be impossible to fathom. She wondered what it took to forge such a friendship. Something more than the ordinary fires of war, fierce though they were. Perhaps it might be better not to know.

'She's a good girl, my Nell,' Ginger continued. 'She don't mind him staying with us. She didn't bat an eyelid over all that business with the nut-house. She's got a right soft spot for him now, she has. The kiddies have and all. The kiddies think the world of their Uncle Midge. Anyone would feel the same, once they got to know him. He's a mate. Know what I mean? He's a real mate.'

Ginger looked down, noticed his cap on the floor and jerked out a hand to scoop it up. At the same time he jumped to his feet, thereby shutting the door on Emily's brief and intriguing glimpse of something deeper, darker behind that freckle-faced, boyish exterior.

'You'll let me know, missus, if you hear anything, if you see him?'

'Yes. Of course. Of course I will.' Emily, too, stood up. She felt unsure of herself, almost as if she was the one who'd turned up unannounced, a stranger, at someone else's house. 'You — you'll do the same — you'll let me know?'

'Will do, missus.' He hesitated. The colour in his pasty cheeks darkened still further and suddenly he said in a rush, 'Beg pardon and all that, but he likes you, missus, any fool can see it. Blooming cheek, I call it. I told him so and all. "You've got a nerve," I says to him, "a bloke like you, and a lady like what she is." But that's another thing about old Midge. Gets big ideas, he does — too big for his boots, you might say. Only, we'd have never started with *The Sparrowhawk* if it weren't for him. He was the one thought we could make a go of it. Ah, well. Reckon that's all over and done with. I enjoyed meself, being a bus driver, but *The Sparrowhawk*'s napoo. It'd cost an arm and a leg to fix it: dosh we ain't got. So that's that.'

With that, he left the room in all haste, not giving her time to summon Andrews to see him out. Pensive, and rather puzzled, she sank back down into her seat and was soon lost in thought.

* * *

Ginger ran down the steps of the big, posh house with a sense of relief. Talk about getting the wind up — he was all in a muck sweat. He'd rather face Jerry any day than go through that again. Mind you, it served him right, served him right for sticking his nose in. But at least he knew now she was on the level. And she was as sweet on Midge as Midge was on her, unlikely though it seemed: it was plain as the nose on her face. Then again, that was Midge for you. Charm the birds out the trees, when he put his mind to it, old Midge. But he needed a deal of looking after — cor blimey, didn't he just! No one braver at a pinch. No one more soft-hearted inside.

Mind you, thought Ginger, his own missus had been known to say the same, but not about Midge, about him.

'Me? Soft? Do me a favour, Nell! You'll change yer tune quick enough when I take me hand to yer.'

'Hark at him! Knock me about? I'd like to see you try!'

They'd fallen about laughing. She was the kind of girl you could have a laugh with. And they still had the laughter, despite everything, and she had the kindest heart you could imagine which was why she'd taken to Midge.

'But I'll tell you this for nothing, Ginger: there's only so much we can do for him, me and you. What he needs is a woman — the love of a good woman.'

She might be right and all, thought Ginger. She usually was. He'd never have got through without her. She'd made all the difference. And she'd been patient with him, when it was all over. Had the patience of a saint, his Nell. She was a good girl, too, didn't want to know what she could never hope to understand, left all that alone.

'You're back now, Ginger. That's all that matters.'

And they'd never mentioned the war again. Mind you, him and Midge: they never talked about the war either. But that was different. When a pal's been there for you the way Midge was — well, you never forgot something like that.

Ginger hesitated at a junction. Left or right? Which way had he come? He ought to be thinking of how to get home, not letting his mind wander. So, was it left? No, right. Definitely right.

Problem was, he'd never been in this part of town before. No end of posh. He felt like he was trespassing. There was no one around, but he could sense it all the same, the feeling he wasn't welcome. He didn't belong here. He was one of 'them', one of the workers: they hated him and everyone like him. Hated him more than ever, with things the way they were. He could feel it coming out of the very walls, waves of contempt and hostility. Well, they needn't worry. He'd no desire to hang around in these parts. He wanted to get back amongst his own kind just as soon as ever he could.

* * *

He likes you, missus.

Emily mulled over Ginger's words as she sat lost in thought in Aunt Margery's drawing room.

He likes you, missus, and any fool can see it.

But she didn't need Ginger to tell her that. Even if she hadn't guessed before, Midge had made it obvious on Friday when he kissed her. It was hopeless, though. The kiss had shown her that. She would never be free of what had happened at Nethercote Hall. She still belonged to *him*. She would always belong to *him*. She could never give herself to another man. *He* had spoiled her for anything like that.

But there was no point in dwelling on it. *What can't be cured must be endured*, as Granny Drage would have said.

Putting all her thoughts and feelings to one side in a way that Granny Drage would surely have approved of, Emily turned instead to the bag which she had thought she would never see again. She checked the contents, expecting to find her purse missing at the very least. But it was all still there, her purse, the letters, the photographs — the book, too.

She'd forgotten about the book. She'd forgotten that she'd brought it with her. It was odd to think that it had been given to her in this very room five years ago.

She took the book out of her bag, turned it over and over in her hands, thinking back to the summer of 1921. Strangely enough, there'd been a coal strike then, too. The post-war boom had been faltering, the troubles in Ireland never-ending, Sir Hubert — still in government — had been at his most suffocatingly bombastic. Escaping for a while from the cloying atmosphere of Heartlands, Emily had taken Chad with her on a visit to Aunt Margery, but with little hope of enjoying herself, forced to witness — as she would be — the consequences of the unhappy marriage between her aunt and the man Emily had never quite got into the habit of calling 'Uncle Charles'.

She had arrived in London on the hottest July day for forty years, and in that week of glorious weather hope had unexpectedly blossomed. The coal strike had been settled. A truce was called in Ireland. And the Ainsleighs' Belgravia home had become a haven of peace and contentment: the transformation had been as startling as it was unexpected.

It had to have been the third or fourth morning of Emily's visit. Lord Ainsleigh had gone out after breakfast — Chad too: he'd been meeting a friend and they were going to the Science Museum. Sitting with Aunt Margery in the morning room, the windows wide open and the sun beating down outside, Emily had felt more relaxed than she could remember in a long time. Aunt Margery, a picture of tranquillity, barely recognizable as the frenzied woman of three years before, had suddenly produced, from a locked drawer, a slim volume, and she'd handed it across to Emily. This was the book, she'd said solemnly, that had saved her marriage.

Emily had looked at it in wonder. This? This was the secret of happiness?

She had opened it. *Dr Marie Stopes*, she had read.

'But isn't she the lady who . . . ?'

Blushing bright red with realization, Emily had covered the book with her hand. She would much rather have drawn a veil over it and forgotten it. She would much rather have talked about anything else — the weather, or even Ireland. But Aunt Margery had seemed compelled to pursue the subject, as if it was a need in her.

During the war, she said, she'd fondly imagined that she had broken free from the prison of marriage (she had thought of marriage as a prison back then), and learned at last to enjoy herself with endless parties and *affaires du coeur*. But all she'd been doing was aping men, the very worst behaviour of the very worst sort of men. It had been a hollow sort of life, born of misery and desperation, born of a desire to get her own back, to pay her husband out. In the end, it proved to be nothing more than a prison of another type.

Then she'd read Dr Stopes's book. Afterwards, she had given it to Charles and he had read it too.

'You can't imagine the effect it had, Emmy. We'd been fumbling in the dark. We didn't understand each other at all. Small wonder our marriage had never worked. Mrs Stopes showed us that our problems, in large part, stemmed from what happened — or didn't happen — in the bedroom. Dear Emmy. You've gone bright red. I'm embarrassing you. But I don't apologize. I was just as embarrassed as you, to begin with. There's really no need. It's all perfectly natural and ordinary. And yet nobody ever talks about these things, it's all swept under the carpet, and that causes no end of harm. When I got married, I was completely ignorant, I had no idea about anything. I'd been taught to shun that side of life, to fear it. It was a duty. It was a chore. "Lie back and think of England." I envied Charles, who seemed so much better informed. I resented him. I didn't realize that he was not much better off than me. He'd been given completely the wrong idea about women. When he turned seventeen, his father sent him to a tart. That was the sum of his education in those matters — that, and what he heard at school, smutty talk. Charles wasn't ready at seventeen. He was still very much a boy at seventeen — he admits as much himself. His experience skewed all his later relations with women. He'd learned all about tarts but he assumed virtuous women were somehow different, on a higher plane. And so, when we got married, he put me on a pedestal, he thought I was a china doll, he was afraid of corrupting me. And I, in my ignorance, was no help whatsoever, with my envy and resentment, and my lying back and thinking of England. You can see where all our troubles started. But instead of talking about it, we stayed silent. We became — well, you know what we became. Our marriage was hell, and it might have stayed that way, had I not happened to read Dr Stopes's book. The book changed everything. That's why I want you to have it now, Emmy. One day it might change things for you, too.'

'Really, Aunt, I can't think why you'd — I've no earthly use for — Alan is dead — all that is over with.'

'You might meet someone else.'

'At my age? And with so many men killed in the war?'

'Dearest Emmy, you talk as if you were old! You're not old! You're in the prime of life! In any case, it's never too late. Just look at Charles and I!'

Emily recalled how determined she'd been not to accept the book. She'd wanted Aunt Margery to take it back. But before she could force it into her aunt's hands, they'd been interrupted and Emily, in a fluster, had hidden the book under a cushion. In doing so, it became her responsibility, and the moment had passed when she could have rejected it outright.

Aunt Margery had never mentioned Marie Stopes again, which made Emily wonder in retrospect if her aunt had been quiet as blasé that day as she'd made herself seem. Quite possibly she'd felt as awkward as Emily herself. But Aunt Margery — the new Aunt Margery, the real Aunt Margery — was kindness personified, and not likely to stand on her dignity if she thought she could be of some help. At the time, however, Emily had only been able to feel that she'd been lumbered, and she had buried the offending book at the bottom of her suitcase. Once back at Heartlands, she had hidden it in her storage box and tried to forget about it.

Whatever Aunt Margery might say, the book had seemed to Emily a mockery. There'd been a rhyme doing the rounds back then which had summed it up precisely: a sort of crude and tasteless joke.

Jeannie, Jeannie, full of hopes
Read a book by Marie Stopes.

But, to judge by her condition,
She must have read the wrong edition.

Emily now looked down at the book in her hands. She had hidden it. But she had never thrown it away. Why?

She glanced guiltily round Aunt Margery's drawing room. A clock was ticking. She was alone. Taking a breath, she opened the book at random.

> *. . . the whole education of girls, which largely consists in the concealment of the facts of life . . .*

Why, that was exactly what Aunt Margery had said in 1921! And it was true. So very true. What had Nanny ever taught her? Only to avoid like the plague the naughty places, the nasty places, those parts of the body one must only ever touch with one's flannel.

Becoming interested despite herself, Emily turned page after page, her eyes darting from one sentence to another.

> *In the kisses and hand-touch of the betrothed are a zest and exhilaration which stirs the blood like wine. To read poetry, listen entranced to music which echoes the song of their pulses, and see reflected in each other's eyes the beauty of the world—*

'To listen entranced to music,' murmured Emily, poring over the page, thinking of Alan, and the cottage, and the Gilbert and Sullivan records she still kept as a memento. 'In the hand-touch . . . a zest and exhilaration . . .' Her mind went back of its own accord to Friday, sitting in the public house with Midge. She remembered the electric shock which had danced up her spine when her fingertip had touched his. 'The beauty of the world . . .' she murmured, and she found herself caressing the words on the page.

Engrossed, she only slowly became aware of voices in the hallway. She barely had time to thrust the book back into her bag before Aunt Margery and Lord Ainsleigh came in.

'Emmy, dear, you've found your bag, how wonderful!'

They were bursting with news.

'We will tell you everything over lunch.'

Emily glanced at the ticking clock in some surprise. It was true, it was lunchtime already. The whole morning had passed in a blur. But how hungry she was, as if she hadn't eaten for days!

She ran upstairs to put her bag away, and to wash her hands and tidy her hair, looking forward to taking luncheon with her aunt and uncle, whose unhappy marriage had been rescued by Marie Stopes.

CHAPTER SIXTEEN

'Chad! Oh darling, it's so lovely to see you!'

He came breezing in at teatime, snatching a moment from his busy day. He looked, as Aunt Margery had said, incredibly handsome in his uniform, incredibly grown up too.

'Mother! You're hurt! You've such a bruise on the side of your head!'

'Your mother has been in the thick of it!' cried Aunt Margery, drawing Chad onto the chaise longue, plying him with tea, sandwiches, cake, regaling him with the story of Emily's adventures.

'Those strikers, what rotters! I should like to get my hands on the man who hit you!' Chad was angry, almost savage, crumbling a piece of cake in his fist.

'Actually, it was a special policeman who hit your mother.'

Emily felt that Aunt Margery was being unnecessarily exact. When she thought of the boy in the Fair Isle jersey, it made her uneasy, it made her wonder about Chad. She heard the savage note in Chad's voice, she watched the cake crumbling in his fist. She wished the strike was over and that Chad was out of harm's way. She tried to block out the memory of the violence around *The Sparrowhawk*.

But that proved impossible. In what seemed a particularly cruel coincidence, it emerged that Chad had been detailed to help protect the few buses that were still in service. He rode with them all day, like the soldier Emily had seen. At night, the buses were gathered in Regent's Park under armed guard.

'The Park is closed to the public,' said Chad, 'but the Zoo is still open. The Prime Minister was there this afternoon, looking at the animals.'

He laughed. It seemed to Emily that it wasn't an entirely pleasant laugh. His remark about the Prime Minister sounded strangely cryptic.

After tea, Aunt Margery and Lord Ainsleigh tactfully took themselves off, leaving Emily alone with Chad: he had only a short time left before he had to go. He was not nearly so nonchalant when it was just the two of them. Indeed, he seemed to Emily a little unsure of himself, a little overwhelmed.

A lot had been happening, much more than Emily realized. In the last few days, there'd been pitched battles between police and strikers in Battersea, Camden, Deptford, Lambeth, Paddington. Chad knew this for a fact, it wasn't another of Aunt Margery's wild rumours.

'It's — it's like a war, Mother. One half of the country is at war with the other. It's nothing like what I imagined, what I expected. I thought it would be something of a rag. I thought it would be rather jolly, being at the centre of things. But — well — it's serious, it's really serious — it's deadly serious.'

He still felt he was doing the right thing, he said, but with his next breath he admitted that the situation was not as black-and-white as it was painted. He'd begun to question the rights and wrongs on both sides. It was wrong to hold the country to ransom, of course, but it surely wasn't right to make bogeymen out of one's own people — English people. He'd seen sights this last week that had opened his eyes. He'd seen desperation, fear, despair on the faces of people he'd been told were his enemies. He'd seen poverty and squalor he'd never known existed. It wasn't right that people had to live like that, people like — like Lily.

'There are good and bad people on both sides, but money's not the yardstick to measure them by. If stars really were souls — like you used to tell me, Mother — you'd not be able to guess just by looking at them who had been rich and who had been poor.'

He gave that little laugh, as he always did when he thought he might have said something that could be seen as silly, childish, embarrassing, but he'd never stopped himself from saying those things in the first place, and he didn't now. He was opening his heart, saying what he felt, like he always had with her, and it was like getting the old Chad back, the true and genuine Chad.

Glossing over his mention of Lily (a slip of the tongue?), Emily was sharply reminded of Alan as he'd been during the war, and of some of the things Alan had said.

You've no idea how some of them live, the appalling places they come from. Such poverty. How can it still exist in this day and age, in Britain in the twentieth century?

'Sometimes, darling, you remind me very much of Alan,' she murmured, looking at him, this engaging young man, her son.

'Father? I remind you of Father?'

'Yes. Your father.' His real father. For he was Alan's son in every way that mattered. She was glad of this. She was glad he took after Alan.

'What was he like, my father?' Chad looked at her shyly, going back to a conversation they had begun a month ago, a conversation that had been cut short, left hanging. 'What was he *really* like?'

'Kind, gentle, strong.'

'And — and you loved him?'

'Yes. Oh, yes.'

'It's — it's funny about love, the things it makes you do.' He was picking at his trousers, fingering a fold of fabric at the knee, a blush of colour in his cheeks, his eyes now avoiding hers. 'The other day, when I should have been sleeping — I'd been on guard all night — I went to see Lily.'

He was not sure why, or so Emily inferred from his rather muddled report of it. It was almost as if he'd been drawn against his will — drawn to that ABC tea shop on Cheapside (Emily remembered it only too well). The truth was, he couldn't get Lily out of his head, even though she'd betrayed him. But when it came to the point, he'd not been able to bring himself to approach her, to speak to her, so he'd followed her instead. He'd followed her home. He'd walked up and down the street where she lived. He'd walked up and down for an hour, maybe more — he wasn't sure — then he'd come away.

'I think, Mother . . . I think one can't stop loving someone all at once. I think it must take time.'

That laugh again. And then, as if to belie his words, he jumped up, shaking himself free, his mood changing in an instant.

'I have to go, Mother. Do take care of yourself. Try not to start any more riots!'

'Oh, darling—'

'I know, Mother, I know. I'll be careful too. I know you'll worry whatever I say but, honestly, you needn't. I shall be quite all right, I promise. Well, goodbye, Mother. Goodbye.'

* * *

Lying sleepless in bed, Emily was tortured by thoughts of Lily Perks. What had Chad been trying to tell her earlier? That he was beginning to get over his infatuation, or that he couldn't get over it? Whatever the case, if he repeated his impulsive trip to the ABC shop — or, worse, if he made a habit of haunting the street where she lived — it made it all the more likely he'd be ensnared once more. Did Lily still hope to get her claws into Chad? But Lily was almost as much a pawn in the game as Chad. It was Lily's mother who was the master of the game.

Emily shifted uncomfortably in the vast bed as she thought of the last time she'd seen Mabel Perks, a day already uppermost in her mind, for by a strange — almost sinister — coincidence, it was the very same day in 1921 when Aunt Margery had given her the book by Marie Stopes.

Emily had been in the process of trying to refuse the book when the butler interrupted. As Emily hurriedly thrust the book under a cushion, Aunt Margery had said, 'Yes, what it is, Hoxley? Not luncheon already? Master Chadwick's not home yet.'

'No, ma'am, not luncheon. It's for Mrs Winmer. There's a — a *woman* asking after her.' A *woman,* not a *lady*. 'I haven't asked her in.' A meaningful waggle of his eyebrows.

'How very mysterious! You must see who it is, Emmy. We can finish our talk later.'

They had never finished their talk. The book had been buried and forgotten only to fully resurface now, five years later. But in 1921 it had loomed only too large, and Emily had been glad of the interruption by the mysterious caller. As she crossed the hallway, she had seen a woman framed in the open doorway with her back to her. Hearing Emily's footsteps, the woman turned.

It was Mabel Perks.

In the cloistered darkness of Aunt Margery's guest room, Emily remembered all too vividly her sense of stupefaction, seeing Perks again. Surprise had quickly turned to shock, then fear. Her memory now presented her, five years later, with an image of Perks that was distinctly menacing, looming up on the doorstep as if risen from the dead. How much of this was the work of hindsight? It would be difficult, for instance, for Perks to *loom up*. She was not a tall woman. Indeed, sifting through a hundred different impressions of that day, it seemed to Emily that Perks had actually looked rather shrunken and shabby, and much older than she actually was.

Emily's overriding instinct had been to stop Mabel Perks entering Aunt Margery's house. The past must be kept apart from the present, or else some terrible cataclysm would occur. Stepping out to join Perks on the doorstep, Emily had pulled the door to as she struggled for something to say. The full force of the heat had hit her like a wall, after the cool of the drawing room. The glare of the sun had half blinded her. Tongue-tied, she had raised a hand to shade her eyes and, as she did so, Chad had suddenly appeared. He and his friend had come bounding up the steps, back from the Science Museum, hungry for lunch.

'Is this your boy?' Perks had stepped aside to let Chad and his friend pass.

Emily shuddered to remember how Perks's eyes had picked out Chad with what seemed sinister precision. Chad had paused, glancing at Perks with boyish disinterest, and Emily had been seized by panic: she was teetering, she'd felt, on the edge of disaster. There was no knowing what Perks might say or do — Perks, who knew far, far too much. One indiscreet word could ruin everything.

'Go inside, darling.' Emily had ushered Chad and his friend into the house. 'Luncheon is nearly ready. Tell Aunt Margery I may be a few minutes, and to start without me.' She had run down the steps, taking Perks by the arm so she had to go with her.

Very probably, Chad did not now remember his one brief encounter with Lily Perks's mother. He had been of an age when his own affairs dominated all else, the blinkered vision of a fifteen-year-old boy.

Wide awake in the guest room, Emily tried to retrace in her mind the route she had taken with Perks, the streets they had walked along. If it seemed hazy now, it had hardly been less so in 1921. Her one and only aim had been to take Mabel Perks as far away as possible — it had little mattered in which direction. She'd left Aunt Margery's without putting her coat on: such was the muddle in her mind that she'd begun to fret about this quite badly, which was absurd.

The heat that day had been stifling. A coat had been the last thing she needed.

They'd reached St James's Park. Blazing sunshine had glinted on the surface of the lake. The green branches of the trees had hung listless in the heavy air. People had been sitting on the grass, others strolling along the paths in a desultory way that somehow seemed un-English, as if they had all the time in the world, as if they were in Italy or the south of France. There'd seemed something altogether false and unnatural about the London heatwave, as if the glorious weather was a glittering, golden veneer stretched very thin over something sordid and tawdry beneath. True, the coal strike had been settled and there'd been peace in Ireland, but the unemployed had numbered more than two million in the summer of 1921, and poverty and destitution had been in evidence even amidst the grandeur of St James's Park. In Emily's mind there was one abiding image which seemed now almost symbolic: a one-legged man sitting on a bench, an ex-soldier perhaps, though he'd looked so old and ragged it might have been the Boer War he'd fought in, rather than the war which had lately ended. His clothes had been little more than grey rags. His makeshift crutches had been propped against the end of the bench. There'd been a little bundle of belongings beside him. His bloodshot eyes had stared blankly, as if he was looking out at a different world — as if he was seeing, not St James's Park in golden July, but the blasted and withered desert that Emily had visited two years earlier with Lady Winmer.

Emily had shuddered and hurried on, but his eyes had haunted her the whole time she was grappling with Perks. Perks had not looked quite as hard-pressed as some of the down-and-outs in the Park, but it had been only too obvious that the sixteen years since they'd last met had not been kind to her.

What had they talked about as they slogged along the summer streets, as they loitered in St James's Park? Emily had no recollection. All she could remember was a growing conviction that what Perks was about was blackmail. What other explanation could there be? Perks knew more than enough to cause a scandal, to ruin Emily's life, and — more critically — Chad's too.

'What do you want, Perks? What do you *want*? Is it money? Is that why you've come?'

'Oh, yes! You would think that! That's the way your minds work, you toffs!' Perks had been bitter, scathing. 'You think you can buy people. You think anyone down on their luck is for sale. You have no human feelings.'

'If I give you money, will you leave me alone? Will you go away and never come back?'

'That's a fine way to talk, I must say! I don't want nothing from you, nothing, though some might say you owed me. Some might say your family owes me a lot, after what happened.'

People like Perks, thought Emily, were all the same: sly and devious, contradicting themselves, talking in riddles, out for whatever they could get.

'I . . . I can't give you anything right now, Perks. I've not got my coat — my bag, I mean: I've not got my bag. But I'll send you money, I give you my word. I'll send you money, as much money as you like, all I can afford, if only you'll stay away — stay away from me and from . . . from Chad.'

'Do what you like. See if I care.'

Perks's seeming indifference had made her all the more menacing. Emily had been desperate to get away. She'd memorized the address Perks had given her. She'd walked off along the path. She had wanted to run. She had stumbled in her haste, unsteady on her feet. The glaring sun had hurt her eyes. She had been drenched with sweat. Yet somehow she had managed to drag herself back to Aunt Margery's in Belgravia. Somehow she had managed to sit and eat lunch, as if nothing had happened.

Emily had promised money, but she had reckoned without Sir Hubert. Sir Hubert kept a close eye on her finances. Every penny had to be accounted for. Why did she need such a large sum all at once? To send to an old servant, Emily had said. Dear old Nanny, who had been so good to her. She couldn't even hint at the truth, the terrible truth about Chad, Sir Hubert's grandson and heir.

No, no, no! Sir Hubert had put his foot down. Such largesse did no good to either party. He couldn't possibly allow it.

Emily had lived in terror for weeks and months, fearing Perks's return, fearing that Perks would wreak her revenge. The danger seemed greatest in London. Emily had avoided going to London. She had become a stranger at Aunt Margery's. But nothing had happened. Perks had never been heard of again.

Until now.

She'd thought Chad was safe now, that it was all over with Lily. But hearing him talk this afternoon about Lily had sparked all Emily's fears back to life. Like he'd said, you couldn't stop loving someone all in a minute. But Emily reminded herself once again that it wasn't with Lily where the danger lay. Perks had to be at the back of Lily's plot to snare Chad. Perks had found another way to extort money.

Emily had seen Perks just that once in more than twenty years, yet she had never truly been free of her. Perks was always with her. They'd become inextricably linked after the ball at Nethercote Hall. Perks, in a sense, had fashioned Emily's whole life: it was Perks who had come up with the plan to 'save' Emily.

Emily was a marionette. Perks pulled the strings.

Staring up at the ceiling of the guest room, which was swathed in shadow, Emily knew that there was only one way to make an end of it. She would have to go and see her. She would have to face Perks. Only then would she be free of her once and for all.

CHAPTER SEVENTEEN

Chad, in recounting on Sunday afternoon how he'd followed Lily home, had unwittingly given Emily precise directions that would take her to Mabel Perks. The address was not the one she remembered from 1921, the address Perks had given her so she could send money. But the fact it was different fitted in with her idea of Perks as somehow slippery and hard to pin down.

All Monday, Emily dithered. She found excuses. It was too dangerous to go out, with the strike on. She needed to plan what she would say. What purpose would be served, in any case, by confronting Perks?

Monday evening came. Emily grew angry with herself. She tossed and turned in bed. This endless prevarication. This shying away from anything too uncomfortable or difficult. All this conjecture, too, trying to second-guess what might or might not happen. She was torturing herself, and she was tired of it. She was tired of not knowing things — not knowing if Chad was safe, not knowing where Midge was. She was tired of the bland, uninformative voice of the BBC. To confront Mabel Perks: this, at least, was something she could do. So why not face up to it, get it over with? Why not be *brave*, just for once?

She fell asleep at last, thoroughly fed up with herself. She woke with an iron resolve.

'My dear Emmy,' said Aunt Margery over breakfast, 'you don't need to ask my permission, you must come and go as you please. If there's something you need to do, then you must do it. I won't ask what it is. I am here to help if required, but I won't interfere. Heaven forefend I should turn into my mother! But at least take the car. Let Fletcher drive you.'

In no time at all, the Ainsleighs' immaculate motor car was drawing up in a street in Rotherhithe, the street Chad had described. The chauffeur glanced at her in the rear-view mirror. 'Are you sure, madam, that this is the place?' The tone of his voice expressed serious reservations.

'Quite sure.' Emily summoned every last vestige of her meagre ration of Drage determination. All the same, she could not stifle doubts of her own as she stepped out of the car and looked up and down the street. 'Would you wait for me here, please, Fletcher.'

'Very good, ma'am.'

It was a grim little street. The once-fashionable houses were now in terminal decline. By the looks of things, they had been divided into many small lodgings. Washing hung from the windows, rubbish was strewn on the pavements and weeds grew in the gutters. The cobbles had a slimy look to them. An overcast sky seemed to press down onto the louring roof tops.

Emily's shoes clicked on the pavement as she walked. Some dirty and ragged-looking children, playing nearby, stopped to watch her. She felt horribly out of place but, to her surprise, her courage held up.

'Hello, there, children. Which of you can tell me where Lily Perks lives?'

They stared at her. She thought for one long moment that they weren't going to answer. Then one of them pointed.

'There. Down them steps, missus.'

As Emily headed in the direction indicated, the child shouted after her, 'Lily's not at home, missus. Lily's gone to work. Only her mum's at home.'

Emily hesitated at the top of the steps. But Lily's mother was the very person she had come to see.

The steps led down to a cramped little area like a dark pit. There was a door ajar, as if someone had left in a hurry and not quite pulled it to. Emily knocked. She didn't wait for an answer, but pushed the door wide — if she gave herself time to think, she would be sure to lose her nerve.

A narrow, shadowy passage stretched ahead of her, but to the right there was an open door with a gloomy room beyond. A thin querulous voice came from the room.

'Who is it? Who's there? What do you want?'

It was a changed voice, a different voice, but all the same Emily recognized it. For a moment her heart quailed but, instead of allowing herself to waver, she stepped immediately through the doorway.

The room was small with a subterranean feel to it, very little light coming in from the area through the one grimy window. As Emily's eyes slowly grew used to the gloom, more and more details emerged, like a picture being developed. There was a bed, and a woman lying in it. There were several other items of furniture, including a battered wardrobe, a rickety bedside table, a chair with the wooden slats missing from the backrest. A picture, hanging on one of the distempered walls, looked at first glance like some esoteric cubist composition, but then resolved into a rather faded chocolate-box drawing of a girl with a puppy. On the bedside table, a plate with a half-eaten, curled-up sandwich sat next to a glass with water and a chipped ashtray from the British Empire Exhibition. There was an air of claustrophobia, a smell of damp, a sense that the room and its occupant were both slowly disintegrating together.

The woman in the bed, her head sunk in the pillows, was Mabel Perks — or rather someone who had once been Mabel Perks. Perks must be, Emily guessed, in her early forties, but she looked twenty years older, thin and shrivelled, grey-haired. Her eyes were dull and glassy. Her hands, resting on the threadbare counterpane, had swollen fingers. This was not the Perks that Emily carried round with her inside her head. There was nothing to be afraid of here.

'Miss . . . Miss Emily? Is it really you?'

'Hello, Perks.'

'Or Mrs Winmer, I should say.'

Perks began to cough. Her body, for a moment, was wracked by it. Slowly she recovered. Emily waited.

At length, Perks spoke again. 'W-w-why have you come?' Her words were interspersed with desultory coughing. 'What . . . what do you want?'

'I've come about your daughter.' Emily found she was able to be calm and matter-of-fact.

'What about Lily? You . . . you leave Lily alone! She's a good girl, is Lily.'

'Then why did she try to dupe my son?'

'That . . . that weren't Lily. That were me. My idea.'

'You always were full of good ideas, weren't you, Perks.'

Emily, looking down at the woman on the bed, was suddenly seized by a savage sense of triumph. Perks, so sly and devious, so pleased with herself, reduced to this! How the mighty had fallen!

Drawing the decrepit chair towards the bed, Emily sat down, waiting for Perks to speak. The last of her fears had fallen away. She felt a match for any situation. She was surely a match for Perks.

'I-I didn't mean no harm, Miss Emily.'

'Oh, didn't you? Then why use your daughter in such an abominable way? What were you thinking?'

'She'd do any — anything for her old mum. She's a good girl. I wanted to see her settled. Is that so — so wrong?'

'Of course it's wrong! It's monstrous, to play with a boy's feelings, to use him!'

'Don't *you* use *us*, you people, you toffs? What do you care about *our* feelings? We're lower than animals to you!'

This little outburst seemed to exhaust Perks. She lay as if spent, limp as a rag doll, coughing feebly. When finally she gathered breath again, her voice was quiet and flat, expressionless.

'I know all about you lot, you toffs. I didn't work in service all them years for nothing. I know how to work you over. I taught Lily how. I taught her, so she could catch your boy. I knew exactly what he'd be like, your boy. I knew how to make him love her.'

'That's horrible! So cold and callous! I didn't think even you could stoop so low, Perks.'

Perks turned her head away, muttered obstinately, 'I just want her settled. Where's the harm in that? At least, with your boy, she'd never want for nothing. At least, with your boy, I know she'd be all right when I'm gone. There's not much time, see.'

'What do you mean, "there's not much time"?'

'Lily won't face it. Lily won't have it. She thinks there's still hope. There ain't. But that's why she done it, that's why she played along, she thought your money might buy me time. She did it for my sake. But it's too late for me.' Perks turned her head back and looked Emily in the eye. 'I'm dying, Mrs Winmer. I'm dying.'

* * *

Look at her, thought Mabel Perks bitterly. Look at her, swanning around like Lady Muck, in her pleated skirt and knitted jumper, and a big hat with ribbons. Look at her, still in her prime, not showing her age, rich and healthy. Some people had all the luck! And she was so high and mighty with it, so prim and bleeding proper, preaching at you, telling you how to live your life. What did she know about working for a living? What did she know about making ends meet? She'd had everything handed on a plate. She'd no idea what it meant, to live hand-to-mouth, struggling to keep your head above water. She'd never been behind with the rent, she'd never gone hungry — she'd probably never even been ill. She had no idea what it was like to be shivering cold all the time, to have a pain in your chest, to feel tired, so tired: so very, very tired.

She'd always been spoilt, had Miss Emily. Even as a little girl she'd been spoilt. She'd had a spiteful streak, too, telling tales on you and pulling your hair, going behind your back, ganging up with Nanny: that mealy-mouthed, self-satisfied old bag Nanny, who'd thought herself a cut above the other servants at Alleyn Dene.

It was about time Miss Emily — or Mrs Winmer, or whatever she called herself — learned some home truths, spoilt as she was, and soft. Still as innocent as she'd been as a girl — naïve — and never having had to lift a finger, never having had to slave away, to scrimp and save. Pure as the driven snow, she looked, but Mabel knew different. Oh yes, Mabel knew all about Miss Emily's little trouble. Yet, even then, she'd still come out of it smelling of roses, she'd never been held to account. *She* hadn't been called a slut. *She* hadn't lost her position because of it. *Her* child hadn't been born a bastard.

Was it so wrong, to want to do your best for your child? All Mabel had ever wanted, was to do her best. Why shouldn't Lily marry into money? It wasn't Lily's fault she'd been born poor. She oughtn't to have been poor, with a father like hers.

It had seemed such a perfect plan, for Lily to snare Miss Emily's boy and marry into money — money that Lily deserved, money that ought to have been hers by right. Mabel had had no compunction, playing on her illness in order to persuade Lily to go along with the plan. Mabel hadn't minded taking advantage of Lily's sweet nature. It was all in a good cause.

But then Lily had started to have doubts. She found she liked the boy. He was nice, he was kind, it was cruel to con him. Why couldn't she tell him the truth, and take her chances? She would much rather tell him the truth.

Mabel had hardened her heart. 'You do what you like, Lily. Tell him, if you think it worth the risk. Tell him. Don't hold back on my account. I won't be around much longer, any road.'

'Oh, Mum, don't say that! Please don't say that! You'll get better. I know you'll get better. Once we're back on our feet — once we're fixed up proper — I'll ask for extra work at the ABC—'

'And you think that'll help, do you, the pittance you earn waitressing?'

'There's nothing else, no other jobs: you know that, you know how I've looked and looked. Oh Mum, I'll do anything! I'll do anything you ask. I won't say a word to Chad, I promise. Just hold on, Mum, hold on a little longer, and everything will work out right — you'll see!'

And so Lily had been talked round despite her scruples. But Mabel had reckoned without Miss Emily. Miss Emily had come along and put the kybosh on all her plans. Spite, that was all it was. Pure spite. She was heartless, Miss Emily — she'd always been heartless. She'd been heartless in that business over the money. She'd promised to send money, that day in the Park five years ago. Not that Mabel had asked for money, not that she would have accepted it on her own account, she'd still got her pride. Only it was Lily's by right, the money: that was how Mabel looked at it. They owed Lily, the Drages.

It had all come to nothing. Miss Emily had not kept her word — a dirty trick to play. Oh, she must have enjoyed herself over that one! She must have laughed herself silly! Spoilt, spiteful, posh, perfect: how Mabel hated her, and all of them — because they were all the same, those toffs, heartless. It wouldn't hurt for Miss Emily to be told, neither. Mabel would take great pleasure in telling her a few home truths, and see how she liked it . . .

* * *

'Why are you being like this, Perks? Why are you saying these hateful things?'

Emily got abruptly to her feet, filled with a horror of the wizened woman on the bed, of the damp, dark, squalid little room. She wished she'd never come. What had she hoped to achieve? She should go at once, now, whilst Perks was once more wracked with coughing.

But as Emily turned to leave, she caught sight of the picture on the wall and she hesitated, staring at it: the chocolate-box picture of a girl and a puppy. For some reason it made her think of Juniper. How she'd loved Juniper! And Juniper had loved her, devoted. What had become of Juniper, in the end? For the life of her, Emily couldn't remember.

As she stared at the faded picture in the gloom of the fetid room, Emily saw in her mind's eye Juniper, not as a puppy, but as a full-grown dog, jumping up at her, pawing at her, seeking attention, devoted as always, but no longer cute or cuddly.

'Get off me, Juniper! Get off!'

Irritated, she had pushed the dog away and — when Juniper wouldn't take the hint — had smacked the recalcitrant animal hard across the nose.

'Leave me *alone*, Juniper! I don't *want* to play! I'm *bored* with you!'

Emily was stunned by this. Had it really happened? But it must have. She remembered it.

A shudder ran up Emily's spine. She seemed to glimpse, in the recesses of her mind, as dim and murky as this room, other memories, memories she'd pushed aside, tried to forget: the girl she'd once been, the girl who'd vanished without trace one night at Nethercote Hall, the girl who'd been brave and fearless, almost feisty, but who'd also been — it had to be admitted — a little spoilt, and used to getting her own way.

Poor Juniper! And poor Perks, too! Staring at the faded picture, torn from a chocolate box and carefully fixed to the wall, its corners curling — the girl smiling: smiling, smiling forever — Emily was ashamed to think how, just now, she had stood over Perks gloating.

But this gave her pause for thought, and she wondered if that girl she'd been had perhaps not quite vanished after all. Even now, Emily realized, she still had, at a pinch, a modicum of that girl's bravery. It had led her here, to Perks's cellar. And even on the terrible night of the ball at Nethercote Hall, she had somehow found her way home through the darkness and in the teeth of a gale. But if she hadn't lost all courage after her ordeal, she'd still been capable of callousness too: Perks was right about that. She had smacked Juniper's nose, she had pulled Perks's hair, she had stamped her feet and said *me, me, me.*

If anything good had come from all she'd been through — anything good at all — then it was that she'd learned compassion. She mustn't forget that now.

She turned back. Perks was still convulsed by her coughing fit, her body shaking with it. Emily crossed to the chair, sat down. She reached for the glass of water. She held it to Perks's lips. Perks sipped. The coughing slowly subsided. Perks lay back. She was breathing in fits and starts.

Emily lifted her a little, plumped her pillows, settled her more comfortably. As she did so, she thought she heard Perks speak.

'What was that, Perks? What did you say? I didn't quite hear.' Emily leaned closer.

Perks's voice was faint and husky. 'The picture. You were looking at the picture. It's silly, Miss Emily, but that picture always reminded me, somehow, of you. Do you remember that dog you had? Do you remember, Miss Emily?'

* * *

It had put a smile on your face, thought Mabel, to see Miss Emily galloping and gambolling with the puppy on the nursery carpet. And the way Miss Emily had pampered and petted it! Oh, it was daft, but there'd been something about the way Miss Emily carried on that went to your heart!

The picture pinned to the wall — the girl who did not really look much like Miss Emily, the dog who was not a duplicate of Juniper — acted as an aide-memoire and put Mabel in mind of another time, another place: Alleyn Dene, years before the war. For all she'd grumbled, for all she'd worked her fingers to the bone, she now looked back on that as a time and place when she'd been happy. Nanny, of course, had been an uppity old bag, but the others hadn't been so bad: Cook, who slipped you morsels on the quiet, the scullery maid with the angel face and whose dirty jokes had you in stitches and Watkins the gardener, who'd do anything for anybody, who'd been like a dad, really (Mabel had never had a dad). The mistress had liked her pound of flesh, it was true, but she hadn't treated you like dirt the way some (most) did. And the master had been a pussycat, a real pussycat. Off his head, of course, and always fussing about the weather or gazing at the stars, but a real pussycat, who'd let you get away with murder. Even Miss Emily hadn't been all bad, despite Nanny's best efforts to turn her into a hoity-toity little madam. It wasn't Miss Emily's fault, after all, that she'd been born rich. It wasn't Miss Emily's fault that she'd been spoilt. What good had it done her, anyway, all that cosseting and pampering? She'd grown up with no idea about the world. She'd been as innocent as a lamb. You could scarcely credit how ignorant she'd been.

All that was in the past. It was long ago. But, lying there in her grubby bed day after day, tired and weak and feverish and with her only glimpse of the world the grey daylight peeping through the area window, Mabel often found now that the past and the present faded in and out, each as real and immediate as the other. Time telescoped, so that she could never be sure what had happened when. The pain in her chest fogged her thoughts and made them hazy. Distant memories were sometimes much more vivid than this room.

Why, she'd never questioned, but Mabel had kept abreast as best she could of the goings-on at Alleyn Dene in the years after she'd left. She had learned of the master's tragic end, flattened by a train. She'd heard that Sutton's Shoes had gone to the wall. It had seemed such a shame to think of the house as she'd known it being broken up and sold at auction. Funny, after all this time, to find Miss Emily here, in this shabby little room. Funny, to have Miss Emily — or Mrs Winmer as she now was — lifting you up and settling you on your pillows. Funny to have Mrs Winmer's arms around you.

Once upon a time, it had been the other way around, Miss Emily dirty and dishevelled, sobbing her heart out in Mabel's arms: Mabel had never forgotten it. You'd have had to be a hard-bitten brute not to have felt something. Mabel had felt something. Cruel, it had seemed, to have that happen, and Miss Emily such a slip of a thing, and so innocent. She'd not deserved it. She'd not deserved it, no matter what.

Mabel had wanted to help — not just for Miss Emily's sake, but for the family, too. And by 'the family' in those days you'd meant the master and mistress, yes, but all the others too: Cook and the scullery maid and Watkins, even old Nanny at a pinch. Everyone at Alleyn Dene, they'd all been your family, one big family, that was what it had felt like. Daft, yes, but that was what it had felt like. And so, muddling and fumbling between them, she and Miss Emily had come up with a plan to save Miss Emily's honour.

All these years later, Mabel was still not sure if it had been for the best. It had seemed the only way out at the time, but had it been for the best? Had Miss Emily been happy with that callow young stripling, the Winmer boy, who'd later been killed in the war? Was it possible to be happy with any man? Weren't all men the same? That had always been Mabel's experience, that all men were the same. Oh, yes, all men were the same, they only ever wanted one thing.

Miss Emily had left home to get married by the time Mabel started to show. Once her condition became obvious, that had been that, she'd been out on her ear. No one had come to *her* rescue. There'd been no plan to save *her* honour.

But, for all her flirting with the village boys, it had not been one of them who'd done for her. It had been someone else entirely.

* * *

Mrs Sutton emerged from Emily's bedroom in 1905, a puzzled expression on her face, concerned. Mabel stood to attention, waited for her to speak.

'Is she quite well, do you think, Perks?'

'I don't know nuffink,' said Mabel stoutly. You had to watch the mistress, she was a slippery one — she pretended to be dotty, when she was sharp as a knife underneath.

'She seemed all right at luncheon,' continued Mrs Sutton, 'though I didn't really pay much attention, with the Winmers here, and my mother — Mrs Drage, I should say. But Emily seemed all right then.'

'She did seem all right, ma'am, yes.'

'But not now. I wonder . . . I wonder . . . She went into the gardens with the Winmer boy. Do you think, Perks, that something might have happened?'

'Like what, ma'am?' Sharp as a knife. Slippery, too. Best to head her off, before she got any ideas. 'If you please, ma'am, I'd say that Miss Emily is sickening for summat.'

'Yes. Yes. I daresay you're right, Perks. Sickening for something. That will be it. She *does* look very pale.'

'Should I go for the doctor, ma'am?'

'That would be best, I think. If you could go right away — if you could hurry. Thank you, Perks. I don't know *what* I would do without you.'

She didn't half give you some flannel, thought Mabel, as she fetched her coat and hurried out of the house, putting on a burst of speed down the drive until she was safely out of sight of the windows. She didn't half give you some flannel, but every so often you fell for it, you sort of felt she meant it, you really did believe you were indispensable.

Turning into the lane, one half of Mabel laughed at the other half: for being such a mug, for letting herself get taken in. The other half dug in her heels, insisting that Mrs Sutton was not a bad old bird, and that this situation at Alleyn Dene was better than most situations, at least you got treated decent. But the cynical half of her wouldn't have it.

That's what they want you to think, you great booby. You work harder that way. You work your fingers to the bone. And for what? For a pittance, and a few fancy words.

Mabel dawdled along the lane. She was in no hurry to reach the village and odious Dr Woodhouse, ninety if he was a day, and with bushy white whiskers and a beard so big and ragged that the villagers said of any mislaid or missing object that it must have 'got lost in the doctor's beard'. It was not as if this was a real emergency. There was nothing wrong with Miss Emily — nothing that could be easily cured, anyway.

Mabel wondered very much if Miss Emily had gone through with their plan. Mabel had her doubts, but she'd not been able to snatch a private word, so she couldn't be sure. Perhaps Miss Emily hadn't been able to manage it, perhaps that explained her collapse, knowing that it would all come out now, her disgrace. Or maybe she *had* done as they'd planned, and the shock of it had knocked her sideways. It wasn't meant to knock you sideways. It was meant to be a slice of heaven. That was what the scullery maid said, anyway. The scullery maid had a young man on the sly (you weren't meant to have followers, it was one of the Rules), and to hear her talk you'd think they were at it — her and her fella — at every opportunity.

A slice of heaven, the scullery maid said. But Mabel wouldn't know. She'd never let a boy go that far. She had a lot of catching up to do, where the scullery maid was concerned.

Halfway to the village, she met two lads from Hopkins' Farm clearing the ditches.

'Hello, Mabel Perks. Give us a kiss, then.'

This was Alfie Collins, a right cheeky monkey, but as handsome as the devil, and he knew it and all. He'd asked her to the harvest supper the other week. She'd managed to wangle her half day. She'd been very pleased with herself, having Alfie Collins dancing attendance. Peggy, one of the village girls who was sweet on Alfie, had pulled her hair and pinched her and called her a foreign hussy. To pay Peggy out, Mabel had allowed Alfie a kiss and a cuddle behind the barn. He'd said she was the nicest-looking girl he'd ever clapped eyes on. He'd put his hands on her breasts and squeezed them through the pleats of her frock.

She'd let him take this liberty in order to spite Peggy, but she didn't want him getting any ideas. It was high time he was put in his place.

She ignored Alfie, said to his companion, 'How are you, Bert Mawsley?' Bert Mawsley had spots and sticky-out teeth. 'I'll let *you* kiss me, Bert, if you like.'

Bert Mawsley went bright red. Alfie Collins went bright red too, but with rage not embarrassment. Mabel laughed. She was the belle. They all lapped her up. But you wouldn't catch her throwing herself away on a farm boy up to his knees in ditchwater. She had her sights set higher.

'I'll come back for that kiss another day, Bert Mawsley.'

Alfie shouted after her. 'Won't you even *speak* to me now, Mabel Perks!'

'I might and I might not,' she flung over her shoulder as she went on her way. 'You'll have to wait and see, Alfie Collins.' (It didn't do to burn all your bridges.)

Reaching the village at last, she delivered her message to the doctor, then idled round the green. The Barford girls passed by with their noses in the air. One of them was wearing a rather nice pair of white gloves. Mabel looked on enviously. She hankered after nice clothes. Nice clothes were better than any boy.

She went into the shop, hoping to have a gossip with old Mrs Wetherall, who knew everything about everyone, but it was Mrs Wetherall's sour-faced daughter who came out from the back room to stand behind the counter, holier-than-thou.

'Do you want anything? I haven't got all day.'

'I might and I might not.'

Mabel prevaricated long enough to get up Mrs Wetherall's daughter's nose, then bought a quarter of barley sugar. She set off back to the house.

The day had started out rather grey and blustery. There'd been rain. But now, mid-afternoon, the rain had cleared and a pale autumn sun was beginning to shine behind the thinning clouds. Meandering along the lane sucking barley sugar, passing the place where Alfie Collins and Bert

Mawsley had been working (there was no sign of them now), Mabel began to whistle and then to sing, swinging her arms in the sunshine.

The boy I love is up in the gallery,
The boy I love is looking down at me;
La, la, la; la, la la (how did it go?)
Waving of his handkerchee—

'*THE BOY I LOVE*!' she began again at the top of her voice, but then fell silent, hearing the clip-clop of hooves on the road. Round a bend in the lane came a large black horse trotting quickly towards her. Mabel eyed it nervously. She did not like horses. She did not trust them. Coming from the city, she liked to see horses safely yoked to carts or carriages.

Only at the last moment, when the horse came to a stop in front of her, did she look up and recognize the rider.

She curtsied. 'We heard you was ill, sir.'

Mr Walter Drage looked down at her from what seemed a vast height. 'Well, I'm not ill, as you can see.'

'But Mrs Drage said—'

'What did she say?'

'She came to us for luncheon and she said—'

'Never mind what she said! That's just Mother. One has to lay a few red herrings, when it comes to Mother. What she doesn't know won't hurt her.'

He grinned, rather devilish, and Mabel felt her stomach tighten. She had a soft spot for Mr Walter, and he looked fine, mighty fine, in his tight jodhpurs and black coat. Alfie Collins was handsome in a rough, unrefined sort of way, but Mr Walter was different. He was smooth and polished and more mature. He looked dark and dashing sat astride his big horse. He was around twenty-eight, just the right age in a man, or so the scullery maid said. Mabel wondered how it would feel kissing Mr Walter. Would he too squeeze her breasts, or was that just farm boys? She was aware of his dark eyes looking her up and down, and she felt herself blushing.

But, oh my, wouldn't she trump the scullery maid if she could boast of a slice of heaven with a gentleman like Mr Walter — wouldn't she just!

'You're from Alleyn Dene, aren't you, girl? I've seen you at Alleyn Dene. What are you doing out here in the lane?'

'I was sent to fetch the doctor, sir. Miss Sutton's not well.'

'Miss Sutton? Emily?' He frowned. A shifty look came into his eyes. 'What — what's wrong with her?'

Nothing, thought Mabel: nothing should be wrong now, everything should be fixed, if Miss Emily had snared the Winmer boy, if Miss Emily had done as they'd planned. But Mabel experienced a twist of jealousy. Everyone was so concerned about Miss Emily. They all fawned over Miss Emily. Where would Miss Emily be now, were it not for her, Mabel Perks?

'Got a soft spot for Miss Sutton, have you, sir?' she asked sulkily.

Colour flushed into his cheeks. His frown became a scowl. What had she said, to make him so angry? She hardly dared glance at his burning eyes.

'What do you mean by that, girl?'

'N-n-nothing, sir.'

'You ought to mind your own business.'

'Yes, sir. Sorry, sir. I didn't mean to offend, I'm sure.' She curtsied again, demure, apologetic, laying it on, soft-soaping, thrusting her jealousy aside.

'Yes — well . . .'

His growling voice sent a shiver through her. She peeked up at him from under her hat.

'If there's anything I can do for you, sir . . .'

His eyes flashed, but the creases in his brow were smoothing out. 'And what do you imagine a girl like you could possibly do for me?'

Mabel's heart skipped a beat. He had a different look in his eyes now. She recognized it. She'd seen it earlier in the eyes of Alfie Collins, of Bert Mawsley. She'd seen it often in the eyes of the village boys. But why play for the village boys, when there were bigger fish you could fry?

'What can you do for me?' he repeated.

'I'm sure sir could think of something if sir put his mind to it.' She held her breath. She'd gone out on a limb. What if she'd got it wrong?

'What's your name, girl?'

'Perks, sir.'

'What Perks?'

'Mabel Perks.'

'Well, Mabel Perks, you're a pert little thing, aren't you.'

'Am I, sir?'

She saw his knuckles whiten as he gripped the reins of his horse. Somehow she knew she'd played it just right. A sense of achievement made her bold, and she looked up at him, batting her eyelids.

Gotcha, she thought.

Now to reel him in.

* * *

'Walter? Walter Drage?' Mrs Winmer's face was pale in the gloom of the basement room. Her voice shook. 'Uncle Walter is Lily's father?'

'You don't believe me. I knew you wouldn't.' Mabel turned her face away, not wanting to see Mrs Winmer's look of shock and revulsion.

Why tell her? Why tell her after all this time? But if it helped Lily in some way . . .

Only Lily was important now.

Shivering with cold, coughing, Mabel pulled the bed clothes close round her. She would have liked to pull them right over her head, to hide from Mrs Winmer's staring eyes, to hide until Mrs Winmer had gone. A feeling of bitterness welled up inside her. Why look quite so shocked? It was not as if Mrs Winmer didn't know what she, Mabel Perks, was like. Mrs Sutton must have told her daughter all about it, how the housemaid had got in the family way and had to be dismissed. Such a nuisance, such an inconvenience!

Tears pricked Mabel's eyes, as she remembered how carefree she had been that day long ago, walking to the village and back, sucking her barley sugar and singing out loud.

The boy I love is up in the gallery,
The boy I love is looking down at me . . .

Seen from a distance of years, that afternoon — that moment walking along the lane, just before Mr Walter came along — shone in her memory as the last time she'd ever been happy. How swiftly things could change. One moment happy, carefree, the next—

She'd been silly, stupid, green as grass but at the time she'd thought she knew it all, she'd thought she'd been no end of clever, flirting with the village boys, getting them to run after her, keeping Alfie Collins dangling, and then her moment of triumph with Mr Walter. What had she imagined would happen next? That Mr Walter would fall in love and marry her? Had she really been so simple-minded? What made it worse was that she'd had the example of Miss Emily, she'd known all about Miss Emily's predicament — and yet she hadn't learned a thing from it. She'd thought herself superior to Miss Emily — to the scullery maid as well — but she'd simply been a fool.

She'd started to show. It had been the scullery maid who noticed first. 'What will you do, Mabel? It won't just be me asking, everyone will know soon enough.'

There'd been a brief stay of execution, with the house in turmoil, Miss Emily's abrupt departure and hasty marriage. Mabel had seized the opportunity and contrived to get a word with Mr Walter. Half the blame was his, after all. It was his child she was carrying.

'Oh, no you don't! You can't pin that on me! I've seen you, you little bitch—' He'd twisted her hair, his dark eyes blazing, he'd thrust his face up close to hers. 'I've seen you making eyes at the village yokels and the peasants. I've seen them sniffing round. How many have you opened your legs to? I'll warrant you spend half your life on your back, whilst they queue up for it. Do you really think anyone will believe a slut like you, if you try to make out that your bastard has anything to do with me?'

It was the injustice of his words that had made her weep. She wasn't like that. She didn't do the things he'd accused her of. She'd always been a good girl. But, as he'd said, who would believe her now?

Mrs Sutton certainly hadn't. 'I expected better of you, Perks, I really did. You are *such* a disappointment to me.'

Mabel, in her attic room, had packed her little bag. She had left Alleyn Dene by the tradesman's entrance. She'd made her way to the village. She'd had one last hope.

'We could make it work, Alfie. If you said the baby's yours, we could get wed as soon as you liked. I'd be the best wife a man could wish for, you know I would.'

Alfie Collins had looked her over. 'Why would I want to bring up another man's child? Turns out Peggy was right about you all along. You're a hussy, Mabel Perks. You're a trollop. I can't think what I ever saw in you. I never want to clap eyes on you again.'

And so she'd made her lonely way to London, where Lily had been born fatherless, a bastard.

But I wouldn't be without her for the world, thought Mabel. *She's the best thing — the only good thing — that's ever happened to me.*

And Lily was all that mattered now, making sure that Lily would be all right.

Mabel reached out a swollen hand, but shrank from touching Miss Emily — who was Miss Emily no longer, who was Mrs Winmer now, aloof and unreachable, and with an expression on her face of such dismay and distress that it made Mabel, hardened though she was, experience all over again the bitterness and shame of her own degradation.

Mabel remembered that once before she'd almost told Mrs Winmer everything. Summer, it had been, five years ago.

Lily was grown up and working by then, she'd got a position as a scrubbing maid. But to see her so worn and tired, to see her lovely hands all red and the skin cracked, to see clear on her face the pain her knees gave her, to hear her crying quietly in bed at night (for her mistress was a cow, a right cow): it had been more than Mabel could bear. Lily deserved better. She didn't just *deserve* it, she was *owed* it. And so, in St James's Park on a blazing July afternoon in 1921, Mabel had been prepared to throw herself on Mrs Winmer's mercy, for Lily's sake. But Mrs Winmer had been cold and distant and had talked about money — she had seemed to think that Mabel was trying to screw money out of her. And Mabel had suddenly seen how it would be. Even if the Drages could be persuaded that Lily was theirs, it would all be hushed up, swept under the carpet. They had no human feelings, those people. They were loathsome. In a sudden flash, Mabel had realized she didn't want Lily to be a part of that, to be a guilty secret with a price on her head, hush money. Also, Mabel had shuddered to think what might happen if Master Walter got involved. She didn't want Master Walter having anything to do with Lily — he who was a selfish brute, and she so gentle and unspoilt. So when Mrs Winmer offered money — offered it off her own bat — Mabel had decided on the spur of the moment to take up the offer and to keep silent. But, of course, Mrs Winmer had never sent the money, because that was what they were like, those kind of people: heartless, faithless.

Things were different now. Mabel knew she was dying. She hated to think of Lily left all alone, and the world such a cruel place. She only wanted what was best for Lily. But why should Mrs Winmer help Lily? What was Lily to her? She obviously didn't believe a word of it, about her precious Uncle Walter. She didn't know what he was like. How could she possibly know?

How could she?

CHAPTER EIGHTEEN

Emily slowly climbed the area steps. It came as a relief to escape the claustrophobia of the basement room. The gloom and the damp had begun to seep into her. Now she could breathe again. The decaying street seemed light and airy by comparison, the grey day as bright as spring.

But it *was* spring. It was May. She had all but forgotten, cooped up in Mabel Perks's dungeon. She had all but forgotten Fletcher, too, and the Ainsleigh's motor.

'Home, madam?' He held the door open for her.

But she couldn't bear it, to be shut up in the motor, to be hemmed in — to have escaped from one confined space, to end up in another. She wanted to be free. She wanted fresh air and time to think. She didn't want to go back to Belgravia just yet.

'I'll take a walk, I think. If you wouldn't mind waiting, Fletcher . . .'

He peered at her with disquiet. 'A walk, madam? In these parts? Is that wise? If I may be permitted to say, madam does not look at all well.'

'Don't fuss, Fletcher!' She knew her words sounded brusque, dismissive. She knew she must seem silly and headstrong. She couldn't help it. Her mind was in a hopeless muddle, she was reeling from what she'd heard. She wanted time on her own, to sort things out. 'Don't fuss, Fletcher. I am quite all right.'

'Very good, madam.' He spoke stiffly, and gave eloquent testimony to his displeasure by slamming the car door.

Emily didn't notice. She was already walking away. She didn't know where she was going. It didn't seem to matter. In normal circumstances, she might have thought twice (*A walk? In these parts? Is that wise?*), but today it never crossed her mind. She felt, in a sense, that she wasn't really there. She was still in the basement room with Perks. She was lost in the past. The present, for the moment, couldn't touch her.

Poor Perks! How diminished she looked, how insignificant! Dying, she'd said — and it might well be true, to look at her. No one could be afraid of Perks now.

But Emily began to wonder as she walked, reaching back in time, if there'd ever been anything to be afraid of at all. Perks, in her own muddled way, had simply been trying to help, and so she'd come up with a plan to 'save Miss Emily's honour'. Emily — inexperienced at seventeen, naıve — had not known to say no. She'd gone along with it, because there had seemed no alternative.

Like Papa's brass telescope, the passage of time had acted as a lens, but instead of bringing Perks into sharper relief, it had distorted her out of all recognition, so that whenever Emily looked back she saw a monster — sly, conniving, grasping — when all Perks had really been was different: a girl from a different world, a blunt working-class girl, out of place in the pampered middle-class milieu of Alleyn Dene. They had never really understood each other at all, Emily realized. That was the crux of the problem. It was as if they had spoken different languages.

Walking at random, barely aware of her surroundings, Emily wondered if what Perks had said was true — what she had said about Lily's father. It would be easy to dismiss the whole story as another of Perks's lies. Except that Perks was no more a liar than she was a monster.

All the same, you'd need good reason to accept what she'd said as the truth. You'd need good reason.

Emily's mind went back to the day of Papa's funeral in 1913. She remembered the sad little gathering at Alleyn Dene, after Papa had been laid to rest. She remembered Granny Drage holding court. She remembered the unctuous sympathy of Alan's father. She remembered Aunt Margery's suffocating misery. She had stepped outside to escape it all.

It had been a dull afternoon, a lowering sky: she remembered it as if it was yesterday. Spring had been showing in the gardens. They had never looked better, Watkins's last hurrah. She had walked across the lawn. She had avoided the summerhouse. She had looked for fish in the stream. There had been no fish. Up in the trees, rooks had been cawing. She had watched them, their black wings, their black beaks. Their harsh calls had echoed in the drab, grey silence.

It was then that *he* had come. He had looked like a rook himself, in his black mourning, with his thick black eyebrows and dark glinting eyes, sinister. Eight years had passed since the night at Nethercote Hall. But eight years had not been enough.

* * *

'Are you going to say nothing to me, Emily — *nothing*? Don't you think this has gone on long enough?'

'Please go away. Please leave me alone.' Emily hunched her shoulders against him. The waters of the stream tinkled over the stones. She looked desperately at the far bank with thoughts of escape. But the rope she had swung on as a girl had long gone.

'You've never told anyone, I take it? Well? Have you? Look at me, Emily! Look at me! And for goodness' sake, stop trying to run away!'

He made to grab her arm. She shrank from him, getting dangerously close to the water, her feet slipping in the mud by the stream's edge.

'Emily, please. You don't understand. You don't know how it was for me. I couldn't help myself, because I was so damnably in love with you.'

'No—'

'I'm still in love with you.'

'No—'

'I want you, Emily, so much. If only you knew.'

'No, no, no! I don't believe in your love! I don't *believe* in it!'

But she realized there was no escape. She had left it too late. Already she could feel her body slowly stiffening, the creeping paralysis coming over her. Suddenly, there were walls all round her, hemming her in — as if she was back in that tiny cloak room at Nethercote Hall.

His whisky breath. His groping hands.

She was at his mercy.

'Emily? Emily, where are you?' The voice broke in on her, faint but coming nearer.

Next moment, Alan was there. She almost sobbed with relief. She barely noticed *him* go sloping off, sheepish.

'So this is where you've been hiding, darling. I was worried, when I couldn't find you. What did *he* want? What were you talking about? What did he say to you, your Uncle Walter?'

'N-n-nothing. I don't know. I can't remember.'

'You look awfully pale, darling. You're shivering. And — oh — Emily — you're *crying*!'

Alan reached for her. She flinched. She couldn't bear it, to have anyone touch her. Her skin crawled at the very thought of it. But then she saw his anxious eyes peering at her from behind his little round spectacles — those brown, gentle eyes — and she remembered his promise: the promise he'd made, the promise he'd kept, never to hurt her, never to give her pain. She was safe with Alan. She was safe.

As he put his arms round her, she felt the paralysis wearing off. Her heart was beating again. She could breathe. The creeping horror that had threatened to overwhelm her started to fade.

He looked at her, concerned. 'Darling, what is it? I wish you'd tell me. Is . . . is it your father?'

'Yes, oh yes. It's Papa, it's everything. It's Aunt Margery. Poor Aunt Margery.' (She couldn't say: *It's* him, *it's Walter.* She would never say his name, never again.)

'Hush, darling. It wasn't right of your aunt to burden you at a time like this.'

'But Alan, she's so unhappy. Marriage has made her so unhappy.' (Better to dwell on Margery's misery than on wounds that wouldn't heal.)

'Ainsleigh is a cad, an absolute swine!' Alan tightened his grip on her. 'But our marriage is different, darling. We'll never be like that. I'd never treat you that way. You do believe me, don't you? Darling, I love you with all my heart. I always have and I always will.'

* * *

'I love you too. I love you, Alan.'

Emily, in 1926, spoke the words out loud, thirteen years too late.

The sound of her own voice brought her back to herself and she looked around, her steps slowing. She was in a narrow street with tall brick buildings — warehouses or factories — but up ahead was a brightness and openness. She hurried towards it, left the narrow street behind. There was a low wall in front of her, and beyond it the river. The sky over the Pool of London was opening up, there were patches of clear blue and a golden radiance behind the clouds. Barges and lighters were moored in rows on the grey water. There were wharves and warehouses and cranes on the opposite bank. The masts and funnels of ships could be glimpsed downstream and to her left was the ponderous grandeur of Tower Bridge. It all seemed very still, very quiet, like a Sunday. Except today was Tuesday.

And then she remembered the strike, and Chad, and everything else: it all came flooding back, like the tide up the river.

She breathed deeply. She was back wholly in the present and the past was fading away. Her mind was abuzz. She thought of Mabel Perks, mouldering away in her basement room. If only Mabel could see this, this incomparable view, the ships, the docks, the brightness glinting on the water, the majesty of Tower Bridge — if only she could breathe this air. It wouldn't cure her — perhaps nothing could cure her — but it couldn't fail to lift her spirits. They could sit here, and talk together, as they'd talked for a while in the basement room — because it had been possible to talk, despite everything, despite the awkwardness and the misunderstandings and the shock of Lily's origins. They had grown calm. They had fallen to reminiscing. They had a lot in common, after all, and Perks had seemed to look back on the days of Alleyn Dene almost as fondly as Emily herself. They had talked of the house and the village, of the Barford girls at Cedar Rise, and old Mrs Wetherall in the shop, such a gossip. They'd talked of Mama and Papa and all the servants, of jolly old Cook, of Watkins the gardener, who'd do anything for anyone. How much they remembered between them and yet how differently they remembered it! It was like seeing it all afresh.

But what they hadn't talked about was Lily or Chad. Instead, they'd taken refuge in the past. They'd gone back to a time before Uncle Walter wreaked havoc on both their lives. (Oh yes, they had a lot in common, much more than Perks knew.) Only when Emily was leaving had the present intruded once more.

'I would like to come again, Mabel, if I may. Would you mind if I looked in on you again?'

'Why? Why would you want to? Why should you care about me?'

'You did your best to help me once. I was never grateful as I ought to have been. I misjudged you, Mabel, and I'm sorry. You were treated badly by my family in your time of trouble and I would like to make up for that. And there's Lily, too. Lily is a bond between us.'

'Then — then you believe me? You believe she's Mr Walter's child?' Sudden hope in Perks's face had given way to sudden fear. 'You won't take her away from me, will you? Your family won't want to take her away?'

'Of course not. You're her mother. She belongs with you. I'm sure she'd never leave you.'

Mabel had gripped her hand. 'Don't let *him* — please, I beg you, don't let *him* — I don't ever want *him* anywhere near her.'

'Don't worry. I give you my word. Uncle Walter shan't meddle with Lily. You see, I . . . I know what he's like.'

Emily had been seized at that point by an all but overwhelming urge to unburden herself. She yearned to confide in Perks, to tell Perks everything — everything that had happened on the night of the ball at Nethercote Hall. But where would she begin? She'd never told anyone, not of her own choosing. Perks only had an inkling because she'd worked it out for herself. And not even Perks knew that it had been Uncle Walter in that cloak room twenty-one years ago.

But what about Lily? What about Lily and Chad? If Lily really was Walter's child, and Chad—

Oh what a tangled web we weave, when first we practise to deceive!

The sound of voices interrupted her thoughts. She looked round, but could see no one. Moving closer to the wall, she peered over. Below, the river lapped at a little muddy beach. There was a group of people by the water, two policemen amongst them. One of the policemen had waded into the river, the other had a long pole with a hook, was dragging something towards the bank. As Emily watched, the policeman in the water reached to grab whatever it was and Emily realized with a shock that it was a body. Somebody had drowned in the river. An accident, or—

Out of nowhere, she remembered Ginger's words the day before yesterday. *He'll not do nuffin stupid. He'll not do nuffin all at once. But he winds hisself up. He gets down on hisself. He starts thinking the worst.*

She was gripped by sudden, unreasoning fear, and leaned dizzily over the wall, heedless of danger, as the body was pulled up, face down, onto the mud. The two policemen stooped to turn it over. For a moment they were in her way, Emily couldn't see. Then one of them stepped aside. She glimpsed long sodden skirts, long hair splayed out on the mud. It was a woman's body. A woman. A stranger.

Emily stepped back, shuddering with relief, and a little ashamed. Was it right to feel so glad when someone was dead? She wondered who the woman was, and why she had ended up in the river. It seemed such a little thing, amidst all the chaos. But someone's life had ended, had been cut short, and that was terribly sad.

It wasn't Midge. But if he wasn't here, where was he? Ginger had promised to let her know, but she'd heard nothing, so Midge must still be missing.

One thought now eclipsed all others: what had happened to him?

What had happened to Midge?

CHAPTER NINETEEN

Another restless night. Emily tossed and turned, racking her brains. But if Ginger didn't know where Midge was, then why would she?

She thought of the body in the river. She couldn't get it out of her head. She thought of Papa, who'd gone walking on the railway and had been flattened by the London express. But why would Midge — unless . . . ?

A sort of breakdown, he'd said: a wound that had healed, according to Ginger. But did such wounds ever really heal, when it was the mind? Did one ever get better? Mama hadn't. Mama's mind had snapped. Might Midge's too?

Why should it matter, Emily asked herself, tossing and turning: why should she care what happened to Midge?

But I do care. Because I love him.

She stopped dead, lying stock-still in the dark. Had she heard right? Had she heard what the voice in her head had just said? She formed the words with her lips: *I love him*. Oh, but how could she? How could she love anyone, ruined as she was, broken by her ordeal in the cloakroom at Nethercote Park more than twenty years ago?

Yet these last few weeks, she'd felt a change inside her. She wasn't sure exactly what it was, whether it was a long frost slowly thawing, or a new and growing awareness of herself: it could be either. Whatever the case, she knew now that she had something to compare it with — for she knew about love now, she knew what love meant. She could say with certainty that she'd come to love Alan during their years of marriage — she could say it with certainty, because the same feelings were stirring in her again.

Yes, it was true. She, Emily Winmer, knew love. She had known it first with Alan, who was dead, and she knew it now with a lowly bus conductor, which was hopeless.

Oh, Emily! She could hear Mama's voice, she could all but see Mama too — Mama as she'd been long ago at Alleyn Dene, shaking her head with a long-suffering look.

Oh, Emily! After Emily had fallen and torn her frock, after she'd got her feet wet trying to tickle the bellies of fish, after she'd trod in cow dirt fleeing the galloping herd. Always the same long-suffering look. And always, *Oh Emily! What am I to do with you?* With a girl who'd been brave and sometimes even foolhardy, a girl who'd not cowered in the face of the world, a girl who — even after the ordeal at Nethercote Park — had managed to find her way home though the black night, a girl who, despite everything, had not completely vanished without trace. Less reckless now, perhaps. More humble now, perhaps. But the same Emily.

Oh, Emily!

Emily dropped off to sleep at long last, a smile on her face, hearing Mama's voice in her head, and remembering the deep affection shining in Mama's eyes as she shook her head at her wayward daughter.

Oh, Emily . . .

* * *

Emily awoke with a start, early. She sat up in the vast bed. Inspiration had come to her, even as she slept. She thought she might know where Midge was.

It had been one of their earliest meetings, her first trip to London on *The Sparrowhawk*. She had been late back. Midge and Ginger had waited for her at the tube terminus. She and Midge had fallen into conversation as the omnibus travelled through the suburbs and out into the countryside in the April dusk. They had talked about London, how Emily found it faintly menacing, how Midge had grown to love it. He had told her how he used to walk for miles on Sundays, getting lost and finding his way. He had told her about his favourite place, Parliament Hill.

Parliament Hill.

It was a faint hope, but it was better than nothing.

Emily jumped up. She threw on some clothes. She ran downstairs for a hurried breakfast.

'You're early, Emmy dear.' Aunt Margery was sat at the table, smoking her first cigarette of the day before facing her bacon and eggs. Smoking was the one habit of the war years she'd not been able to quit. 'Charles had me up at some ridiculous hour, then he went rushing off. I thought you'd be having a lie-in, Emmy, after yesterday, whatever it was you were doing, so mysterious!'

'I'm going out again, Aunt.'

'Out again! And you used to be such a sedate and stay-at-home sort of person! Where are you going this time — or shouldn't one ask?'

'On a wild goose chase.' Emily gave a penitent smile. 'I'm sorry, Aunt, to be such a nuisance.'

'Don't be silly, Emmy. You're not a nuisance. We love having you here, Charles and I. But are you sure it's quite safe to go out, with things the way they are? Won't you have Fletcher again?'

But Emily did not want to be hampered in her search. This was something she had to do alone.

Her nerves were jangling as she let herself out of Aunt Margery's Belgravia house and ran down the steps, but there was — undeniable — a sense of adventure too. She hastened along the street, with only the vaguest idea where Parliament Hill was and how to get there.

To her surprise, she found Hyde Park Corner station open, and a tube service of sorts running. She was whisked by the London Electric Railway to Leicester Square, where she changed onto the Hampstead and Highgate line. The train rattled and rolled through the dark tunnel. She wanted to clutch her bag, but she had come without it. She was a woman alone, unencumbered, on a wild goose chase, afraid — and wonderfully free.

The past, since yesterday by the river, had receded further and further into the far corners of her mind. The future could not even be guessed at. Which left only the present.

* * *

Emily looked out at London spread below her — timeless London, stretching to the far horizon. Midge had been right about the view. It was magnificent, even on a day like today, breezy, cloudy, rather cold: one could scarcely believe it was May. But from up here, the great strike seemed like nothing, a mere ripple in history, and her spirits soared as she gazed into the distance with the wind in her face. Even so, she was shot through with disappointment, for her wild goose chase was over and she had not found Midge.

With a sigh she turned away, remembering as she did so Chad's words on Sunday. *It's funny about love, the things it makes you do.* Love had brought her here on the hopeless quest. Now she had to leave the dream behind and retrace her steps, calm and stoical.

But somehow she missed her way, and she found herself walking down a path she didn't recognize. And there on a bench, sitting — just as she'd given up all hope — was Midge.

She walked towards him a little warily, as if she half suspected he was a mirage that might vanish at any moment into thin air. His conductor's uniform, usually so neat, was badly crumpled. He had no hat. He'd lost it, she remembered, in the melee last Friday. His hair was tousled, his face grey and unshaven. Almost she expected him to be muttering like a madman but, as she got nearer, she saw that he was sitting completely still and staring into space, as if a cavalcade of thoughts was marching through his mind.

He didn't see her until she was almost on top of him, then he got to his feet with a look of dismay and confusion.

'Mrs Winmer — you — here?'

'It was a guess, a chance. I hoped I might find you. I thought I'd failed. Why haven't you been home, Midge?'

He looked away, said dully, 'Tint my home. Not really. It's theirn: Ginger's, Nell's. I only get in their road.'

'They've been desperately worried about you. We . . . we all have.'

'Y-y-you, Mrs Winmer?' He looked at her, and then looked away, troubled.

'I do wish you'd call me Emily. I would like it, if you called me Emily.'

'Emily . . .'

'Shall we sit?'

She sat, he sat, on the bench. There was a sound of wind in the trees, the branches dipping and swaying. London might have been a million miles away. Emily's hands rested in her lap. Midge's fingers fidgeted, picking at the folds of his trousers.

'Where have you been, Midge? No one has seen you since Friday. It's Wednesday now.'

'I've been sleeping in garage, where we used to keep *Sparrowhawk* of a night. I-I needed time by mesen, I suppose.'

'Imagine if it had been Ginger missing. Imagine how you'd feel.' Emily was suddenly angry, remembering the fear that had clutched her on the bank of the river, watching the body being dragged out of the water. 'You could have let us know. We hadn't the first idea what to think. Ginger came to see me and—'

'He dint ought to have mithered you. I've been note but a nuisance since you first met me.' He rubbed his knee. He rubbed and he rubbed it, working himself up until he burst out, 'I can't tell you how sorry I am. I'm ashamed of mesen, of everything that happened, bus being set on and — and what I did in shop doorway. I've no right to expect you'll ever forgive me.'

'Forgive you? But I don't want to forgive you!'

Emily was no longer sure if her anger was really anger, or if it was something else: exasperation or impatience — or what was it, what? All she knew was that she was tired of sitting demure in a corner, tired of effacing herself, tired of it all — when she wasn't that sort of woman at all, when she was the girl who had caught fish by tickling their bellies, who had swung on a rope across a stream, who had found her way home in the dark from Nethercote Hall.

'I don't want to forgive you, Midge. What you did in the shop doorway — I want you to do it again.'

Well, of course she did. Of course. She saw it clearly now. She saw it clearly at last, even as she was speaking. She wanted him to kiss her. It was what she'd wanted all along.

But that was impossible, an impossible dream.

Oh, why couldn't they just go back to being friends? Why couldn't they go back to sitting in *The Sparrowhawk*, as it wound through country lanes, looking out at the setting sun and talking lightly of life and London, expecting nothing of each other, at ease with each other? Because that was the best she could hope for, that was the best she could manage.

Only — it was too late to turn back the clock. It was too late, now that she'd given him renewed hope. He was looking at her, a sudden light in his eyes — he was taking her hand. And she'd brought this on herself. She'd brought this on herself, and she'd ruined everything. Already she could feel it, the creeping paralysis triggered by his touch. Already it was taking hold, her body stiffening like setting cement. What was the use in trying to fight it? She wasn't strong enough. She'd never be strong enough.

She shut her eyes tight, suddenly afraid of him — of his rough, unshaven face, of the light in his eyes, the light she'd mistaken for love but which was nothing but lust, ravening lust. She felt herself dipping and swaying like the branches of the trees. She had the wind in her face, heard it whispering in her ears. The whispers sounded strangely like words and, unbidden, there rose in her mind something she'd read, something that the whispering words seemed to be repeating gently in her ear.

In the kisses and the hand-touch—

The words took shape, the words she'd read in that book of Aunt Margery's.

> *In the kisses and the hand-touch of the beloved are a zest and exhilaration which stirs the blood like wine . . .*

His lips touched hers. She could feel the bristles of his jaw. His cheek was cold against hers. His arm was snaking round her. The touch of his hand on her waist made her shudder.

His breath was a little sour — but there was no hint in it of whisky, and this sweetened it beyond measure. His hand, too, rested lightly, holding her, but not grasping or groping.

He was kissing her on the bench in full view, where anyone could walk by and see — and she didn't care. She didn't care about people seeing. Nothing mattered except this moment, this kiss.

What a discovery, what an extraordinary discovery, to find that she didn't care, to find that nothing else mattered!

She felt marvellously alive, and so incredibly lithe and supple in his arms. He was holding her, but she was free — free of the creeping paralysis — free, even, or so it seemed, of the gravitational pull of the Earth. She was flying through the air, flying like a bird, and it was a million times more wonderful, a million times more exhilarating, than swinging on a rope across the stream — for she didn't need to hold on, she could let go and be free.

'Mrs Winmer — Emily — Emily —' His voice was full of concern. 'You're piping your eyes out.'

It was true. Her eyes were brimming over with tears. They flooded out and rolled down her cheeks. She blinked them away as best she could, so that she could see him. He was sitting a little apart now, bewildered, troubled, watching her.

'Oh, Midge!' She took his hand. She let the tears flow. She couldn't have stopped them. 'It's all right, Midge. It's all right. I'm only crying because I'm happy. I can't tell you how happy I am!'

* * *

They got off the tube at Hyde Park Corner and walked, holding hands, through the quiet streets, Midge following Emily's lead. It seemed to him that a hush had fallen over London, as if the city was waiting for something. He felt horribly dirty and dishevelled. He was ravenously hungry. He was anxious, too. She was taking him to her aunt's house, and he couldn't even begin to imagine what they would think of him — Emily's posh relations — a man of his sort.

You could have knocked him down with a feather earlier, when she'd appeared out of nowhere as he sat, despondent, on that bench. He'd thought he'd seen the last of her. To find that she'd actually come looking for him seemed, well, too good to be true. He couldn't quite believe it, couldn't help thinking it wasn't the real Emily but some sort of apparition, a figment of his diseased imagination. He'd begun to wonder, these last few days, if he wasn't going doolally again. He'd spent a lot of time just sitting and thinking, and that was all he could come up with, that he was going doolally: what other explanation could there be?

And then — he wasn't sure exactly how it happened, but he'd kissed her. He'd kissed her again, but this time she'd wanted him to, she really had. He'd been trembling like a leaf, trembling all over: his congenital cowardice, of course. But, by heck, coward or not, it had taken some nerve, kissing her.

Everything changed. To hold her in his arms, to kiss her gently, almost chastely, to see the tears in her eyes, to hear the happiness in her voice — it had been like a dose of salts, clearing his head, so that he could see at last: see, know, understand. She was not a figment. She was only too real. Indisputably real. And he was not going doolally. He was utterly — devastatingly — sane.

If he was a little afraid, hadn't he good reason? What he'd felt for Evie under the railway bridge all those years ago — all that seemed a pale imitation compared to what he felt now. What he'd felt for Evie had been safe, homely — child's play. What he felt for Mrs Winmer — for Emily — well, he couldn't even begin to describe it.

He'd sat with her on the bench. They'd talked, leaping from one subject to another, in no sort of order. As far as he could remember, most of what he'd said had been nothing but a load of old bull, yet he couldn't help feeling that he'd never had such a deep conversation before. And they'd barely scratched the surface.

They had quite a lot in common, when you came to think about it. Family tragedy. The shadow of the war. But there was even more that divided them. There was an age gap as well as a social gap, he a penniless nobody, she with an uncle who was a lord, and a father-in-law who'd been in government. And he told himself he wasn't mad! What could be madder than this? Here he was, embarking on a journey with no destination board and no return ticket, and with no idea who was driving. It was sheer lunacy, that's what it was. They had put him in a straight jacket for less.

Eventually, she'd got to her feet. She had held out her hand. 'Will you come with me, Midge?'

He had let himself be led. 'Where we going, Mrs Winmer — Emily?' (He couldn't get used to calling her Emily. It gave him a little shock every time, daring to say her name.)

She'd said, 'There's Ginger—'

He'd groaned. 'Ginger! He'll clonk me one, I shouldn't wonder, way I've treated him.'

'But first, I thought, Aunt Margery—'

'What in heaven's name will your aunt make of me — me, in all me scruff?'

But he would soon find out, for they were almost there.

'It's that house,' said Emily, pointing.

A huge, grand, white-fronted house with a forbidding black door and a heavy, polished brass knocker. Enough to put anyone off, thought Midge as he hesitated at the bottom of the clean-swept steps. His anxiety was now almost too much to bear. He was shaking again. Symptoms of his sick mind, they'd said in the nut-house, this anxiety, this shaking — symptoms of congenital cowardice.

But what did they know?

He squared his shoulders. He'd gone over the top in the war. He'd crawled around no-man's land on patrol. He'd sat through endless enemy bombardments. He'd almost been buried alive, when a trench wall collapsed on him. If he could face all that, he could face Emily's aunt.

He put one foot on the bottom step, but Emily hung back, suddenly gripping his hand, holding on as if her life depended on it. He turned back, saw her stood there as if frozen, staring wide-eyed along the street. He could sense her fear.

Midge looked, but he could see nothing, just a couple of pricey motors parked by the kerb, and a pillar box on the far corner. What was it, then, filling Emily with such dread?

'Emily? Is summat wrong?'

But his words appeared to go unheard, as she shrank in terror against the stone post at the bottom of the steps.

CHAPTER TWENTY

Lurking behind the red pillar box, Walter Drage had peered out as his niece Emily came walking along the street, heading for Margery's house. What was she doing here, and who was that man with her, a rather unkempt-looking man?

By Margery's front steps, the man had come to a halt as if reluctant to go on, and Emily, waiting patiently for him, had happened to glance along the street. Walter had ducked back, pressed himself against the pillar box. Had she seen him? He couldn't be certain. But here he was, still lurking, his heart racing.

Why was he hiding? He wasn't sure. It had been a reflex action, perfectly ridiculous. He clutched his stick, angry. He was entitled to visit his sister, if he wanted. He ought to stop dithering and just do it. But somehow, knowing Emily was there, he couldn't bring himself to go on.

Emily! Silly little bitch! Always running away from him! Like a sheep, she was, with big scared eyes. And yet — and yet . . . there she was, and here he was . . . and who was running away now? Somehow, at some point, their roles had got reversed. When had things changed? It must have happened slowly, gradually, because he hadn't even noticed, not until now. But it had come to this, there was no getting away from it: it had come to him lurking, skulking, hiding behind a pillar box.

He pressed himself against the pillar box, panting slightly, waiting a moment before he snatched another look. His mind reached back. All this had begun years ago. All this stemmed from that evening at Nethercote Hall, the ball. That was when things had taken a wrong turn.

He licked his lips, agitated to remember the way Emily's skirts had flared up as she danced, revealing a trim, stockinged ankle, unbearably desirable. She had followed him like a lamb into the cloakroom. All he'd wanted was one kiss. But then—

And yet — and yet — why not? Why shouldn't he have taken what he wanted? Why shouldn't he? That little minx! She'd known exactly what she was doing. And she'd wanted it, too. She'd been asking for it. She'd deserved it. She'd not tried to stop him, either, only a token show, the way women did, playing on their pretended virtue. All the same, he didn't like to think about that evening. It had left a nasty taste. He'd wanted just one kiss, but somehow she'd tricked him into more. Yes, yes, it was her fault, all her fault, and — well — it was best forgotten.

Why, then, *couldn't* he forget? Why, at night, alone, did it all come back to him? Why did he dream about it? She'd struggled like a rabbit in a trap, until he took charge of her. She'd struggled in his arms, playing on her pretended virtue. Then she'd suddenly stopped struggling. She'd given way. Because she wanted it, because she'd been asking for it: what else could it be? And yet somehow she'd shifted the blame. She'd been very clever. Devious, artful, slippery — like all women. She'd shifted the blame, so that now, at night, alone, he shuddered to remember, he woke up sweating after dreaming of it, he wished it had never happened.

Walter risked a look. Emily and that common-looking man had gone. It was safe to move. Patting his sweaty brow with his handkerchief, he turned away. He didn't want to visit Margery whilst Emily was there. He wasn't sure why he ever went to Margery's at all. Margery only nagged, like all women. She asked questions and she interfered. She treated him as if he was a baby still, her baby brother. And she was so insufferably pleased with herself these days. He much preferred not to have her smug happiness thrust in his face.

He passed into the next street, swinging his stick as he always did when he was in a jaunty mood. Why bother about Emily? Why think of her at all? There were other women he could think of. He'd been pleasingly successful in that department. Perhaps none of the others had been quite as pretty as Emily, perhaps rather too many had been of a somewhat lower station. But, all the same, he'd had his little conquests when he was younger, sprightlier. He'd not often had to pay for his pleasure, either, back then. That maid, for instance, at Alleyn Dene. What had been the name of that maid, so pert, so tempting, just asking for it? No. No. He couldn't remember her name. What he did remember was how eager she had been, how easy — the little strumpet! He salivated, thinking of how he'd had her, right there and then, behind a hedge in the lane. By God, she'd been asking for it! She'd left him with no choice! And she'd not cried or struggled at all, she'd had no virtue to play on, she'd been neither sheep nor rabbit. But she had turned out to be a rat. She'd come gnawing at him later. Oh, God, yes — he'd all but forgotten until now. Why must these old memories always come with a sting in the tail?

She'd come gnawing at him, pestering him. She'd gotten into trouble, she'd told him. She was having a child. His child. A likely story! A girl like that, it could have been anybody's, some hobbledehoy or bumpkin. She was the type who spread her legs for anyone: that had been only too obvious. He'd told her so, too, when she'd begun to make herself a nuisance. He'd put the fear of God into her. She'd thought better of her blackmailing ways, by the time he'd finished with her. She'd known not to go telling tales.

He patted his pockets as he walked, pleased to think that he'd put the fear of God into her, pleased to think that he'd had the measure of her — of all those strumpets, those trollops, those doxies. Oh, yes, he'd had the measure of her, and it pleased him to remember it, though he had sometimes wondered, over the years, about the child, wondered if it really had been his: perhaps it had. At the time, it hadn't seemed to matter. He'd been young. He'd had his life ahead of him. There'd be lots of children by and by, there'd be a wife by and by. And yet . . . and yet . . . Somehow, it had never happened. Somehow, here he was, a bachelor and childless — though sometimes he wondered — the child — yes, he wondered—

But, ah, here was an omnibus! He waved his stick for it to stop, he got on board, he handed the conductor a half-crown (he had a pocket full of pennies and ha'pennies, but he didn't like to use them, it gave the wrong impression). Lucky, he thought, settling himself into a seat, lucky to have found a bus with this strike on. It was getting past a joke, this strike. It was getting to be inconvenient. Shoot a few of them, those riff-raff and troublemakers. Shoot a few, and they'd soon buck up their ideas. Shoot a dozen or so — a score — whatever it took. They'd soon fall back into line.

Looking out as the omnibus passed along Piccadilly, he found himself feeling thankful that Mother had never found out about the child, or the maid whose name he couldn't remember. Mother didn't know about any of them, his little conquests, though sometimes she gave him looks, as if she guessed more than was entirely comfortable. Why, he asked himself as he gazed out at Green Park, did he bother with Mother? Why didn't he just leave her? It was meant to be daughters who stayed home to look after their aged parents, not sons. But somehow his sisters had both wriggled free. They'd evaded their responsibilities, the selfish bitches. Beatrice had jumped first, marrying that common little shoemaker, who'd later gone bankrupt and done away with himself, whilst Margery had fallen on her feet with the Ainsleigh millions. (It wasn't *millions*, she insisted. It wasn't as much as that. But whatever treasure trove she was sitting on, she was extraordinarily parsimonious when it came to sharing it round — and he her own brother!) So much for his sisters, selfish bitches both. As for Frank, his brother Frank — God, how he hated Frank, how he *loathed* him. He was consumed by jealousy, even now. Frank, everyone's favourite. Frank, who'd found the courage to run away. And to top it all, Frank had even had the great good fortune to die, so that he'd never had to come crawling back with his tail between his legs, he'd never had to face the consequences of his actions.

Mother had washed her hands of Frank. She'd written him off as a bad lot. 'But I shan't make the same mistake with you, Walter.'

Walter chuckled, remembering how, after news of Frank's death finally reached them, he had often, when taking his nap after lunch, amused himself by picturing Frank's self-satisfied, selfish body lying at the bottom of the sea, somewhere off the coast of South America: Frank's body, wreathed in seaweed and being nibbled by clouds of little fish with sharp teeth, fish that nibbled and nibbled until there was nothing left of Frank, nothing but a pile of white bones on the sea-swept sand.

Walter chuckled, shifting in his seat as the omnibus swung round Piccadilly Circus (why did they make these seats so damned uncomfortable?). Frank'd had his fun, and he'd paid the price. It was a price Walter had not been willing to pay. Because he'd had his chances too. Mother, for all her vigilance, had not been able to watch him night and day — he'd not actually been locked in his room, or chained to his bed. When he turned twenty-one and the South African War was on, he could easily have slipped away and joined the Army, covered himself in glory. But if the price was death, was it really worth it? In any case, he'd not been entirely sure that he could manage on army pay alone. He liked a few comforts, he was not cut from the same cloth as Frank, who'd not minded roughing it, who'd not seemed to have any sense of his own worth. That had been Frank all over, slapdash and shoddy. Which made it all the more of a mystery as to why he'd been so popular, everybody's favourite. People hadn't been able to see through him, that was the problem. They hadn't been able to see through him, the way Walter could.

Walter sighed as the omnibus turned down Haymarket. What was the use of going over it and over it? He could have joined the Army, but he hadn't, and that was an end to it. That particular escape route was now closed to him. He was too old and too fat, nearly fifty. Nearly fifty, and still trapped at home, still enmeshed in Mother's webs, the evil old spider. Why was she even still alive at the age of eighty-two? Wasn't it time she died? He'd been waiting twenty years for her to die. She'd used up twenty years of his life. And yet, at eighty-two, she seemed hardly changed, she looked as if she could go on forever, another twenty years. At this rate, he'd be in his grave before she was.

He groaned out loud, not caring about the stares he got, contemptuous of the other passengers, riff-raff. Why, why, why had he not joined the Army when he'd had the chance? He'd threatened her with it, he remembered, as he looked out at Trafalgar Square, the tall pillar of Nelson's Column. He'd threatened her with it, but she'd laughed in his face and exerted her will — her indomitable will. Then, and always, she'd got the better of him. She'd slowly cowed and crushed him.

'The Army would only encourage you in your dissolute habits, Walter. You will *not* join the Army, you will do as I say, do I make myself clear?'

Dissolute habits? An occasional wager, the odd hand of cards, a girl or two — and not always the sort one paid for, not in those days — a drink now and then: was that dissolute?

'You are dangerously addicted to gambling, Walter.' (Gross exaggeration.) 'You drink far too much.' (Because of *her*, because she drove him to it: because of her constant nagging, because of her tyrannical ways.) 'You are weak, Walter. You have no backbone. You cannot resist temptation. I, therefore, must resist it for you. Without me to watch over you, you would come to ruin. I learned my lesson with

Frank. I will not make the same mistake with you. I will not let you throw your life away, as the others have. Don't think I won't cut off your allowance if I have to. I will do whatever it takes. You *will* obey me, Walter! You *will*!'

Walter grimaced, ringing the bell and then getting to his feet, as the bus slowed in the Strand. There was a nice little restaurant just along here. He'd been looking forward to lunch all morning. But, as he stepped down into the street, he felt the pangs of indigestion already, before he'd touched a morsel.

This was *her* fault. This was what she did to him. She made him ill. She sucked the life out of him. Nearly fifty, old and fat. To think of it kept him awake at night. How much time he'd wasted, waiting for her to die! How he hated her!

He rapped his stick angrily on the pavement, thinking of the lunch he wouldn't now enjoy, thinking of the row there'd be in a week or so when she got the bill (he'd charge it to her account), thinking of the little knot of pleasure he'd get from making her rant and rave — the only pleasure he ever got now, the only pleasure left, when he couldn't even eat his lunch without getting indigestion.

Eighty-two and going strong. Would she *never* die? Would she *never* set him free? He couldn't think what he'd done to deserve such a life. It was worse than a life sentence — it was worse than being in gaol . . .

* * *

'Emily? Is summat wrong?'

Midge's voice slowly brought Emily back to herself. For a moment, she'd had been mortally afraid, frozen in place. For a moment, a pall had descended. She had been certain that, at the end of the street, something — someone — was waiting, cold and menacing and indescribably sinister. But now she looked again, and there was no one there. The street was quiet and empty. Brightness welled in the sky where the sun was beginning to break through. Her fears evaporated. They were no more real than a will-o'-the-wisp.

She felt, just then, that she would never be afraid of anything again. It was like being set free.

She turned to look at Midge. She took his hand. She took his hand, not because she needed to, but because she wanted to. Not because she was weak and seeking reassurance, but because she was strong — strong enough to know her own mind, and to stick by it.

She smiled at him and watched as an answering smile slowly unfolded on his face, the smile she had once thought of as wolfish, but which she now saw as full of life and hope and laughter, and — dare she say it? — love.

As they stood there on the steps, hesitant, suddenly the door flew open and Aunt Margery appeared.

'Emmy, do hurry, you're just in time! There's going to be an announcement on the wireless — an announcement from Number 10.' Her words were addressed to her niece, but her eyes slid round to look inquisitively at Midge.

Emily led the way up the steps. 'Aunt, this is Mr Midgely, Mr George Midgely, a friend.'

'Mr Midgely. Delighted. Am I to take it that you are the friend who saved Emily's life in the riot last Friday? I can't tell you how awfully grateful we are.'

Midge flushed. 'I dunna think—'

Aunt Margery interrupted. 'So modest. But that must wait. Do come in, Mr Midgely. Do come in, both of you. We mustn't miss the announcement.'

They gathered round the wireless. A piano was playing over the airwaves.

'A voice just now asked us to stand by—' Aunt Margery began, but at that moment the music stopped.

The BBC announcer, ponderous, pompous, read out a message from 10 Downing Street. The words took shape, the meaning became clear. The General Strike was over.

'Oh, my dears!' Aunt Margery's eyes shone. 'Such a relief! Charles said he felt the end would come today, but it hardly seemed possible. It's all been such fun, but really—'

Midge broke in on Aunt Margery's sibilant tones. His voice sounded very gruff, almost coarse, and his East Midlands accent shockingly alien in the genteel drawing room. Emily shivered, as if a breeze had blown in, cold, crisp, bracing.

'No fun for men living on strike pay, me lady. No fun for miners, struggling for decent way of life.'

Aunt Margery looked at him soberly. 'You may have a point, Mr Midgely. "Fun" is the wrong word.'

The old Aunt Margery, standing on her dignity, might have bristled at such treatment as this, being contradicted in her own home. The new Aunt Margery, however, was a match for any situation. She had all of the Drage insouciance, but with none of Granny's haughty disdain. Catching Emily's eye, her face was a picture of surprise and curiosity.

'Fun or not, it's all settled now. That can only be a good thing.'

'Seems rather sudden-like, to my way of thinking,' said Midge gloomily. 'I've got a bad feeling about it.'

'Is that so? Well, I can see we will have a lot to discuss over luncheon. You will be staying for luncheon, Mr Midgely, I hope?'

'I-I dunna know. I'm in no fit state—'

'That is easily remedied. Andrews, if you would be so kind?'

Faced by Aunt Margery's punctilious butler, a look almost of panic came over Midge's face. He was led away, but glanced over his shoulder before he left the room. His eyes sought Emily's. She held his gaze and smiled. To her surprise, the panic showing on his face subsided at once, as if all it took was a smile — her smile. Squaring his shoulders, he followed Andrews resolutely out of the room.

The door closed. 'Dearest Emmy!' Aunt Margery could barely contain herself. 'So this is your bus conductor! So dour, and so young, and so very, very handsome!'

There were other words, Emily felt, on the tip of Aunt Margery's tongue. Her cheeks burned at the thought of them. 'Aunt, I—'

'No, Emily. You don't need to explain. He is your guest. That is enough. If there's one thing I've learned, it's that life is too short. Of course, if it was anyone else, I might have cause to worry, but with you, Emily, I know I don't have to. There's no one I know more sensible and level-headed than you. But enough of all that. Lunch. We must get ready for lunch.'

In the guest room, Emily washed her hands and face, brushed her hair, took off her blouse and skirt, put on a clean frock. Her mind grew more and more muddled with every passing moment. Ever since she woke up that morning, her one thought had been to find Midge. But now that she'd found him, everything else came rushing back, Chad first and foremost. How much could she — dare she — tell Chad? Must she tell him about Lily, the connection between him and Lily? Would Lily learn the truth too, from her mother, Mabel?

Poor Mabel! She couldn't just be abandoned, Emily was determined about that. And there was Jarvis too — the promises she'd made to herself about Jarvis. So much to think about, so much to consider — so much she was letting herself in for. She couldn't ignore Heartlands, either. She couldn't disregard Sir Hubert and Violet and Lady Winmer. And always there was Mama, dear Mama. How, Emily asked herself, could she ever hope to juggle all these things? How could she walk such a tightrope? She'd thought, after facing Mabel, after finding Midge, all her troubles would be over. She saw now that her troubles were only just beginning.

Her mind was still churning as she sat down to lunch with Midge and Aunt Margery. Midge had spruced himself up. His hair was brushed rigorously flat, his face was scrubbed and shaven. His uniform had been pressed and was now free of all creases.

'Tell me, Mr Midgely,' said Aunt Margery, shaking out her napkin. 'How does the strike look from your point of view?'

'Well, your ladyship—'

'Please. Call me Margery.'

'Well . . . Margery . . . way I see it . . .'

Emily was barely listening. As she spooned her spinach soup, she asked herself what exactly she intended by her resolve not to abandon Mabel Perks. She recalled something Mabel had said in St James's Park on that hot July day in 1921.

I don't want nothing from you, nothing, though some might say you owe me. Some might say your family owes me a lot, after what happened.

Mabel was right. But she was owed more than a few visits to her sickbed. She was owed more than gratitude and a belated apology. If she really was dying, if there really was nothing anyone could do for her, then she at least deserved a little comfort, a little dignity, in her last days or months — however long she'd got. That would mean spending money. Where was the money to come from?

If anyone ought to pay, Emily said to herself, it was Uncle Walter. He should be made to provide for his daughter, Lily, too. But Mabel had begged her not to let Uncle Walter anywhere near Lily, and Emily could well understand Mabel's fears. When she thought what might happen if Uncle Walter ever discovered that Chad was his son — well, it didn't bear thinking about. And Uncle Walter was just the tip of the iceberg. He had no money of his own, only the allowance Granny Drage apportioned him. If Uncle Walter was made to provide for Lily, then Granny Drage was sure to find out. Emily shuddered at the prospect of Granny Drage getting involved. Indomitable, invincible, overbearing, Granny Drage would take charge and arrange things as she saw fit. Chad's life — and Lily's — would no longer be their own. *You won't take her away from me, will you*, Mabel had said: *your family won't want to take her away?* But that was exactly what *would* happen if Granny Drage ever got wind of Walter's by-blows.

Granny Drage was best left in blissful ignorance, and Uncle Walter must be kept away from Chad at all costs. Chad must never discover who his real father was. And Emily was sure that Mabel must feel the same way about Lily.

But how were Chad and Lily to be kept apart if their mutual attraction proved intractable? In that case, they would have to be told the truth, Emily could see no other way. And though she might try to convince Chad that Alan would not have rejected him had he too known the truth, doubts would remain. Doubts would fester in Chad's mind that only Alan could have dispelled. Without such reassurances — well, it would be like taking Chad's father away from him: the only father he'd ever known, the only father who mattered.

Emily's soup plate was removed.

'You're very quiet, Emmy.' Aunt Margery was regarding her anxiously from across the table.

'Aye.' Midge had his eyes on her too. 'Is summat wrong, Emily — Mrs Winmer?'

But just then Andrews served Midge with a veal cutlet and Midge looked round at the tall manservant. 'That for me? Tah very much, mate.'

'That's quite all right, sir.'

Andrews was admirably po-faced as he continued round the table, but Aunt Margery cast a look in Midge's direction and she continued to watch him as he hesitated over the array of cutlery in front of him. The look on Aunt Margery's face suggested that she still wasn't sure what to make of him. If Aunt Margery had her doubts, what would Lord Ainsleigh think, and Sir Hubert? Emily's heart sank. Her troubles were weighing ever more heavily on her. She couldn't see how she'd cope.

'You'll manage, darling.'

The voice sounded so real and immediate that for a moment Emily thought there must be someone else in the room. But the voice was Alan's, and the words were words she remembered — words from a long time ago. He'd been going away, the last morning of his embarkation leave. The thought of having to carry on in the cottage without him had sent her into despair.

'Dearest, darling Emily, do you really imagine for one second that I'd leave you on your own if I thought you wouldn't manage? I'll always put you first — and Chad, too — whether my country needs me or not. But I have nothing to worry about, nothing at all. Oh my darling, you do sell yourself short! You are so very much stronger than you think. How else do you think I'd have got were I am, without your strength behind me? That's why I can leave Chad and our cottage without a qualm, because you will take care of them, you will keep them safe until I return.'

Oh, Alan — dear Alan! The cottage and Chad had been waiting — she had been waiting, too — but Alan had never come home.

He'd known her better than she knew herself, she saw that now. And at last, after all this time, she felt she knew him, too. Had he still been here, she would have had to tell him the truth about their marriage. But that wouldn't have been the end of it. He'd have found a way they could have carried on, he would not have abandoned either her or Chad. If, by some slim chance, he continued in existence somewhere, floating in the ether perhaps (but Madame Bobatska had not been able to find him) — or if he was merely a presence, a memory, in her heart, in her soul — if anything of him remained at all, then she could be sure that he would still believe in her, and that he would want her to be happy.

Alan's voice faded, a last distant echo of the receding past. Emily was back in the drawing room with Midge and Aunt Margery and they were both looking at her, lunch in abeyance and concern written on their faces.

But seeing Aunt Margery jogged Emily's memory and she suddenly thought about the allowance or lump sum she'd been promised. She'd been embarrassed by it, she'd tried to forget it, but now it seemed the obvious solution. She could use the lump sum to help Mabel, Lily too for that matter — and perhaps Jarvis as well. She could at least look into finding Jarvis somewhere nearer his family: his mam and dad and sister Vera, and the nippers he'd not seen in a while, the nippers who 'must have growed up quite a lot by now'. Mabel, Lily, Jarvis — they came first, her own needs must come low on the list, she was determined on that. After all, she didn't need much. A little flat somewhere would suffice. A little flat where she could live independently at last. But would she live there alone? What about Midge? Where did he come in the list? Did he come in at all?

As she glanced uncertainly at Midge, she found herself repeating in her head some words she'd read in Aunt Margery's book, some words on the last page of all.

> *When knowledge and love go together, the joy of that new unit, the Pair, will reach from this physical foundation of its united body to the heavens where its head is crowned with stars.*

Was it possible she needn't be alone? Was it possible, at her age, to find all-embracing love at last? Was it possible to reach for the stars, when she'd always had her feet so firmly rooted on the ground?

But how could she doubt it? All she had to do was think of the kiss, the way he'd kissed her on that bench where anyone could see them, and the way she'd felt at that moment: untrammelled, free, lighter than air. There was her answer — the kiss.

'You seem in the oddest mood today, Emmy,' said Aunt Margery. 'Are you sure you're all right?'

'I have a lot on my mind, Aunt.'

'Haven't we all!' exclaimed Aunt Margery with another doubtful glance at Midge.

'I'm making plans, Aunt. I'm looking to . . . to the future.' Emily stumbled over the word — future — for she'd shied away from thinking about the future for so long. She turned her eyes towards Midge. 'We have a lot to talk about, Midge and I. We have decisions to make.'

She reached out a hand. After a moment's hesitation, Midge took hold of it. Colour flared in his cheeks but he met her gaze head-on and he gripped her hand ever tighter. Emily smiled at him. A real smile, not feigned. A smile that spread over her face and lit up her eyes.

Aunt Margery was watching them, half puzzled, half amused. 'Well, Mr Midgely,' she said at length, taking up her knife and fork. 'I've only known you half an hour, but anyone who can put a smile like that on Emmy's face gets my seal of approval.'

But even now the voice of doubt was still whispering in Emily's ear: what if . . . what if . . . ? What if Sir Hubert took a dim view of Midge? What if Chad could not be separated from Lily?

Emily refused to be discouraged. With Aunt Margery's money, she was no longer reliant on Sir Hubert. And yes, Chad had said, 'One can't stop loving someone all at once,' but he'd not said it was impossible. And if it proved to be that he couldn't get over Lily — well, she would cross that bridge when she came to it, Emily told herself firmly. She would not shy away from anything — even the bitter truth, should that be necessary. Alan had believed in her. Midge did too. It was time she believed in herself. She would manage. She was ready.

She laughed, because she *was* ready — ready for anything — and she had so much to look forward to. She really did have a future now. And with that she let go of Midge's hand and set about her cutlet.

THE END

THE JOFFE BOOKS STORY

We began in 2014 when Jasper agreed to publish his mum's much-rejected romance novel and it became a bestseller.

Since then we've grown into the largest independent publisher in the UK. We're extremely proud to publish some of the very best writers in the world, including Joy Ellis, Faith Martin, Caro Ramsay, Helen Forrester, Simon Brett and Robert Goddard. Everyone at Joffe Books loves reading and we never forget that it all begins with the magic of an author telling a story.

We are proud to publish talented first-time authors, as well as established writers whose books we love introducing to a new generation of readers.

We have been shortlisted for Independent Publisher of the Year at the British Book Awards three times, in 2020, 2021 and 2022, and for the Diversity and Inclusivity Award at the Independent Publishing Awards in 2022.

We built this company with your help, and we love to hear from you, so please email us about absolutely anything bookish at: feedback@joffebooks.com

If you want to receive free books every Friday and hear about all our new releases, join our mailing list: www.joffebooks.com/contact

And when you tell your friends about us, just remember: it's pronounced Joffe as in coffee or toffee!

ALSO BY DOMINIC LUKE

BRANNANS FAMILY SAGA

Book 1: AUTUMN SOFTLY FELL
Book 2: NOTHING UNDONE REMAINED
Book 3: DREAMS THAT VEIL
Book 4: THE LIVES WE LEFT BEHIND
Book 5: REMINDERS OF HOME

STANDALONES

THE SECRETS WE KEEP
WAITING FOR THE SUN

www.ingramcontent.com/pod-product-compliance
Lightning Source LLC
LaVergne TN
LVHW091114080826
845145LV00008B/1915

* 9 7 8 1 8 0 4 0 5 9 1 5 9 *